Homecoming Queen

PRAISE FOR CHAD BOUDREAUX'S AWARD-WINNING DEBUT NOVEL *SCAVENGER HUNT*

An intelligent thriller. Boudreaux makes the most of his [story in *Scavenger Hunt*], populating his page-turning plot with plausible characters and developments.

-Publishers Weekly

Boudreaux weaves a daunting story of treachery and puppeteering in this finely crafted race for survival. As terror and history come to bear, it will be through grit and determination that justice is delivered and wrongs are made right in one giant *Scavenger Hunt*.

-Best Thriller Books

Boudreaux's unique voice and page-turning storytelling packs a plot-driven punch that readers won't be able to put down.

-Indie Crime Scene

Boudreaux delivers an action-packed thriller in *Scavenger Hunt*. [The book] provides an intense thrill ride with well-developed characters and realistic events.

-Novels Alive

Scavenger Hunt . . . has no flaws and instantly grabs your attention. Blake's personality pulls the story together, and his witty character makes this book all the more enjoyable to read.

-Review Tales Magazine

AWARDS FOR *SCAVENGER HUNT*

Literary Titan Book Award, *Scavenger Hunt*, Winner

2023 Bookfest Award, *Scavenger Hunt*, Winner

Book Award Pro Global Book Award, *Scavenger Hunt*, Winner

Speak Up Talk Radio Firebird Book Award, *Scavenger Hunt*,
Winner – Legal Thriller

2023 American Fiction Awards, *Scavenger Hunt*,
Winner – Thriller: Legal

2023 Pacific Book Award, *Scavenger Hunt*, Finalist

2023 Indies Today Awards, *Scavenger Hunt*, Semi-finalist

A SMALL TOWN POLITICAL THRILLER

HOMECOMING QUEEN

CHAD BOUDREAUX

NEW YORK

LONDON • NASHVILLE • MELBOURNE • VANCOUVER

HOMECOMING QUEEN

A SMALL TOWN POLITICAL THRILLER

Published in New York, New York, by Morgan James Publishing. Morgan James is a trademark of Morgan James, LLC. www.MorganJamesPublishing.com

Proudly distributed by Publishers Group West®

Morgan James BOGO™

A **FREE** ebook edition is available for you or a friend with the purchase of this print book.

CLEARLY SIGN YOUR NAME ABOVE

Instructions to claim your free ebook edition:
1. Visit MorganJamesBOGO.com
2. Sign your name CLEARLY in the space above
3. Complete the form and submit a photo of this entire page
4. You or your friend can download the ebook to your preferred device

ISBN 9781636983677 paperback
ISBN 9781636983684 ebook
Library of Congress Control Number:
2023949079

Cover Design by:
TLC Book Design
www.tlcbookdesign.com/

Interior Design by:
Chris Treccani
www.3dogcreative.net

Morgan James is a proud partner of Habitat for Humanity Peninsula and Greater Williamsburg. Partners in building since 2006.

Get involved today! Visit: www.morgan-james-publishing.com/giving-back

For Nana and Papa. They never left.

MIRANDA

MIRANDA RIVER

UPPER WEST SIDE

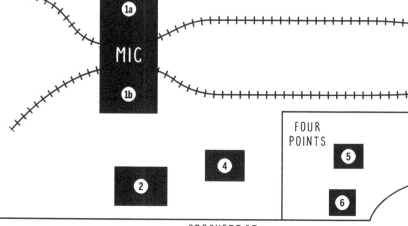

MIC
1a
1b

FOUR
POINTS

5

2

4

6

CROCKETT ST.

← TO HARBOR
BRIDGE

7

3

REVOLUTIONARY
PARK

LOWER WEST SIDE

MAP KEY

1. MIRANDA INDUSTRIAL COMPLEX
   A. REFINERY
   B. TRAIN DEPOT
2. DANFORTH DISTRIBUTORS
3. MATHIS RESIDENCE
4. SHERIFF'S HEADQUARTERS
5. SHIP AHOY GRILLE
6. ALAMO OPERA HOUSE
7. OLD MEXICO RESTAURANT
8. WHATABURGER
9. ZED'S MUSIC STORE
10. BLOUSES & BOOTS BOUTIQUE
11. HOSPITALITY CENTER
12. KWIK MART
13. LIGHTHOUSE RESTAURANT
14. KENNY'S SPORTS
15. WATER TOWER
16. MISSION CENTER MALL
17. DANFORTH HACIENDA
18. CHURCH GROUNDS
19. MIRANDA HIGH SCHOOL
20. CLOCKWORKS NIGHTCLUB
21. ENDLESS SUMMER SURF SHOP
22. ETHAN'S BUNGALOW

TOWNSHIP

THE FLATS (15)

UPPER EAST SIDE

BEACH

(16)

(17)

(8)

(9)

(20)

CAUSEWAY

(11)

(10)

GULF OF MEXICO

CROCKETT ST.

(21)

(13)

(12)

(18)

WATERWAY

(14)

(19)

(22)

LOWER EAST SIDE

BEACH

BOWIE ST.

PROLOGUE

FIVE YEARS AGO
INTERVIEW OF RICK HOLLOWAY

FBI Special Agent Brian Maxwell: State your full name and age.

Witness: Ricky Holloway. Just turned eighteen.

Agent: Mr. Holloway, what can you tell me about Miranda, Texas?

Witness: Something's terribly wrong here.

Agent: Like what?

Witness: Miranda needs to eat.

Agent: Not sure what that means. We're talking about the town itself, not the fat lady who sings at the Alamo Opera House, right?

Witness: You think that's funny?

Agent: Okay, I'll take the bait. Eat what?

Witness: Miranda feeds on conflict and pain.

Agent: You believe that nonsense, Mr. Holloway? Listen, I need you to remember three things for me. *One*, lying to a federal officer is a crime; *two*, this is a homicide investigation, not Texas hold 'em; and *three*, I'm not a psychiatrist.

Witness: You asked me a weird question. That tells me you're still figuring things out. You know there's something wrong here in Miranda, my friend. *Terribly wrong.* I can see it in your eyes. You just can't put your finger on it. Not yet.

Agent: Anything else?

Witness: The old timers say Miranda isn't the end of the world, but you can see it from our water tower.

Agent: See what?

Witness: The end of the world.

Agent: Let's stay away from folklore and wives' tales, shall we?

Witness: Stay in Miranda long enough, and you'll forget what's fact or fiction.

Agent: Mr. Holloway, were you born here . . . in Miranda?

Witness: No doubt. Miranda Underground. [Holds up arms covered in tattoos.]

Agent: Miranda Underground?

Witness: With all due respect, if you must ask . . .

Agent: Is that a local gang?

Witness: More like a multicultural posse. All on the up and up, my friend. You're either in or out; but when you're in, you're family.

Agent: I'm from Texas, Mr. Holloway, and you know the bond. '*Born* anywhere in Texas, *welcome* anywhere in Texas.'

Witness: You memorize that from a convenience store coffee mug? Look, just be glad you didn't drive to Mirando City. Completely different town. Other side of the state somewhere, they tell me.

Agent: I guess I'm not welcome in Miranda.

Witness: Let's be clear, my friend . . . self-proclaimed Son of Texas. You're *welcome* here. You're just not *trusted* here because—

Agent: Because I'm from Houston and not from Miranda?

Witness: No, you're not trusted here because you're from anywhere in this whole wide world *but* Miranda. I don't care if you're from Mirando City, San Antonio, San Angelo, Los Dos Laredos, or even closer still—Corpus Christi or Harlingen. It *don't* matter.

Agent: You clearly have a problem with trust. Is that why you have the nine-millimeter pistol?

Witness: I pack a nine because I'd rather be judged by twelve than carried by six. And I got a permit.

Agent: Tell me what happened the night that Johnny Delgado committed suicide.

Witness: [Pause] Johnny didn't commit suicide.

Agent: Well, that's an interesting theory. He was the only one in the car. He missed his jump over the gully, and his car crashed, exploded, and burned. Had explosives in the car.

Witness: Heard about all that.

Agent: With all due respect for your friend, that goes beyond the standard rebel-without-a-cause or devil-may-care mishap.

Witness: [Nonresponsive.]

Agent: Don't you think?

Witness: Doesn't mean he committed suicide.

Agent: Mr. Holloway, he tried to jump his muscle car over the Miranda River with explosives in his trunk. Evel Knievel himself wouldn't have tried that. You wouldn't say that's suicide?

Witness: It's only suicide if he's dead.

Agent: Wait. You think he's still *alive*?

Witness: [Nonresponsive.]

Agent: Mr. Holloway?

Witness: I went to the funeral, but I never saw the body.

Agent: Funeral was closed casket. Explosion like that . . . the remains would've been a charred mess of ashes. When's the last time you saw Johnny Delgado?

Witness: Few hours before the homecoming dance.

Agent: The Miranda High School homecoming dance?

Witness: [Nods.]

Agent: So you haven't seen him since the incident in question?

Witness: Nope—not since before he jumped. Before he *tried* to jump, I mean.

Agent: His car *exploded* and was engulfed in flames. Houdini couldn't escape a tragedy like that. If you haven't seen him, what on earth makes you think he's still alive?

Witness: Y'all never found his bones.

Agent: So what? What conclusion can you draw from that ridiculous rumor?

Witness: Bones don't burn.

1

PRESENT DAY

Refusing to knock, Anika Raven busted through the front door of her childhood home. She snatched the letter opener from the kitchen bar, weaponized it between her middle and ring fingers, and charged deeper inside the house. Enraged, she struggled to adjust her vision and locate her target. The afternoon's sunlight couldn't penetrate the living room's drawn shades, and the television and jellyfish lava lamp provided the only lighting. In an instant, however, she homed in on his shaggy blond hair.

And then she attacked.

Ambushing her stepdad from behind, she followed no codes of war. Her means and direction of attack, though stealthy, didn't affect movements on the battlefield. He sat motionless on the couch, drunk and stoned in his tighty-whities, watching Samuel L. Jackson talk about tasty burgers in the movie *Pulp Fiction*.

"Where's Sam?" she demanded with gritted teeth, lodging the makeshift weapon against his throat.

"Easy, darlin'," Scotty Mathis said, intoxicated but clamoring for life's spark. His flailing arms missed the bong on the coffee table but knocked over the pyramid of empty beer cans as he searched for his bearings. "Samantha's around here . . . somewhere."

"Don't you dare call me *darlin'*," Anika said, pulling the letter opener from his throat. The pungent smell of body odor, bar rot, and loaded ash-

1

trays nauseated her. "I'm not your daughter, thank heavens. You should be ashamed of yourself. You need a hazmat shower. You reek!"

"Not fair," he said, stammering to his feet, a full can of Shiner toppling from his lap to the floor. As beer sloshed onto the carpet, he added, "You didn't tell me you—"

"Sam!" Anika screamed. "Where are you?"

"Probably in her room," he mumbled, his curly, sun-bleached hair covering his face.

"Quit talking," Anika barked. His blatant sin was neglect, not physical abuse, but they were equal in her eyes. She hated him with a passion. Her sister, and even her deadbeat mom, deserved better. "You're a pathetic excuse for a human being and a horrible husband and father. Put on some clothes and wait outside."

"Darlin', listen," he said, stumbling toward her. "I don't know why—"

"Stand back and get on the lawn! If your pinky toe so much as creeps back inside, I'm calling 911."

He mustered a look of disappointment over what he considered Anika's overreaction. His attempts at drama, though, fell short of an Oscar-worthy performance. In fact, like most things in his life, his effort failed miserably. The alcohol and weed controlled his functions, so his facial expressions were more pathetic than serious. Another scene of "Drunk Pothead on Stage," one that filled the bill every night during amateur hour in Miranda's Lower West Side. Eventually, after all the hemming and hawing, whatever small remnant of shame he possessed took over. He grabbed his frayed jean shorts and, after losing his balance more than once, slid them on and stumbled outside.

Anika marched down the dark hallway toward her sister's room. As she walked, she experienced an eerie resistance in her steps, a slight but noticeable pull not unlike the lane-keeping assistance in her rental car. Two deadbolts secured Samantha's bedroom door, and Anika noticed the doorframe's splintered casting and bent strike plates. Someone had broken down this door many times. She knocked lightly and whispered, "It's me . . . Anika." She heard the pitter-patter of bare feet scrambling behind the door.

Samantha carefully unlocked each bolt, one at a time, as if each turn and click signified a courageous, life-changing choice.

"Samantha!" Anika said, clutching the blonde eight-year-old with the pointy nose. She had sapphire blue eyes so prodigious that she'd require time and puberty to grow into them. Anika ran her hand through her sister's tangled, bird's nest hair and kissed her forehead. "You okay?"

Samantha, wearing a yellow polka-dot sundress, nodded and squeezed her big sister like she'd never let go.

"Haven't seen you in forever," Anika said, kissing her again. "Where's Mom?"

No response. Nothing but vacant eyes.

"You know where mom is?" Anika asked again, pulling away from the hug. For a moment, she feared Sam had forgotten how to speak.

Samantha shook her head, sat on her bed, and slipped on a pair of red rain boots.

"Honey, why are you wearing those boots? It rains here five times a year." Anika surveyed Sam's bedroom, once her own. At least one thing hadn't changed. The iconic self-portrait of Mexican folk hero Frida Kahlo still anchored the room over the bed. Everything else, however, seemed different. In addition to the locks on the doors, someone had boarded the windows. A naked bulb hanging from the center of the ceiling cast the only light. Once pink and yellow, someone had painted the walls black. The walls, in turn, provided the canvas for several white pencil drawings of different cube variations. The macabre look and feel of the space unsettled Anika.

More unsettling, though, was Scotty's yammering psychobabble from the front lawn. "You come home with your self-righteous moralism!" he slurred. Despite his blithering nonsense, he'd recaptured a measure of spunk and soon would regain enough sobriety and confidence to frustrate the sisters' escape.

Scotty Shortshrift, through every fault of his own, always found himself on the receiving end of the Town of Miranda's billy club. An excellent surfer before shredding his knee, he'd driven eighteen-wheelers until the Texas Highway Patrol stripped him of his commercial driver's license for blowing twice the legal limit. Now, he was a bum bent on excuses, rationalization, and conspiracy theories. Societal forces had conspired against him and facilitated his demise. "Blame your mom, not me!" he continued. "I'm here! What about her? Where's she?"

His last question was valid, the answer unknown. Barbara Mathis's drunken benders sometimes took her to faraway places where few lifeforms travel. But Anika was a survivalist, not a philosopher, and found no interest in trading barbs in a world of whataboutisms. She grabbed Samantha's wrist and said, "Let's get out of here. Sisters in the bond!"

Samantha, remembering something important, pulled away from Anika, lunged across the bed, and grabbed the orange object nestled against her pillow.

"Faux Pooh!" Anika said, referring to the fake Winnie the Pooh stuffed animal her grandmother had crafted and gifted to Anika as a child. Before leaving home, Anika had stashed Faux Pooh—more a guardian than a keepsake—behind a cutout in the sheetrock inside the closet. "How'd you find him?"

Samantha smiled, pointed to the secret compartment, and shrugged. Anika's hand found Sam's, and they darted from the room.

Once they entered the hallway, the eerie resistance returned with a vengeance. Scampering to the living room was like swimming against a fierce rip current. The sunlight shone through the open door, providing a clear escape path, but the indescribable force made it hard to move forward. Confounded by its presence, Anika kept fighting. Grasping Sam, she bulled forward until she reached the splintered front door. She descended the three dilapidated steps, where she confronted her stepdad again.

"You're gonna pay for that door," he growled. "You busted the lock."

"Plenty of locks to cannibalize in that dreadful place, but she won't need deadbolts anymore."

"You just wait one—"

"I'm calling family and protective services," Anika declared. "Sam's with me now."

"Take it up with your mom, not FPS. She never loved you or me; she left us all. She's probably face down in a gutter somewhere in Matamoros."

"I hate you! For all her faults, Mom deserves better!" Anika said, walking to her compact rental car with Samantha in tow. "And so does Sam!"

"Hate me all you want, darlin', but you won't keep Sam," he threatened.

"We'll see about that," Anika responded, opening the door as Sam crawled into the passenger seat.

"Bring her back tomorrow, or I'll release the hounds. The sheriff, his deputies—maybe the mayor herself."

"You're evil."

"I may be evil in your book, Anika, but I'm not the one hiding my dirty laundry."

Anika closed her eyes. She knew what was coming next. Drunks rarely keep their promises, and alcohol is the skeleton key for the most secure locks.

"You're the one with the dark secret, darlin'," he continued with a vicious smile, his bloodshot eyes hovering over his red, bulbous nose and tar-stained teeth. "You'll pay for this!"

2

Time was ripe for another big, nasty one. The old timers in Miranda, Texas—those who played 42 on the porch of the Alamo Opera House—measured time by hurricanes. They were the survivors of the last big, nasty one. The clicking of dominos by arthritic fingers intensified during the late summer months in South Texas, when tropical disturbances progressed into depressions, strengthened into storms, and ballooned into hurricanes. And hurricanes often advanced in intensity as they barreled west in the warm waters of the Gulf of Mexico.

Category 3 hurricanes changed a culture's worldview. Categories 4 and 5 converted unbelievers to religion. And for whatever reason—Texas Democrats blamed karma—Republican presidents bore the brunt of Category 3s and 4s on their watch. Nixon had Celia, Reagan had Alicia, Bush 43 had the Katrina-Rita-Wilma one-two-three knockout punch, and Trump had Harvey, a Category 4 that ravished Miranda.

But the old timers didn't care a lick about *those* storms. Nor did they give a hoot about federal or state politics. In Miranda, on that expansive porch outside the Alamo Opera House, only the mayor's authority mattered and only three storms garnered much attention: the Storm of 1900, Hurricane Carla in 1961, and the Category 5 hurricane the mayor believed was on its way. Those two prior storms mattered because they hadn't just ravished Miranda, they had *decimated* her—torn her down to the dirt and mesquite roots. And they mattered because they signaled something more ominous.

Time was ripe for the next big, nasty one.

The old timers weren't superstitious, but they *were* paranoid. And their paranoia didn't mean they were wrong. Facts mattered. The old timers shaking dominos knew that every sixty years or thereabouts a hurricane ripped the soul from Miranda and stripped her to the bones. Legend said it happened in 1779, a few years after America declared her independence from Great Britain. It happened in 1840, a few years after Santa Anna marched his Mexican Army through Miranda on the way to the Alamo (the real Alamo, three hours away). And it happened again in 1900 and 1961.

"Need to update the coordinates," the leader of the old timers said, the vintage radio resting in his lap. Cyrus Kleberg, known as Cyclops, listened to weather radio as he rocked in a rickety chair and puffed on his pipe. In the background, not as loud as the blaring weather update, Hank Williams bellowed through porch speakers manufactured the same year he recorded the song. The air was heavy and sticky, but wind funneled through the porch in intermittent gusts, and the multiple ceiling fans circled at high speeds, making a *click, click*, clicking noise after each rotation that sounded like Newton's Cradle.

Cyclops entered the world during the 1933 summer of terror, when eleven consecutive storms pummeled Miranda. The lives lost to Mother Nature that season included his mom and two older brothers. His dad had escaped death only because he'd been stranded with his mistress in Corpus Christi. He hanged himself soon after the Catholic priest had tossed dirt over their bodies, the toxic dish of shame proving too much to stomach. Miranda had eaten well that year. For reasons no one could explain, however, Baby Cyclops (deemed "the boy who lived" by the *Miranda Caller Times* sixty-four years before Harry Potter) wasn't on the menu.

"Cyclops, you reckon this here's the one?" Curtis Worden asked, walking through the swinging saloon doors onto the porch. Some believed the creaking doors—seasoned with chipped paint and hues of green and red—were originals, having survived the Storm of 1900 and Hurricane Carla. Curtis had thumbtacked an old hurricane tracking map near the doors, and he enjoyed moving the magnetic markers to the correct latitude and longitude.

"No, this ain't the one. But she's the forerunner—Tropical Storm Joyce. Joyce'll likely poop her drawers as a Cat 2 and turn north before reaching the Gulf. Won't affect downtown much, but the waves'll pound the Laguna Madre and Padre Island like a meat mallet on a chicken-fried steak."

"Water temp's just right for the big one," an old timer named Vernis announced from the domino table.

"Water temp's just right," Cyclops noted.

"*Timing's* just right for the big one," another old timer named Peanut added.

"Timing's just right too," Cyclops parroted again, blowing tobacco smoke from his cream blend, its smell monopolizing the porch. "Sixty-year storm's right on schedule. Time for the cleansing."

"Read me the coordinates," Worden said. Worden, who was at least twenty years younger than the others, was the fastidious caretaker of the Alamo Opera House. He spent considerable time sweeping the porch, managing daily affairs, and listening to the old timers fuss, cuss, and discuss things concerning their hometown. Born just a few months after Hurricane Alice in 1954, which produced a two-thousand-year flood in Miranda, Worden was too young to be an old timer. They allowed him access, though, to their seedbed of daily gossip and wellspring of local predictions—predictions that often came to pass.

Like most of Miranda's infrastructure, the townsfolk rebuilt the Alamo Opera House in 1962. Despite the reconstruction, it never changed locations. Across the street from Revolutionary Park, it was smack dab in the middle of Four Points. No longer an active theater for live entertainment, it was now an amalgamation of quaint office space, a general store, and a beer hall where the town's elderly-but-restless contingent loitered on the porch. The small store sold sundry items that resembled the inventory in the early 1960s, featuring duct tape, band-aids, and painkilling powder (now available in more user-friendly packets). The primary draw was the Lone Star beer on tap and the award-winning breakfast tacos, heralded as the best in town (and second in Texas only to San Antonio's Pete's Takos, a place that Cyclops said cooked so good they forgot how to spell). Timmy, who was Worden's righthand man, wore a Gary P. Nunn "Adios Amigo" concert T-shirt. He served the food and drink from behind a sixteen-foot Brunswick antique bar that rivaled any bar in the best westerns.

Those who rebuilt the Alamo in 1962 repurposed some of the square footage once dedicated to the theater and its vaulted ceilings. Sleeping quarters and living space serviced employees upstairs. Everything else was downstairs, including some modest office space, the General Store, the Commons, a large commercial-grade garage, and a holding cell for those who committed serious misdemeanors or low-grade felonies. Depending on the mayor's mood, she'd often allow petty criminals placed in the holding cell to sleep it off, think about it, and go home the next day.

The repurposed Alamo maintained most of its Theater Hall, replete with stage and seating, and it never forgot its roots. Signs from old theater shows and concerts peppered its walls. This included mostly Tejano and Country-Western singers but also Rock 'n Roll, Blues, Jazz, and vaudeville acts. Of course, the Alamo had hosted barn dances and family variety shows (similar to *Hee-Haw*), broadcast by WBAP in Fort Worth. Besides an opera house, the Alamo had been a storied dancehall, rivaling the Broken Spoke, Luckenbach, John T. Floore's Country Store, the Armadillo, Billy Bob's, and Gruene Hall.

One of Worden's many odd jobs included decorating the Alamo, and he thumbtacked his favorite concert poster next to the hurricane tracker on the porch: Bob Wills and the Texas Playboys. The famous Western-Swing band had played here in April 1948, a few days after headlining the inaugural *Louisiana Hayride* in Shreveport, Louisiana, the venue that launched the careers of legends Hank Williams, Elvis Presley, and Johnny Cash.

Cyclops recited the coordinates of Tropical Storm Joyce, still not to Cuba, and refilled his pipe with fresh tobacco. "When the big, nasty one gets here, won't be no need to board up windows."

"How long before she hits land, you reckon?" Worden asked.

"Days not weeks."

"What about that girl? She comin' back?"

"Suspect she'll be here soon," Cyclops said as he spat. "Been five years, Curtis, and she ain't a girl no more. She graduated from Rice and is now off at some fancy DC school. I hear she wants to be one of them lawyers."

"So they say. Figured she'd stay gone after losin' her boyfriend like that."

"When Miranda wants you, she gets you. Surprised y'all allowed her to leave town. I ain't never said much to her, Curtis. You?"

"We've not met proper. Doubt she'd recognize me. Mayor wants to meet with her for some reason."

"Curious to know what all the hubbub's about," Cyclops said. "Few ever leave this place."

"And no one leaves twice. You figure she's already come back?"

Cyclops peeked at the cubes he'd doodled on his napkin. The muddied picture denied him a clear answer. "Reckon we'll know when she gets here."

"Even so, maybe I should walk down to the stores, ask some questions, and have a look-see."

Cyrus Kleberg scratched the back of his neck, tipped up the front of his straw cowboy hat, and relit his pipe. After an uncomfortable pause, he tossed the napkin on the porch and said, "I already sent somebody down there . . . to ask some questions and have a look-see."

3

Anika slammed her palms on the steering wheel so hard the airbag should've deployed. She couldn't escape the neighborhood fast enough. Scotty had threatened to expose her secret beyond the family. He had made a clown of himself, raising his fist and tripping on the steps before reentering the house. Driving off, Anika smelled general-vicinity marijuana smoke, ubiquitous in Miranda's Lower West Side. She heard the car's air conditioner revisit its losing battle with the Gulf Coast summer heat. The neighborhood had become a junkyard for jalopies, some parked in yards. Most of the yards hosted unkempt flowerbeds and mesquite trees of various vintages, shapes, and sizes. The mesquite tree outside her old bedroom window—the one that had scared her for two years after she'd watched *Poltergeist*—looked like a mangled hand of death. Its multiple trunks sprouted from the ground. Its limbs stretched like lanky fingers into her yard, where the thorny branches would *screech, screech, screech* against her window on windy nights.

And there was the gate. The one gate on the chain-link fence surrounding the backyard. The blasted gate that changed everything. It was open. Of course it was open. *Why is that cursed gate always open?*

Sam remained mum, presumably traumatized by the abrupt home extraction. She had texted Anika a day earlier to express her loneliness and longing for Mom. Little did she know, her older sister would roll into town before the next sundown like Tasmanian Devil from *Looney Tunes*, tearing to pieces what remained of Sam's home life. But enough was enough.

11

Bald vultures swirled overhead, attracted by the decaying flesh of Miranda's Lower West Side roadkill buffet. On this day, armadillo and possum competed for the title of main carrion delicacy.

"You okay?" Anika asked as she patted Sam's leg. Sam smiled, squeezed her sister's hand, and nodded. Her eyebrows danced, and her pupils contracted and expanded in rhythm with the conversation. "Not sure where we're sleeping tonight," Anika continued, "but we need junk food! Just like old times!"

Long ago, city planners had organized Miranda into quadrants like Manhattan, just without New York City's grid system. Like other towns, city officials had zoned Miranda for residential, commercial, and manufacturing at different locations within each quadrant. Of course, manufacturing was forbidden in the Upper East Side, and zoning was more of a recommendation than a requirement in the Lower West Side, enforced not by restrictive covenants but by peer pressure and intimidation. Miranda's Central Park, so to speak, was named Revolutionary Park. Located in Four Points, it served as the heartbeat of Miranda. This lush—the old timers called it *hallowed*—twenty-acre park was where townsfolk of all ages and quadrants would gather, picnic, dance, play music or games, and frolic under towering trees.

Approaching Four Points, Anika spied the trees' majestic canopies. Revolutionary Park boasted an assortment of Mexican oak, live oak, and burr oak that—magically, the old timers argued—had survived every hurricane since the eighteenth century. This phenomenon did not go unnoticed. Indeed, legends of monster hurricanes from generations past and images captured of Category 5s that had crushed Miranda all shared a common story. A story that caused even skeptics to scratch their heads. Despite the storms obliterating everything in their paths, they all had spared the oak trees. And there was more. Pictures of the park hanging in the Alamo Opera House—taken in the aftermath of Hurricane Carla in 1960—showed without a doubt the oaks had barely lost any leaves.

Townsfolk had rebuilt Miranda around those trees after Carla. They had prioritized the reconstruction of the Alamo Opera House because that's where the mayor worked. To the old timers' delight, many of Miranda's long-established restaurants returned. They had rebuilt the Whataburger first, of course, but Old Mexico, Ship Ahoy Grille, and the Lighthouse Restaurant soon followed. New construction didn't stop in the early sixties; more contemporary establishments opened, including Zed's Music Store, Blouses & Boots Boutique, and an overpriced sporting goods store called Kenny's. What's more, construction now continued beyond the quadrants. Across the causeway, for instance, Ethan Danforth built his Endless Summer Surf Shop, which resembled the Dockside Surf Shop in the movie *The Legend of Billie Jean*. That was the same Ethan Danforth with the fantastic abs who was looking down, larger than life, at Four Points from a billboard that towered over the Kwik Mart. Anika gaped at the gigantic image of her hunky friend until she parked the car on the curb underneath him.

A bell jingled as Anika and Sam entered the Kwik Mart. Anika smelled barbeque brisket, and she spotted a few locals loitering next to the gambling machines. Walking toward the back, the sisters passed Big Red soda in two-liter bottles, pickles the size of gourds bobbing in vats of vinegar, and Lone Star beer in twenty-four-ounce cans floating in drums of ice. Anika noticed bags of pork skins (Mirandarites called them *chicharrones*), a Dr. Pepper Icee machine, and beef jerky in all shapes, sizes, and spices. In the back, Anika spied the neon lights that advertised myriad beer and wine cooler choices in refrigerators.

Sam shrugged when Anika asked what she wanted to eat. Anika, presently a vegetarian, frowned at the Giant Slim Jims and buffalo-wing-flavored *chicharrones* and grabbed two boxes of strawberry Pop-Tarts. That's when the bell jingled again. An old man, likely a few years short of a century, shuffled in with a worn cowboy hat. She paid him little mind, other than to notice his fragile frame, gray handlebar mustache, and liver spots on his face. Minutes later, she walked to the front counter. Standing near one of the gambling machines, the weathered man leaned on a cane and stared at her. He didn't blink. Didn't smile. He just stared and chewed on a toothpick. Growing uncomfortable, she smiled as a courtesy, but he didn't respond. He just stared . . . and chewed.

She kept one eye on him as she checked out. The slight pulling force she'd felt at the house returned, nearly causing her to panic. She had never responded to pressure or fear like this before. *Why is my body doing this?* She wanted to ditch the Pop-Tarts, grab Sam, and sprint to the car. But she waited. She handed the cashier cash as the old man tightened his stare and the force grew more palpable. When she completed her transaction, she rushed Sam out the front door. Tossing the grocery bag in the backseat, Anika and Sam hopped in the car, bound for the causeway, and fastened their seatbelts. Before they drove away, however, the bell jingled again, and the old man shuffled outside. Once there, he spotted them in the car, leaned on his cane, and twirled his mustache.

Looking in her rearview mirror, Anika noticed the old man didn't break his stare until they disappeared. Only then did the strange, pulling force stop.

4

The Endless Summer Surf Shop was located over the causeway on the beach. The place smelled of surf wax, new leather, and coconut sunscreen. C101 Radio was playing the Red Hot Chili Peppers when the sisters walked in. Anika witnessed Sam's knees wobble when she laid eyes on the authentic version of the man on the billboard. Startled by sensory overload, Sam retreated behind Anika and lost herself among the countless clothes racks. She peeked through cheap T-shirts at twenty-one-year-old Ethan Danforth, now the most famous person with whom she'd shared a room. She watched his every move as he abandoned his customer at the cash register and bounced like Tigger toward Anika.

"Wonder Woman returns!" he said, smiling ear to ear, giving Anika *la bise*, the customary Miranda quick kiss on both cheeks, which she reciprocated. "You wore a rubied tiara the last time I saw you. A beautiful sight to behold."

"Your brother looked better in his crown of fake jewels," she said, embracing him with a comfort that displayed familial affection. He lifted her and spun her around.

"Not many of us are royalty, even for a day," Ethan said, walking back to the counter. A young surfer waited to buy some strawberry-scented surfboard wax and an *Outer Banks* tank top (from the Netflix show). Completing the transaction, Ethan continued, "I always knew you'd be homecoming queen. My older brother, on the other hand . . ."

"Logan was a brilliant homecoming king," Anika said, feigning interest in a sale rack of surfing attire too big or small for those not employed by Barnum & Bailey.

Ethan addressed the young customer. "Dude, thanks for the biz, and long live the Pogues!" His attention returned to Anika and Sam. "If you say so. Seems like forever and a day since that night."

"Five years," Anika said as she watched the customer flash a hang loose sign on his way out. Anika pivoted to a more important line of questioning. "How's your brother?"

"Believe it or not, Logan got hitched."

"Really," Anika said, trying to hide her emotions, her heart stealing away her breath. The primary reason she'd driven to the Endless Summer Surf Shop was to reconnect with Logan through Ethan. The marital news hit her like brass knuckles to the jaw. She knew, though, that Logan's dalliance with bachelorhood eventually had to end. He was a big catch: handsome, smart, successful, and rich. No, not rich, not even filthy rich—*wealthy*. His parents owned the biggest Lone Star Brewery beer distributorship in Texas, making him and Ethan heirs to the Danforth fortune. Unlike Ethan, who always dreamed of owning a surf shop, Logan worked for the family business and wasn't interested in charting an independent course. Anika would reflect more on his marriage later. Time being of the essence, she would need to look elsewhere for a place to sleep.

"Yeah, he married a UT cheerleader."

"That's great. I'm *so* happy for him," she lied. "Must be a special woman."

"She's okay. Dude acts weird when she's around, but I guess that's to be expected. She's wicked hot."

Anika rolled her eyes. Ethan's priorities, simple to decipher, hadn't changed. Though handsomer than his older brother, which said a lot, he lacked Logan's emotional depth, couth, and humility.

Picking up on Anika's reaction, Ethan added, "But not nearly as pretty as you."

Ethan's compliment sounded like a hackneyed pick-up line, but it didn't land that way. Taking things in stride, she received it as more mechanical than flirty; but seasons had come and gone since anyone had flattered her so brazenly. Then again, this was Miranda, where confidence permeated the gene pool. "Thank you, Ethan, but you didn't need to say that."

Ethan leaned behind the counter, out of sight, to fetch some coins. "Always thought you and Logan would tie the knot. He was bonkers for you . . . but I know you and Johnny were a thing." Reemerging, he added, "May he rest in peace."

"That's interesting to hear, Ethan," she chuckled awkwardly, dismissing the comment about Johnny. "I doubt Logan would agree. Besides," she said, holding up her left hand, "I'm engaged!"

"Congrats! Uh . . . I mean, best wishes!" He grabbed her hand. "Nice ring. Who's the lucky winner? When's the date? And blah, blah, blah—all the other girl stuff I'm supposed to ask."

"Thank you . . . I think," she laughed. "He's a young professor in DC, and the date's still open." She released her sweaty hand from his, seeking to change the subject. "Do you remember my sister, Samantha. She's why I came home for the weekend. Sam, come meet Mr. Danforth. He doesn't bite."

"Hi, Samantha."

Sam smiled, lifted Faux Pooh, and waved the stuffed animal's right arm before scampering off to play with the hermit crabs. Ethan turned his attention back to Anika, who eyed Sam with sisterly pride as she skipped away.

"She doesn't talk much, does she?" Ethan asked.

"To be fair, she's crushing on the owner of the place. She saw you on a ginormous billboard near downtown. Haven't seen her this giddy since—"

"She's a doll," he interrupted.

"Apple of my eye," Anika said. "But don't take her for Pollyanna. She has a mischievous streak."

"Hmm. Sounds like her older sister. Everything good with you, Anika?"

"Not really, but it's a long story, and we need to find a hotel room before it gets dark," Anika said, straightening her hair and touching her flushed cheeks as if she'd stayed too long. But her voice, singed with anxiety, betrayed her desire to linger and continue reminiscing with Ethan. Ages had passed since she'd regarded life in Miranda. "So we should—"

"I'm fixin' to shut down the store. Y'all are welcome to stay at my bungalow. Ten-minute walk down the beach."

"That's so nice of you, but . . ."

"Come on," he insisted. "Miranda's most beautiful homecoming queen can't pay for room and board. Visions of your orange eyes, olive skin, and chocolate hair would haunt me for months."

Anika grinned. A true alpha dog, Ethan let his instincts run without a leash. "You have a roommate?"

"Two roommates, but they won't mind; and there's plenty of room for five, especially if you're only staying a few nights."

"One night," she insisted, "but my fiancé wouldn't approve of me shacking with three guys."

"You wouldn't be *shacking*. And I'm the only dude. You're like my big sis, so that should bury the optics."

Of course, Anika thought. *If there was ever a real-life Jack Tripper from* Three's Company, *Ethan would own the part.* Sam had returned, so Anika grabbed her hand. "Would that be okay, Sam?" Sam stared at the engagement ring. "*Sam*," Anika repeated, "you okay if we sleep at Mr. Danforth's place?"

Sam squeezed Faux Pooh, smiled bigly, and nodded in excitement.

Anika consulted her watch and panicked. Two minutes shy of five o'clock. "Ethan, you're a saint, and we accept. May I ask another favor? Keep an eye on Sam for a sec?"

"Of course. And before we leave, pick out some swimwear. The waves are rockin', and I'm surfing tonight."

"*Tonight?* I haven't surfed in years," Anika said, dialing a number. "Need to step outside for a private call."

"No problem, Anika, but remember that jealous fiancés are *no bueno*," he joked.

"Tell me about it," she replied, opening the door. Her choice not to correct him was a dishonest omission. A tiny white lie. She wasn't calling her fiancé. She remembered what her old priest had said: a half-truth masquerading as a whole truth was nothing but an untruth. But half-truths were horseplay in Miranda, where big lies came quick and easy. And they were about to come a lot easier. Her heart racing, the recipient of her call picked up with only ten seconds to spare.

And Anika breathed a sigh of relief.

5

Against her better judgment but consistent with drinking one too many margaritas, Anika joined Ethan in what daredevils call moonlight surfing. Ethan's roommates—Amber and Chelsea—were no-shows at his bungalow. Sam had crashed on the couch. The bungalow itself was a long five iron from the second sandbar over which Anika's surfboard now floated. Her legs straddled the longboard as she watched Ethan's muscular body maneuver on, over, and through the four-foot swells. The Comanche Moon lit up the ocean, providing ample light for him to navigate the surf breaks with masterful skill and ease. The night was otherwise calm, even as the larger waves signaled the imminent arrival of what news reports were calling Hurricane Joyce, now a Category 1 predicted to transition north before reaching the Gulf of Mexico.

After riding a spectacular wave to shore, Ethan climbed back on his board and paddled toward Anika. "You see *that* ride? Radical!"

Anika smiled, marveling at his many gifts, including his chiseled jawline. His cobalt eyes, presently reflecting the moonlight, paralyzed the strongest of women with their Medusa-like power. But an immature child lived inside that beautiful man, a child who'd never experienced any meaningful adversity. "No wonder Billabong pays you so much."

"Not gonna surf?"

"Couldn't catch a wave sober," she noted, "and I'm a bit over-served. Wanna join me over here?"

"Would your fiancé approve? Not sure how things roll in DC."

"Approve of me drinking too much, or what?"

"It's all harmless. Drinking, surfing, listening to Jane's Addiction records."

"You said it yourself; you're like my little brother," she said, growing less convinced.

"True, but you're only two years older."

"Speaking of older women," she said, steering the conversation else-where, "where are your roomies tonight?"

"They're vampires."

"Oh, Ethan, I ruined your Friday night!" Anika said, remembering single Mirandites barhopped on weekends. "I'm being selfish and didn't even think to—"

"Not at all. I'm moonlight surfing with an amazing woman. Life doesn't get any better. Besides, it's cool reconnecting. If you don't mind me prying, what's up with your sister?"

Anika jumped to the point. "She's in a neglectful home and needs out before it's too late."

"That bad?"

"She won't even talk. I had my suspicions before, but once Mom flew the coop on her latest bender to who-knows-where, Sam started texting me. Her dad gets wasted and checks out, leaving Sam alone to fend for herself."

"Terrible."

"Once he forgot to pick her up at softball practice, and she walked home in the dark. She's eight, mind you! Last year, he left her alone for two days. For some reason, she has two deadbolts on her bedroom door. That's *inside* the house."

"And your mom?"

"She's guilty, too, and bears equal responsibility. But Mom needs med-ical help, and she's not my impediment to helping Sam. If it weren't for Scotty Scumbag, Sam could live with me."

"So what's the plan? Run away?"

"Ethan, I don't know what to do," Anika moaned, tilting back her head and running her hand through her mane of soaked hair. Moonlight caused the water droplets on her arms and legs to sparkle. "I'm no good at this. Just waiting for her dad to call in an AMBER Alert. Not to be confused with your Amber . . ."

"Yeah," he chuckled, "I have my own *Amber* Alerts. Much different, of course."

"For all I know, the police want me for kidnapping. I'm so confused. Long way of saying that I plan to call FPS tomorrow . . . and we'll go from there."

"You don't sound confident they can help."

"I don't have concrete proof of neglect. Sam's silence is 'Exhibit A,' but, ironically, she needs to talk. Who knows? Like other abuse victims, she may not implicate her dad. Maybe she's silencing herself intentionally—to protect him. She's a shell of herself, Ethan, scared of her own shadow. I can't let them send her back to that monster." Anika buried her face in her hands, her tears visible even with hair dangling over her eyes.

"Grab my hand," Ethan said.

"Thank you, Ethan, but I'll be okay."

"That's not what I meant. There's a rogue wave coming for us, and you're gonna topple."

Embarrassed, she complied an instant before impact. The wave propelled them high on its crest and threw them down with a mighty force. They didn't release their grip, however, and somehow stayed upright on their boards. Anika screamed in triumph. And when the water flattened out between waves, she refused to release Ethan's hand. She wouldn't look at him, and she wouldn't let go. She just floated there, holding his hand.

Her engagement ring rubbed against his fingers, but she didn't care. Ethan didn't say a word despite the awkwardness. His next step, she knew, would be automatic. He was hardwired for this occasion; he'd mastered it with repetition like he'd mastered the surfboard between his legs. But to her surprise, he didn't make a move. She could only guess his thoughts. She wasn't Amber or what's-her-name or any of the others. She was like a sister. Many had predicted she'd be his sister-in-law, the love of his brother's life. Logan was now married, of course, but . . . none of this was right. Ethan, Anika surmised, didn't know how to paddle back to his comfort zone, so he waited for her to make the next move, waited for the next wave to break.

But that wave never came. "What's that sound?" Anika asked.

"Don't hear it."

"Sounds like a roar. And look there," she pointed, "at those lights!"

"Four wheelers . . . driving on the beach. Several of them."

"It's ten o'clock. We're the only ones out here. Who would—"

"Be quiet," he whispered. "It's the cops! Sheriff Karnes and his deputies."

Anika panicked and squeezed Ethan's hand. *Did Scotty call them? If so, how does he know I'm here?*

"They're coming from my store," Ethan observed. "Likely saw your rental. Be still. Maybe they won't spot us."

Anika thought that was unlikely given the bright moon overhead and nary a cloud in the sky, but no better plan came to mind.

The police piloted the ATVs like bloodhounds tracking a feral hog. The four-stroke engines' roar echoed into the ocean. The officers were searching for something . . . or someone. The two surfers held hands as they witnessed the action unfold under the canopy of moon and stars. The aggressive noises unnerved them. The four-wheelers groaned in intermittent bursts as their drivers revved the engines to maneuver through deeper sand and along steeper inclines. The search team zig-zagged closer to Ethan's bungalow. Anika prayed they wouldn't stop.

But they did stop.

Ethan now squeezed *Anika's* hand—a gesture that increased her anxiety. Her only mooring of safety was signaling uncertainty. The five ATVs had decelerated, their roaring sounds transformed into muffled *chop-chop-chops*. The cops formed a perimeter around Ethan's bungalow. All but two remained seated. One of the deputies climbed off and traversed the driveway, past Ethan's vintage Volkswagen hippie van, past the volleyball court in the front of the house, where he knocked on the door.

Paralyzed, Ethan and Anika bobbed in the water like abandoned fishing corks. They wondered whether Sam would wake up and answer the door. The deputy was far enough away that a recognizable time lag existed between sight and sound. He rapped his knuckles on the door so fast that the resulting sounds couldn't keep up. Instinctively, the two let go of one another and lay down chest to board. But they had another problem. The officer facing them, hands on his hips, had focused his attention on their general vicinity.

"That's Sheriff Karnes," Ethan whispered. "Total jerk."

Karnes's interest in the moonlit surf evidenced more than an admiration for God's creation. Had he spied them lying on their boards? They tried to remain calm. He dismounted his ATV as his deputy banged on the front door, now knocking uncontrollably and barking indecipherable words. Anika hoped that, were Sam to wake up, she wouldn't open Ethan's door for a stranger, especially one banging like a banshee. Parents taught kids from the Lower West Side not to trust cops, but predicting the actions of an eight-year-old was the work of fools.

An eerie calm overtook the beachfront. Crashing waves and distant engines provided the only sounds. The four-wheelers idled softly as if to catch their breaths. The deputy at Ethan's front door had stopped hollering and banging. Instead, he had placed his ear to the door, listening for signs of life. Sheriff Karnes—likely looking for floating objects, maybe looking for Anika—fixed his gaze without moving a muscle. Ethan and Anika, pretending to be invisible and one with the ocean, remained flat on their boards. Heads down and eyes up, neither moved, nor said a word, nor took a breath. The wait continued, with no end in sight.

But then something happened. A dorsal fin broke the water's surface!

Anika nearly screamed at the prospect of a shark—any kind of shark—swimming around them. Particularly at night, the thought was too frightening to fathom. Jail was one thing; Jaws was worse. But thankfully, Jaws it wasn't. Fluids exploded from the bottlenose dolphin's blowhole as it unleashed a booming snot rocket less than ten yards from Anika. The mammal's chuffing sent her blood pressure overboard, but her body managed to stay upright and balanced. Barely. The pod of dolphins, now surrounding her, paralyzed her faculites.

A few seconds later, things broke their way. The dolphins had captured Sheriff Karnes's interest, but his attention eventually returned to the beach, and he yelled, "Move out!" The deputy at the door obliged and walked to his ATV. Others revved their engines, waited for their boss, and then sped off. Anika felt her heart pounding on the surfboard. She refused to exhale until the ATVs vanished beyond the dunes.

"If the water gets warm," Ethan said, sitting up on his board, "I promise it wasn't me."

Anika followed course, grabbing Ethan's hand for balance. She remained shaken but grew more exhilarated than fearful. Unsure what the cops wanted, she felt like a fugitive who'd escaped capture. Her heartbeat racing, she tugged on Ethan until his surfboard floated closer. Even at night—especially in the moonlit dark—her amber eyes shone like hardened resin reflecting a sunset. Their seductive glow refused to entertain any prior inhibitions. Her intentions now blindingly clear, there would be no more uncertainty.

None whatsoever.

"Where were we?" she asked.

"That's quick. A pod of dolphins just assaulted us. And didn't the sheriff and his merry deputies almost arrest us?"

"Probably. Me for kidnapping; you for aiding and abetting." She tugged harder, not breaking eye contact.

Ethan weakened. "Not sure what you're doing."

"You're about to find out."

"You'll hate yourself tomorrow."

"Come here," she demanded.

"You'll regret this."

"That's my problem, not yours."

"But . . . your fiancé."

"You don't even know him, and he'll never find out."

Ethan mustered as much resistance as his DNA allowed, but he didn't possess the tools to quash this temptation. He wasn't equipped to say no when he wanted to say yes.

Anika leaned into him, grabbed his wet head with both hands, and violently kissed his luscious lips until neither of them could ever forget this moment.

Today's secrets would give way to tomorrow's problems . . . but tomorrow would need to wait until sunup.

6

Anika awoke to a rattling A/C unit blowing from the window. Closer still, she heard faint snoring that sounded like the purring of a well-nourished housecat. Sunlight pierced the cracks in the wooden shades. Her mind climbing through the cobwebs, the recollection of last night's events returned—but not entirely. The pounding in Anika's head signaled that she and Ethan may have exhausted the town's supply of tequila. She had wanted only to reminisce with an old friend (a brother of sorts, they'd assured themselves) after a horrific day. But the Serie 2 Patron had other ideas and refused to be recorked and returned to the top shelf.

The consequences of dirty dancing with potent potables had come home to roost. She was scared—terrified, really—to roll over and identify her bedmate. Had the kissing transpired into something more? That hadn't been the plan, nor was it her style. Anika, however, like many before her, now found herself in Señor Tequila's chamber of remorse, begging for mercy and lying prostrate at guilt's feet. If Ethan was sleeping beside her, how embarrassing would the walk of shame be? Were his roommates, Amber and Chelsea, awake and in the living room?

Anika panicked. She had slept in her contacts. Not a good sign. Was she naked? *Please no.* And what about Samantha? Was Sam still sleeping—no pillow or blanket and wearing those stupid red rain boots—on the living room couch? The thought of being a worse caretaker than Sam's no-account parents caused her to fret. What was she doing with her life? She had never been a drinker, and no one in Miranda, before last night at least, had legitimate cause to question her moral compass. She had triumphed as high school valedictorian, for goodness' sake. Her classmates had elected her homecoming queen. Little girls had looked up to her, and the town's businesses had tried to recruit her. And now this? Hungover, ashamed, and unfit to care for her neglected sister? With all her talent and potential, why all the poor choices? Was she really this bad?

Anika peeked under the covers. She was wearing her bra, unfamiliar cotton pajamas, and someone else's Elvis Presley T-shirt. That was a good start. Wearing others' clothes wasn't ideal, but clothed was better than nude. Beyond the wardrobe, her engagement ring was on her finger, and her smartphone was on the side table. That, of course, left one remaining item of immediate concern: the snoring. Who was sleeping next to her? Tired of lathering herself up in a frenzy, she marshaled the courage to turn over and . . .

Spying her sleeping partner, she exhaled. Samantha, curled under the sheets, was in Neverland, sawing logs, or at least tiny twigs. After months of neglect and uncertainty, Sam's body had cried, "Uncle!" and crashed. Anika would allow her to sleep until Sam's operating system rebooted. Grabbing her device, she ruled out making any embarrassing witching-hour calls or sending any regrettable texts. The gods of shame, while punitive, often showed mercy.

Unfortunately, everything wasn't sunny in Miranda. Scotty Scumbag, true to form, had sent a series of late-night texts, the contents and spelling of which revealed his mental state. They began with words of love and negotiation, seeking a truce. Scorned by her silence, his next salvo reiterated his initial demands. *Return Sam by tomorrow night . . . or else!* He obviously hadn't called the police, but it had crossed his mind and could happen any minute. The next series of texts, sent at one-thirty in the morning, were more harrowing. He had issued threats about AMBER Alerts, threats about exposing her dirty little secrets, and a new one, likely sent as he stumbled along the narrow precipice of overdose—threats to life and limb.

The man was sick. Anika's image of him getting wasted and texting threats made her want to puke. He had promised to be their protector, not their nemesis. The thought of returning Sam to him made her want to scream. She closed her eyes and tossed her phone aside as she prepared to crawl out of bed and face the day.

Anika walked into the living room wearing her glasses. Ethan, shirt off, the morning light glistening from his athletic frame, had returned from dawn patrol. His sandy surfboard leaned against the wall near the front door. Anika, having just repented for last night's dalliance, found it hard not to marvel at Ethan's strapping muscles, which worked like a finely tuned engine underneath his flawless tanned skin. He was watching a *Dude Perfect* video on the couch and eating a fried egg on top of an avocado. With the sliding glass door open, the living room smelled like a blend of bubble gum-scented surfboard wax, Kona coffee, and the sea.

Nearby, a brunette with legs a mile long sat on a brown recliner, wearing a white T-shirt and boxer shorts. She had zero visible imperfections. The recliner matched her catlike eyes, which scanned pictures in *Vogue* before turning their attention to Anika.

"Good morning . . . everyone," Anika said with a hesitant smile.

"Anika!" Ethan replied, mouth full of breakfast, craning his head to make eye contact. "Cool glasses."

"You surfed already?"

"Can't pass up Joyce's waves," he said. "Meteorologist said a hundred-year storm's coming to Miranda, so I need to train for the monsters." After the small talk, his attention slingshotted back to his video where dudes were performing wild tricks with a basketball. Anika had noticed no wink, no stutter, no smirky grin—*nada*. Last night's hookup was business as usual for Ethan, and he showed no signs of a headache or morning-after regret. The guy was a machine, a poster child for extreme sports and endless revelry. He had likely jumped in the water before sunrise for a three-hour workout in the gulf. "Coffee's in the kitchen," he said. "Wicked beans from Maui."

"What do you mean by a hundred-year—"

"Good morning, Anika," the young woman interrupted. "I'm Chelsea. Hope my bed was comfortable, and you look *so* beautiful in my PJs. Love how you rolled them at the bottom."

"Thank you," Anika replied. Chelsea's comments appeared genuine, without a hint of implication. To Chelsea, an unknown visitor emerging from her bedroom and wearing her pajamas was apparently as natural as dogs lifting their legs on fire hydrants.

Before Anika could continue, Amber emerged from Ethan's bedroom in a fitted black hoodie. She was a natural blonde with a celestial nose, a confident gait, and a sculpted body. The small smattering of freckles on her nose—what Anika's mom called Tinker Bell kisses—was the desire of many. She wasn't as tall as Chelsea, nor did she have her sidekick's elevated cheekbones, but she was equally gorgeous. When Anika saw her emerald-green eyes, she knew she'd finally met a woman's stare more penetrating and mesmerizing than her own.

Amber seemed startled to see Anika standing behind the couch. "Oh, hello," she said, stopping in her tracks and wiping her hands on her khaki shorts—no doubt a nervous tic. "You must be Anika. Ethan has talked a lot about you . . . *this morning.*"

His attention occupied by Tyler Toney going Rage Monster on *Dude Perfect*, Ethan said, "Yeah, Anika's like a sister."

"Yeah," Amber said with her eyes locked on Anika. "He keeps saying that . . . for some reason."

The housing arrangement came into focus, and this was no *Three's Company*. Amber was more attached to Ethan than Chelsea. Chelsea, Anika surmised, relished the role of clueless beach bunny in search of the next high. Amber, on the other hand, likely grew tired of single life. Not content with a seasonal fling, she disliked other gals crashing her party. That made things difficult for Anika, who suddenly found herself in the blonde woman's crosshairs.

Anika spotted the tattoo on Amber's wrist. "Cool tat. Rubik's Cube?"

"I see you also dabble in ink," Amber ventured, staring at the three dots near the base of Anika's thumb. "What does that mean?"

"Holy Trinity. To remember my dad's faith."

Amber's eye roll was less than subtle. She had no time for outsiders. Despite Anika being the only one in the room who *hadn't* slept with Ethan, she obviously threatened Amber in a way Chelsea didn't. Anika's diplomatic instincts intervened as she flashed her engagement ring. "Thanks for letting me and my sister crash here. My fiancé slept well knowing we were with Ethan and not an old crush."

"So where did your fiancé sleep?" Amber asked.

The tone of Amber's question carried enough tart to capture Ethan's attention. Not known for his awareness, he displayed expertise in spotting gathering storms. "Chelsea," he said, squirming and closing his laptop, "play some music, will you?"

Chelsea, too, had noticed Amber's snark. Her neck had snapped to attention once Amber's frigid breath collided with the warm morning air. As tensions mounted, she thumbed through a healthy stack of vintage Led Zeppelin albums.

Anika, meanwhile, played it cool. She sympathized with Amber, up to a point, and had no time for beachside drama. Besides, this love triangle did nothing but distract from getting Sam to safety. Anika wasn't chasing Ethan—they'd had their first and last tryst. The clock was ticking, and she needed to call FPS and scram before the cops returned and arrested her for kidnapping. News of a hundred-year storm only heightened the stakes. "He lives in DC."

"That's forever and a mile," Amber pounced. "You must really miss him." The comment shone a piercing light on her insecurity and desperation. Her affection for Ethan had clearly warped her mind. Did she not realize that Ethan wasn't the relationship type? Did she not understand that he was the archetypical permanent bachelor? Anika's sympathy turned to pity as she considered Amber's wasted efforts to wrangle an unbreakable stallion.

Her pity turned to shock, however, as Amber removed her hoodie. The white T-shirt underneath grabbed Anika's attention. It wasn't that the shirt was too tight, or that it revealed Amber's black embroidered bra underneath, or that it left little to the imagination. All that was true. Instead, it was the words emblazoned on the front, magnified in big navy-blue letters.

Bones Don't Burn

"Where did you get that shirt?" Anika asked. The time for tiptoeing around Blondie had come to an abrupt halt.

"Ethan's store."

"What's that mean? Ethan, you're peddling this?" she said, her voice elevated, her hand pressed against her forehead. "I didn't see it on the racks yesterday. Do you have any idea how wrong—"

"Wait," Ethan said, leaping over the couch, putting on a button-up shirt as he addressed Anika. She was spiraling into a bad place. "The saying's popular with the younger crowd. It's a clarion call for justice."

"You're making money off this? Off Johnny's death?"

"That girl needs to chill," Amber said. It was the worst thing she'd said so far . . . until it wasn't. "What's your problem?"

"What's my problem?" Anika seethed, charging Amber, no longer playing nice.

Ethan intervened, swooped her up, and with one fluid motion, threw her over his shoulder. "Let's go outside, Anika. Let me explain."

On the way out, sprawled over Ethan's shoulders, Anika writhed and yelled at Amber, "That's my boyfriend! The love of my life! *That's* my problem! And now *I'm . . . your . . . problem*!"

7

"You're hyperventilating, Anika," Ethan observed, dumping her from his shoulders. "Before you kill me, hear me out."

"How could you?"

"You're thinking about this all wrong."

"Are you *kidding* me?" she asked.

"Bones Don't Burn is a tribute to Johnny, a call for police transparency. It's a radical slogan, and you of all people should embrace it."

As her shock wore off, Ethan's explanation made more sense. She was overreacting and not thinking clearly. Clouds and lies had surrounded the whole investigation into Johnny's death. And she remembered the day—two days before she left Miranda—when Ricky had played Joan of Arc on the sheriff's department steps, raising his fist and yelling to the crowd: *Bones Don't Burn!*

Though not on the level of Make Love, Not War, she confessed the slogan carried a punch. "I don't like people profiting off his death."

"No profits. All proceeds from the Bones Don't Burn campaign go to St. Jude Children's Research Hospital. You'll recall, Johnny was a huge fan."

Anika closed her eyes, shook her head, and lifted her left hand to display her engagement ring. Neither she nor Ethan understood why. Only later would it make sense. Ethan hugged her, this time truly like a brother, and she put her cheek on his shoulder. "I'm so sorry, Ethan. I've had a terrible week. I'm so scared of losing Sam . . . or getting arrested."

"No way to work it out with her dad?"

She shook her head. "I guess moral outrage isn't a good strategy."

"Why do you hate him so much?"

"Because he abuses Sam with his willful neglect," she replied. "She's fragile in stature but normally strong in spirit. When she contacted me for help, I didn't expect the stark change in her demeanor. And I will not allow that white trash to crush the soul of my baby sister. No way."

That was bad enough, but it was only half the story.

Van Halen was the other half. Long ago, her mom had gifted her a beautiful fawn pug for her birthday from the rescue shelter. But Scotty didn't like dogs with breathing problems, especially those who snored. In fact, he'd told Anika not to name "it" because "it" may not live long. Scotty had called him dog, or mongrel, or mutt. Disobeying a direct order, Anika had named *him* Van Halen (perhaps because Scotty was Sammy Hagar's doppelgänger). When she had returned from a week at 4-H camp the following summer, Van Halen was missing. Vanished. Scotty had claimed the dog caught canine parvovirus ("the parvo," he called it), and the vet had to put him down. "*Pobre perro*," he'd said with a twinkle in his eye.

The neighborhood gossip, however, had told another story. After receiving multiple calls, the Miranda Humane Society picked up Van Halen. The pug was a serial flight risk, the true story went, because Scotty always left the gate open. *Of course it was open.* Beyond that, even when Scotty had kept Van Halen fenced in, he'd failed to provide adequate food and water. Anika didn't have the wherewithal to investigate further. But she hoped that Van Halen was still alive somewhere. Maybe his new owners had renamed him Otis or Scrappy. Scotty would've long forgotten about Anika's mutt, but she would never forget Van Halen. *Never!* Nor would she ever forgive the scoundrel who took him away. More important still, there was no way she would allow Scotty to deprive her of another loved one.

"Worried about you, Anika. If you keep tackling everything at once, you'll stop functioning altogether. Did you have Mr. Torres for algebra?"

Anika nodded.

"Remember what he taught us?" Ethan continued. "About how to eat an elephant?"

"One bite at a time," she said.

"Anika, you need to take one step at a time. I'm going back inside so you can call Miranda FPS. That sounds like step one."

"Any news regarding the cops?" she asked, pulling from his embrace. "Last night was messed up. They combed the beach, dismounted their four-wheelers like a SWAT team . . . banged on this door."

"No one else saw them," Ethan said.

"Nothing this morning?"

"I surfed all morning. Only signs of life were the blue hairs in long sleeves picking up sand dollars. Oh, and I might've spotted the Midnight Rider from afar before the sun came up."

"Midnight Rider?"

"You haven't heard of the Midnight Rider? Some dude—or dudette, maybe—who ships drugs late at night in his car. Legend has it he wears night vision goggles, turns off his lights, and . . . hammer down. Goes so fast that Sheriff Karnes's deputies won't chase him."

"Nuts, if true," she said. "Listen, Ethan, it's not just Sam or the cops that have me on edge. I woke up thinking all was good from last night, but based on Amber's hostility toward me—"

"She gets jealous. Don't take it personal."

"Ethan, did we . . ."

"You don't remember?" Ethan asked, looking down at Anika's engagement ring.

"I remember kissing—*very innocently*, of course—in the water and coming back to the house."

"And dancing . . . and drinking."

"And drinking too much," she added.

"And running a needle through a bunch of vintage records."

"And . . ."

"Relax," he said. "There wasn't another 'and.' You'd already moved Sam from the couch and tucked her into bed with her stuffed animal. You don't remember talking about the adventures of Faux Pooh?"

"No," she chuckled, biting her bottom lip.

"We turned up the music, danced, and played air guitar until midnight. Your Artist-Formerly-Known-As-Prince impersonation was brilliant."

Anika covered her face and laughed. "I could use Dr. Everything'll-Be-Alright right about now."

"I don't know any Beverly Hills doctors, but I know Miranda's Dr. Feelgood. We can smoke a joint if that'd be helpful. Amber could use one too—like you read about—and Chelsea smokes weed like they're about to stop growing it."

Anika demurred, making it clear without being judgy that she'd never used drugs and didn't intend to start. Tequila was bad enough. Ethan didn't push the issue but continued to chronicle the remainder of the night. "I walked you to the guest room, pulled those clothes from Chelsea's chest of drawers, handed them to you, and walked out. Called Chelsea and Amber to come home from Sharkey's. It's all good, Anika."

"Really?" Anika asked, not hiding her relief.

"You act like hooking up with me is the problem," he said half-joking. "Do me a favor, okay? Don't crush me with that 'very innocent' malarky when talking about our kiss. I know you're engaged—you'll need to process that issue yourself. And I realize you French kissed my brother back in the day, and this is all very awkward for you. But I've got a rep to protect."

"Where are you going with this?" she asked.

"You hurt my feelings."

"Please! Give me a br—"

"Really. Our kiss last night was anything but innocent. It was epic! Mischaracterizing it robs me—*us!*—of an amazing memory. Plus, it ruins my weekend, especially since Amber thinks we did more than kiss. I'm getting punished for something I didn't do, so I need to celebrate what I did do. Make sense?"

For someone who lived with two women, Ethan sounded genuinely upset, and maybe a tad heartbroken, by Anika's blasé description of their ephemeral twirl of passion. His response reeked of alpha male, but he was right. It had been epic. A moment so memorable that a bottle of tequila failed to drown it all out.

"Enough with the charades," Anika said. "You live with professional models. I can't compete, so stop it."

"Wrong. You may not have their height and cheekbones, but you have the secret sauce. You have the entire package they covet: beauty, passion, *and* brains."

As Ethan stomped toward the door like a bear stung by a honeybee, Anika couldn't resist. She dedicated this one to Amber. "Ethan, my love," she said, with Shakespearean elocution, "you took my breath away last night."

He stopped, turned around, and smiled.

And then came the hook, line, and sinker. Her next words carried more seduction and manipulation than the first. "I will remember that moment for the rest of my life. You were amazing."

"I knew it!" he said, holding up his clenched fist. "Better than my brother, right?"

Anika panicked. "You better not tell him!"

"Whoops . . . already did. He'll be here in twenty minutes."

"Wait! What? Logan's coming? You told him?"

Anika stood still, caught unaware, as the door slammed shut.

8

Anika sat head down and crisscross applesauce on Amber's light blue Volkswagen bug. She didn't care about denting its hood. Her long brown hair covered her face. She heard an annoying voice squawking in the distance on her phone, which she had hurled into the sandy yard. The phone had landed in the yard only after crashing against a wooden pole that held the volleyball net. Somehow, it still worked. Anika's call with FPS hadn't gone well. It had caused her to pace, snort, tug on her hair, curse, and scream. And now she was zapped of energy, left paralyzed by the venom of incompetence that dripped from the fangs of bureaucracy.

A low-level FPS apparatchik named Mary—from the town's We-Know-Your-Child's-Best-Interest-Better-Than-You Bureau—continued chirping through Anika's abandoned phone. Wielding power beyond her abilities, Mary had declared she couldn't help Sam without demonstrable evidence of abuse. The law required that Anika return Sam to her home. Mary promised to send some part-time gumshoe next week to interview the little girl who couldn't speak, her abusive father, and her drunkard of a mother—assuming, of course, mother returned from her boondoggle in la-la land. But meanwhile, *hey, everything'll be alright* and best interest of the child *blah, blah, blah*.

Sam, of course, would be fine, Mary had said. She had performed a thorough clinical evaluation over the phone. The conversation frustrated Anika so much that she didn't end the call or say goodbye. Instead, she activated her smartphone's propulsion system and launched it across the yard.

When she thought things couldn't get worse, a white Ford F-250 King Ranch Series truck turned into the driveway. The powder-coated Ranch

36

Hand front bumper and grille combo, outfitted with an industrial-size winch, was a dead giveaway. Logan always purchased expensive toys that reflected his inner urban cowboy. His truck, more expensive than a BMW 7 Series, had every piece of equipment known to the Marlboro Man, short of a gun rack. Logan wore a straw cowboy hat, but no one accused him of being all hat and no cattle. The Danforth empire had more money than some Miranda banks. To make the point, they didn't raise cattle for food or sale. No, they raised cattle for the sake of raising cattle.

Logan had been Anika's "friend-boy" since they rode ponies in spurs, but she had taken him for granted, and now he'd turned the page without her. Several pages, in fact. Now president of his family's local beer distributorship, he'd married someone outside their inner circle. Someone not named Anika. Someone not even from Miranda.

The Anika-Logan relationship was complicated. For years, he'd chased after her, and she'd gambled with his heartstrings. She found him attractive, interesting, and a barrel of fun; but despite all the glimmer and glam his money bought, he'd never been the shiny new thing. She had assumed he'd always be available, that they'd eventually wed and ride off into the sunset. But a shiny new thing named Johnny thwarted that plan when he transferred to Miranda High and swept her off her feet. Anika and Johnny had described their first interaction as love at first sight.

Johnny now gone forever, she considered what love at second sight entailed. Unfortunately, until now, the opportunity to reconnect with Logan had never presented itself. Every fairy-tale scenario had her rolling into town in a luxury car, her life in complete order, looking and feeling like solid gold, and rewrapping him around her pinky.

Today's scenario, though, didn't meet expectations. She was hungover, without makeup, her forehead broken out, and wearing another woman's clothes. Worse, she had tears in her eyes and had just chunked her phone in the yard. For a cloudless morning in Miranda, Texas, life was raining a kennel full of mangy mutts on her homecoming celebration.

Logan's ostrich-skin boots barely touched the ground before he bounded toward her. He stopped short of a bear hug when he saw the tears. With familiarity and trust cultivated over years, he removed her glasses, and said, "There she is. The prettiest star in Texas. Been lookin' for you . . . a long time."

His words hit hard, and she struggled to frame a response. "Having a really bad day, Logan."

"Well, I'm here now."

"You found me," she said, fighting back more tears. "You always find me."

"Got you right here, gorgeous," he said, kissing her cheek. Unlike the *la bise* double kiss, this was more intimate, evidencing a relational history.

"You're married," she stated the obvious.

"Last I looked, that has no bearing on your being gorgeous," he chortled. "Facts are facts. And I'm not the only one wearing a ring."

"Long story."

"Think it will get any longer after you kissed Ethan last night?"

"Ouch. Word travels at light speed in South Texas," Anika said, deflated and feeling betrayed. "He shouldn't have told you that."

"He's my baby brother. We don't keep secrets."

"Yes, I should've remembered: brothers in the bond. He's not a baby anymore, Logan. And again, you're married."

"You keep telling me that. To the extent it matters, Anika, I'm happily married."

"You mad I kissed your baby brother?"

"Want me to be? That why you did it?"

Anika demurred, slowing down the conversation and looking past Logan toward the ocean. "It doesn't surprise me that you're *happily* married; you were always an old soul. But it's still weird. What's her name?"

"Sarah."

"She take your name?"

"Sarah Danforth," Logan said, nodding.

"Can I be happy for you and unhappy about the marriage?"

"I'm confused. You've been gone for *five years*, Anika. You never reached out *one* time—never returned my calls. Not one. No emails, no texts, no social media. Nothing. Disappeared into your college world. You never came home, never came up for air, so I gave up."

"So I'm not the only one who's rehearsed for this moment."

"What do you expect, Anika? Didn't we take a serious step forward at homecoming? Wasn't I the last one you kissed before running away to college?"

"That mistake was bigger than last night's," she said.

"Wow! You're out for scalps. Thanks a lot."

"That's not what I meant, Logan. Unlike last night, what happened at homecoming had devastating, irreparable consequences. My betrayal of Johnny is something I'll spend the rest of my life regretting."

"He was just your boyfriend. What about your fiancé? Him finding out could have its own irreparable consequences."

"Even if my fiancé found out, he wouldn't react like Johnny. Johnny, as you remember, had an animal spirit."

"So that's why you ran and hid?" Logan probed. "Why you avoided me like the plague? You blame yourself for Johnny's death?"

"Like you said, facts are facts. After he saw us kissing, he lost his mind. I cheated on him, Logan! I'm a terrible person."

"You're not a terrible person. For heaven's sake, we were teenagers. And we never left first base."

"Say what you want, Logan, but the hits keep coming. I found myself on first base again last night. And by kissing your brother, I've now burdened you."

"I appreciate your concern for *my* feelings, but I'd be more worried about your fiancé. What's his name?"

"Doesn't matter. That's my problem. At least I keep my mistakes in the same family."

"You have feelings for Ethan?" he asked.

"No . . . *heck no!* Of course not. We shared a special moment when I needed someone to hold, that's all. He's a beautiful creature, but he's too much of a creature of habit. Not for me and vice versa . . . and I don't know why we're having this conversation. I'm engaged!"

"Ethan told me Samantha's with you. What is she, about seven now? What are y'all's plans? Are you taking her—"

"She's eight."

Seeing that Anika was frazzled, Logan moved into problem-solving mode. It's what he did best. The idea of passive listening never crossed his mind. He was wired to fix things, especially things outside of his area of expertise. Sarah, though, likely would beat that out of him over time. "How can I help you, Anika?"

"Sam and I need a place to sleep until Mom comes home. I've worn out my welcome here, and I'm low on cash flow."

"Worn out your welcome? Amber?"

"She hates me. Ethan tell you that too?"

"Easy guess. She's jealous of anyone who grabs his attention. I'm not surprised she's suspicious of unfamiliar women crashing at Ethan's pad."

"Whatever. I have no time for her," Anika said as the sounds of sirens became audible in the distance. "You make it sound like this is all my fault."

"For once, no. You in trouble?"

"Yeah, I forgot to mention that I kidnapped Sam from her dad. Not taking her back. Just waiting for the sheriff to show up."

"Yikes! Can't help with the cops. We donate a bundle to the *100 Club*, which helps with speeding tickets, but Mayor Dodd has her investigative eyes on my distillery right now, so—"

"You're making moonshine? Those sirens could be coming for you."

"I don't think so. Moonshine's legal in these parts, and it's more of a science project." He smiled. "Dodd's after my taxes, trying to fill her coffers with civil penalties. Do you have a play?"

"FPS won't help, so I'm running out of cards."

"If you want something done in this town, the plays run through Mayor Dodd's office at the Alamo Opera House. Small-town politics is the name of the game. Just don't tell her I sent you."

"I'm allergic to politics of any size. Any leads on a place to stay?"

"Would love to host you, Anika, and we have a mile of rooms, but Sarah's out of town, and—"

"Understood. I'm not walking into that buzzsaw again, especially with a married couple."

"I have an idea, though. A place where you can probably stay. Grab Sam and hop in my truck; I'll drop you at your car. You need to figure this out fast." He grabbed her chin. "Time to take care of business, Anika. Hurricane Joyce will miss us, but the meteorologists predict a generational hurricane to follow."

"I should know this, but when's hurricane season?"

"Runs from June 1 to November 30, and August is the danger zone."

Anika nodded, reflecting on her situation as the sirens grew louder. Danger zone, to be sure. She looked up at the clear blue sky and saw swarming seagulls squawking and crooning. She had some time, but cops, hurricanes, and jealous women weren't the party favors she'd expected for her homecoming parade.

9

Anika drove the rental car onto the caliche driveway of the "Church Grounds," as Logan called it. She parked under a sign that read, "Reformed Baptist Church of Miranda, Est. 1962." The sign below that, made from a paper bag and black Sharpie, read, "Room for Rent: Inquire at Lodge."

"We're here, Sam," she said. Sam reached into the backseat to grab Faux Pooh, nestled next to a stack of napkins on which she'd drawn myriad cubes.

The Church Grounds comprised twenty acres, a sizeable chunk of property in Miranda's Lower East Side. (Anika figured the property was the size of Mission Center Mall in the Upper East Side.) Logan had characterized the location as spitting distance from Four Points. From a cursory internet search, Anika learned it once was the "Running J Ranch," owned by Belton Johnson. The Kings (of King Ranch fame) had booted Johnson from their family for killing a man for no good reason.

Exiting the car, she saw several structures, including the church sanctuary and a two-story lodge that also served as the office. Barbed wire fencing surrounded the property. She noticed the absence of mesquite trees or invasive plants. Instead, the manicured grounds included some of the most beautiful gardens and hardwoods she'd ever seen in South Texas.

The place seemed peaceful and welcoming, the air somehow cooler. Before the car doors shut, though, a man sprinted from the front office and hollered, "Stand still! Don't run!" Anika's knees buckled. She lost her breath. Sam screeched in terror as enormous figures ran right for them, aiming to take them down.

Two Great Danes—ears cropped, each weighing over one hundred pounds—came barreling toward Anika and Sam at high speeds. For a few seconds, all bets were off on chances of survival. Once the beasts neared the car, the fawn veered toward Anika, the harlequin toward Sam. The man with the ponytail kept hollering, "They won't hurt you!" but even Sam knew never to trust strangers.

They soon learned, however, that he was right. The dogs slid to a stop short of their targets like champion reigning horses. The fawn dug his head into Anika's abdomen, seeking attention with Anika's hands in the air. Her self-defense system froze. On the other side of the car, the male harlequin licked Sam's face as she hopped, turned in circles, and laughed uncontrollably.

"That's Luther," the man said, catching his breath, pointing at the fawn. "And the one that resembles an oversized Dalmatian is Calvin. And my name is Joshua Molina, or you can call me Pastor Josh. And you are Anika, and she is—"

"Samantha," Anika exhaled, answering for her sister. Sam waved. She presently had no time for other humans. She gave her full attention to Luther and Calvin. The dogs traded sides of the car, panted, sniffed, and tried to discern which guest had more to offer. The answer to the question soon arrived, as Sam and Pooh broke for the open pasture with the prodigious beasts in playful pursuit.

Anika guessed that Joshua, with his aquiline nose and stubble beard, was ten years her elder. With his modest clothes, hip sandals, and youthful looks, he looked more suited to lead Miranda's Church Under the Bridge than a reputable brick-and-mortar establishment. "I guess Logan called ahead?" she asked.

"Logan's my South Texas connecter. Introduces me to all the right folks. I've only lived here about eighteen months. Says you need a place to stay?"

"Temporarily, yes. Sam needs . . . well, something different."

"Logan mentioned something about that. She okay?"

"She's not talking, but I'm hopeful she'll come around. I'm not licensed in . . . well, I'm not licensed in anything useful. But I suspect she's dealing with some mild trauma."

"Any other unusual behavior?"

"Not really . . . other than the cubes."

"Cubes?" Joshua inquired, a less than subtle swing in attentiveness that Anika noticed.

"Yeah, it's no big deal. She doodles boxes . . . or cubes. Mostly three-dimensional. Normally wouldn't catch my attention, but she drew them on the walls of her bedroom. Little creepy."

"Interesting," he said, staring at Sam in the distance. "Does she draw cubes often?"

"It's just a coping mechanism, but she's religious, so to speak, about her drawing."

"They say discipline is the handmaiden of genius. If you're willing to share some examples, I'd be happy to review her drawings. Meantime, let's give you a tour, shall we?"

Joshua escorted Anika around the Church Grounds. Inside the sanctuary, solid oak pews provided comfortable seating for about three hundred worshippers. Vaulted ceilings and organ pipes stretching to the heavens gave the place a celestial feel. The building looked centuries older than its 1962 birthdate. According to Pastor Joshua, average Sunday attendance filled about three-quarters of the room. Stepping on stage and around the four-column pulpit, Anika learned that Joshua had covered the modest stained-glass windows depicting Jesus with dark drapes. His concern, he said, was that images of the Son of God may violate the Second Commandment. That was a far cry from the church down the road that Anika had visited as a child. Inside the ornate splendor of the Four Points Catholic cathedral, one couldn't spin around and spit without hitting a picture of Jesus (and Mother Mary).

Sam returned from play before Anika and Joshua exited the sanctuary. In the connecting hallway, photos of the 1962 Church Grounds rebuilding effort captured Anika's attention. She wondered how many of those churchgoers were still alive. The faces within the frames were haggard, solemn, and kissed with the blunt instrument of unspeakable suffering. During that time, while their countrymen had focused on the Cuban Missile Crisis, civil rights, and Vietnam, Mirandites hammered and sawed, sowed and pruned, painted and cleaned. Most frames contained action photos, but there were also isolated pictures of family units and other congregants with arms around one another in solidarity. Men, women, and children wore hats and clothes from a different era. Anika's ears started to buzz, and the disconcerting pull on her body—like the undertow at the beach—returned. She moved over a few steps, hoping the uncomfortable force would recede. But it didn't. Another eerie feeling overtook her. She sensed the figures in the photographs were watching her.

"Pretty cool photos, huh?" Joshua said, startling her.

"I keep forgetting that few town photos survived Hurricane Carla in 1960."

The two walked to the lodge, which in addition to the front office, included a large living area with a thirty-foot ceiling, a kitchen, and bedrooms upstairs. They also visited the barn, a greenhouse, and a three-acre pond stocked full of largemouth bass and crappie. Eventually, they arrived at the modest brick cottage for rent on the edge of the property. The exterior was quaint and the interior more utilitarian than memorable, a mixture of white paint on plaster and natural wood surrounding a bevy of garage sale furniture. No one would mistake it for the Waldorf Astoria, but it checked all the boxes.

"Honestly, Joshua," Anika said. "This cottage is just right."

"Our cup overflows, to be sure."

"Perfect for our needs. Sam will be comfortable here," she said, pausing to reflect on her sister enjoying herself for the first time in who-re-members-when. "I mean, just look at her dancing around like a ballerina with Calvin and Luther. Takes my breath away."

"But?"

"But trouble follows me like my shadow. I don't wanna bring my curse to your church. Trying to be a good person, and it's just not working out so well."

"You've come to the right place. We're all sinners saved by grace. We start by confessing that we're not good people, but—"

"I hear all that religious mumbo jumbo, Pastor, but I'm talking about something real. If I don't get things worked out pronto, the sheriff will come for me and Sam. I don't want him arresting me on your property. I don't want the cops believing you're harboring a fugitive."

"Theology is real, Anika," he replied, struggling not to launch into an ad hoc sermon, "but that's for another day. As for the cops, I'm not that concerned, and I choose not to borrow trouble from tomorrow. We've had to deal with Sheriff Karnes before."

"Did somebody—"

"Nobody did anything wrong. We submit to the governing authorities unless they take measures that keep us from obeying God. In our case, we had some overzealous cops abuse their authority regarding mask mandates and undocumented migrants attending worship services. No biggie. We worked through it with the mayor."

"A friend of Logan's scheduled a meeting with me and the mayor first thing in the morning. I need to talk to her about Sam's predicament. Anything I should know?"

"Mayor Dodd runs this town with an iron fist. She has more power than the Pope and micromanages the town's affairs from the Alamo Opera House."

"Can she help me? Can she help Sam?"

"If anyone can help you in Miranda, it's Mayor Auntie Dodd. But be careful what you ask for. She's a political animal, and small-town politics is her game. She chews up the innocent and spits them out . . . all to advance her power and influence. I shouldn't gossip, but . . ."

"I'll keep that in mind."

"And I wouldn't mention a word about Sam drawing cubes."

"I don't understand."

"We can discuss it later, but I have a strong suspicion Dodd will take a self-serving interest in that girl."

Anika wanted to explore his concern but decided to press forward, growing anxious about her standing phone call back home. "I'm broke and can't pay you for the first month."

Joshua looked at Sam. "Not a problem. I'll waive rent for the first month. You can move in right away. If the weatherwoman's prophetic, you may never pay a dime. Storm may wash everything away."

"Joshua, I don't know much about theology, but I do know this: Mirandites don't leave for hurricanes. That could be a safety challenge for you and your congregation when we have another big one."

"That's what Logan said," Joshua noted. "I'll draft a lease contract for you to sign."

"Sorry to be rude," she said, "but I need to make a call before five o'clock. Otherwise, I'll be in a doghouse big enough to hold Luther and Calvin."

"Cottage is open, and keys are on the counter. Oh, I almost forgot. With one exception, you and Sam have full access to the entire property, including my kitchen and the living area. Don't be shy. *Mi casa es su casa.*"

"Awesome. What's the exception?"

"There's one place where you and Sam can't go. Under no circumstances—none whatsoever—are you allowed in my bedroom."

10

A nika and Sam, holding sweaty hands, walked up the creaky steps of the Alamo Opera House. Even at sunrise, the humidity held moisture like a sponge, but Anika would've perspired anyway. Though the sheriff's headquarters was located in the Upper West Side of Miranda, several deputies lingered around the mayor's office, and Anika knew there was a holding cell in the back. She had only felt this vulnerable once before, five years ago, when the terrible secret she now carried was birthed. As bad as that day was, the stakes were higher now with Sam's welfare on the line.

Pasty old men on the porch played Texas hold 'em using Old West playing cards without numbers. They sipped joe and flashed toothless smiles as Anika and Sam marched toward the Alamo entrance. Though their smiles appeared genuine, even endearing, these weren't the innocent grandpas from central casting. And they didn't possess the eyes of casual observers but of scheming men with an agenda. Eyes of small-town henchmen who orchestrate meaningful events. Eyes of mischievous malcontents who delight in their roles as instruments of fate.

Anika recognized one of the old men, the one who had stalked her at the Kwik Mart. The one with the thick handlebar mustache.

Walking through the swinging doors, Anika and Sam entered the saloon-cum-General Store. Relics from another generation covered the walls, including a huge shoulder mount of a buffalo. The smell of eggs and bacon overtook Anika's senses. Unlike the solemn card playing on the porch, lively activity filled this room. She noticed the Western-era bar and three circular card tables, each surrounded by four wooden chairs. Beyond the aged furnace extending from floor to roof, a young man wrapped breakfast tacos in foil behind the bar. He wore a "Don't Mess with Texas" apron with his name, Timmy, imprinted in cursive.

"Welcome to the Alamo, Anika," a male voice of authority emerged from behind. "Probably don't remember me; name's Curtis Worden. I'm the caretaker here. You're here to meet with the mayor." It was a statement, not a question.

"We have an appointment," Anika said, turning around to address the man, still trying to process her surroundings. Light-years from her comfort zone, she contemplated swooping up Sam and sprinting to the car. Instead, she patted Sam's head, mustered additional courage, and said, "We need some help."

"Help with . . ." Worden asked as a coo-coo clock with tiny deer heads and horns next to the Buffalo Bar announced it was seven o'clock.

Anika considered the gravity of her next response, a waterfall of words flooding her mind. "Life."

"Life, huh?" He chuckled. "Never heard that one before . . . but it makes good sense."

"We've reached the end of our rope," she added.

"The end of a rope is a terrible place to be," said another voice, one with even more authority, from the hallway. Anika and Sam turned to see a squatty woman dressed in thrift shop attire with lunch-lady arms, graying hair, and eyes discolored from decades of crises. "Curtis, I've got this. Ladies, come on back."

After brief introductions, Mayor Auntie Dodd invited them into her office. The spacious area was under the same roof but set apart from the General Store. As the sisters sat in front of Dodd's wooden desk, Anika noticed a framed remnant of the "Come and Take It" flag in the corner, several photos of children on the credenza, and a strange picture on the wall. In the picture, five men in top hats huddled around an old car that had a box on top labeled "Precinct 13."

"Anika Raven," she said, staring at Anika's engagement ring. "I remember you. I presided over your graduation ceremony. Handed you an honorarium, right? Weren't you salutatorian?"

"Valedictorian. Don't want to boast, but—"

"No, please—brag all you want, girl! What an amazing accomplishment! I'm always happy when a woman takes home a blue ribbon. Tell me what's going on."

Anika scarcely began her story when, distracted, Mayor Dodd said, "Excuse me, darlin'," and turned her attention to Sam, who was eyeing the thingamabob at the corner of her desk. "Young lady, do you know what that is?"

Samantha squeezed Faux Pooh and shook her head.

"That's called a Rubik's Cube," she said, picking it up and tossing it in Sam's lap. "You have to match all the same colors on the same sides." Sam set aside Pooh, picked up the toy puzzle, and began fiddling with it. Only then did Mayor Dodd turn her attention back to Anika, repeatedly glancing down at her engagement ring. Something about the ring disturbed her. "Go ahead, darlin'. Sorry to interrupt."

Anika continued her story as the mayor nodded along, cradling her "Mayor Days Be Merry and Bright" coffee mug. Occasionally, Dodd would take a note, and her squinty eyes kept darting to the Rubik's Cube as Sam worked her tiny fingers over the square contraption. Anika took her time outlining the facts concerning their plight. She was careful to include specifics but avoid hyperbole. Meanwhile, Dodd seemed to be listening, but she was obsessed by Sam's pursuit of matching a color on one side.

Anika's description of events and cries of injustice, delivered with impassioned pleas, proved to be a command performance, better than anything she'd ever pulled off in Ms. Stubblefield's tenth-grade theater class. Absolute truth often stirs convictions that are compelling and persuasive. But something was wrong. Dodd remained unmoved and unengaged. Something had her distracted or disinterested. Was it Sam's goofing around with the toy? Was it something about Anika's engagement ring? Did the ring remind Dodd of a bad memory, perhaps a topsy-turvy marriage?

Anika thumbed her ring, spinning the diamond toward her palm, and said, "I hope all this makes sense." After the mayor dutifully nodded but said nothing, Anika sighed. She needed to reset the conversation. Perhaps she'd made a tactical error by foregoing the customary South Texas pleasantries and jumping right into business. "By the way," Anika said, pointing to the strange picture on the wall, "that's an interesting photograph. Relatives of yours?"

"That's my dad on the left," Dodd smiled, turning around. "He's the landmass of a man leaning against the car. And sitting atop the car is the infamous Box 13. That box, full of 'late-discovered votes,' handed LBJ the democratic primary for the 1948 US Senate seat from Texas. He won by eighty-seven 'votes' and earned the nickname Landslide Lyndon. One hundred and ninety-eight of the two hundred 'votes' in the box had his name on them. Just two 'votes' against," she laughed, using air quotes when she mentioned *votes*. "They didn't even try to hide the corruption back then."

"Fascinating," Anika said. Dodd confirmed Joshua's assessment of her. Politics made her tick. "Did that happen in Miranda?"

"Down the road in Jim Wells County. That was another era, and it's one of the few photos that survived Hurricane Carla. Speaking of hurricanes, you weren't here for the last one."

"Correct, ma'am. I live in Washington, DC. Start my second year in law school at Georgetown this fall."

"So the plan is . . . what?" the mayor asked, not impressed that Anika attended one of the top law schools in the country. "To get your law degree and return home? Use your talents to give back to your hometown? I suspect our Miranda law firms don't pay but a fraction of the DC and New York firms."

That line of questioning raised yellow flags. Suspecting it related to her ability to care for Sam, Anika deflected. "My future's unclear, but one thing isn't: I'd suspend my legal education and come home. Anything to help Sam."

"I doubt you'd wanna drive my rusted ol' El Camino and live in the Alamo," she snorted. "And this job's about as sexy as it gets in this town. Lawyers are more like servants than leaders, and few wanna be consigliere to some clown with no power."

Anika hid her frustration. She remained focused on finding a solution for Sam, but Dodd kept talking about Anika's career path. If she ever moved back to Miranda, she'd apply for a job with the wealthy Danforth family, but she remembered Logan's warning not to invoke his name with the mayor. "Again, my path follows the best interest of my little sister."

"I admire that, but I'm not sure I can help. Unfortunately, in this fallen world, kids living with substance abusers isn't uncommon, and with no signs of physical abuse . . ."

"With all due respect, neglect is equally bad."

"Preachin' to the choir, sister, but rules is rules. When's your interview with FPS?"

Anika remembered Joshua's warning of Dodd's penchant for bartering. *She's a political animal, and politics is her game.* Her actions, albeit subtle, betrayed a woman who wanted to negotiate. The magnanimous mayor who'd started the meeting was now starting to resemble Monty Hall of *Let's Make a Deal*. "Next Wednesday," Anika answered, "and that's too late."

"I'll see what I can do about moving that up. But here's what I can't do: I can't keep the sheriff away from you. If Daddy calls 911, then I can find you a lawyer. Not a fancy-schmancy DC or New York lawyer, a *Miranda* lawyer."

"Anything you can do is a gift," Anika said, alarmed by the mayor's tribalism, making sure to avoid the Freudian slip—*grift*.

"If I'm gonna help you, Anika, you must be honest with me. My reputation's too valuable to be played, particularly by a flight risk. Will you be truthful about all the details related to this matter?"

At this point, Sam was going berserk with her new toy, swaying her head and making a ruckus that was borderline disrespectful. Anika placed her hand on Sam's leg, signaling for her to quiet down, and turned her face back to Dodd. "Yes, ma'am."

"Including details about yourself?"

Anika thought this line of probing was odd, but she had no leverage. "Of course."

"You okay with Sam stepping out for a sec? Curtis is a good caretaker, and I'd like to speak in private."

"Sure," Anika said as Sam left the Rubik's Cube on the mayor's desk, grabbed Pooh, and walked to the door. "What's going on?"

"This will only take a minute," Dodd said. With the door closed and Sam in the Commons, the mayor's eyes tightened, and her voice lowered to an intense whisper. "This will be the last time you lie to me, Anika. Do you understand?"

Anika's heart sank. "No, ma'am. I don't understand. What are you talking about?"

Dodd grabbed Anika's left hand, the diamond on her engagement ring still facing her palm. "Don't give me your 'ma'am' sandwiches. I'm no fool! We both know that you're not engaged. This is all a ruse—a big lie!"

Anika pulled her hand away and recoiled. "That's none of your business! Why would you say that?" The course of her denial was exhausted. "How did you *know* that?"

"It's my job to know these things. And if you're asking for my help, then everything about you is *my business*. That's the deal—take it or leave it. I don't do favors for liars, cheats, or charlatans."

Anika buried her face in her hands, perplexed and ashamed, not knowing how Mayor Dodd had uncovered the falsehood of Anika's fake fiancé. Faux Pooh was more real than her Washington beau. Left speechless, she worried that she'd squirreled away any chance of favor.

"So what'll it be?" the mayor asked. "My way or the high—"

"Your way," Anika said without hesitation. Her words leaped from her lips before the question ended.

"I'll make some calls today. Come see me again tomorrow afternoon."

"Whatever works best with your schedule."

"I'd like for my best educators to test Samantha," Dodd said. "Perhaps tomorrow. She's very gifted."

"Test?" The yellow flags turned red. As Joshua had predicted, the mayor exhibited a keen interest in Sam. Why had she said that, and how did she know anything about Sam? Sam hadn't said a word in at least two days. "I appreciate you saying that, but she's an average student. Just needs someone to take her to school."

"Average student!" the mayor roared and pointed to the edge of her desk. "Honey, there ain't another child under ten years old in South Texas who can do what Samantha just did."

Shocked, Anika stared at where the mayor was pointing. She couldn't believe her eyes.

On her first try, and in just a few minutes, Sam had solved the Rubik's Cube.

11

For all the chatter about ominous weather forecasts, the night's sky was calm. The same couldn't be said for Anika's nerves as she stepped into the backyard party with Sam. Her return to the Danforth hacienda unsettled her. Before Logan's and Ethan's parents moved into an apartment on the Upper East Side, she had spent much of her teens here—playing hide and seek, swimming, and flirting with Logan. In fact, she and Logan were *firsties*, as he called it, when it came to holding hands. She remembered it like yesterday on the diving board. Everything looked the same as it did five years ago. The ivy-covered stucco walls, the wrought iron fixtures, the uplighted trees—even the algae in the fountain beckoned like a familiar friend.

During her last visit, she had donned her homecoming tiara and drank Lone Star beer around the pool. That last visit marked another memorable moment. Despite being steady with Johnny, she had French-kissed her *firsty*, who was now hosting a welcome-home party for his newlywed wife, Sarah.

Life had a cruel sense of humor. The infamous kiss was more regrettable than royal, fueled by the beer and Logan's "for old times' sake" plea to end the historic night. Anika—who loved Johnny and never meant to betray him—had intended it as Logan's goodbye kiss, not a gateway to romance. Tonight, however, life would rub Anika's nose in her goodbye decision. Tonight, Anika would be a commoner invited to witness the pomp and pageantry she'd forgone for a dead man. Tonight, she would live a tale of two cities, and the contrast would be striking.

Sarah, dressed to the nines, had on designer clothes and boots valued more than Anika's rental car. In contrast, Anika wore khaki shorts, a Bob Marley T-shirt, and flip-flops—clothes she'd purchased at the thrift shop. Sarah resided in the biggest estate in Miranda, whereas Anika slept in a rental cottage she couldn't afford. Sarah boasted a Tiffany's wedding ring that could light up the Roman caves and, if placed around their necks, drown small children. Anika had discarded her fake engagement ring after the mayor exposed her as a fraud. Sarah dined on lobster and chateaubriand—cooked medium-rare-plus—and swilled first-growth wines from Bordeaux. Anika had some strawberry Pop-Tart wrappers tossed in her backseat.

No one had ever prepared her for the grave consequences of goodbye kisses.

Sarah likely knew little of her husband's childhood crush. It wasn't Logan's style to acknowledge failure; he wouldn't mention the girl who got away. A manufactured blonde, Sarah was the shiny new Miranda transplant. She had just returned from a week's-long shopping spree in Highland Park, a wealthy neighborhood in Dallas, where jewelry and Rolls-Royces cost about the same. One of her former Texas Longhorns cheerleaders (now a Dallas Cowboys cheerleader) had accompanied her. Referring to her big-budget boondoggle, Sarah told party guests that she *just had to get away with Emily for a week.*

Logan had invited Anika and Samantha to the party, along with Ethan, Chelsea, Amber, and two other friends from high school, Ricky Holloway and LeSean Brown. It wasn't Sarah's idea of a good time. She preferred the company of her out-of-town socialites, flown in on the private jet. Her presence here, though, was a small price to pay given the truckload of lavish clothes and loot she'd shipped from Dallas. Her credit card, Anika thought, was probably still hot to the touch. Overhearing Sarah brag, Anika figured that Saudi royal heirlooms cost less than what Sarah had tallied on her Dallas jaunt.

Though hard to admit, Anika conceded Sarah had a mesmerizing personality, which explained Logan's attraction to her. To be fair, she was an attractive woman by any standards, with features one would expect of a

Division I college cheerleader. She didn't have the looks or proportions of an Amber or Chelsea—few did. Marketers paid real money for their beauty. But Sarah didn't want or need to be a model. She possessed her own talents, and few could match her presence and control of the crowd.

Watching Sarah work Logan's guests, Anika reflected on their first meeting a few minutes ago at the front door. Sarah had owned that introduction and left Anika feeling as if she was the most important *visitor*—to Sarah's house, to Miranda—in the whole wide world. Surveying the backyard that held so many of her memories, that's what stung the most. The perception of Sarah as the longtime Miranda resident and Anika as the outsider. Anika had countless Logan stories to share but stayed mum. *Firsties*.

As the crowd waited for the concert, Ricky and LeSean approached Anika. "Here comes trouble," Anika joked, winking at the two young men, watching Sam walk toward the stage and take a seat at a glass table. With Ricky and LeSean at her side, Anika kept a casual eye on Ethan. He ignored her because Amber was clinging to him like a tick. She found that drama more amusing than disturbing. Anika's world had moved on, but Amber's hadn't—maybe never would. "You boys look lost."

"Lost and found," Ricky said, kissing Anika on both cheeks. Ricky managed the Miranda Depot, located in the Upper West Side. No trains, drugs, or migrants traveled in or out of town without his express knowledge and consent. He governed with know-how, street smarts, and the help of his ruffian gang, which added to his power and influence. Through hard work, a strategic mind, and whatever illegal tactics he employed, he was, at the ripe age of twenty-three, an effective and formidable business-person in Miranda. "How's life?"

"Better than I deserve, I guess." It was a half-truth but the best she could summon.

"Beautiful as always," LeSean followed, kissing her on the forehead, a sign in Miranda of tested friendship. LeSean had legendary status as the town's star football player, but his NFL dreams fizzled after he tore his ACL playing linebacker for Baylor University. Instead of opting for a lengthy rehab after surgery, he decided to apprentice under his dad, who was the CEO of the Miranda Refinery, located in the same industrial complex as

Ricky's depot. Like Ricky, LeSean was a successful businessman; unlike his friend, LeSean refined his Texas tea on his daddy's motto, *Performance with Integrity*. If the Danforths held the blue ribbon for the wealthiest family in town, the Browns held the red one. Third place was so far in the distance that no one cared to speculate. "You look tired."

"Met with Mayor Dodd this morning. Need her help protecting Sam. Interesting meeting, to say the least."

"Interesting how?" Ricky probed, sharing glances with LeSean as if they'd discussed the mayor before. He tilted back his head, lifted his chin in the air, and fanned his white Houston Astros jersey (Altuve 27), which draped over his wife-beater V-neck and concealed a handgun attached to his belt. With his casual dress and countless tattoos, most underestimated Ricky's business savvy, a mistake he monetized and used to his advantage. "And what's this about *protection and help*?"

"Protection from the police . . . help from family and protective services."

"Say no more! I got the po-po right here!" Ricky said, tapping his firearm.

LeSean, who wore a green Polo with an oversized emblem, khaki pants, and vintage Air Jordans, shook his head. His friend's antics no longer surprised him. He put his gargantuan bicep around Ricky's neck and said, "Let's get another Lone Star before you and Anika end up in the crowbar hotel."

"Wait," Ricky said. "Dodd's a political hack. Been busting our chops for several weeks, messing with our business. Believes a big hurricane's coming. But we don't pack up and leave just because a few storm clouds roll in."

"True," LeSean added. "Auntie Dodd acts like a despot. My family's gotta business to run, same as Ricky, and financial statements to sustain. Trying to go public . . . crack the *Fortune 1000*. I can't be a charity case for an old hag worried about bad weather."

"Pals and gals," Logan interrupted, already intoxicated and putting his arms around Anika and Ricky. "How's ya mom and them?"

"Having a blast, Logan," Anika said, wondering about his moonshine distillery. Even the rich and famous needed pet projects, she guessed. The servant dressed in a tuxedo had offered her an apple pie, and it certainly wasn't a dessert from Grandma Danforth's recipe book. Unless Grandma was baking up 151-proof concoctions. "Thank you for inviting Sam."

Keeping hubby on a short leash, Sarah expedited her poolside carousing. "I'm so jealous of your eyes," she said, wrapping her arm around Anika's neck. "It's sooo nice to have you here. Know that you're *always* welcome in our home." Sarah had put a dent in her 2005 Bordeaux, but Anika didn't care. Sarah was getting clumsy, but her words, however untruthful, were a balm to Anika's wounds. "And Samantha is . . . a . . . *doll*," she continued with a half-measure cadence. "I would love to enroll her in sailing lessons. I already feel like she's family."

Sailing lessons? The idea of sailing lessons was a pipe dream, the farthest thing from reality for Anika and Samantha. Anika tried to hide her emotions. If anyone deserved the very best, it was Sam. Sarah, swinging her wine glass around like a magic wand, failed to notice Anika's watery eyes, as if she'd majored in bringing people to tears with her promises and charm.

But Sarah did something else that caught Anika's attention. She did it as Logan walked away to grab another drink. It was subtle but seemingly important. Pulling out her phone and swaying side to side, Sarah mumbled her answers to texts. And as she typed, she smiled, looked across the pool, and voiced, "Logan will never find out."

"Logan will never find out what?" Anika repeated, causing Sarah's eyes to widen. But as soon as Anika confronted Sarah about what she'd said and meant, the country musician—an Evan Felker look-alike with a white cowboy hat and rhinestone button-down—addressed his small audience.

"I'm told that we're dedicating this night to the homecoming of a special woman," the crooner said, as Anika's heart raced in anticipation. "A woman who Miranda loves and respects. A woman who has overcome great adversity to be here tonight and who makes the lives of those around her so much better."

Anika couldn't believe it. Was Logan honoring her publicly? Had he scheduled this party to celebrate her return home? She felt like she was walking on clouds.

"Sarah Danforth!" the musician announced with a toothy grin, toasting Sarah and the crowd. "Thank you for making this world better. And for making Logan happy—that's important . . . to all of us. Cheers!"

Anika stood paralyzed with a fake smile, staring at Sarah as she pirouetted in the spotlight. Logan, clueless as usual, believed he'd brought everyone together as one happy family by honoring his wife. And Ethan still hadn't mustered the manhood in front of Amber to speak to Anika, playing a romantic card game with himself. What he thought was five-card stud, she snickered, would likely end up as solitaire. The middle-school drama was comical.

After a few Red Dirt songs, Anika thanked her hosts, grabbed Sam, and marched toward the exit. Before she departed, however, Ricky pulled her aside, outside the earshot of her younger sister. "Are y'all safe?"

"I don't know, Ricky."

"Bring me in; let me take care of it."

"I'm not ready for that. Love you like a brother, but you're too comfortable with crime and . . . other things."

"Here's the deal. *Someone* better take care of it. FPS and the po-po can't be trusted. And the mayor is the devil, or at least a vaulted demon. I'm not saying you need to," he made a slit-the-throat gesture, "but you need to play hardball. Understand?"

Anika hesitated. She hoped the police would arrest Scotty at some point, but hope wasn't a good strategy.

"Promise?" he insisted.

Anika looked at Samantha, realizing that she hadn't brought Faux Pooh to the party. Sam was finding her courage, whereas Anika was wallowing in pity and fear. Ricky was right. Anika needed to face reality head-on.

Time to play hardball.

"Promise," she said, her nostrils flaring.

12

The next morning Calvin and Luther played near the Church Grounds pond, pouncing and pawing at the diamondback rattlesnake they'd killed. Serpents weren't allowed in the garden. Sam attempted to coax the Danes away with a tennis ball, but she failed to disrupt their interest in the viper. Texas herpetologists, Anika had read, believed that South Texas rattlesnakes were evolving without rattles. Luckily for the dogs, microevolution took time because the snake's warning signal had saved Luther's life.

Anika sat on the bench next to Joshua, facing the church from the screened-in porch of her cottage. The sky was gray, the air cool for August. The porch smelled of blueberry pancakes, which Joshua had delivered in a wicker basket. The dancing wind chime signaled the arrival of Hurricane Joyce's remnants. A storm with so much potential had pivoted north, leaving but a whimper of wind, rain, and storm surge. For Miranda, so accustomed to life-changing storms, Joyce was a yawner. But Anika sensed the increased anxiety around town as the whisper campaign peddled news of a sixty-year storm brewing off the west coast of Africa.

Watching Sam's antics through the gaping hole in the screen brought Anika joy. She was encouraged to hear her sister scream with excitement as the dogs abandoned the serpent and chased the tennis ball. The return of Sam's voice meant that her speech was not far behind. Sam's colorful persona showed signs of returning, too, along with her innocent devilry. In addition to providing breakfast, Joshua had stopped by to drop off the lease.

"Before I forget, Anika, there's a large hunting knife in one of the kitchen drawers. Might want to hide it over the fridge, or I can take it with me. Our last pastoral intern left it behind."

"Maybe I'll carry it to my meeting with Mayor Dodd," she joked with her eyebrows raised. "Not sure why I'm a nervous wreck."

"Because Dodd wields incredible power, and she's torched the rulebook. Don't like to gossip, but she plays dirty."

"What makes her tick?"

"She's beholden to political power, but she may have a remnant of a soul. I'm told she had a husband and three young children who died in a car accident. Hit by a drunk driver. Leniency toward DWI laws caused her to quit her teaching job—primary ed, I think—and run for office. She's flourished as mayor for two decades, amassing inordinate power and influence."

"How'd you change her mind on covid masks? She doesn't strike me as a constitutional scholar wedded to First Amendment religious-rights issues."

"Definitely not. She's more tactical and programmatic than principled or ideological. I won because I had leverage."

"Meaning?"

"I had hundreds of local taxpayers with strong religious convictions lathering up. She didn't want Christian protesters besieging the Alamo Opera House. She's got bigger things on her plate."

"What's the biggest, I wonder?"

"Sixty-year storm. No one here takes hurricanes seriously. You said it yourself: There's a stubborn refusal to evacuate. Some unwritten code."

"Mirandites don't leave town much anyway, but since I was born, we've never evacuated for hurricanes."

"Why is that? If you were to evacuate anyplace in the world, it would be Miranda. Multiple recorded hurricanes destroyed everything here and nearly wiped out the population."

"My dad told me that, back in the seventies and eighties, people evacuated as far as Waco or Dallas. That was before they opened all lanes to northbound traffic, when many got stuck in traffic for days. Huge mess. Then, in the nineties, after repeated cries of wolf, townsfolk bought generators, hunkered down, and rode out the storms. In the new millennium, it became a pride thing. You'll be ostracized from social circles if you fly the coop."

"That's unfortunate. Where's your dad now?" Joshua asked.

"Died several years ago in a motorcycle accident. Sam's my half-sister."

"Was your dad from Miranda?"

"Los Angeles. Aspiring movie producer."

"Interesting work."

"He never took opportunities for granted. 'Work hard, never complain, win everything, no excuses, Anika,' he would say," she sighed. "He always told me I was special. I miss him."

"He'd be proud of you, no doubt. What about your mom?"

"Mom's a mess. She's also from SoCal, a failed actress who dabbled in adult film. Many believe she looks like Sharon Tate from *Valley of the Dolls*, who was—"

"Slain by Charles Manson's maniacs," he said, finishing her sentence.

"Get this," she said. "My parents' first date was at El Coyote, where Sharon Tate dined the night she died. It was eerie watching that scene in the Tarantino movie."

"Never saw it. Your folks stayed together, so the enchiladas must've been good."

"More likely, the margaritas. As the story goes, they went on a field trip to South by Southwest in Austin, married in a rush, and moved to Corpus Christi. Dad clearly wanted Mom far removed from the toxic environment in LA. He took a job as an insurance salesman."

"Bravo. He abandoned his professional dreams to care for his family."

"After he died, she remarried. I don't know where she is this exact moment. When she escapes the world, she forgets to pay her phone bill. Not sure you wanted to hear all that."

"The context is helpful, particularly as it relates to Sam's situation."

"Speaking of Sam," she said, "not even Dad could've rescued me from this mess. I have zero leverage with the mayor."

"You might have more than you think."

Anika turned her eyes to Joshua. "How so?"

"Samantha."

"You keep alluding to Sam, but I don't get your point."

"She still drawing cubes?" he asked.

"Yeah, but I don't understand how that—"

"I saw the drawings you left for me, Anika. She has a gift. Have you ever heard of the term *soothsayer*?"

"You think she's a witch because she draws squares?"

"Not a witch."

"A sorceress then?" Anika said, floating somewhere between anxious and impatient. "Or someone who communicates with the dead?"

"You're getting warmer, but it's more complicated than tinkering in fairy tales."

"I'm not tinkering in anything. Listen, Joshua, I struggle with your religious beliefs, but I grew up Catholic and believe God exists. Whether he's personal or three-in-one is beyond me, but I never took you for selling make-believe. Now I'm having second thoughts."

"Hear me out."

"No offense, but I'm trying to solve real-world problems, and something tells me you're about to wax on about wizards and warlocks. I don't have the time or energy for nonsense."

"What I'm proposing is more nuanced. The Bible refers to spiritual warfare but doesn't reveal all the details behind it. And to be clear, the only Spirit I'm aware of is the Holy Spirit, and I believe He's the only one who illuminates Scripture. But cults and freaks and unhealthy religions take this concept of spiritual warfare to another level, so we get hokey beliefs such as voodoo, hoodoo—other variants of false religion in Mexico and South Texas. It gets even kookier when you travel to New Orleans."

"What's your point?" she asked.

"If spiritual *warfare* is real—and, through my experience as a pastor, I'm certain it is—then it's not a huge leap to say that spiritual *forces* are also real."

"Where does that leave Sam?"

"Dodd might say Sam's an instrument, or conduit, for spiritual forces. I call that a soothsayer, but maybe that's imprecise."

"An instrument for good or evil?"

"Those who believe in soothsayers would say they're usually neutral. Their gifts are used for good or evil depending on who's using them."

"You know how crazy you sound?" she said.

"To be clear, I don't believe in sorcery or necromancy. I do think, however, Dodd believes that nonsense. Soothsaying, depending on how it's defined, is more nuanced. Here's an example. Dodd will look at someone like Sam and think she can magically predict the future. A bona fide soothsayer."

"And you'll look at her and see a prophet, a messenger from God?"

"Far from it. The only prophets I recognize are Jesus and others mentioned in the Bible. I look at Sam and see a young girl with the gift of observation that's off the charts."

"Now you make her sound like a Jedi with a high midi-chlorian count."

"That's getting closer to reality," he said, "but it's still fantasy. I'm talking about something in her brain—IQ, instinct, and observation, maybe a combination of things—that helps her anticipate future events."

"I understand how we draw on past experiences to anticipate future happenings, but this takes that concept to another level."

"Trust your instincts, Anika. Once you realize that spiritual forces exist, then you'll realize that wild coincidences don't. You've lived in Miranda most of your life, and the spiritual forces are powerful here. You may be numb to them. You've never wondered if this town is alive?"

"New York City is alive," she said. "I'm told Paris is alive."

"Not like this. Be honest with yourself. This town breathes and guides and tugs and pulls. You've never felt that force? A pulling that's hard to describe but that's manipulating time and space to influence your movements?"

"I felt it in the church, in front of the paintings on the wall." She chose not to mention the eyes that she thought followed her. No need to introduce more awkwardness. She didn't know Joshua well, nor did she trust him. Presently, she didn't trust anyone but Sam.

"Right. There you go!" he said.

"Felt it in my old house, particularly in the hallway."

"That's called the *koya*, and once you accept that the *koya* exists, the more you'll remember it from your past and recognize it in the future."

"*Koya* sounds like it's—"

"Comanche," he interrupted. "Likely derived from the local tribe that occupied Miranda in the eighteenth century."

"I grew up hearing stories about Native American rituals and hocus pocus. Never this. Where'd you hear about it?"

"Around the church watercooler . . . from some elderly saints."

"Spiritual forces. Soothsayers. And now the *koya*? It's all too much, Joshua."

He shrugged. "How else would you explain strange phenomena that occur in this town? Like the trees in Revolutionary Park left unscathed by hurricanes that eviscerate everything else in their path?"

"I heard it was air pockets," she said, "created by cool winds from Colorado colliding with warm winds from the Gulf of Mexico."

He chuckled. "Air pockets? The same air pockets happen to form right over the park every hurricane? Now who's tinkering in fairy tales?"

"It's not that I don't want to believe. I do."

"Not for nothin', the leverage you have over the mayor doesn't require *you* to believe. It only requires the *mayor* to believe. And she will. One look at Sam's cube drawings, and she'll recognize her gift. In fact, Mayor Dodd uses an old timer named Cyclops who, I'm told, practices soothsaying. I'm not sure who interprets his work, though, or how accurate it is."

"Wait. There are two Nostradamuses in town?" she said. "That sounds even more absurd."

"If the legends are true, then there'll be more."

Anika stared at him with suspicious eyes.

"Back to Revolutionary Park," he continued. "The three largest trees exhibit carvings from centuries past."

"Let me guess . . . carvings of cubes."

"Indeed. Legend has it that soothsayers increasingly manifest their gifts right before the sixty-year storms."

"Legend also has it," Anika said, "that kiddos with pocketknives carve shapes into trees. You believe that malarky?"

"Fair point," Joshua reasoned. "I believe some folks possess gifts of observation that allow them to be more perceptive—and yes, predictive—than others. That's not supernatural or magical. It makes sense that some within that group, like Sam, have more talent than others. I'm still trying to figure out, though, why gifted Mirandites manifest their talent through cubes."

"Let me know when you figure that out, Joshua. By the way, does Cyclops wear a scary eye patch?"

"No, but people say he's got an eye in the back of his head. Knows all the town gossip. Some say he's a former Nazi hunter."

"Is he always in the rocking chair on the Alamo porch?" she asked.

"That's him."

"Saw him yesterday . . . thought he looked familiar."

"Listen," Joshua reemphasized, "I could care less if you believe in soothsaying or the *koya*. Not sure anyone can adequately explain them. But if I can't convince you to believe in spiritual warfare, at least believe that you're at risk negotiating with the mayor. She wields the power to make or break you and Sam. Behind her gentle smile lies a ruthless politician bent on manipulating everything. She won't take no for an answer, and once she pulls you into her lair, you'll never crawl out."

"I'll keep that in mind, Joshua, and thanks for the wise counsel," she said, smiling. "Even if it's a bit coo-coo."

"We'll both figure it out one day."

"Fine, but I demand proof before I hop on the crazy train."

"I *can* give you some proof."

"How do you figure?" she probed.

"Bet I can interpret Sam's drawings."

"I don't believe you."

"Hand me one. Where's the most recent?"

"Here," she said, handing it to Joshua. "What does it say?"

Joshua's face went ashen, and a ghastly expression came over him.

"Joshua?"

"It says you'll be arrested tomorrow."

"Come on!" Anika howled. "Really? Now you're just playing with my head. *Magic Eight Ball, will I be arrested tomorrow? It is decidedly so.* You're more mischievous than Sam, and that's quite a feat."

"I wouldn't joke about this," he said, pulling out a red pen and writing in another condition to the lease agreement. "I'll leave this lease for you to read. After signing it, slip it under the lodge's front door. First month's free. If we survive hurricane season, and you're still here, we'll talk about a payment plan. Fair?"

"Fair." She thanked Joshua, who got up to leave—still disturbed by Sam's drawings.

The screen door, tethered to a loaded spring, slammed shut as he left. Before he walked too far, he told her, "My phone number's on the lease. Call me tomorrow if you need a ride . . . or a lawyer."

Anika rolled her eyes, picked up the lease, and read the terms and conditions. The only typed prohibition was the one he'd already mentioned: Under no circumstances will Lessee enter Lessor's bedroom. That was strange enough, but his handwritten addition in red ink was even more ominous.

Sam will not walk or play alone beyond the barbed wire fence.

13

Anika obsessed over Joshua's lease addendum. *Sam will not walk or play alone beyond the barbed wire fence.* What kind of creepy term and condition was that? She didn't know what it meant, but she knew she needed to leave town. First things first, she had to focus on the mayor. Approaching the Alamo Opera House front porch, she noticed nothing changed much here. The old men—whom Joshua had referred to as "old timers," as if they were plank owners of AARP—clicked dominos and carried on. She chalked up their continued interest in her to elderly curiosity. New faces—whether arriving to eat breakfast tacos, visit the mayor, or purchase a suppository—captured the attention of folks who no longer kept calendars.

Anika paid closer mind this time to her surroundings. The Kwik Mart stalker, whom they called Peanut, occupied his same seat, gnawing on his toothpick and playing dominoes with a man they called Moon. Moon had squinty eyes attached to a gaunt face that was hidden behind a silver, braided Viking beard. He sat next to a loose-jowled fella named Vernis, whose droopy overalls revealed a malnourished frame.

She focused on the one with the tattered cowboy hat in the rocking chair. She remembered his always-around-town face from years ago. Unlike the others, he hadn't committed his full stare. One eye followed her every step, but the other was on the doodling project in his lap. By the looks of his napkin—covered with cubes that were shaded, stacked, twisted, tilted, and connected—she figured this was the old timer that Joshua had called Cyclops, the mayor's soothsayer. The wise one with the eye in the back of his head.

Ascending the creaky steps, she heard the old timers discussing the weather. But this wasn't the usual small talk. They ranked Texas storms. Not by category, wind speed, or monetary damage, but by casualties—body count. The Galveston hurricane of 1900, which the old timers called the Great Storm, was the deadliest in US and Texas history. Galveston was but a stone's throw up the coast from Miranda, and the Great Storm had killed nearly ten thousand people, many of them Mirandites. Vernis believed Hurricane Carla, which hit Miranda in 1961, had killed almost as many. Though the official calculation was less than fifty deaths, the man called Moon was arguing that Miranda had a penchant for under-reporting its body count, and the actual death toll edged toward twelve thousand. Peanut agreed with all the comments voiced, even when they conflicted.

Reaching the top of the porch, Anika spied Curtis Worden leaning his broom against the wall underneath the vintage concert bill of Bob Wills and the Texas Playboys. Though she remained allergic to thoughts of the supernatural, she couldn't dismiss Joshua's explanation of the *koya*. She didn't fully embrace the notion of its existence, but she knew something had affected her senses near Sam's bedroom, in the Kwik Mart, and inside the church sanctuary. Thankfully, nothing held her back as she strode toward the swinging doors. That was a good omen. The last thing she needed was spiritual forces disrupting her meeting with the mayor.

"She's in her office," Worden said, skipping the pleasantries. "Would you like a breakfast taco? I recommend potato and egg."

"Not hungry, thanks."

Worden escorted Anika to Auntie Dodd's office, and she walked right in, took a seat, and straightened her hair.

"Where's your little sister?" the mayor asked.

"Probably wrestling with two dogs that together weigh as much as a baby elephant."

"With adult supervision, I trust?"

Adult supervision? Given the circumstances, Anika thought the question revealed an utter lack of awareness. Didn't Dodd know that adult supervision was the problem? "I've asked a pastor to babysit," Anika responded with an assassin's smile, "so both her life and afterlife are in good hands today."

"Brava, Anika! Wasn't trying to call ticky-tack fouls, but with the plays you're wanting to run, you need angels on your team. No unforced errors."

Not interested in sports metaphors, Anika said, "I'm curious if you learned anything more—if you can help with FPS."

"Well, it's not that easy."

Here comes the negotiation, Anika thought. "I didn't expect it would be."

"I rescheduled your FPS interview, but there's an issue with your mother."

"There are several issues with my mother; that's why we're here in the first place."

"FPS believes she's abandoned Samantha. That means her dad must acquiesce to your having custody."

"But her dad's the real problem."

"Rules is rules, and it's hard to remove a kid from a parent. Lots of talk about 'best interest of the child' and whatnot, but this one's hard. And the lack of direct evidence of abuse and, quite frankly, your living up north in DC without a job isn't helping things. No way they let you take Samantha away from Miranda with the status quo."

The reference to the District of Columbia being *up north*, Anika thought, was a rich dish of Texas home cooking. But it wasn't surprising. She expected the parochial, xenophobic attitude from a Texas politician. The way Dodd had said *take Samantha away from Miranda*, however, was downright creepy. Everything, in fact, was creepy in the mayor's office. "Again, I'm willing to move back home and get a job. Whatever it takes. I'm renting a place on the Lower East Side. Have the lease in my purse if anyone wants to see it."

Uninterested in the lease, the mayor peered into Anika's eyes. "Let's cut to the chase. Samantha's a gifted child. The way she mastered the Rubik's Cube . . . a sight to behold. Is she doing other things, such as drawing or painting?"

The critical juncture was at hand. If Anika refused to mention Sam's habit of drawing cubes, the mayor would wash her hands of their troubles.

That much was clear. Sam would return to the squalor and neglect of the Mathis homestead in the Lower West Side. But that was the only thing that was clear. Scotty, for instance, had become an enraged lunatic, and Anika feared that, if Sam returned, his neglect could morph into physical abuse. If Anika came clean, however, the mayor could make all the uncertainty, trouble, and pain vanish. In the end, it wasn't even a close call. "She draws pictures of cubes."

"Not surprising." The mayor smiled. "Well, I bet we can find a path forward."

"I'm all ears."

"How about this? You come work for me, full-time, and Curtis takes care of Samantha's schooling until the end of the year. That'll give you a steady job, and I can attest to FPS that Samantha's getting the best education and care in town."

"Work here? For you? What would—"

"Beggars can't be choosers, my dear," Dodd said, growing agitated, "and we'll figure out specific responsibilities later. I just handed you a golden key, Anika, but you don't seem thankful or interested."

"I'm both, Mayor Dodd," she fibbed, remembering Joshua's warnings of becoming the corrupt mayor's puppet. "Just saddened about leaving law school."

"Let's talk about that. What *exactly* would you be leaving?"

"One of the top law schools in the country."

"Yes, indeed. Georgetown Law. Very impressive. Leaving in what capacity?"

"As a second year."

"Second year *what*?"

Anika paused. "Student." Her answer came across more as a question.

"What did I tell you about lying to me, Anika?"

Anika paused again, now confused and anxious. "Not to do it."

"But here you are again, Pinocchio without the long nose, lying about this and that and everything in between."

"I don't understand."

"You're not a student at Georgetown Law School. You don't even live in DC. You're an administrative assistant to an insurance salesman outside Lockhart, Texas."

Anika closed her eyes, deflated. She no doubt had drained the mayor's reservoir of trust and goodwill. "How did you—"

"When will you get it through your thick skull? It's my job to know. I know you didn't go to law school. You didn't even go to college."

"What else do you—"

"I know you're a convicted felon. That three-dotted tattoo below your thumb is a prison tat that means *mi vida loca*." *My crazy life.* "You served five years in prison . . . were just released. I know you call your probation officer every day at five o'clock. How long did he give you to travel? A week?"

"Another reason FPS won't allow me to care for my sister."

"Wrong again!" Dodd yelled, slamming her fist on the desk, her empty eyes dilating. "Here's my little secret! Miranda FPS does whatever I tell them to do!"

"I just was saying—"

"And I own the criminal justice system! I can have them transfer your probation down here! I have the power to take care of all this for you! They do whatever I tell them to do!"

"That sounds . . ."

"Enough chitchat. You have my terms. Lie again, you're back in the slammer. I'll snap the cuffs back on you, dump you in the back of my El Camino, and drive you to the poky myself."

"I'm not sure I can accept your offer right now," Anika said, intrigued but frightened. "I'd like to speak with Sam and sleep on—"

"Suit yourself," the mayor said, clearly vexed by Anika's vacillation. "You have until noon tomorrow." As Anika walked toward the door, the mayor stepped in front of her. "This is your opportunity to be a *queen* again, Anika! To hop off your mule and climb back on the Clydesdale!"

Staring at the floor, Anika nodded hesitantly and felt the lump in her throat.

"This is your opportunity to save *Samantha*," the mayor continued, digging in her pudgy but razor-sharp talons. "Otherwise, she'll remain in danger so long as her dad is alive."

Lying in bed, Anika stared at the ceiling fan and combed her fingers through Sam's hair. A nightlight plugged in nearby cast ominous shadows throughout the bedroom. The coyotes yip-howling in the distance—in the backwoods beyond the barbed wire fence—caused Anika to shutter, but they weren't loud enough to drown out Sam's gentle snores. Anika grasped Faux Pooh with her free hand. Pooh had comforted Anika through many childhood trials, but this predicament proved too much for his soothing balm. She considered what else lay beyond the barbed wire fence; what evils other than wild dogs and rattlesnakes lurked outside its hedge of protection; what had caused Joshua to write that addendum concerning Sam in the lease agreement. Was it the mysterious drug courier who people called the Midnight Rider? Anika thought she kept seeing a vehicle late at night with its lights off, circling the property. Was he also a kidnapper?

Anika released Pooh to grab her phone on the nightstand. Incoming texts revealed ghosts, goblins, or spiritual forces weren't the immediate threat. Instead, Scotty Scumbag remained the most pernicious problem. Over the last two days, his texts had evolved from silly to sad to irritating to troublesome to threatening. Tonight, they had taken on new characteristics: startling, disturbing, alarming . . . actionable.

Actionable. Anika let that word marinate. Agonizing over her next steps, she felt the walls closing in. Scotty posed a clear and present danger to everything she loved. And he left her with few options. His latest texts revealed he'd lost his mind and soul. That said, his words, too wicked to reread, wouldn't be enough to influence FPS. Not unless Anika heeded the mayor's demands. And she refused to do that. Dodd's devil's bargain promised the world but, alas, fell short on details and guarantees. In the end, Anika knew, working for the mayor would only lead to more headache and heartbreak. Dodd's idea of small-town politics rose to a whole new level.

One viable option remained. Anika slid from under the sheets and into her pants and shoes. She walked to the kitchen, grabbed the Bowie knife from atop the refrigerator, and returned to the bedroom. The double-sided blade—normally used for skinning game or splitting firewood—was monstrous, perhaps fifteen inches in length. The knife nestled in the small of her back, Anika tucked Pooh in Sam's arms and wrapped the covers over her shoulders. She kissed her little sister on the forehead and whispered, "I love you . . . to the moon and back."

And then she was off.

14

Before tonight, the idea of killing her stepdad had never crossed Anika's mind. Despite what Ricky Holloway had in mind, the promise she'd made to him at the Danforth's party only spoke to the ends, not the means, of solving the problem. She wasn't a murderer, and even though she'd spent five years in jail, she'd never taken someone's life. But things had changed, and now she sat in her car outside her childhood residence staring at an open gate with a fifteen-inch Bowie knife in her lap, thinking.

Scotty had never sexually or physically abused Sam. But that wasn't the standard for parenting young children. Sam lived in a toxic environment of neglect, fear, and hostility, exacerbated by rampant substance abuse—booze and weed, but also the occasional pills and blow. Some experts would claim emotional abuse, while others called it fancier names. Anika's simple mind boilded it down to one word: abuse. And no sane person would call any of it a *home*. Anika's mom was AWOL, and her stepdad had license to blame her mom for much of life's ills. But that didn't give him the right to make it worse.

Things had to change. And they had to change now.

Anika palmed her old house key, exited the car under a hidden moon, and strode to the front door. The knife was sheathed but in plain view. The porch light was an exposed, flickering bulb that shone just enough to attract bugs and reveal the doorknob. Surgical gloves pulled tight, she cracked open the door. Scotty had forgotten to lock it, signaling he was likely passed out.

He was going to make this easy.

Taking a deep breath, she walked inside, pulling the sheath off the knife and setting it on the kitchen table. She had zero doubt that killing Scotty Scumbag would improve her sister's life. Sam, of course, may suffer temporary grief—Scotty was her flesh and blood, after all—but his absence would bear fruit in the long run. Perhaps this was a zero-sum game: taking one life to save another. Better yet, she rationalized, perhaps her actions would epitomize justice: taking a guilty life to save an innocent one.

When she stepped inside, the *koya* returned. The faint nudging and tugging in different directions. The thrumming in her ears like someone blowing into the hole of an empty glass soda bottle. She didn't want to admit the existence of the *koya*—the word itself sounded mystical. She wondered if it was nothing more than the sound of electricity humming from a nearby electrical substation. Maybe that palpable, intrusive noise was throwing off her balance. Perhaps she was experiencing early signs of tinnitus. Focused on the task at hand, her feet desired to walk toward the master bedroom, but the thrum, or the tug, or the force—whatever the heck it was—signaled that walking in that direction was not a good idea.

She marched forward nonetheless, her memory and the lava lamp her only guides. The gravity of each step weighed on her, the *koya* intense. Approaching his bedroom, she noticed the door was ajar. She raised the heavy knife and peeked in, prepared for any sudden attack, prepared for Scotty Scumbag to pounce.

He didn't. He was right where she'd expected him to be. She walked into the bedroom, noticing the thrumming and tugging—the *koya*—had stopped. The ambient light coming through the window in the room framed the image. He was passed out in the bed, lying face down like he'd attempted to land the plane headfirst without engaging the landing gear. Knife in attack position, she grunted to elicit a response, to discern his level of awareness. He normally snored like a freight train—certainly louder than her dog, Van Halen, ever had—but tonight, he lay eerily quiet and still. Nothing but a big, overweight blob of disappointment mushed together on top of stinky cotton sheets. Adding to his disgrace, his customary stench of booze and body odor was laced with the menthol scent of pain relief cream. Little did he know that, after tonight, he'd experience no more pain. At least not on planet Earth.

He didn't respond to her grunts, which she elevated incrementally to a shout, so she assumed he was out cold. This would be easier than planned. She put down the knife at the foot of the bed, beyond his toes, and fetched what normally would be her mom's pillow. Grabbing the pillow with both hands, she took a deep breath . . . and hovered over Scotty Mathis.

The moment of truth. She could smother him and rid the world of his evil forever. Not even the best sleuths in Miranda's sheriff's department would suspect foul play. No prints, no hints, no nothing. Just another out-of-work, overcooked bum who overdosed on his coping devices. The house contained enough illegal drugs and alcohol to kill a pride of lions. No one would be surprised to learn that tonight's toxic concoction proved lethal. The line of credit for substance abuse was longer for some than others, but the bill eventually came due. It *always* came due.

She thought of another reason for finishing this. No one would ever miss him. No one but . . .

Tears welled up in Anika's eyes. No one would ever miss him but . . . Samantha.

The ugly truth is that little girls love their daddies even when their daddies don't deserve it. Anika's dad had been dead for more than ten years, and she still cried herself to sleep every year on his birthday. He had been a good dad, but it didn't matter in Sam's case. She only knew one daddy, and little girl hearts can be fragile, naïve, and poor barometers of good and evil. Anika also couldn't erase from memory the drawing from Sam's pile, the only one without the cubes. A drawing of a dad and his daughter holding hands in the park. With all the urgency this crisis demanded, that drawing, above all things, had summoned Anika to this room. It had scared the daylights out of her. It pictured the control Scotty Scumbag had over Sam's heart.

And now that Anika was here, one step away from unspeakable evil, reality came knocking live a Jehovah's Witness. This wasn't who she was. She wasn't a murderer. She wasn't the villain. *He* was the villain. The town's authorities—*they* were the villains. She wanted to save her sister's life. She didn't want to return to jail, this time for life or until they squirted the night-night serum into her veins. What's more, this sorry excuse for a human being crashed face down on the bed—his curly blond hair disheveled like an industrial mop—no longer posed a threat to Anika. For all his wild threats of exposing Anika's secrets to the world, he never did. And now it didn't matter—those cats had clawed themselves free of the bag. The mayor of the town—now her employer—knew Anika's criminal history. So why was Anika standing over her stepfather with a pillow in her hands?

She tossed it to the floor, turned on the bedside lamp, and then . . .

Screamed at the top of her lungs!

She noticed the vomit on the sheets. That was scarring enough, but things got worse. She rolled Scotty over and saw his ghost-white face. His jaundiced eyes stared into Neverland. She spied a half-empty bottle of Jack Daniels next to some nondescript pills on the nightstand. To an outsider, the whiskey bottle alone would tell the whole story, but she'd witnessed him drink more than that for breakfast. That the bottle was only half empty was more notable.

She panicked! His threatening texts to her likely remained on his smartphone. His texts tonight had been especially incendiary. He had threatened to call the police, threatened to reveal secrets, even threatened physical harm. If the police read those texts, the booze and pills alone wouldn't be enough to close the case. Detectives would make Anika a prime suspect in his death.

She rushed to the living room, turning on lights and scouring the house for his phone. She frantically pulled up the couch cushions until she heard a voice behind her at the front door.

"Ma'am, put your hands in the air! Slowly!"

Anika noticed the blue and red lights flashing on the wall. "I'm unarmed," she declared, her lips trembling as she raised her gloved hands in the air.

"I see an empty sheath on the table. If you're unarmed, then where's the knife?"

"Officer, I know this looks bad, but it's not—"

"Answer my question!"

"The knife's on the bed in the main bedroom."

"Listen to me very carefully. Turn around slowly, keeping your hands in the air where I can see them."

Anika, now looking down the barrel of a pistol, followed orders. A second police officer, his pistol drawn, entered the scene. When he saw Anika, he holstered his gun and walked toward her.

Sheriff's Deputy One lowered his weapon but continued his questioning. "What am I going to find when I walk back there?"

"It's not good," Anika said.

"Anyone else here?" Deputy Two asked.

"There's a dead body on the bed."

Deputy One walked to the bedroom and within seconds called for backup. He returned to the living room, his face ashen.

Deputy Two said, "She has a prison tat below her glove."

Anika felt the cuffs wrap around her wrists as she heard the same words she'd heard five years before.

You have the right to remain silent. Anything you say can be used against you . . .

15

FIVE YEARS AGO
INTERVIEW OF LESEAN BROWN

FBI Special Agent Brian Maxwell: Please state your full name and age.

Witness: LeSean Brown. Eighteen years old.

Agent: Middle name?

Witness: No. I have a nickname, though. People call me LB.

Agent: Your initials.

Witness: And because I'm a linebacker on the football team.

Agent: Yes, I know. One of the best in the country. You playing college next year?

Witness: Yes, sir. Baylor.

Agent: Great school and fantastic football program. Maybe you'll be the next Mike Singletary.

Witness: Samurai Mike! One can dream, I guess, but I'll take it one step at a time.

Agent: Listen, Mr. Brown, I won't keep you long. You aren't in trouble. We're trying to figure out what happened to Johnny Delgado. He was a friend of yours?

Witness: Best friend. Johnny and I were thick as thieves.

Agent: Best friend? Didn't know that. Was he an athlete like you?

Witness: Blacktop warrior. Fierce competitor on the basketball court. But no, he didn't play organized sports, if that's what you mean.

Agent: Very sorry for your loss.

Witness: Tragic accident.

Agent: You know, I keep hearing people say that word: "accident." And I guess I'm struggling with it, so maybe we can—

Witness: Not trying to be cute with words. Would you prefer I say "incident?"

Agent: To be blunt, the word I'm looking for is "suicide."

Witness: Painful enough thinking about this as an accident . . . or incident. Hard for me to associate suicide with Johnny—not his style.

Agent: You see Johnny the night he died? . . . You do believe he's dead, correct?

Witness: I have no doubt he's dead. The night he died I saw him after school in the parking lot. He called me right before . . . the incident.

Agent: Okay, let's focus first on the parking lot. Was he acting unusual? Anything out of the ordinary?

Witness: Yeah, he was fit to be tied.

Agent: Meaning upset, right? Upset about what?

Witness: Upset at Anika. Not really *at* Anika . . . that would come later. But he was upset by the situation—that she was going to the homecoming dance with Logan.

Agent: Who is Anika?

Witness: Sorry. Anika Raven. Johnny's girlfriend.

Agent: And who is Logan?

Witness: Logan Danforth is a fellow student. Miranda High's homecoming king. He was taking Anika to the homecoming dance because she's the homecoming queen. King and queen go together to the dance, at least that's the tradition at my high school.

Agent: Makes sense. So that left Johnny out of the picture and had him, as you said, *fit to be tied*?

Witness: Correct. But he was more upset when he called later that night, right before the incident.

Agent: What about? Wait . . . what happened from the time you saw him in the parking lot until the time he called you?

Witness: He saw Anika and Logan kissing. You know, not just a peck on the cheek, but making out.

Agent: Ouch. I guess that's not a tradition at Miranda High School—cheating on your boyfriend.

Witness: He was ticked, but he didn't mention doing anything drastic. I would've talked him off the ledge . . . so to speak.

Agent: Of course. What about drugs? You ever see him use drugs?

Witness: He smoked weed sometimes.

Agent: That it? Never saw him use anything else?

Witness: He might have dabbled with scripts. He took some of my OxyContin when I had knee surgery.

Agent: ACL tear?

Witness: Just an MCL, thankfully. Doctor says it's now stronger than before.

Agent: Great. But when I hear OxyContin, I think about the morphine molecule. And that gets me thinking about heroin.

Witness: Heroin? Nah. Johnny wasn't on heroin. I guarantee you that. Maybe I've been unclear. Johnny had his act together. He had some tattoos, and he wore a leather jacket and all that, but that dude was solid. He scored like a 1560 on his SAT and nearly had straight *A*s. Everyone talks about Anika being valedictorian and getting accepted to Rice, but Johnny could've gone anywhere.

Agent: I'll apologize in advance, but I'm required to ask these questions. There's a criminal syndicate out of Mexico that's been selling black-tar heroin around Miranda. Mexican immigrants call them the Xalisco Boys.

Witness: Yeah, I've heard of 'em. Learned about them in school. But that wasn't Johnny's bag. He had a little James Dean in him, but he took care of himself. We'd shoot hoops with some boys who don't mess around. You can't be a druggie with his game and his grades.

Agent: What about Anika? Is she on drugs?

Witness: With all due respect, Agent Maxwell, I don't understand what you're asking. Do you suspect that drugs were involved in Johnny's death?

Agent: Let's move on. We may come back to drugs, Mr. Brown, but I'd like to turn now to the issue of explosives.

83

16

PRESENT DAY

Pastor Joshua Molina marched with resolute cadence through Four Points, his shoulder-length hair now unleashed from its ponytail, his gray eyes determined. Some of the passersby—those who only attended church on Easter Sunday—recognized the pastor from Reformed Baptist Church of Miranda. Depending on where their walk was taking them, they'd go out of their way to greet him or try to hide in the traffic. Approaching the Alamo Opera House, he heard Cyclops yell at Timmy to play Willie Nelson's "Time of the Preacher." The lyric in that song about a preacher killing people was inappropriate, particularly for this morning, but Joshua refused to swallow the bait. "You're quite the showman, Cyclops," he said, walking up the steps, "but there's no need to be afraid of me."

"Oh, I'm not afraid of *you*, Preacher," he said, pointing to the sky. "I'm afraid of the one you work for."

Joshua shook Cyclops's hand and said, "Fear of God is a good sign. Never too late to come to church. Y'all live here?"

"We live over yonder ways . . . upscale trailer homes on the Lower West Side."

"Curtis live with you?"

"No, he lives in a brick home somewhere."

"Never had you over, huh?"

"Preacher, you're startin' to look like the Son of Man himself—long hair, beard, sandals," Cyclops said as the pack of old timers at the domino table chuckled. "Reckon you could skim off some of that tithe and buy you some boots. Had Jesus been born in Miranda instead of Bethlehem, he'd a wore cowboy boots, not them Birkenstocks."

"For the record, we don't know what Jesus looked like, only that he had no beauty that we should desire him. But I'll take that as a compliment coming from you, old timer. You think Jesus would've worn a cowboy hat?"

Cyclops tapped his hat's brim as if to say *touché*. "What does 'reformed' mean, anyhow? Why can't y'all just be plain ol' Baptists or Catholics like the rest of the sinners 'round here?"

"Means he's a Calvinist," Moon sneered from the domino table.

"Means we preach the whole counsel of God," Joshua explained, "not just the parts that make people feel good. You sit in that rocking chair, shoot the bull, and draw pictures all day?"

"Storm's a comin', Preacher," Cyclops said. Hopping from religion to weather, his tone grew more serious. "Better stock up on some plywood for them stained-glass windas. Pull out that insurance policy . . . give her a look-see."

"Cubes on that napkin telling you that?"

"Gonna be a big one," Vernis declared.

Cyclops nodded. "Gonna be a big one."

"When's it get here?" Joshua asked.

"Hard to tell. Days not weeks, I reckon."

"You interpret those cubes yourself?" Joshua asked, prompting Vernis, Peanut, and Moon to stare at Cyclops.

Cyclops thought long and hard before answering. "I'm pretty good at predictin' the weather."

"What about cubes that don't concern the weather?"

Cyclops glanced at the other old timers, who'd inched to the edges of their seats. "Curtis is pretty good at readin' them."

"Mr. Kleberg sometimes talks too much!" Curtis Worden said from the swinging doors, his head shaking in disapproval. "Must be gettin' senile."

"Reckon that's right," Cyclops said, cowering in his chair like a puppy about to get punished for wetting the kitchen floor.

"You're here for the girl," Worden said, addressing Joshua but still glaring at Cyclops.

"I'm hoping you have both girls."

"Come with me."

"You boys come see us at Reformed Baptist," Joshua said as he followed Worden inside. "We meet every Sunday morning. Ten sharp."

"Little girl's with FPS," Worden said. He led Joshua through the General Store and the Commons, past the mayor's office, and down a narrow hallway that opened into Theater Hall.

"That in this building?"

"Down the road aways."

"Where's the mayor?" Joshua inquired, already knowing the answer. Mayor Dodd was with Samantha *down the road aways*. He only hoped Sam was heeding the counsel he'd imparted last night as the sheriff's deputies carried her away from the Church Grounds. *Don't draw pictures for anyone.* It would be Anika's only chance, the only leverage she had left.

"Mayor should be here later," Worden demurred. Prior to reaching the theater, they arrived at the door leading to the holding cell. Worden pulled out a large key and rotated it three hundred and sixty degrees until the bolt made a loud click. Keyless entry or more sophisticated electronic access control, now commonplace in prisons, wasn't in the Alamo's budget. Another reminder that the town resisted transitioning into the twenty-first century. "Welcome back, Preacher."

Never an inmate himself, Joshua had visited the mayor's holding cell often since becoming pastor of Reformed Baptist. A few times a year the shepherd needed to spring a sheep who'd drank too much, escalated a domestic dispute, or viewed illegal images on the dark web. Most sinners tried to clean themselves up before coming to church, but effective pastors knew the depth of human depravity. Joshua, to be sure, felt right at home among prisoners. Jesus himself had said, "It is not the healthy who need a doctor, but the sick. I have not come to call the righteous, but sinners to repentance." Inmates, nonetheless, found it awkward when a man of God walked into their jail.

But today brought with it a different vibe. Anika was curled in a ball on the floor in the corner of the cell. Three men of different sizes and skin colors sat socially distanced and hunched on the two wooden benches inside the vertical bars. Nothing more than a holding cell, the place smelled like jail. And jail, Joshua knew, had a unique scent that couldn't be described with words, unless the words were *complete* and *hopelessness*.

Joshua looked at the deputy sitting at the small desk littered with fingerprint cards and manilla folders. "Did she really need to be locked up all night, Carl?"

"Preacher," Deputy Carl said, finding his feet and pointing to a locker of caged compartments, "based on what's in that evidence box and down at the morgue, she may be locked up for the rest of her life . . . if she's lucky."

"Well, lucky for her, you don't get to decide—that's left to a jury of her peers where she'll be presumed innocent until proven guilty."

"You're right about that, Preacher, but I decide where she sleeps tonight."

"You and the mayor," Worden interjected, making sure everyone in the room understood the power dynamic.

"I'm appealing to y'all—Mayor Dodd, Sheriff Karnes, and anyone else in authority—to allow me custody," Joshua said.

Deputy Carl said, "Preacher, there's a legal process that we must—"

"Carl," Joshua said, pointing his finger, his voice escalating, "don't play games with me. We all know there's a process inherent to Miranda justice. But it's not a bail hearing or a meeting-with-a-judge kind of process." Dodd had dirt on every person who mattered in town—local judges, city administrators, you name it. "We all know the mayor's calling the shots here, and she has the authority and discretion to let Anika go."

"Preacher," Worden said, "you're askin'—"

"Mr. Worden, I'm not asking for much. She's already staying on Church Grounds, and you know I'm not a flight risk. Throw an ankle bracelet on her, if it makes you feel better, and release her into my custody."

"I'll need to speak to the—"

"You've already spoken to the mayor. Otherwise, I wouldn't be back here. She anticipates every detail, down to the gnat's eyelash. Enough with the games, gentlemen."

Worden nodded to Deputy Carl, who opened the cell. "Let's go, Ms. Raven."

Anika stood up slowly and, with a blank, listless face, stared at Joshua. Her eyes, normally a vibrant shade of amber, barely revealed a hint of orange—drained of color and bleached with pain, sorrow, and complete hopelessness. This experience, Joshua observed, had drained the life from her as she hobbled toward him with a puffy face and tousled hair.

Worden, no doubt trusting his spies more than technology, disregarded talk of an ankle bracelet. As he marched them back toward the front entrance, Joshua stopped him. "You mind if we slip out back? Humiliating enough without perp-walking her in front of Statler, Waldorf, and the rest of the Muppets on the front porch."

Worden smiled and changed direction. Opening the back door into the sunlight, he said, "She's got a meetin' at noon with the mayor."

"She'll be on time."

Once she heard the door slam shut, Anika asked in a raspy voice, "Where's Sam?"

"Safe. With FPS."

FPS taking Sam was another gut punch in a series of psychological beatings. "What'll happen to me?"

"That'll depend on Sam. I'm certain the mayor's with her."

"Why would the mayor be with her?" Anika asked as Joshua opened the passenger side door of his Jeep.

Her question hung in the air until he walked around the vehicle, climbed into the driver's seat, and faced her. "I'm not sure how to explain it. Things crystal clear to me about this town don't align with your worldview."

"I stayed up all night reflecting on what you said—about this town, about the *koya*, about Sam's cubes, about my getting arrested. I'm reconsidering my worldview."

88

"Then you'll understand how Mayor Dodd values Sam's gifts. I did my best to warn Sam before the police snatched her, but it's crucial that she refrain from drawing cubes."

"I'm expendable if she draws for the mayor," she pondered as they drove toward the Church Grounds, "but I have value if she only draws for me."

"Exactly. And the fact they released you tells me Sam isn't drawing. Not yet."

"But they'll work her over, day and night, and tempt her like—"

"Like the serpent tempted Eve."

"I didn't do it. Didn't kill anyone."

"I know."

"How do you know?"

"I saw it in your eyes, clear as day, as soon as they released you. And they wouldn't have released you if they thought you were guilty."

"Joshua, remember what you said? The thing about unexplained things happening in town? Supernatural things?"

"Yeah, sure."

"I recently had a dream where I was trying to escape town but couldn't."

Joshua wondered how to respond to the odd remark, curious if she was experiencing some form of trauma. "Go on."

"The first time Sam and I were in the car, driving westbound, I thought we were free and clear. But I stopped at the red light at the bottom of the Harbor Bridge. An old man came out of nowhere and said they were repairing the bridge, and we couldn't get out that day. Sure enough, and right on cue, people walked out into the road with orange cones. Weird, right?"

"Little weird, yeah."

"The second time I was by myself. I wasn't really leaving town for good—Sam was at the cottage—but I needed to know I could leave. Driving back to the Harbor Bridge, I had a green light this time. Home free. Coast clear. Except there was a sign nailed to a tree on the side of the road that caused me to slam on the brakes."

Arriving at the Church Grounds, Joshua parked the Jeep and walked Anika to the guest cottage.

"What did the sign say?"

"It said, 'REMEMBER SAM.'"

"Creepy dream. Sounds more like a nightmare."

"Yeah, but here's the really creepy part. It wasn't a dream . . . or a nightmare. It was real."

"I don't follow."

"All that happened. I stopped and took down the sign, and it's still in my car. Wanna see it?"

"Maybe later, Anika. You need some sleep. This will be another challenging day for you, I'm afraid."

Returning to the lodge, Joshua grabbed his acoustic guitar and picked a tune from another era as the sun continued its ascent. Before finishing the song, however, he heard a cry of rage so piercing that it echoed across the Church Grounds and seemingly shook its foundation. Blackbirds and mourning doves, flapping their wings, fluttered away in fright, as the screaming and wailing and smashing of household items in the guest cottage continued without ceasing.

Anika had found Faux Pooh left behind on Sam's bed.

17

Anika, face nonplussed and hands on her knees, sat in the same chair in the mayor's office. Today's lecture felt like an arraignment hearing. The mayor had a ball framing Anika's indictment. Anika didn't mind, though, because it meant Sam wasn't drawing cubes. Anika still had value. Otherwise, the mayor would've placed her on the morning train to the hoosgow. And this time—shackled with fresh murder charges—it wouldn't be a women's prison in Lockhart but the Walls Unit in Huntsville. Home of the Texas execution chamber.

Once idolized by her schoolmates, she struggled to process her current predicament. Life's twists and turns conspired to destroy her future. What had she done to deserve this? Was this the result of one stupid kiss? She caught herself wallowing in pity and realized second-guessing was counterproductive. She didn't have the luxury of being defensive. She needed to play offense. *Remember Sam.* Focus on getting her back. Then they could run to the hills and flee this heaven-forsaken town. For that to happen, she needed to play Dodd's political game. Anika would either embrace the politics, or politics would devour her. And looking at the power-hungry charlatan in front of her, she made a silent promise. She would *win* this game.

"Were this a crime novel," Mayor Dodd said, "no one would believe it. You've dropped incriminating evidence everywhere. You were at his house, uninvited, in the dead of night. You had on gloves. You were brandishing a Bowie knife. The pillow used to suffocate him was on the floor. You accused him of abusing your little sister. He'd sent you texts with all sorts of physical threats, clearly establishing your motive. You've already spent five years in prison. How do you explain that?"

"I had second thoughts," Anika said.

"Second thoughts don't explain the dead body."

"He was dead before I arrived."

"Intent to kill is not changed by mistake of fact."

"I'll take your word for it, Mayor. As you know, I didn't attend law school."

"You don't sound heartbroken. Hand me your phone."

Anika obliged.

The mayor turned it off, tossed it on the desk, and yelled at Worden to close the door. The Alamo caretaker, Anika observed, excelled at following directions. After he shut the door, the mayor continued her inquisition.

"Why don't you just own this?"

"I'm sorry?"

"You've already signaled you wanted him dead."

"I wanted Sam away from that house, away from her dad. That's all."

"But I handed you the path of least resistance, and you refused my help. You wanted to do the job yourself," the mayor insisted, rubbing her hands together, "didn't you?"

"No."

"Oh, admit it. He was abusing your sister and your mom. Poor little Samantha had two deadbolts on her bedroom door. FPS turned a blind eye. No one would help. Samantha texted you to come home, to come to her aid. She stopped talking. But despite doing everything in your power, you couldn't help. He was more powerful, had the law on his side, and nobody cared."

Anika's blood boiled. Losing control, her body trembled.

"He was laughing at you," the mayor continued. "Threatening you. Threatening to reveal your secrets. You hadn't attended Rice . . . or George-town Law. You went from high school valedictorian to convict. Locked up in Nowhere, Texas. Worst of all, he was threatening to keep Sam from you. Threatening to call the cops . . . report you for kidnapping."

Anika clenched her fists. Her surroundings grew blurry.

Smelling blood, the mayor ratcheted up her intensity. "The door's closed, the phones turned off. No one's here but you and me, *Anika Raven*! Own this! He was a rabid animal and so you grabbed that pillow and—"

Anika snapped to her feet, raised her finger, and screamed, "I wanted him dead! I'm glad he's dead! And I hope he becomes the devil's slave for eternity!"

"Yes . . . *yes*!" the mayor laughed. "Now we're getting somewhere, Anika. Feels good, doesn't it? Feels good to put a man like that in his place, to put a monster like that in the ground."

Anika nearly hyperventilated but maintained consciousness. "But I didn't kill him."

After a dust-settling pause, Dodd broke the silence. "I know you didn't."

Perplexed, Anika stared at the mayor, trying to discern what she'd said. "You believe me?"

"Anika, you're the last person on earth I believe right now. You'll say anything to save your bacon, and you've already lied more in two days than my ex-husband did in fifteen years."

"But you outlined all the reasons why I'm guilty. Now you're saying you know I didn't do it. I don't understand."

"Never said you were guilty. I just cataloged the irrefutable evidence. I need you to understand how much trouble you're in, to realize there's no way out unless I provide you with one. Even if everything at trial broke your way, no jury in Texas would acquit. Heck, in some parts of the Rio Grande Valley, you'd be lucky to escape mob justice. And if everything didn't go your way, then, well . . . you'd likely get the needle. I wanted you to see that, without me, you have no hope. No hope *what . . . so . . . ever*."

Once she pulls you into her lair, you'll never crawl out. "I know how bad it looks, and I know I need your help. But I still don't know why you think I'm innocent. Did the medical examiner perform an autopsy? Was there a toxicology report?"

"I don't *think*, I *know* you're innocent, Anika," the mayor said, slamming down her fist in a fit of madness, "because I'm the one who killed that pig!"

Shell-shocked, mouth and eyes wide open, Anika struggled to breathe. No wonder Dodd had turned off the phones. Even amateur sleuths could transform them into listening or recording devices. Dodd wanted no evidence whatsoever. The revelation itself was knee-buckling, forcing Anika to collapse into her seat. More troubling, Anika marveled at the delight this deranged woman took in claiming credit for her butchery. Anika regarded the depth of depravity required to celebrate cold-blooded murder without remorse. She had heard others say politics was a blood sport, but this felt different.

"Only wish I'd done it with my own hands," Dodd said, continuing her confession, raising her arthritic meat hooks in front of her face.

Anika's thoughts jumped to Sam. This psycho-killer had Sam in custody at a hidden location. She held every card in every deck that mattered. And now she'd demonstrated with deliberate cunning that the house always wins. Anika tried to process the questions raised by this new information. How did Dodd frame her so easily? How long had her stepdad been dead? Was it just a coincidence that the cops arrived on the scene soon after she arrived? Her thoughts bounced back to what Joshua had said. *Once you realize spiritual forces exist, then you'll also realize that wild coincidences don't.*

Had the old timer on the Alamo porch—Joshua had called him Cyclops—foreseen the event unfold? Joshua, of course, had predicted her arrest using Sam's drawings. Had the mayor used similar intelligence to manipulate events? If the mayor hadn't done the dirty work herself—a fact she lamented—then who had Scotty's blood on his hands? Was it this madwoman's aide-de-camp, Curtis Worden? He was older but capable enough to be her cleaner, plenty strong to suffocate an out-of-shape, intoxicated loser like Sam's dad.

Things began to make sense. That explained why Dodd cared so much about Sam. By drawing the cubes, Sam, perhaps like the old timer Cyclops, could provide the mayor with actionable intelligence. That intelligence, in turn, could inform her decision-making and help defeat her enemies. The more accurate and prophetic the intel, the easier it would be to preserve political power. Perhaps Dodd expected Sam to apprentice under Cyclops;

or perhaps Sam's skills already exceeded his, making her the master crafts-woman in what Joshua had called *spiritual warfare*.

Anika had more to learn. Along the way, she needed to play the mayor's deadly parlor game and hope to survive another day. She found combat-ting hopelessness difficult, especially when she didn't know the extent of the mayor's knowledge. How much did Dodd know about Anika's past, her present, and—she struggled mightily with this one—*her future*? But hopelessness had a way of clarifying one's options. Anika needed to earn the mayor's trust and do her bidding. Beyond that, she hoped Sam didn't start drawing cubes for Dodd.

Anika forced a smile. Looking straight at Dodd and regaining her con-fidence, she heard herself say, "Thank you. *Thank you so much, Mayor!*" Anika's words of appreciation seemed to hit Dodd like dopamine, and the mayor experienced a rush of euphoria, her flushed cheeks giving away her realization that her cards were hot, her chips stacked high.

"What would you have me do?" Anika continued.

The mayor had turned myriad dials to maintain control, but one area remained beyond her claws and caused her fits. "Another hurricane's com-ing."

"I heard the rumors but chalked them up to fear-mongering."

"It's coming. Sooner than expected. I need help preparing the town. The situation's made worse because—"

"Because Mirandites don't evacuate."

Dodd repeated in a chorus of newfound chemistry between the two, "Because Mirandites don't evacuate. And when it comes to hurricanes, they also don't *cooperate*. And that's where I need your immediate help."

"Of course," Anika said as if they'd already pricked index fingers and exchanged blood.

"Two businessmen—boys, really—are pushing back on me: Ricky Holloway and LeSean Brown. You know them?"

"Friends of mine."

"That means they should be easy to convince," Dodd said. The look on Anika's face said otherwise. "You know something more?"

"Yeah, convincing them to evacuate won't be easy. Let's just say . . . they're not fans of your administration."

"I won't be a failed leader because thousands of imbeciles refuse to heed life-saving advice."

Any hint of altruism, Anika realized, flew from the building with that comment. "But people have chosen not to evacuate in every major hurricane ever recorded. It's a free country."

"You're too young, Anika, to remember the shame the New Orleans mayor experienced in Katrina. Guy looked like a moron. Forced out of office for his incompetence and even sentenced to prison for his corruption. That's not gonna happen to me. No way, no how."

"Just seems like a long walk for a small beer."

"Anika, let's be clear about small-town politics. To be in power, you must be assertive and not let the common people drag you down. This is especially true in the face of existential crises. Folks are either with you or against you. So are you with me . . . or against me?"

Remember Samantha. "I'm all in."

"Excellent. Call me, Auntie," Dodd said as she stood up and returned Anika's phone. "Let's go see your little sister."

18

A few hours ago Samantha had winked at Anika when Anika visited her at FPS headquarters. Until that moment, Anika had considered the phrase "It's the little things in life that matter" nothing more than a hackneyed Hallmark cliché. But Sam's wink was a little big thing, signaling to Anika that Sam had heard Joshua's warning—*no drawing cubes for strangers*. And Anika had also made clear to Sam, when Dodd wasn't looking, another no-no: *no playing with the Rubik's Cube*. Anika wasn't sure if Sam knew the *why* behind the *don't*, but Sam knew enough to keep everyone safe . . . for now. Everyone was safe, that is, until Auntie Dodd turned up the heat on her eight-year-old hostage.

"How was your little sister this mornin'?" Worden asked, escorting Anika beyond the Alamo holding cell and through the same backdoor she and Joshua had exited that morning.

"Okay, I guess, considering the circumstances." Anika wondered if Worden interpreted Cyclops's drawings. If so, had he interpreted Sam's cube craft that Sheriff Karnes's deputies had confiscated from the Church Grounds?

"Reckon she'll be back by week's end," he said, approaching an industrial garage door connected to the rear of the Alamo. "Mayor's good at cuttin' red tape."

Anika knew that no tape of any color stretched between the mayor and Miranda FPS, but she would play make-believe until a plan emerged. The FPS facility was nice enough. Disney characters painted on the walls, video games, friendly staff; of course, plenty of craft paper and markers to draw cubes. Anika had spent an hour with Sam, enough time to put both sisters at ease. Anika dreaded acting in Dodd's sinister tragedy of *Hurricane Evacuation*, billed as the Alamo Opera House's most harrowing production. She did savor one thought. Though she had no poltical experience, she'd excelled in high school theater class.

Presently, Anika played the role of the mayor's assistant. That involved spending time with the mayor's septuagenarian henchman. She figured the more she could learn about Curtis Worden, the more she could discern the mayor's strengths and weaknesses.

For someone in such a powerful position, Dodd couldn't crack the code on hurricane preparedness. Experts had penned the natural disaster playbook after Hurricane Katrina slammed into New Orleans. If a monster hurricane was advancing toward Miranda, evacuation was the only solution. Beyond that, the specifics of the playbook were clear. People should board up their windows, grab their family heirlooms, fill up their tanks, and check their tires.

One thing unclear to Auntie Dodd was how electric vehicles would fare sitting in stalled traffic. Scores of Mirandites had purchased Teslas after Elon Musk opened a plant in Austin, but Texas interstates lacked enough EV charging stations. In any event, the mayor would open all roads and lanes to the west, diverting evacuees down country roads until they reached Interstate 37 (toward San Antonio). Driving farther, they'd travel north on Interstate 35 to Austin, or Temple, or Waco, or Nowheresville, until they escaped the storm's deadly reach. Hurricane preparedness and response 101.

But nothing was easy in Miranda where, as the mayor acknowledged, people didn't evacuate or cooperate. That left Dodd in the lurch because any advancing Category 5 would obliterate everything in its path. Where that would leave the mayor after the destruction was anyone's guess. She would be lucky to save her own life, much less those of her stubborn constituents. Of course, she didn't care about the loss of life, per se. Instead, she cared more about how a high body count would damage her legacy. Were she willing and able to evacuate, the surviving townsfolk—including her fellow evacuees—likely wouldn't welcome her back. And why would she come back? With her political power dwindled or gone, she'd struggle to find purpose and probably go mad. Madder than her current state, if that were possible.

These thoughts seeped through Anika's mind as Worden lifted the industrial garage door, and its rollers clanked and lumbered along the tracks. Cool air crashed into her face as it escaped the cavernous area. The familiar and pleasant smell of motor oil and gasoline filled her nostrils. Viewing the object in front of her, she grew dizzy and her stomach contracted. She couldn't believe her eyes. "What's *that?*" she asked, afraid to hear the answer.

"Figured we'd return the rental car."

Somehow her legs found the wherewithal to tread forward into the garage, which was now touched by the alleyway's filtered sunlight. "Is it his?" she asked as her voice cracked, unable to take her eyes off the polished black paint.

"The 1970 Dodge Challenger R/T is one of the most iconic muscle cars ever made," he said proudly.

"This can't be," she whispered to herself, rubbing her fingers along the passenger side door.

"This one's special, closest thing to the infamous Black Ghost Challenger from Detroit."

However innocent, the fact that Worden had associated the term *ghost* with this car caused her angst. Her wounds, which she thought had healed, resurfaced. She fought her emotions, trying to maintain her resolve. "Black Ghost?"

"She's better than the Ghost. Performance hood with dual scoops. Rallye wheels. One-hundred and ten-inch wheelbase. Quad headlamp and full-length tail lamps. Thing of beauty."

Anika had spent time with Johnny at Delgado Auto Pros, where he'd worked for his family's company in the main garage. She was familiar with some of the lingo and tools: air hammers, welding torches, and sanding disks. "You rebuilt this yourself?"

"Most of it," Worden said, now dragging his fingers on the hood, admiring his handiwork. "Know much about cars?"

"More than I should, I guess."

"I was able to handle the panelin', blastin', weldin', grindin', and paintin'. Rebuilt the inner structure by using triangular braces for increased strength. Replicated the curvature of the original by manipulatin' the steel here and here," he said, pointing to various parts of the car.

"I assumed everything was incinerated or scrapped after the crash."

"Skeleton of the car survived. She lost her organs but kept her bones."

"That's because bones don't burn, Curtis."

"You've heard that too," he said, staring at her, likely surprised that she'd addressed him by his first name. "Salvaged a few original parts. Cannibalized the rest from South Texas junkyards."

"And the engine?"

"Original engine was a 440 Six Pack that could do zero to sixty in seven point seven seconds. Replaced that with a 436 Hemi, which can do the same distance in six seconds flat," he said, pulling out a set of keys and reaching inside. "Listen to this."

The car jumped to life, and the engine growled and roared. The roar, amplified by the garage's acoustics, was so powerful that it sounded less like a muscle car and more like an F-22 fighter jet. Anika, once again, smelled the gasoline burning and felt the vibrations rumbling from the concrete floor, up her legs and arms, and inside the cavities in her teeth.

"Anything else to do?" Anika asked, raising her voice to speak over the Hemi engine.

Curtis killed the engine and said, "Just added a serpentine belt and finished the suspension upgrades last week. This mornin', I sinched down the fans on the radiator. If you could fetch me that grinder over yonder in that cabinet, I see a few welds I forgot to dress."

Anika walked to the workbench, which was flanked by two metal cabinets. She opened the cabinet on the left and spotted sundry items—nails, paint, and whatnot—that one expected to see. Even the rat poison with skull and crossbones on the bag made sense. She also saw, however, several boxes wrapped in white and labeled, "Explosive Plastic Comp-4 (C-4)." Paralyzed, she tried not to panic or stare.

"Other cabinet," he said.

"Gotcha," she replied, forcing her lungs to resume function, opening the cabinet on the right, and grabbing the grinder. "And after you grind and blend those welds?"

"She'll need a driver."

"You want me to drive Johnny's car?"

"Your car now." He smiled as he plugged in his grinder. "So long as you're working with us. You'll need to get a feel for her."

As he ground the welds, she marveled at his craftsmanship. After he finished and blew off the shavings, she said, "Not sure I'm comfortable driving this car—for several reasons."

"You have to drive a car like this or she loses her soul. We need to gauge her performance and get a baseline. Then we'll make adjustments," he said, walking away and placing the grinder back in the cabinet. "Go ahead and hop in. Let's take her to the Flats for a spin."

As Anika turned the key, she remembered what Johnny had taught her. *The starter engages the flywheel; the flywheel rotates the crankshaft; and the crankshaft starts the engine.* After a brief *ruh, ruh, ruh*, the Challenger roared to life again, tugging from side to side when she revved the engine. When Curtis climbed in the passenger seat, Anika confirmed what she'd suspected earlier—he smelled of Icy Hot. The same scent she had smelled on Scotty's warm cadaver. She looked at Curtis's hands, which were peppered with liver spots, scrapes, and knicks. They were the hands of a mechanic but also those of a cleaner or a fixer—someone who made problems disappear by any means available. *Dirty deeds done dirt cheap.*

Anika would have to worry about that later. Presently numb to the threat Curtis posed, she found herself lost in the past as she drove from the garage. Being in the ghost car brought back memories that she'd suppressed for years. This car symbolized the highs and lows of high school. There was the high of her and Johnny, hands extended from the windows, singing Violent Femmes on the way to the beach, juxtaposed by the low of this deathtrap being the contraption that took his life.

"Power steering?" Anika asked. "It's hard to turn."

"I added it," he said with a laugh. "She ain't as nimble as that rental."

Anika drove around the corner toward Revolutionary Park, where a blindfolded kid swung a stick at a Cookie Monster piñata. Nearby, a child performer—dressed in a light blue Elvis Presley jumpsuit replete with sequins and silk scarves—lip-synched the words to "Suspicious Minds" on an elevated stage with hundreds of onlookers. "Wanna stop and watch Little Elvis?" she asked.

"Cyclops said that kid drew an audience of thousands a few weeks ago at Bayfest in Corpus. Eyes on the road. You familiar with the history of this park?"

"Can always learn more."

"Town was founded by three Texian soldiers who escaped the Goliad Massacre in 1835, the famous battle where we got the 'Come and Take It' flag. They stopped to rest and make camp right over yonder." Curtis pointed. "But before that, legend has it that Comanches had rituals in the park right after the American Revolution. And before that, around 1000 AD, Aztec refugees and their children escaped and camped here to avoid the human sacrifices of Quetzalcoatl."

"That's fascinating history." *But you left out the part about the* koya *and carving cubes into trees.* "Speaking of ancient history, I see the original eight-track player. I guess you didn't equip the Ghost with Sirius/XM?"

"Same tape player Johnny had. I even replaced his four tapes. They all burned except the one in the player."

"Which one was that? I remember his tapes."

"I don't know the names. It's back in there, though."

Anika hit the button and Iron Maiden's "Run to the Hills" blared through the speakers.

Anika pushed eject. "What else did he have?"

"Let's see," Curtis said, grabbing the three other eight-track tapes. "Elvis Presley . . . Led Zeppelin . . . and—not sure how to pronounce this one—Violent Femmes?"

"It's pronounced *fems*. Let's try that one."

As she drove toward the Miranda Flats for a test drive, listening to eighties alternative, Anika took stock of her surreal situation. She had a job with the crooked mayor of her hometown, who was holding her sister hostage. Anika had days to ransom or rescue Sam and escape town before a monster hurricane killed everyone in its path. Meantime, she was driving to the location where her *ghost* car had blown up, and she was sitting in the seat where her boyfriend had died. Sitting next to her was the mayor's mercenary, the ostensibly kind and gentle grandpa-like figure who had boxes of C-4 explosives hidden in his garage and who had, not long ago, murdered her stepfather.

It's the little things in life that matter.

19

The following morning Anika drove westbound on Crockett Street toward the outskirts of the Upper West Side. Clear skies hosted an intemperate sun poised to bake the Miranda terrain. The typical coastal breeze—caused by the sun kissing land faster than it heated the Gulf of Mexico—had arrived early. Otherwise, the weather's rhythm was normal for August, so Anika predicted that weather-as-usual would be a topic of conversation during her scheduled meeting with Ricky and LeSean.

The magnificent growl of the refurbished '70 Challenger masked the sounds of its tires crushing the gravel on the road leading into Miranda's Industrial Complex. The MIC (pronounced "mick"), as locals called it, included sundry local enterprises providing decent-paying trades jobs, but its train depot and refinery anchored and fueled Miranda's economy.

Awestruck passersby, ogling Anika from afar, struggled picturing a petite woman driving a muscle car. Her muscles hurt from yesterday's track run at the Flats, where Curtis had pushed her and the car to the limit. She felt a symbiosis with the new and improved Black Ghost. Even refurbished, the Ghost had some flavor to it, like a cast-iron skillet that families pass down through generations. Questions remained, of course, as to the car's reincarnation and existence, not to mention how she came to possess it. But she wasn't about to give it up. Of all the daggers life threw at her, driving the mayor's company car seemed the least dangerous.

Slowing down for a parking spot, Anika spotted a familiar face and reciprocated LeSean's exuberant, welcoming wave. He was walking to Ricky's office in a hard hat and, she assumed, steel-toed boots from the refinery. He had put on weight since retiring his football helmet and pads, but he still possessed the Travoltan strut and swagger of a gridiron super-star. And why not? He had leveraged his Big 12 rushing title and straight *A*s in college to skyrocket up the corporate ladder and position himself as the heir apparent to his father as the refinery's president.

Miranda's refinery resembled an industrial playground for danger-ous, imaginary creatures. Flare stacks bursting into the blue sky reminded Anika of dragons spewing flames. The labyrinthine piping system, inter-spersed with three hundred heat exchangers, resembled robotic spiders coiled together and wrestling on the ground. A variety of pumps, com-pressors, and mammoth white storage tanks participated in the creaturely activities. And these creatures needed a diaper change, Anika thought, as she exited the vehicle. Even with a westerly wind, she noticed the acute rotten-eggs smell of the refining process as the flares burned off excess sour gas. Walking to the meeting place, she heard the grunts and beeps of equipment and vehicles, pressure being released, and a sleepy cargo train traveling west toward San Antonio.

She had scheduled the meeting at Ricky's office because he demanded the most respect. The South Texas railroad provided the steel arteries for egress and ingress, so the Miranda Train Depot was the heart of com-merce. Ricky knew the exact location and dimension of every rail, tie, fastener, fishplate, and spike in the vicinity of his train depot. The depot itself consisted of one level and two platforms for freight to be unloaded, loaded, shipped in, and shipped out. The building at the center of the depot resembled a Spanish mission, replete with colorful, hand-painted tile and stucco walls. It provided offices for employees and a resting area with two vending machines for operators and guests. The scene around the building, however, was rough and less attractive, with aged steel freight cars covered in profane graffiti of all sizes, colors, languages, and offensive drawings. This train depot, to be sure, was no place for respectful folks like Thomas the Tank Engine and his band of merry friends. Eighteen-wheel-ers increased the flow of sketchy traffic, coming in and out twenty-four-seven in the never-ending movement of product.

Ricky's men loitered about. Dressed like gangsters, they guarded areas of the terminal station while spewing clouds of vape smoke that rivaled the refinery flares. Ricky, Anika knew, ran more than trains through this operation. She also knew something else. The MIC would be a logical exit point to evacuate—or escape—town. The tracks, which continued farther east toward the Gulf of Mexico, crossed north of Four Points in an *X* and departed toward Laredo and San Antonio.

Anika followed LeSean into the maroon high-roof Wabash boxcar. It had corrugated steel ends and sliding doors on both sides. Someone had spray-painted in silver on the outside: RICK'S PLACE. Its dimensions were thirteen feet high, sixty feet long, and ten feet wide. That was enough space for a makeshift office in the center of the MIC devoid of hidden listening devices. The old timers had an adage in Miranda that many learned too late. It went something like this: *There are two kinds of enemies of the mayor—those who know she's bugged their office and those who don't.* Inside the boxcar, there was a picnic table posing as a conference table surrounded by four chairs and a buffet table lodged against one end. Nothing more.

"Welcome to the Wabash Cannonball!" Ricky said. "Thought I saw a ghost when you drove up."

"You did," Anika said, climbing up the three stairs into the boxcar. "The Black Ghost."

"Reminds me of Johnny's car," Ricky said with a double-cheek kiss.

"That's because it *is* his car. Or it was. It's mine now."

"No way!" LeSean said, disrobing his blue hard hat and giving Anika a light hug. "How'd you swing that?"

"The mayor's guy, Curtis Worden. He kept the salvage and rebuilt it."

Ricky's eyes met LeSean's.

"You seem skeptical," Anika observed.

"Odd that a stranger rebuilt Johnny's car," Ricky said. "I don't trust strangers."

"Johnny was your boyfriend," LeSean added. "Makes it even weirder."

"And dude just hands over the car after you start working for Mother?" Ricky continued.

Mother? "He handed over the keys, Ricky, not the title."

"Let's talk about the car later," LeSean said. "Breakfast is served."

Anika's hosts served a Mexican buffet from chafing racks set up at the end of the boxcar, where the smell of fresh eggs replaced that of rotten ones. The racks housed the stainless-steel water and food pans that hovered over Sterno cans that kept the *migas*, bacon, and flour tortillas warm.

"No beans?" Anika asked, filling her plate and grabbing an avocado slice.

"You eat beans in the morning?" LeSean asked.

"Come on, LB," Anika said, walking back to the center table. "You don't remember our parents' stories of the infamous Destroyer from Elva's?"

"You mean the greatest breakfast taco ever created?" LeSean asked, chuckling. "Always thought that taco was part of an old wives' tale. Did it have refried beans?"

"Refried beans, eggs, tomato, shredded cheese, and bacon," she said. "Best salsa in the world, according to the old timers."

"My dad called it supernaturally good," Ricky said. "When Elva died and her restaurant closed, she stole Miranda's soul . . . and the mayor stole *el Tesoro*."

"What's that?" LeSean asked.

"Not *what* but *who*," Ricky said. "Tesoro is Elva's son with special needs. He now goes by—"

"Timmy," Anika interrupted, shaking her head in mild disbelief at this revelation. "Timmy's the cook at the Alamo Opera House, isn't he?"

"No wonder those tacos are so good," LeSean said.

Ricky smiled. "Nothing's changed, Anika. You always had the super-charged brain. After Elva died, Tesoro's family cared for him, raised him, and no doubt showed him around a kitchen. But something happened along the way, and he ended up with FPS."

"What?" Anika asked, now more interested in Tesoro-turned-Timmy.

"At the time," Ricky continued, "he wasn't even a child. He was our age, but he still functioned like a child and needed support."

"How'd he end up working at the Alamo?" Anika asked.

"How do you think?" Ricky said, looking outside the boxcar and cueing the woman waiting outside. "Same way you did."

"What's that supposed to mean?" Anika asked.

"The mayor collects people she needs to run her operation," Ricky said, nodding at the woman stepping into the boxcar.

"Please stand up and raise your arms," the athletic, black-haired woman with a tattoo of the Mother Mary on her neck demanded, preparing to frisk Anika in search of recording devices.

"Are you kidding me?" Anika said, sneering at Ricky as she complied. "I guess breakfast is over."

"I could've asked Diesel to pat you down," he said, referring to his oversized bodyguard. "You're working for the enemy now, little sister, so you should know that I'll be skeptical. Besides, you lost your engagement ring and found a prison tat. Perhaps you're—"

"I'm disappointed in you, Ricky. And don't call me your little sister if you think I'm your enemy."

"She's clean," the woman said.

"And don't act like you're doing me any favors," Anika continued, retaking her seat, jabbing her finger at Ricky. "I told you what I'm up against. I told you Mayor Dodd—the one you call *Mother*—is holding Sam hostage and extorting me."

"And I told *you* that I'd handle that!" he said.

"I'm scared to think what that means, Ricky, and I'd rather you not explain it."

Ricky raised his palms. "You think Mother's beyond using brutal means to solve her problems?"

Anika knew Dodd had ordered Scotty's execution. "Let's just say I don't see her tossing bodies in a trunk," Anika replied. *Suffocating someone with a pillow on the other hand . . .*

"Wouldn't be so sure," Ricky said, "but you're questioning whether *I* run a legitimate business? I thought we were family."

"You just had your people frisk me, Ricky," she said. "That the way you treat family? And you implied that you'd use *brutal* means to solve my problems, so color me cautious."

"Quit watching *The Sopranos*. I don't deal in waste management. That said, my trains *will* run on time."

"Family shouldn't fight," LeSean said, tossing a stack of letters on the table. "Let's talk about *this*."

"What's that?" Anika asked.

"Threats," Ricky said. "Intimidation. Bullying. Mother flexing her administrative muscle to get her way."

"She's predicting a hurricane's on the way," Anika said, "and that it's gonna wipe out the entire town."

"Covid already wiped out the town," Ricky said. "It crushed our businesses and robbed us of our freedoms. We can't afford to shut down again and evacuate because the mayor has nightmares."

"We just hired a bunch of welders, pipefitters, and experts in other trades from a local shipyard that laid off people who wouldn't get vaccinated," LeSean added. "I'm not about to shut down early and let them walk."

"Ricky," Anika asked, "can't you make money by evacuating people and bringing them back by rail?"

"I don't have passenger cars, and the summer freight biz is lucrative. Besides, Mirandites don't evacuate."

"And the demand for oil and gas is through the roof," LeSean said. "I'd be committing financial suicide if I followed her despotic fiats."

"What do you want from me?" Anika asked.

"Tell her to back off," LeSean said. "She isn't about saving lives. It's all politics. And there are no morals in politics, just expediency."

"Her bark's worse than her bite," Anika said. "Don't let her threaten you with a feckless letter campaign."

"Interesting that you'd mention barking and biting," Ricky said, dropping a pile of photos in front of Anika. It landed with a thud. "The mayor's political gamesmanship includes more than harsh words and letter campaigns. She's employing deadly intimidation tactics . . . and this means war."

Shocked, Anika was at a loss for words.

20

After viewing photos of three dead rottweilers, Anika realized she hadn't noticed any guard dogs at the MIC. That wasn't Ricky's style. His gang in high school—the same toadies working at the train depot—always ran with dogs. It was part of the 361 (area code) bad-boy bravado. Ricky's Miranda Underground would bring rottweilers, Dobermans, and pit bulls to the beach as religiously as Christians carried Bibles to church.

She remembered the rat poison in Curtis Worden's metal cabinets—the same cabinets containing explosives. She wondered what other weapons Miranda's Colonel Mustard and Miss Scarlet employed as part of their cleaning duties. Did those unusually dangerous cabinets house the pewter, rope, and candlestick? The dagger, wrench, lead pipe, and revolver? *The pillow?* Had Curtis or Mayor Dodd already chosen a specific weapon to dispose of *her?* Faulty brakes or a gas leak on the Black Ghost?

Anika empathized with Ricky's and LeSean's writhing over Dodd's fierce intimidation. The mayor dished it out in spades. And Anika knew first hand the anguish the mayor's turning of the screw caused. Earlier in the morning, FPS had denied her visit with Sam, and Dodd would cancel any future interviews. FPS officials would obey their puppet master. The mayor held the keys to unlock the door to child custody. Anika's only hope was that Dodd and her FPS thugs wouldn't break Sam, that Sam would hold fast in her refusal to draw cubes. Otherwise, to quote the old timers, Anika would become as worthless as a sidesaddle on a sow.

Before today, Anika hadn't considered the threat of surveillance. Had the mayor bugged her cottage at the Church Grounds? She cringed at that prospect. Were Calvin and Luther in danger of Curtis poisoning them?

One would need enough poison to kill a giraffe to take down those two gargantuan Danes. Did she need to warn Joshua of Curtis or his old-timer adjutants?

Anika parked her car on the street separating the Blouses and Boots Boutique from Revolutionary Park. Winds continued to pick up, but the heavens had painted a powder blue sky to greet the late afternoon. Exiting the vehicle, she noticed the Alamo Opera House down the road. Cyclops and his ancient quislings—Vernis, Peanut, and Moon—watched her every move with unabashed interest from the porch. For the old timers, Anika thought, seeing her drive a muscle car through Four Points was probably like seeing a unicorn gallop through the Texas State Fair. Less transparent and predictable were the thoughts of Miranda's finest. Anika observed two sheriff's deputies patrolling the park on horseback, still a common practice in some Texas towns. One of them stared at her as he guided his quarter horse around oak trees, tables, and benches. Approaching the boutique's massive front windows and towering door, she felt the intensity of his eyes searing through her, but the *koya* remained dormant.

Entering the store, Anika held the door for the parting woman with fogged Jackie O sunglasses. Escaping the humidity, Anika welcomed the intense cool air and the smell of leather and coffee. The fading sunlight glistened off the high-end merchandise in Sarah's Blouses and Boots Boutique. Mexican dresses and blouses, concho belts, and straw and felt cowboy hats anchored the store. Anika saw racks full of the upscale and chic Johnny Was apparel from LA, a definite contrast to the tacky *Bones Don't Burn* T-shirts peddled at Ethan's Endless Summer Surf Shop. She could see along the walls displays for handcrafted leather luggage, Consuela bags, and boots made from the hides of cow, shark, and ostrich. One pair of boots stood alone as the centerpiece of the store. Handmade in Texas, the Lucchese (pronounced "loo-casey") Romia Nile crocodile boots—dyed in cavalry blue on a wooden heel—beamed like the Ark of the Covenant.

"You know your boots," Sarah said as George Strait sang "Amarillo By Morning" through hidden speakers. Emerging from under the imposing Texas Longhorns shoulder mount that policed the store, she pranced like a peacock in her cowboy hat and boots toward Anika atop the reclaimed pine floors. "I'm fond of my vintage Taxco bracelets and necklaces, but those crocodiles are my crown jewels."

"They're exquisite," Anika said, touching the crocodile scales and peeking down at her threadbare sneakers.

"That's my last pair," Sarah said, snatching a Resistol cowboy hat off the rack, cordially embracing Anika, and placing the hat on her head. "Cool Elvis mugshot T-shirt. I trust you know your hats. No respectful Texan wears anything but a straw hat in the summer. As for those boots, they have an awkward size and a Texas-sized price tag, so they'll be hard to sell."

"Well, I hope you find your Cinderella," Anika said, adjusting the new hat on her head, trying to discern whether to thank Sarah for the gift. Anika knew she should just accept the hat as a nice gesture. She found it presumptuous, though, and somewhat insulting, as if the princess needed to dress up Wharf Rat Barbie before dragging her to the country club dance.

Sarah laughed, locked the front doors, and began closing the boutique for the evening. "If not, they'll still lure customers. Want a mimosa before we jet?"

"I'm good, thanks."

"You sure, *darling*?" Sarah insisted with Holly Golightly pizazz, a pitcher full of orange juice and champagne in hand. She played the part well, Anika thought, and even had the colossal Tiffany's wedding ring to add to her mystique. "But I *mustn't* let it go to waste."

"Well, if you're having one," Anika said, realizing Sarah had probably danced with mimosas all day.

"Just a sip, of course."

"Of course." Anika smiled as she sat down on a stool made from an old leather saddle. Looking around, she saw the oversized oil painting on the back wall of college cheerleader Sarah in action. One could scarcely distinguish the painting from a life-sized photograph. Sarah was dressed in a blur of white, brown, and burnt orange and suspended in midair, suspended in time. Her twiggy legs extended parallel to the ground, and her pearly whites blinded the sixty thousand Longhorn fans.

"Can't imagine being part of the Texas Spirit Squad," Anika said. "What an accomplishment."

"It's no high school homecoming queen, but being a UT cheerleader was a great honor."

"Your entire boutique is beautiful," Anika continued, making a mental list of the obvious slights. "You must be so proud."

"Isn't it *so* great? When I learned that the King Ranch Saddle Shop opened another store in Fort Worth instead of Miranda, I knew there'd be a market here. My dad was a sweetie and helped me launch. Ready?"

Sarah made it clear that her Daddy Warbucks, not the Danforth family, funded her business. She wanted her customers—*clients*, that is—to smell something more than leather and coffee when they entered Blouses and Boots: *old* money. Her family didn't take handouts. And they didn't need the in-laws' beer money to fund their operations. She had no qualms, Anika discerned, with her husband's business. Indeed, his wealth made her a popular and powerful figure in town. She wouldn't allow anyone, though, especially her friends back in Dallas, to confuse her for *nouveau riche*. If the Danforth beer trucks all drove off a cliff bound for the deadly waters below, Sarah would land safely on Daddy's mega-yacht—cocktail in hand, *darling*.

"Ready when you are," Anika said, her response meant for Sarah . . . and anyone else waiting outside.

21

Exiting the store with Sarah, Anika noticed that twilight had overtaken the square, and the old timers and sheriff's posse had departed with the sun. "Want me to drive?" Anika asked, now standing next to her car, unsure how many mimosas Sarah had *sipped* throughout the day.

Sarah took one look at the muscle car, turned up her nose, and darted toward her pearl-colored Range Rover Autobiography. "Let's take mine."

Sarah, perhaps with alcohol-inspired honesty, spent the ride to the Clockworks saying things like, "I would never insult Logan, *but . . .*" Or, "I'm not criticizing his family, *but . . .*" And, "You know what I mean?"

As they drove over the causeway toward the beach, Anika spied Ethan's new billboard. Like the one it replaced, he was larger than life and beautiful, holding a surfboard with his tanned skin, hulking muscles, and perfect abs. "Ethan's new ad looks great," she said.

Sarah expressed an unusual interest in the billboard and even took credit for the ad. She explained how she'd worked with Ethan's agent to create a more effective brand. Her commentary, interesting if true, was saddled with so many uses of "I" and "me" that Anika's ears received it as more *yadda, yadda, yadda* from a woman craving the limelight.

Once they arrived at the Clockworks, Sarah valet parked the Range Rover, rushed to find Logan, and jumped into his arms, leaving Anika in her tracks. Logan's wife had checked her "Befriend Anika" box. Sarah, Anika observed, was always on stage (or on the field), dancing, smiling, entertaining, soaking up the spotlight, and reveling in the attention.

And there was something else. Anika observed that Sarah Danforth had roaming eyes. Eyes that surveyed a room for reciprocal eyes. Eyes on the constant lookout for the shinier object to attract her attention.

Clockworks was an outdoor nightclub on the beach that served strong drinks and cheap pub food. It featured a clock six feet in diameter and frozen in time: its little hand on the eight, big hand on twenty-nine. Specializing in edgy music and expansive ocean views, a seemingly endless string of lights twisted their way around the property like an invasive ivy. Those serpentine lights, coupled with the prodigious moon, illuminated the club's large wooden structure and platforms.

The nightclub wasn't far from where Anika and Ethan had surfed, kissed, and witnessed Sheriff Karnes's men scour the beach on ATVs. Despite all the unruly human activity that night, nature's elements had slept. Now, however, Anika noticed the first signs of hurricane season. She could hear the pounding surf over the drums, guitars, and singing. Ropes snapped, flagpoles swayed, and flags flapped and popped. Likely the beginnings of a summer squall, Anika couldn't rule out that this disturbance foreshadowed a nastier storm to come.

As she walked closer to the throng of usual suspects, Ethan approached Anika with a concerned look. "Where's Sam?" he asked, raising his voice over the blaring music.

"Oh, you're talking to me now?" Anika giggled as she leaned toward Ethan to be heard.

"I'm concerned about her, Anika."

"She's in FPS custody."

"Is that what you wanted?"

"Good enough for now," she said, refusing to extrapolate on her half-truth. "I'm working for the mayor this summer and hope to get Sam released soon."

"Working for the *mayor*? What about your fiancé?"

"I don't have a fiancé, Ethan. I made him up and lied to you. I wanted my friends to believe I still had my act together. It was stupid. Sorry about that."

"You're having a difficult homecoming."

"You don't know the half of it. I'm trying to do better."

"You're a good person, Anika. Stay focused, keep grinding, and let me know how I can help. You know what the old timers always say. When life gives you lemons—"

"Make Lynchburg Lemonade."

"No doubt. Speaking of . . . Amber and Chelsea are walking back with drinks. Talk later," he said, melting into the crowd.

Leaving so early? Anika thought. *Don't wanna show Amber the sandbar where we kissed?*

After dancing to an hour's worth of songs with strangers, Anika scheduled an Uber ride home. The mayor's apparatchiks at FPS had taken from her the only soul she trusted. And tonight, for the first time, Anika felt isolated by her supposed friends. Even Logan acted distant, probably to appease his wife, her majesty. Unlike the smaller event at the Danforth hacienda, Anika's acquaintances segregated into their tribal groups and paid her little attention. Even those with good intentions—the Danforth brothers, in particular—had no true understanding of her plight. The adversity mounted against her like powerful waves pummeling a helpless child who wanders too far into the surf.

To make matters worse, Ricky and LeSean, huddled with their factions across the dance floor and ignored her. Pegging her as the mayor's marionette, they likely plotted to save their businesses at her expense. Amber, now glaring at Anika with her drug-induced china-white eyes, didn't even try to fake her disdain for the new interloper. Unlike Sarah, Amber viewed Anika as an immediate threat to the future she hoped to cobble together. Chelsea was just along for the ride and, as far as Anika could tell, hadn't formed a point of view of her. Ironically, Curtis—the mayor's henchman who had ruthlessly killed Sam's dad, a few dogs, and no telling what or who else—had shown her the most kindness over the last few days.

Anika neared the exit when the local crowd demanded Ethan play a small set. He obliged, hopping on stage and grabbing the house guitar. He saluted the crowd, now going wild, pulled the microphone close, and began strumming.

Of all the raving fans and fawning women, one stood out near the stage's footlights. The one with lascivious moves and hungry eyes locked on Ethan. The one with the fake blonde hair flowing from her straw cowboy hat. The one with the glistening diamond ring on her hand so big that it resembled a disco ball from Studio 54.

Sarah had found her shinier object.

22

Eager to see Sam, Anika bounded up the front steps of the Alamo Opera House at dawn. She noticed Curtis and four old timers gathered around the table under a yellow porch light. "You boys here early for reveille?"

"Reveille? I'm your 'Boogie Woogie Bugle Boy' of Company B, girl," Cyclops said. "Reckon you're too young to know that song."

"You'd be right."

"I've been around since Moby Dick was a minnow."

"*Reckon* you're not huddled up for morning prayer," she poked.

Cyclops, surprised by her newfound wit, smiled. "Board meetin'," he said with "meetin'" somehow coming out in one syllable.

"Hope y'all are productive, Mr. Chairman," she said. "Your pals need something else to do besides follow me around."

"The only thing we produce around here are bathroom breaks," he said, tipping his cowboy hat as Peanut and Moon chuckled.

Anika winked and entered through the swinging doors. She approached Timmy, who was busy behind the bar rolling breakfast tacos in foil. Speaking broken Spanish (an Anglo-Tejano variant), Anika ordered two egg-and-cheese tacos.

Timmy's work ethic was legendary. He had all the hallmarks of Down syndrome but was twice as efficient as the most gifted business school graduate. He worked like a well-oiled machine. His head stayed down, and his hands never stopped moving. Every blue moon, he'd engage in conversation, but he was allergic to small talk. Time was precious behind the Alamo bar.

"*Buenos dias*, Timmy," Anika said.

He didn't answer, his hands toiling around the tortillas, eggs, cheese, and potatoes.

"You must get up early," she continued in Spanish.

No answer. *Eggs, cheese, potato.*

"You live here at the Alamo, Timmy? In the loft?"

Nothing. *Cheese, potato, foil.*

"Timmy, can you make an Elva's Destroyer?"

The world stopped. Timmy looked up for the first time and responded in English. "I'm the only person on the planet who can make a Destroyer."

"That's the rumor, but I'm not convinced. Sounds too good to be true."

"Would you like one?" he asked, unbuttoning the cuffs of his white bartender shirt. Rising to the challenge, he prepared to whip up something sacred.

"I hate to disappoint, but I'm a vegetarian. Maybe later?"

"I can make it without bacon. Just eggs. Cheese. Refried beans. Shaved potato. Tomatoes. Tortilla. *Voilà.*"

"Deal," Anika said, looking over her shoulder. She spied a thin, gray-haired man wearing a pinstriped suit and carrying a leather briefcase leaving the mayor's office.

"Pleasure doing business with you, Judge," Mayor Dodd said, before turning her attention to Anika. "When you're done with Timmy, come see me, Anika. I'll grab Curtis."

"Auntie," Anika said. "You said we could visit Samantha."

"Sam's thriving," the mayor said, walking through the swinging doors onto the front porch. "She can wait."

Frustrated, Anika thanked Timmy, grabbed her vegetarian Destroyer, and entered the mayor's office. She surveyed Dodd's lair, waiting for the furry, poisonous arachnid to return with her fixer. The office looked more disheveled than usual. Stacks of papers, soda cans, and junk food wrappers distracted attention from the mementos pinned to the walls.

"Anika Raven," the mayor said with Curtis in tow. Everyone sat. "Give us the update on your rendezvous at the MIC. I assume everyone's ready to evacuate."

Anika set her half-eaten Destroyer on the side table. "Afraid it's not that easy. They're pretty upset. Apparently, someone killed their guard dogs. That's got them piping mad."

Dodd peered at Curtis, confirming who'd killed the rottweilers. Returning her attention to Anika, she declared, "That's not good enough."

"Meaning what?"

"Meaning that if you know what's good for you, you'll convince your friends to evacuate. And I mean by *any means necessary*. Whether it's homework or something else, people always weave dogs into their excuses."

"Well, I don't think you can—"

"This isn't open for debate. Directly or through supply chains, they employ more than *thirty percent* of Miranda's workers."

"That's not fair," Anika said, leaning forward. "You're asking the impossible, Auntie. I can't convince them."

"Impossible? Need I remind you of Sam? Don't you have your interview soon with FPS? Or should I remind you of the police, waiting to arrest you for the murder of your stepdad? I just spoke to the judge who'd hear your case. And did you forget about your mom?"

"My mom? Wait . . . you know where my mother is?"

"Don't underestimate my power, Anika."

"Where's my—"

"We need to discuss a path forward," Curtis interrupted. "I'm getting pressure from the old timers to start preparations."

"What would you have me do, Curtis?" Dodd asked. "I'm doing everything possible to evacuate the town . . . to save lives."

"I suggest we divert resources—money and manpower—to fortify this building and other government installations. Outfit at least two school buses with armor and replenish our weapons cache."

"Good heavens, Curtis!" Dodd said. "You sound like you're preparing for war, not a hurricane!"

He didn't respond. Anika, still reeling from the mention of her mom, remembered Ricky's battle cry during her meeting at the MIC. *This means war!*

"Is this what you're hearing?" Dodd asked. "Folks wanting a fight? Sounds like urban legend."

"The picture's murky," he said, choosing his words with care, "but I think it warrants girding for conflict under the cover of hurricane prep."

"I don't make rash decisions based on murky pictures! Bring me better intel!" the mayor said before pointing her finger at Anika. "Which brings me back to you. Your friends best evacuate their people. Period. No dog excuses. Make it happen. Then you'll get Samantha back, and we can get to work."

"Get to work on what?" Anika asked, already knowing the answer.

"We all know your sister has a gift," Curtis said. "She sees things others don't. We need her back here with you so she can start drawin' again."

"Time is of the essence," the mayor said. "The storm's a comin'. You have a company car. You have an unlimited budget. You have an office next to the bar. And you have the town's fixer at your beck and call."

"If time's of the essence, Auntie, then ask FPS to release Sam now . . . today," Anika insisted. "Please."

"They still haven't interviewed you," the mayor said. "We just discussed this."

"With all due respect, Auntie," Anika said, "you were the one who demanded honest discussions. You said it yourself: FPS will do whatever you say. Just like Curtis here, the police, and the judge who left your office ten minutes ago. You warned me not to underestimate your power. Believe me, I don't."

The mayor wriggled in her chair and stared at Anika with one eye squinted and the other one wide open under an arched, bushy eyebrow. Unaccustomed to internal challenge, she conceded, "That's a fair point, Anika. I canceled your interview. Sorry for being dishonest."

"May I have Sam back, please? The threat of going back to jail is enough to ensure my loyalty, and this whole ordeal is nothing but a distraction."

"I'm not sure that—"

"I miss Sam, and I don't function well without her. Bring her back, and let's solve some real problems."

"Sam is no longer with FPS."

"Where is she?"

"She's at a clinic on the Upper West Side."

"A clinic for what?" Anika asked, her heart pounding. "What are you talking about?"

"Something isn't right with her, Anika. She's no longer drawing. She's not talking."

"*Of course* she's not drawing or talking. She's suffering from trauma. She's only eight years old. Her dad neglected her, and he died an unexplained death," Anika said, looking at Curtis, who was emotionless. She turned her attention back to Dodd. "You took her from me and left her with a bunch of strangers. What did you do to her?"

"I get your point, Anika, but there's more to it. I sent her for tests."

"For *tests*? What does that mean? Now you're treating her like some lab rat? You think that's gonna help her trauma? Are you giving her a lobotomy to decipher how she draws cubes?"

"Calm down," the mayor demanded. "No one's treating her like a lab rat or performing experimental, dark age medical procedures. You're more excitable than Cyclops."

"When can I see her?"

"Couple of days. Plenty of time for you to solve our problem at the MIC."

"Can we revisit the issue of my mom?"

"No."

"Again, with all due respect, I think that demands an honest discussion."

"*With all due respect*," the mayor said, now leaning forward over her desk, "you start bringing me solutions, and I'll bring you answers. Your mom's safe. That's all for now."

"Can I see her? Can I talk to her? Is she in town?"

"We got work to do," the mayor said, standing up. "I want a daily report on the MIC issue, and hopefully, the next report will be the last. Lives are at stake."

"But, Auntie, I—"

"Good day, Anika."

Curtis patted Anika, signaling that the meeting was adjourned. Anika, reluctant to leave without pressing harder, begrudgingly snatched her breakfast, stood up, and walked out. Timmy remained hard at work behind the bar, and the line for breakfast tacos stretched out the door onto the porch. As the sun ascended, its rays sneaked through the swinging doors and penetrated the windows above the bar.

"Your Destroyer is amazing, Timmy," Anika said on the way to her new office. Timmy smiled without looking up.

Anika's new office was spartan and included a library desk, a large whiteboard, a tufted leather chair that sat atop four casters, and a three-foot-tall cactus growing from a Mexican pot. No pictures on the wall. No phone. No computer. No windows. No style.

Anika finished the rest of her breakfast taco, thought about the deep hole she was in, and considered how to climb out of it. Savoring the last bite, she grabbed the napkin Timmy had handed her earlier. She froze. She hadn't noticed it before.

Timmy had doodled cubes all over it.

23

Back at the Church Grounds, Anika approached Joshua outside the sanctuary complex as he crooned and picked "A Mighty Fortress Is Our God" on his Taylor acoustic. Luther and Calvin, ears perched, tongues unleashed, rose to greet her.

"You okay, Anika?" he asked. "Haven't seen you since our jailbreak."

Anika skipped the chitchat. "Am I safe here, Joshua?"

"Why wouldn't you be?"

"You tell *me*. You indicated in the lease that Sam couldn't go beyond the fence, but you never said why. That's spooky. You tell me I can't go in your bedroom, which is a creepy thing to say . . . on multiple levels."

Joshua laughed.

"The force-pull thingamajig you call the *koya*," she continued, "which is also creepy, is heavy inside the church complex for some reason. And we casually talk about soothsayers like we'd talk about accountants or plumbers instead of how we'd talk about leprechauns."

"You don't believe in leprechauns?"

"Not funny, Joshua. My life's in shambles. I'm working for the town's diabolical mayor, who uses any means possible to keep her throttlehold on power. Once she gives the order, Miranda's finest will arrest me again for a murder I didn't commit. Oh, and she's holding my eight-year-old sister hostage."

"I know there's—"

"Wait. It gets better. Outside the Church Grounds, the person nicest to me is a maniacal killer who *did* commit the murder in question. In fact, he suffocates and poisons people with the same lack of emotion that you strum a D chord."

"Interesting . . . but I'm not surprised about Worden. Listen, Anika, I apologize for making light of evil. Evil is—"

"Now I have *you*, an enigma, giving me advice. You've entered the picture, a thoughtful lunatic with a mane of hair, translucent eyes, and a congregation of hundreds—a protestant preacher who speaks of magicians, necromancers, and sorcerers."

"I'll take all that as a compliment," he smiled, "but I don't recall discussing necromancy. That's make-believe, Anika. People can't predict the future by speaking to the dead. Don't confuse black magic with real life."

"That's just it. I can't make heads or tails of my *real-life* world anymore. You've introduced this *supernatural* world—along with the *koya*, soothsayers, and whatnot—that I don't really believe or understand. It's overwhelming."

"Let's make this simple. You and I have different worldviews, but that shouldn't matter."

"But it *does* matter," she said.

"Not in how we address the creepiness, as you call it. Just hear me out. I believe in spiritual things and science. You believe in science . . . at least. We can probably reconcile most of this on those grounds. For instance—"

"Yes, please explain."

"Take the *koya*, or whatever you wish to call it. You and I both experience it. That it exists is something we'd both say is fact. And we'd also contend that science plays a role in the *koya* pulling us. We aren't sure how that works—the Comanches thought it was black magic—but we can affirm that science factors into the equation, right?"

"Right," Anika said, noticing his play on words.

"If we just stop there—before our worldviews diverge—then we're able to acknowledge that the *koya* is creepy. It's certainly unusual and uncomfortable. And the next step is how to address it."

"And that's where our differing worldviews matter," she said.

"Not so fast. We aren't sure what causes the *koya*, so our finite minds wander to things beyond science. I attribute the cause of the *koya* to spiritual forces, whereas you attribute it to, let's say, a physiological or psychological response to the immediate environment."

"I get it. The *koya* is easier to explain without pointing to the supernatural. Soothsayers, on the other hand . . ."

"They, too, are explainable without delving into the supernatural," he said. "Certain brains can predict behaviors and events better than others based on how they process the information around them."

"If you say so."

"Artificial intelligence does it all the time. Since we last spoke, I've done some internet research on quantum mechanics and computing. Those concepts have taken ones and zeroes and turned them into—"

"Cubes."

Joshua's eyes widened. "Cubes! Cubes to better inform predictive decision-making. The fact that certain human savants manifest their predictions in cubes is odd but not necessarily supernatural. Drawing cubes or working through a Rubik's Cube, to be sure, is a phenomenal vehicle for expressing complex, multidimensional thoughts."

"That helps," she said.

"That's as far as I can go without being dishonest."

"Dishonest about what?"

"Anika, I don't believe in superstition, but I *do* believe in the supernatural. I believe Jesus was raised to life on the third day after hanging dead on a Roman cross. The Bible says that if that's not true, then I'm to be pitied the most. But I believe it with all my heart, mind, and soul. And I think the supernatural is causing the things you find so creepy. My point is that you don't need to believe what I do to overcome spiritual forces."

"Did you know the chef at the Alamo, Timmy, is a soothsayer?"

"How so?" he asked.

"Draws cubes on this," she said, handing Joshua her napkin. "Take a look."

"That would explain why they protect him like a child," Joshua said, putting down his guitar. He examined the napkin with his hypnotic eyes like a wizard analyzes a crystal ball. "These are raw, basic visions."

"How can you tell? I still don't know how you interpret the cubes."

"Being able to understand the cubes is not dissimilar from learning writing symbols for an Asian language, such as Mandarin Chinese. It takes time and practice. When I stare at Timmy's cubes, however, I see a lack of focus and clarity."

"He has Down syndrome," she said. "That may explain it."

"His condition may explain why he's a soothsayer to begin with."

"What do you mean?" she asked.

"Cognitive disabilities and cerebral trauma can trigger the gift."

"But the cubes don't look blurry. They appear well drawn and symmetrical."

"True, but they're not detailed and multidimensional like Sam's drawings. Think of it this way," he said, holding up the napkin. "I look at these drawings, and I see people fighting in the streets. I can't tell *what* streets or whether the streets are here in Miranda. I assume this is a future event— I've never known soothsayers to draw things in the past or present—but there's no discernable sense of timing. And I can't tell the reason for the conflict or whether those fighting are men or women, boys or girls. If Sam had drawn this, I'd see more detail. Her sophisticated artwork would paint a more fulsome picture and, with a skilled interpreter, perhaps provide useful intelligence."

Anika, listening with laser focus, rubbed the dogs' ears as Joshua continued.

"That would explain something else: I'm now convinced that Timmy, not Cyclops, is providing the cubes to the mayor. Cyclops is likely a poseur, a wannabe soothsayer."

"Why do you think that?" she asked.

"I peeked at his drawings on the Alamo porch . . . before I picked you up. They're trash—unactionable. Makes perfect sense why the mayor obsesses over Sam. That woman craves information, and Sam's a wellspring of intelligence when she's drawing."

"Joshua, help me understand how the cubes translate into actionable intel."

"Pick an event in history . . . anything."

"I don't know. The September 11 terrorist attacks?" she posited.

"Okay, 9/11. Let's just focus on New York City. I've never met a sooth-sayer sophisticated enough to orchestrate visions involving multiple cities at once. You with me?"

"So far."

"If Cyclops had drawn cubes predicting the 9/11 attacks on the World Trade Center, he would've doodled on a napkin something that I'd inter-pret as a third grader's sketch of Manhattan from 10,000 feet. No time stamps. No specificity. No use."

Anika nodded.

"If Timmy had drawn the cubes," he continued, "we'd see more. Maybe a focus on Wall Street with buildings and planes. No specific time stamps, but we might see through the cubes the sun rising from the east, showing us a morning event. By itself, not very useful. Coupled with other intel, however, who knows? Better than nothing, I guess."

"And Sam?"

"Had Sam drawn the cubes, I'd see a detailed, sophisticated picture of Manhattan with a focus on the World Trade Center towers. There's an architectural and autistic savant named Stephen Wiltshire who draws cityscapes, including Manhattan, with precision. That's what I'd expect to see through her cubes. I'd also expect time stamps. Not exact times, mind you, but she'd let us know the attacks would occur in the morning in September. She'd tell us it would be commercial planes used as weapons, flying into the buildings."

"Wow, that's impressive," Anika said before pivoting to her original concern. "When FPS releases Sam, will she be safe here?"

Joshua gazed beyond the fence line. "I can't be sure."

"That's unsettling."

"She'll be safer here than anywhere else."

"That doesn't make me feel any better."

"Do you care about facts or feelings?" he asked. "I'm just telling the truth."

"You need to be more specific," she said. "This is crucial. Should we fear ghosts, goblins, and gremlins, or are you talking about the mayor's henchman or evil old timers?"

"You can rule out the make-believe, Anika, but I'm told there's something that happens to this town right before a big hurricane. People act crazy. They do things you'd never expect them to do. Likewise, they don't do things you expect them to do."

"And I get to decide whether it's natural or supernatural, right?"

"You don't get to decide. It is what it is. It's your job to protect yourself and your sister from whatever it is. Because of her gift, she'll likely be a target if and when trouble comes. Hence the reason I want her close by, especially when the sun goes down."

"How do you know all this?" she asked. "You talk like someone who's lived through it."

"I'm a student of history. Miranda has a sordid past when it comes to natural disasters, including a hurricane every sixty years that destroys the town."

"When's the next one due?"

"Now," he said. "It might be on its way."

"You sound like you should be working for the mayor. You're speaking her sky-is-falling language."

"You can be evil and still be right."

"Would you suggest we evacuate, then?" she asked.

"Not necessarily. When I said *sordid* history, I chose my words intentionally."

Anika stared at him.

"I think I've said enough," he said. "You already think I'm a lunatic."

"You can't leave me hanging on that cliff. Cough it up, Joshua."

"I'm convinced the town destroys itself before the hurricane arrives."

"You talk like the town's alive."

"Perhaps, but I could've also said the *townsfolk* destroy themselves . . ."

"But you didn't, and you choose your words *intentionally*."

"One day," Joshua chuckled, "we'll figure out whether certain things are natural or supernatural."

"Let's hope that day is far off," she said. "This town will never allow us to leave, will it?"

"I don't know," he admitted.

"You keep staring at Timmy's napkin. Something else you need to tell me?"

"It's blurry."

"You see something more than townsfolk fighting in the streets, don't you?"

Joshua took a deep breath. "I see gnashing teeth, runaway trains, fire-bombs, machine guns . . . utter chaos."

"Anything I should do with that interpretation?"

"Yeah . . . get a good night's sleep. You're gonna need it."

24

Anika sipped her second cup of coffee from the "Texas Est. 1845" mug. She sat in a rocking chair next to Curtis on the Alamo front porch. The sun struggled to climb from its slumber, cumulus clouds blanketed the sky, and intermittent wind gusts pushed out the otherwise salty morning air. The hurricane tracker on the wall had a new magnet moving west from Africa.

On the lawn, near the far corner of the porch, Cyclops loaded split wood into an Aaron Franklin-style barbeque smoker made from an abandoned propane tank. Moon, Peanut, and Vernis surrounded him. They engaged in various chores required for a full day's cook. Anika could smell the billowing mesquite smoke and hear the sizzling sounds of Timmy's bacon. *Not the most welcoming place for a vegetarian*, she thought. *Wonder what Timmy's drawing while preparing breakfast.*

"Here's some advice," Curtis said. "You shouldn't upset the mayor. Doesn't help things."

"I'm exhausted, Curtis. Doing everything she's demanding. And she continues to keep my loved ones from me. It's not fair."

"Lower your voice, or you'll make it worse," Curtis whispered. "Fair's got nothin' to do with it. You need to be more strategic."

"She shipped Sam off to heaven knows where. She knows where my mom is and won't tell me. This is unacceptable!" For the first time, Anika challenged Curtis directly. The mayor had programmed him long ago. Anika needed to discern whether he was reprogrammable. "Do *you* know where my mom is?"

He took the question in stride. "No," he said. After a pregnant pause, he married his asphalt-colored eyes with Anika's. "But I'll find out."

She smiled, thanked him, and patted his leg, hoping the moment would mark a breakthrough in their relationship. *Perhaps he is reprogrammable.*

She cast her eyes on the Blouses and Boots Boutique. Logan, for some reason, was dropping off Sarah at work in her Range Rover. She was probably hung over. He parked it in front of the store, hopped out like a bunny after a carrot, grabbed his wife before she reached the boutique door, and kissed her on the lips. After Sarah entered her store, Logan waved toward the Alamo and waited for an Uber or Lyft.

Pathetic, Anika thought, refusing to return the wave. *What a whipped puppy dog.* Sickened to her stomach, Anika rocked out of her chair and marched toward Cyclops. *Maybe the old timers are reprogrammable too.* "Sorry to interrupt you fine gentlemen."

Startled, Cyclops looked up to the porch through the smoke at Anika. "Yes, ma'am. What can we do for ya?"

"See that guy over there?" Anika pointed.

"Over *yonder*?" he corrected her, cleaning his hands on a dirty towel. "Logan Andrews?"

"That ol' boy's as smooth as Tennessee whiskey," Moon interjected.

"Makes the best moonshine in these here parts," Peanut added.

"You know his wife, Sarah, the owner of the boutique?" Anika asked. "The one you saw me with a couple of days ago?"

"Know of her," Cyclops said. "Every beer guzzler in town knows her in-laws."

"I need you to follow her."

"*Follow her*?" he laughed.

"Oh, don't act so innocent. I know you old timers are masters in surveillance and reconnaissance. You've been following me since I hit town. Right?"

Cyclops's keen eyes searched for Curtis, visible through the porch balustrade, clearly seeking permission to say more. After further direction, he said, "That's the mayor's business." *Permission granted.* "We do special services for her from time to time."

"Do you know who my boss is?"

"President Hindenburg? Every field marshal needs a strong chancellor."

"Sorry to disappoint, Cyclops, but you aren't Himmler, and your old timers aren't the SS."

"*Touché*, ma'am. Curtis tells me you work for the mayor."

"Bingo," Anika said, learning the machinations of small-town politics on the fly. "So . . . I'm asking you to do the mayor's business."

Cyclops's sidekicks interrupted their chores near the smoker to rubberneck. When he looked at them, they shrugged, signaling that Anika's logic passed the smell test.

Sensing acquiescence, Anika continued. "You have a camera?"

"Yes, ma'am," Cyclops said.

"Digital? Don't want your spies getting caught with a Polaroid Instamatic."

Cyclops chuckled.

"Know how to use it?" she asked.

"One of our youngsters can figure it out, I reckon."

"Youngsters?"

"Someone under ninety years old," he said. "What are we lookin' for, anyways? Butts and elbows?"

"You'll know it when you see it. Keep me updated," she said as she walked back to Curtis.

"Personal vendetta or business?" Curtis queried.

"I work for the mayor now," she said with a wink, "so it's nothing but politics."

Anika relished Curtis's smirk, but it didn't last long. His face contorted into an expression of surprise and disturbance at the sound of distant voices. The words still indecipherable, the crowd drew closer and grew louder.

"That better not be . . ." Curtis said, popping out of his chair and walking to the edge of the porch. "Cyclops, y'all hear that? Sounds like—"

"Protesters and *pistoleros*," Cyclops said. "Best put yer boots on."

25

Anika heard the growing cacophony of chanting, banging of pots and pans, and cowbells. She could see the multitudes marching around the corner as the sun spread its rays over the neighborhood. Scores of minutemen and women emerged from the west and entered Four Points. Most of them wore hard hats and overalls, and a few numbskulls had on *Bones Don't Burn* T-shirts. Some carried signs that read, "Freedom Not Intimidation," "MIC Workers for Liberty," and "We Ain't Leaving!" One sign that read "Remember the Alamo" had an ironic twist. Another sign that caught Anika's attention had a green-faced rendition of Mayor Dodd superimposed on the body of the Wicked Witch of the West.

Several protesters were waving vintage flags from the Texas Revolution. Anika noticed the Flag of 1824, with its green, white, and red bars—the "1824" smack dab in the middle—symbolizing Mexico's reneging on promises made in the Mexican Constitution of 1824. Many believed that flag flew over the original Alamo in March 1836 when Santa Anna attacked. That event, hardwired into the DNA of every Texan born since, had spawned the war cry, *Remember the Alamo!*

In addition to the traditional Texas flag, protesters waved the dark-blue Lynchburg Flag with its white star in the middle atop white letters—"INDEPENDENCE." Beyond that, they showcased the vivid and macabre Bloody Arm Flag, with its severed red arm, sword, and blood on a white canvas. And if that wasn't provocative enough, one protester unfurled the Troutman Lone Star Flag, emblazoned with a bold star and the words, "Liberty or Death."

Texas Revolution flags were sacred in Miranda, especially the *Come and Take It* flag. That flag, with its star and cannon, emerged from the first skirmish of the Texas Revolution, the Battle of Gonzalez. The saying, borrowed from the battle cry at Thermopylae in 480 BC, was again apropos in 1835 when the Mexican army attempted to remove a bronze cannon from the Texian fort in Gonzales. After several failed attempts, Texians screamed, "Come and take it!" and held strong. No one was removing that cannon.

Miranda's roots stretched deep into the Texas Revolution with Mexico in 1835–36. Miranda's teachers catechized their students on their town's rich history like it was the almighty gospel. Three Texian soldiers had escaped the Goliad Massacre with the *Come and Take It* flag, fled from Mexican Emperor and General Santa Anna, and found refuge in what was now Revolutionary Park. They planted that flag in the middle of the park, and the flag's remnants were framed in the mayor's office.

As protesters gathered in the park across the road, Mayor Dodd launched from the swinging doors like a rabid dog and thundered toward the porch steps. Curtis grabbed her by her bat wing as she thrashed, wrestled, and screamed from the pit of her stomach. "How dare you burnish that flag in Revolutionary Park!? This is hallowed ground, you mongrels! You're all guilty of apostasy!"

"Shut up, fascist!" a protester yelled, throwing a Big Red bottle that barely missed the mayor's face and crashed against the swinging doors.

"Send lawyers, guns, and money!" Cyclops guffawed as he stared at Curtis from the smoker. He was enjoying the escalation of tension.

"Your demagogic leaders promise much but deliver little!" Dodd screamed. "You're all gonna be killed if you don't evacuate! It's suicide!"

"Go pound sand, you evil witch!" another yelled. "Your words are trash!"

"These people are idiots!" the mayor said to Anika and Curtis, her flabby neck jiggling like Jell-O.

"If evacuation's your goal, Mayor," Curtis advised, "then perhaps you shouldn't call them mongrels or idiots to their faces. A touch of grace may be more persuasive."

Anika noticed that LeSean and Ricky were AWOL. "I bet most of these folks are paid protesters," she said. "They represent the train depot and refinery, but I doubt they work there."

"You mean they're Antifa-types?" the mayor asked.

"No," Anika said, as Curtis nodded his head, "professional protesters who are less hostile and polemic."

"Less hostile and polemic than who? Stalin? These hooligans—paid or otherwise—just got here, and *already* they've threatened my life with projectiles and vicious insults."

"What I meant was—"

"Where's your line, Anika?" the mayor continued. "Molotov cocktails that burn down the Alamo? My likeness as a green witch burned in effigy? Machine gun fire cutting me in half?"

I'd love to see all of the above, Anika thought. But wisdom prescribed silence, and Anika swallowed the pill . . . except to say, "Machine guns, no doubt, would qualify as hostile."

The protesters' boisterous spirit simmered somewhat as they got settled. They clearly had plans to demonstrate for days, not hours. As the more restless continued to bang, yell, and fuss, others set up chairs, standing umbrellas, and tents at the edge of the park.

As the old timers continued their cooking preparations, Timmy, over the mayor's soft objection, walked a tray of foil-wrapped breakfast tacos into the maelstrom. Minutes later, he emerged from the congestion of professional malcontents with an empty tray and a pocket full of cash.

"Quit feeding the enemy, Timmy," the mayor scolded.

"He's depletin' their cash reserves," Curtis said, playing the role of a protective father. "Good thinking, Timmy."

No one lays a glove on Timmy with Curtis around, Anika observed.

"Protect him all you want," the mayor fumed, "but he failed to warn us of this catastrophe."

"No," Anika interjected. "He predicted it."

The mayor and Curtis froze.

"I know about Timmy's gift," Anika said.

The mayor and Curtis looked at each other.

"Timmy handed me a napkin with my breakfast," Anika continued. "I didn't realize until later, but he'd doodled cubes on it." Before now, Anika hadn't considered whether Timmy had handed her the napkin on purpose. "I guess he forgot to remove his handiwork from the napkin pile."

Anika had failed to anticipate the next question from the mayor.

"Can you interpret cubes, Anika?"

My answer could be life-changing, Anika thought. "The preacher's teaching me. As you may know," she said, debating whether to say more, "Sam only draws cubes for me."

Mayor Dodd seethed and, with labored breathing, stared at Anika for what felt like minutes. Anika sensed Dodd was processing this new information and deciding what to make of it. Several lives hung in the balance. Anika regretted bringing Joshua into the fold, but she had little choice.

"Guess we should've expected the town preacher to be a prophet," Curtis said, breaking the ice.

"He's not a prophet. He's an interpreter like you," the mayor barked. "It's of no moment. If you and Anika would just *do your jobs*, then we can save lives and get out of this mess! The MIC is threatening to withhold production and transportation. That's blackmail. They'll deprive us of energy, commerce, our basic needs. They'll shut down our supply chain."

At that point, something happened. Mayhem ensued across the road as the park crowd jumped and screamed.

"Something else you need to tell us, Anika," the mayor inquired, "about Timmy's cubes?"

"Uh, yes. Joshua said something about train runners and—"

Before she finished her sentence, they heard the runaway trains coming from multiple directions toward Four Points, locomotives and train cars screaming toward town. And they heard the staccato gun fire from automatic weapons.

The mayor turned to Anika. "There's your machine guns, honey. Right on cue."

26

Gunfire doesn't startle real Texans, particularly those from rural towns. Miranda's children mastered pistols, shotguns, and rifles like magicians master top hats, rabbits, and playing cards. Texas bravado aside, however, fully automatic gunfire wasn't kosher. Not even close. Mirandites cowered at the ominous sounds of hoodlums firing M-16s and AK-47s from train cars barreling through the town's arteries on largely secluded tracks.

Anika and Curtis, waiting for supper at the porch table, had spent dusk till dawn pacing, kibbitzing, scheming, and watching the protests unfold. Of primary concern was protecting the Alamo Opera House from attack. Through it all, Anika had spent considerable thought on Curtis. Presently, she wasn't certain what made him tick. She did come to realize, though, that the transition from mayor's assistant to mayor's assassin was likely a short leap.

The multitudes across the road continued to fuss, but even the towering park trees hadn't shielded protesters from the sun's blistering heat. As the day had worn on, their once boisterous chants had evolved into indecipherable mumbles.

"Soup's on—best barbeque in Texas, by gosh!" Cyclops declared as he shuffled the length of the porch, holding two plastic trays of brisket, potato salad, and pinto beans on top of butcher paper. The trays shook as his gnarly, arthritic fingers eased the food's landing on the table. "Be right back. Gonna tell Timmy to play some Johnny Cash on his jukebox."

Anika stared at her plate and glanced at Curtis. She wasn't sure if he knew.

He slid his tray toward hers. "Give me the meat. You eat the other stuff."

As the sun crawled back to sleep, the trains continued to run every forty-five minutes. The tracks crossed north of the park. To the relief of the townsfolk, including those protecting the Alamo, the gunshots had ended, replaced with fireworks. Protesters on the ground lighted smoke bombs, shot bottle rockets, and fired Roman candles. Those farther off in train cars painted the sky with a kaleidoscope of colors from chrysanthemums and aerial repeaters.

Mirandites, believe it or not, welcomed the fireworks display. Weeks earlier, the mayor had canceled the town's Fourth of July celebration and forbade personal fireworks. When it came to fire safety, Miranda summers resembled pallets of kindling. Few townsfolk had objected to the mayor's executive fiat or abuse of power. Truth be told, even first-generation Mexican Americans in Miranda celebrated Texas Independence Day, which fell on the second day of March, with more fervor than July Fourth. That didn't make them secessionists, at least not from the United States; but they relished shaking their fists at Mother Mexico, a hallmark of Miranda's homogeneous culture that perplexed outsiders.

"Mighty kind of 'em to pop firecrackers to celebrate my barbeque," Cyclops said, taking his seat at the table opposite Anika and Curtis. "But shootin' them military guns all day long . . . that ain't right, Curtis."

"More like Woodstock than Tiananmen Square," Curtis observed, slicing up his moist brisket and dousing it with Stubb's barbeque sauce.

"You say that, Curtis, but these folks are dangerous! They ain't just a bunch of juvenile delinquents. They keep it up, Mayor'll need to toss 'em in the hoosegow."

"Come on, Cyclops!" Curtis chuckled. "You can't be serious."

"Gotta keep the peace! This ain't no Washington, DC, or Chicago! And it sure ain't no San Francisco!"

"We ain't got room to detain hundreds of nincompoops."

"Detain them?" Anika interjected. "These people have a First Amendment right to protest."

"Go figure," Cyclops said. "Girl lied about going to law school . . . now she's a constitutional scholar."

"Ouch!" Anika said.

"Enough!" Curtis snarled, pointing his plastic fork at Cyclops. "You best reattach the muffler on that mouth of yours, Cy."

"Bygones," Cyclops said, tipping his misshapen Stetson. He focused his attention back on Curtis. "You best put that fork away, young man, before somebody gets hurt. Lunatics'll shoot you with a machine gun . . . or a Roman candle. Nothin' but anarchy around these parts on the mayor's watch."

"You're outta control tonight, old friend."

"Oh, *I'm* outta control?" Cyclops said. "I'm a concerned citizen. These millennials and Gen-somethin'-or-others got no right to destroy our property and threaten people! Where's the mayor been all afternoon? She needs to *lock up* these criminals before it gets worse!"

"Calm down, Cy. You're swallowin' their bait—hook, line, and sinker."

"You calm down! You should worry less about protecting this amber-eyed princess and more about protecting *our town*," he said, grabbing his plate and ambling back to the lawn, where the other old timers had noticeably departed. "Not sure what's crawled in that head of yours, boy."

Curtis kept talking as Cyclops departed. "These knuckleheads are makin' minimum wage to camp across the street, hold up some signs, and bark a little bit. They're harmless." After Cyclops walked off the porch, Curtis added, "He's acting like the Third Reich's rollin' tanks into Paris."

"Is the mayor coming back out?" Anika asked, changing the subject. "I haven't seen her in a few hours."

"Be careful what you ask for," Curtis said.

"You know I struggle with that woman," Anika said without reservation, "but she can't be hiding. Shows weakness, and weakness fuels bad behavior."

Anika pushed open the squeaky swinging doors. Timmy had cleaned up the bar and was drudging upstairs to his bedroom. Once he reached the second floor, she entered the mayor's office. The light was off. Dodd, too, must have retired early to her bedroom on the second floor. Anika was about to walk back outside when the stacks of paper on the mayor's desk caught her attention.

The *koya* was heavy here, the pull intense. Or was it just the *boom-boom-boom* of bass guitar reverberating through the office from Cash's "A Boy Named Sue?" The mélange of noise from distant fireworks, muffled protester conversations, and outlaw country music would mask any sounds of the mayor returning. But Anika pressed forward and turned on the bankers desk lamp. The light was just bright enough to cast shadows on the walls of Dodd's lair and bring to life the eyes of the dead . . . captured in black and white photos.

The mayor had taken her laptop. Anika thumbed through the stack of documents on the desk. A quick perusal evidenced nothing but administrivia: receipts, bills, and letters of recommendation. Glancing at the door, Anika opened the desk's file cabinet drawer. If the mayor returned now, she would certainly fire Anika, or worse, turn her over to the sheriff for murder (perhaps for the second time in five years). Anika observed sundry categories, labeled in various colors. She expected to see most of the files: FINANCES, TAXES, CAPITAL PROJECTS, HOLIDAY EVENTS. Near the back, though, crammed in the depths of the cavernous drawer, hid the unexpected: MALCONTENTS, EXPUNGED, and . . . JOHNNY D.

Anika pulled the folder marked JOHNNY D. as Johnny C. crooned the lyrics to "A Boy Named Sue." Her heart raced. The room thrummed, and she scanned the doorway again to see if anyone lurked. If the folder's title wasn't provocative enough, its contents sparked her interest. Someone had redacted the first section of a document titled, "Cause of Death." The next section, however, was littered with photos of Johnny and maps of the Flats. Someone, presumably the mayor herself, had scribbled notes on the maps, indicating a keen interest.

The thrum inside the room turned to a palpable vibration. The walls and floor shook. Anika could hear the coming revelry and roar of train cars full of riotous protesters. They were seconds away and nearing the crossing north of Revolutionary Park. Agitators across the street largely ignored what Anika hoped would be the day's last salvo from Ricky's and LeSean's hired help. The protest in the park had long settled into a harmless hootenanny with an occasional outburst of indignation. The healing balm of Timmy's second round of tacos had helped to soothe tensions.

Anika struggled to breathe, and her knees wobbled as she saw Johnny's beautiful face in his family photo . . . his high school photo . . . and the photo from the article in the *Miranda Times*. He had all the hallmarks of a Hollywood star—cleft chin, wavy hair, and spellbinding eyes. He was an absolute doll.

The contents of the folder grew darker the deeper she dove. She squeezed the official police photos of the accident scene so hard that she left permanent creases. She saw the pictures of the smoldering, overturned Challenger—now her refurbished Black Ghost. The sun setting on the dusty Flats. The scores of nosy onlookers, some of whom she recognized. Working her way through the folder, however, one thing haunted her more than anything else. The car doors were closed . . . and there were no pictures of Johnny's body.

Bones don't burn.

She closed the Johnny D. folder with more questions than answers. Cause of death . . . *redacted?* No body in the official police photos? The tacky T-shirts, Anika thought, now made more sense.

The *koya* grew in intensity. It pulled Anika's arms, legs, and midsection with such force that no truthteller could ascribe it to Johnny Cash's bass guitarist, tinnitus, or any other natural phenomenon. But she had one more area to surveil—the credenza behind the desk. That's where Dodd staged her prized possessions, like her second-place ribbon from the seventh-grade science fair and photos of her lost children. Amidst those heirlooms rested an abandoned document from Miranda's Center of Neuro-oncology. Someone had attached to it a bright green Post-it Note, beckoning like crystalline Kryptonite.

The words on the note read, "To Anika Raven."

When Anika read the document, she screamed a guttural cry so loud that even those protesters riding on the trains trembled, wondering if the lunatic prophets had been right, wondering if a dark, supernatural force had just landed on planet Earth.

27

urtis Worden was leaning his tall frame over the edge of the Alamo porch, chewing his last bite of brisket and listening to Cyclops's surveillance report, when he heard Anika's blood-curdling scream. He hadn't heard a sound like that since the war.

The arthritis (he pronounced it with a "the") made running difficult. It had grown worse in recent days, particularly in his hips. He had re-tweaked them working over Sam's sorry excuse for a father. In fact, Curtis had contorted his body like the young'uns do when they play that game in the park . . . *Twister*. He'd bent over the bed awkwardly as he'd mashed the pillow down for a few minutes. That drunken fellow hadn't struggled much—he had wiggled a tad (*or was it* wriggled?). So Curtis had thrust his body into an unconventional position, and he was now paying the price. He had cussed at himself for not stretching beforehand. He excelled at performing odd jobs—the mayor called it *dirty work*—but without repeated practice, he wasn't immune to minor mistakes. That said, he eventually convinced himself that *stretchin' ain't got nothin' to do with it*. The arthritis always got worse before a big storm.

Complaining didn't matter anyway. He needed to fight through the pain. Business was booming, and there'd be another odd job—more dirty work—today. Cyclops had just told him the old girl was up to no good. He had figured as much.

Unable to run, he scampered like a seasoned dog who'd spotted the mailman coming. He had no idea what or who had caused Anika to scream. The mayor had departed hours before. Little Timmy (he would always think of him as *Little* Timmy) had retired to bed and was watching one of them *Star Wars* movies. (Curtis often watched with him.) Timmy, of course, wouldn't hurt a fly. And Anika's shriek wasn't in response to whacking a funny bone or witnessing a Texas-sized rat. It was something much more agonizing—but what?

He was hobbling by the time he reached the mayor's office, but the invigorating force—the *koya*—had carried him on dragon's wings. That force rarely let him down. When his will aligned with the *koya*, he could accomplish anything. Anika's hypnotic eyes—usually painted a sunset auburn or blazing like smoldering coals, depending on her mood—now resembled the orange golf balls the young'uns use at the Miranda Putt-Putt. Big, round, and dimpled with globs of tears. She held up an official-looking document, her hands shaking like she had that Parkinson's disease.

"What's all the fuss about?" he asked. "What's that?"

"Did you know about this?" she asked, her lips trembling.

"Anika, I don't have Superman's eyes. I have no idea what that says."

She tossed it at him. It swirled around and hit the floor like a poorly crafted paper airplane. "Some doctor diagnosed Sam with a brain tumor!?"

Curtis clinched his teeth, took a deep breath, and closed his eyes. He knew what he had to do. Anika had disobeyed orders and snooped around the mayor's office. By doing so, she'd learned information the mayor wasn't ready to share. *No telllin' what else she found*, he thought. He walked toward her. His moves were cautious but intentional. She didn't budge, not an inch. She girded for battle, looking for a fight. She kept those savage eyes locked on him. He could see the orange, dimpled golf balls turning to smoldering coals. Her nose flared, and her eyes furrowed. She had reached the point of no return—*madness*!

Curtis knew Anika's disobedience had placed the mayor's plans in jeopardy. Just before reaching her, his shadow looked like a monster's as he raised his arms and . . .

Hugged her. "I'm so sorry, Anika. I didn't know."

She welcomed his hug and squeezed him with all her might. "I'm getting Sam back tonight, Curtis. And I need to find my mom. Where's the mayor?"

"I *do* know about that. Cyclops just told me. We've got a runner."

"A runner?"

"A traitor. I'll fix this. I'll fix all of it."

Fixers fix stuff. That's what they do.

Curtis didn't worry about locking his pickup truck. The MIC was familiar territory for his odd jobs (and would continue to be). Over yonder ways, Ricky, LeSean, and others sympathetic to the protests partied in the train depot. Smoke filled the air from . . . whatever: cigarettes, fireworks, bonfires, remnants of the locomotives' diesel fuel. Who knew for sure in the dark? The train cars rested after a long day of terrorizing the townsfolk. Mirandites didn't deserve that, particularly with a life-threatening storm on its way.

The refinery lights lit up the MIC like the fully operational space station in *Empire Strikes Back*, Little Timmy's favorite movie. But the abandoned train car that Curtis approached sat in relative darkness. It was marked only by three wavy flashlights held by the same three stooges who'd cooked Curtis's supper. The mayor had parked her rusted El Camino nearby.

"You boys eat any barbeque?" Curtis asked.

"Not yet, C-Dub," Peanut replied.

"Our runner in there?" he pointed.

"Reckon so," Moon replied sullenly.

"I'll make this quick," Curtis said, looking down at his scuffed-up work boots. "Open it up."

Vernis, the youngest old timer—Curtis pegged him around eighty-five years old—opened the squeaky doors. Curtis entered. Employees of the train depot had repurposed this train car into a makeshift storage facility with fluorescent lights on the ceiling. As for furniture, it was empty now except for two chairs facing one another. Two of the fluorescent bulbs needed replacing and flickered like a strobe light on a low-flash cycle. Curtis heard in the distance the toasts and victory shouts from the train depot as he sat in the chair facing Auntie Dodd, a woman who looked more like a trapped armadillo than Miranda's mayor.

"You got anything to say?" Curtis asked. His eyes were fatigued, his heart broken.

"Based on my research, and Timmy's cubes, it was the most probable means of escape. Reckon Timmy tattled?"

"He had you runnin' somewhere. Old timers did the rest. Were you takin' a train out?"

"Eighteen-wheeler. It left about an hour ago. A guy named Leon, headed for Waco. Thought I'd visit Joanna Gaines and shop the Magnolia."

Curtis didn't catch the humor. He had never heard of Joanna Gaines or Magnolia. Pop culture wasn't his strongest subject. "Reckon you would've made it without Cy's bloodhounds?"

"Perhaps. You never know with Miranda's jealousy."

"Green as a husband with a curious wife."

"You don't have to do this, Curtis."

"Reckon you know what I gotta do, Auntie Dodd. As much as I hate to do it."

"That hurricane's gonna destroy this town. There'll be nothing left. You know that."

"Town's pretty clear about what she'd have me do."

"You've bucked the town before, Curtis. Don't act like you're a Puritan. And who's to say the town's leading you aright?"

"Don't talk crazy," he said, remaining remorseful but growing agitated. He sighed. "My word, Auntie, what have you done?"

"I didn't do *anything* but try to save lives, Curtis!"

"Anika learned about Sam's brain tumor."

"And I saved her life. Had I not sent her for further testing, Sam would've died."

"Even so, Anika ain't happy."

Dodd squirmed in her seat and tried to reset the conversation. "Anika? What do I care about Anika? Curtis, you know me! All I want is for Mirandites to live in peace and prosperity. But they don't listen, and they won't evacuate unless we mandate it. Period."

"But you fled. You know you can't do that. Miranda's never allowed her leaders to leave. That's treason."

"Didn't know it was treason, Curtis. I was just frustrated . . . and scared."

"Rules is rules, Auntie. You've said it yourself: can't tolerate runners. Besides, without rules, we just got anarchy."

"But you've broken the rules before . . . when it suited you."

"Not sure that's right."

"Need I remind you of your family?"

"Family ain't got nothin' to do with it."

"Oh, but doesn't it?"

"Ain't got time to play word games," Curtis said, standing up and pulling out his gun. "I have a Glock nine-millimeter. You choose."

"So that's how it works? I choose who does it? You or me?"

"That's how it works for treason."

"How convenient. Give it to me."

Curtis handed her the weapon and walked away. Before he reached the doors, she said, "I love you, Curtis. Thank you for everything."

He responded, "I love you, too, Auntie. I'm sorry it came to this. You ruled well . . . until the end."

"Sure there's no other way?"

He paused but didn't answer. He stepped outside the train car and signaled to Vernis to close the doors. The doors crashed shut as Curtis and the old timers waited for a gunshot.

The gunshot never came. Curtis reckoned Dodd was regarding things—her career, her dead children, her accomplishments—before taking her life. He paced and grew impatient. His sympathy morphed into irritation as he checked his watch. He could tolerate indecision but not cowardice. After twenty minutes, he nodded to the old timers, a directive to finish the job. They pulled their pistols, took position like they'd done this for a living in another era, and opened the door . . . but there was nothing more to do.

Curtis took a knee as he watched the mayor swing in the strobe light from a rope she'd apparently snuck into the train car.

Curtis shook his head. *Stubborn as the day is long*, he thought. "Figure y'all better cut her down before that party over yonder wraps up."

"Roger that, C-Dub," Peanut said. "You know what this means?"

"The queen is dead!" Vernis declared.

"Yes, she is," Curtis said, now switching his thoughts to Anika. "Long live the queen."

28

FBI Special Agent Brian Maxwell: Please state your full name and age.

Witness: Logan Danforth, and I'm eighteen.

Agent: And you're here represented by your attorney. Counsel, would you like to state your name for the record?

Attorney: You have my card.

Agent: I'll take that as a no.

Attorney: Listen, my client's here voluntarily, but I still don't know why the Bureau's involved in this.

Agent: The FBI's part of a joint federal and state investigation into the circumstances surrounding the death of Johnny Delgado.

Attorney: For a homicide? That's a state issue.

Agent: And drugs smuggled through Mexico. And explosives. And heaven only knows what else. I have a whole Santa's bag of jurisdiction, pal. May I proceed with the witness?

Attorney: Nobody's stopping you.

Agent: Mr. Danforth, let's start with the obvious because some of the witnesses seem confused. Do you believe Johnny Delgado is dead?

Witness: I'm familiar with the campaign *Bones Don't Burn*.

Agent: That's not what I asked. I'll ask it another way: Any reason to believe Johnny is still alive?

Witness: Well, I'm no scientist, if that's what you mean. I don't know if he's alive or not. How do you explain there were no bones if bones don't burn?

Agent: Bones *do* burn. There was C-4 explosive in the car. Did you know that? Do you know what C-4 does to bones?

Attorney: Good grief! He already said he's not a scientist, Agent Maxwell, and we'll concede further that he's no explosives expert.

Agent: Just answer the question.

Attorney: Logan, he wants to know if you have any evidence that Johnny's still alive.

Witness: I don't.

Attorney: Move on, Detective. For heaven's sake, we all know the boy's dead. You're wasting our time.

Agent: Mr. Danforth, did you know Johnny well?

Witness: Yes, we went to school together, and he dated a good friend of mine.

Agent: That would be Anika Raven?

Witness: Correct. I was with Anika the night that Johnny . . . killed himself, I guess.

Agent: I'm told you and Ms. Raven went to the homecoming dance together?

Witness: Yes, I was homecoming king. She was queen. In Miranda, the king and queen attend the dance together.

Agent: Did you see Johnny the night he died?

Witness: Yes, I did. He showed up at my house.

Agent: Did you expect him at your house?

Witness: No.

Agent: Why was he there?

Witness: Looking for Anika. She was at my house for my after-dance party. She stayed later than expected.

Agent: Anyone else there when he arrived?

Witness: No, just me . . . and Anika.

Agent: And what were you doing when he arrived?

Witness: Kissing.

Agent: Kissing his girlfriend?

Attorney: Objection.

Agent: This isn't a deposition, Counselor. Logan, you can answer.

Witness: Correct. Kissing Anika.

Agent: How did Johnny respond when he witnessed that?

Witness: Didn't like it, I'm sure, but he didn't stick around to share his feelings.

Agent: What happened next?

Witness: Anika rushed after him.

Agent: Did she go with him?

Witness: No, he sped off in his car. That's when he went to the Flats.

Agent: And?

Witness: And the rest is history.

Agent: Did you take Anika home?

Witness: No, sir. She drove herself home. I went to bed. I didn't learn about the incident until the next morning.

Agent: If I were to tell you that the local sheriff found traces of heroin in Johnny's car after it exploded, would that surprise you?

Witness: Didn't realize he was into that.

Agent: And explosives?

Witness: I realize the car exploded. Didn't know how. Just assumed it blew up on its own . . . with the gas and whatnot.

Agent: What if I said that Anika Raven was responsible for providing the heroin and explosives? Would—

Witness: That would be ridiculous. I've never—

Attorney: But Logan, you don't know for sure.

Witness: Come on! That's not—

Agent: Following up on your lawyer's comment, you don't know with one hundred percent certainty that she *didn't* provide those things.

Witness: Yeah, but—

Agent: So if the mayor and the local sheriff have proof that she was involved, you wouldn't have much to say about that, right?

Witness: What proof?

Attorney: I'd like to talk to my client outside for a couple of minutes.

Agent: Take all the time you need.

29

PRESENT DAY

The next morning—as if Auntie Dodd's decomposing body was shaking its fist and screaming, "I told you so"—the clouds resembled the phlegm of a productive cough and the wind gusts roared. Anika, however, was in a good mood. Her body had acclimated well to Miranda's climate. All traces of her mild acne had cleared, and for whatever reason, she no longer needed corrective lenses to see 20/20. She hadn't worn glasses or contacts in days. Presently, she was eating a Timmy Destroyer with her feet propped on the mayor's desk. Breakfast taco in one hand and stopwatch in the other, she watched Sam master each Rubik's Cube challenge with lightning speed.

"Forty seconds!" Anika said. "New PR!"

Sam, still wordless as a rock, smiled ear to ear, tossed the Rubik's Cube aside, and grabbed Faux Pooh off the couch. Her Betty Boop eyes told a story of thankfulness that words couldn't capture. She squeezed Pooh with such force that Anika expected his button eyes to pop out. No one had told Sam about the brain tumor. Other than her inability or unwillingness to talk, no symptoms presented. That was assuming, of course, that her ability to forecast future events wasn't a symptom of the tumor. Whether it was or not, that skill would likely be needed in the coming days if they were to survive.

"Sure you're ready to start drawing cubes again?"

Sam nodded.

"Not too tired?"

Sam shrugged.

"Wanna wait till tomorrow? Or the next day?"

Sam shook her head.

"Did you miss me as much as I missed you?"

Sam rushed to Anika, spun her chair around, and answered her with a hug for the ages . . . a sign of affection that poets couldn't describe. Only Pooh's eyes stayed dry.

"I love you too," Anika said. "I won't let them ever take you again. I promise. Do you believe me?"

Sam wiped away her tears and nodded.

"We have work to do," Anika said before her voice softened to a whisper, her lips pressed against Sam's ear. "We need to find a way out of here, sissy."

Sam's eyes widened.

"Meantime, we play it cool. You trust me? Sisters in the bond."

Sam didn't respond. She was staring at the figure in the doorway.

"Mornin' girls . . . ladies. I brewed you some fresh coffee, Anika," Curtis said, raising a smoking mug that read, "The Boss." The thought of ordering Starbucks or buying a Keurig machine had never crossed his mind. "You take it black, I recall."

"Morning, Curtis. You have a good memory," Anika said, spinning her chair around as Sam retreated to the couch with Pooh, curious how long Curtis had been standing there. "Ever consider investing in an espresso machine and cappuccino maker?"

"You know the answer to that," he said, handing her the mug. For a moment, she noticed his lips edging toward a smile. "If my finger don't fit the handle, I don't get near it."

Anika forced her own smile through the exhaustion. She had stayed up late. After Curtis had returned with Sam, Sam had fallen asleep on the couch. Curtis had explained how he'd found the mayor's body swinging from a train car. He expected foul play, but even though Curtis had found her dead—likely murdered—at the MIC, he didn't mention any names. Anika kept waiting for Ricky's or LeSean's name to cross his lips as suspects. To Curtis's credit, however, he didn't speculate or prejudge. They would need to wait for answers. Miranda's best detectives were on the case.

The irony was thick. Anika remembered the first words Auntie Dodd ever spoke to her: *The end of a rope is a terrible place to be.* Beyond that, the mayor's death brought about good news. The local Pinkertons had ruled out Anika as a suspect in their murder investigation concerning Scotty Mathis. Miraculously, overnight, Miranda's finest had cleared her of all charges. Curtis Worden didn't possess Superman's eyes, but the Man of Steel's cape fit him just right.

Fixers fix things. That's what they do.

Curtis, too, had informed Anika of her mother's whereabouts. According to his account, Barbara Mathis, after returning from her latest jaunt to Mexico, had sought Auntie Dodd's help in finding Sam. After a long discussion to which he wasn't privy, Curtis had checked Barbara into Miranda's four-star rehab clinic. Too exhausted to think clearly, Anika tried to make the details jive. For all her faults, Barbara knew how to operate a phone. Had she returned home to find her house empty, wouldn't she have called Anika first? Barbara, however, didn't even know Anika had returned home. Anika couldn't say with certainty—her mom's behavior being predictably unpredictable—but she had a nagging suspicion Barbara didn't make first contact with Dodd. More likely, Dodd's Gestapo had staked out her house, waited for her to return, and spirited her away to be used as leverage.

For now, though, all was well with Mom. Medical providers and clinicians cared for her; she was safe and sound. Anika and Sam could visit her anytime their schedules permitted and their hearts desired . . . during visiting hours, of course.

Ready for her day's next challenge, Anika asked, "What now?"

"We need to announce you as acting mayor," Curtis said.

"You're joking, right? That's not funny."

"Your title is assistant to the mayor. According to local ordinance, that makes you next in line. Law says that in case the mayor can no longer carry out—"

"No! This is nuts. You can't just name me acting mayor and—"

"Ain't namin' you anything. By law, you're already acting mayor. The real mayor can no longer carry out her duties. That's black and white code."

"Why can't *you* do it?" she asked.

"Rules is rules, and I ain't pretty, well-spoken, or smart like you."

She pondered whether it was less about following rules and more about Curtis salvaging his own reputation. "I don't want this, Curtis. People will throw a fit, even those who like me. Not long ago, I babysat some of their kids for gas money."

"Let me explain the—"

"I'm *way* too young . . . with no relevant experience. I hate politics, especially the small-town variety. And I don't have time for this. I need to get Sam out of this town before it's too late."

"Things don't work like that, Anika," he said impatiently, wagging his finger at her, his tone one of clear warning. "Can't have the town's leaders runnin' off during a crisis."

"Miranda's no cosmopolitan center, but it's not Podunk either. There must be a better way to—"

"Look," he emphasized, "we're talkin' days, not weeks. Get through the hurricane and hang up your spurs. Ordinance calls for a special election in a month's time. People will understand your role as a gap-filler in a pinch, and they'll tolerate you if Cyclops blesses it. We'll ask him to swear you in. He ain't got no formal authority, but he does have plenty of influence 'round these here parts."

Anika chewed her fingernails while contemplating her options. For now, Curtis's sinister warning had dashed any hopes of skipping town with Sam. The town—the townsfolk—had thwarted her every attempt to leave, and Curtis would be of no help because he was hardwired to do the town's bidding. If she couldn't leave, then her best option—likely her only option—was to be in charge. "Will you ask Cyclops to come in?"

"I'll do what you say, Anika, but I recommend you walk out on the porch . . . as a show of respect."

"You want me to kiss the ring?"

"Ain't gonna hurt you none to kiss a few rings until you get settled."

"That's wise counsel, Curtis."

Curtis waited for Anika and Sam to exit the office before he followed them. Passing the Buffalo Bar, Anika winked at Timmy, wondering if he'd predicted this moment. His mouth agape, he stared at her like royalty. Once she flung open the swinging doors and marched onto the front porch, the *koya* overtook her, this time in a positive way. She felt invigorated—like heroic knights from Camelot were carrying her on their shoulders—without the slightest hint of nervousness.

As if on cue, Timmy cranked up the volume, testing the limits of the front porch speakers. The music caught the neighborhood's attention. On the porch, Cyclops and Moon charted the new tropical disturbance on the hurricane tracking map. They didn't need cubes on napkins to convince them the big one was coming. Some things you just knew. Despite their important work, they stopped, smiled, and watched Anika's grand entrance.

Onlookers beyond the porch, throughout Four Points, gathered closer to the Alamo. Rumors swirled about Auntie Dodd's demise. The late-night scuttlebutt spoke in terms of "homicide," whereas the morning gossipers dropped the term "murder" as if a jury had already returned a verdict in a heretofore unopened case.

Whatever the cause or crime, the town's citizens processed the sudden death of their leader in different ways. Some protesters blew in the wind like discarded trash. They decried a corrupt political system where a tenderfoot—a "baby!" they shouted—could govern. Ironically, they sought "vengeance!" or "justice!" for a woman whom, a day earlier, they'd rallied to unseat. Others welcomed the transfer of power and mumbled meaningless nothings like, "May Dodd rest in peace." Many in Miranda loathed politics. Some of those folks made the sign of the cross and quickly moved on. Some prayed for sundry things. Still others secretly rejoiced and wished that little people would appear out of nowhere and start singing, "Ding-Dong! The Witch Is Dead."

Anika stood before them all, the centerpiece of the prodigious porch—a porch that was now the true stage of the Alamo Opera House. She wasn't wearing a dress or tiara, but it was a coronation nonetheless, a far cry from the perfunctory administrivia Curtis had foreshadowed in her office. She stood before the gathering multitudes in torn jeans, Chuck Taylor shoes, and a T-shirt with the face of Charles Manson on the front. Emblazoned on the back of the shirt were the words "Charlie Don't Surf," a wordplay on Lieutenant Colonel Kilroy's declaration in the film *Apocalypse Now*.

The music died, and Curtis moved toward the business in order. "Cy, she'd like for you to do the honors."

"Mighty honored, Curtis," Cyclops said. He tipped his hat to Anika. "Ma'am."

"Someone slide me that chair over yonder," Curtis directed. "Anika, you stand on this while you take the oath."

"Gonna need a Bible, Curtis," Cyclops said as Anika climbed onto the wooden chair. A Texas flag hanging on the porch snapped in the morning wind. "King James preferably."

"Timmy's got one of them New King James Bibles behind the bar. Reckon that'll do?"

"Reckon so," Cyclops said, slapping his hands together in excitement. "Let's get this show on the road!"

"Ready when you are," Anika said, her ponytail draped over the front of her shoulders as she stood like a statue despite the formidable wind gusts.

Anika nearly forgot she was standing on the chair as she scanned the horizon at Four Points. Beyond the protesters, she saw hundreds in the crowd, including familiar faces. Word had spread like COVID-19 of the big event at the Alamo. She noticed former classmates and teachers from Miranda High. She saw school children, all dressed in bright orange shirts, on a field trip to Revolutionary Park. She recognized proprietors from the local shops and eateries. Surprised to see him, she waved to Joshua. Her impromptu installation had interrupted his jog around the park with Calvin and Luther.

Before her attention wandered back to the Alamo, she witnessed Logan parking Sarah Danforth's Range Rover outside of her boutique. His sickening chivalry commenced once again, a product of being henpecked or, worse, flogged with a gold-plated cat o' nine tails. He exited the driver's side, walked around the vehicle, and opened the door for his wife. She grabbed his hand and stepped out. They stopped and stared at Anika as she stood on the chair—on the grand stage. Anika licked her top front teeth, took a deep breath, and cast her eyes on Cyclops.

"Anika Raven," he said, reciting off the cuff, "do you solemnly swear that you will faithfully execute the office of Acting Mayor of Miranda, Texas, and will, to the best of your ability, preserve, protect and defend the people of this here town?"

"I do."

"That you will bear true faith and allegiance to the same?"

"I do."

"That you take this obligation freely, without any mental reservation or purpose of evasion?"

"I do."

"That you'll build a jail facility big enough to hold all them wacko protesters over yonder?"

"Cyclops!" Curtis snapped.

"Bygones, C-Dub. Couldn't help myself," Cyclops laughed. "Now, Anika Raven, by the honor vested in me as leader of the Miranda Old Timers, I now pronounce you acting mayor of this town!"

"This ain't no weddin', Cy," Curtis said, shaking his head in disgust.

"She's official, ain't she?"

"Reckon she is," Curtis said.

"Let the big dog eat!" Cyclops yelled.

"Congratulations, Anika!" Curtis said, walking toward the swinging doors. "Time to get to work!"

"Might've been the best show ever performed at this here Opera House," Moon said.

But Anika, who continued to stand on the chair, wasn't paying close attention. She was too busy basking in the morning glow, too busy riding on the wings of the *koya*, too busy taking in her moment and, for a few more seconds, forgetting about the challenges ahead. She was too busy smiling at Sarah Danforth.

But Sarah wasn't smiling back.

30

To celebrate Anika's installation, Timmy's free catering included Lone Star beer on tap and *huevos a la Mexicana*—scrambled eggs colored like the Mexican flag with tomatoes, onions, and jalapenos. Unless one was an alcoholic, beer in the morning and beer served with eggs weren't familiar doubles partners. But that didn't matter. The line entering the Alamo General Store snaked onto the porch, slithered down the steps, and stretched its long tail down the road. Wind gusts becoming more frequent, bystanders witnessed an occasional straw cowboy hat tumbling on the lawn. Inside the General Store and spilling into the Commons, the lively townsfolk chinked glass mugs and raised their voices in hopeful scuttlebutt.

Off the porch, Cyrus Kleberg looked like a zebra at the rodeo. Anika suggested that, in her role as mayor, she meet with him first. Cowboy hat in hand, along with a weathered leather portfolio, he shuffled into Anika's office like Luca Brasi in a meeting with Don Corleone. Anika, seeing that he'd lost his trademark swagger, wondered if the *koya* was affecting him. Curtis nodded to the old timer, indicating he could take a seat.

"Mayor Raven," Cyclops said, issuing a quick nod in salute. He noticed Sam on the couch drawing cubes. "We good?"

"I don't keep secrets from her," Anika said, knowing that wasn't true. She still hadn't told Sam about the tumor, which was the biggest secret in the room.

"You're good, Cy," Curtis added, "but there ain't gonna be no cussin' in front of that girl, you hear?"

"I hear pretty good for ninety-plus, C-Dub," he said, playing with his hearing aid until it made a piercing, high-pitched noise. He turned it off, looked at Anika, and smiled. "That's how I manage my selective hearing."

"Thanks for swearing me in, Cyclops."

"My pleasure, darlin'," Cyclops said. "Not for nothin', I figured Mayor Dodd was too mean to die." He pointed at the credenza behind Anika. "I see you already have your pictures up. I recognize the girl with the microphone, but her name escapes me."

"That's Selena."

"Oh, yes. The famous singer who was killed. Was she a family friend or—"

"Idolized her growing up. Famous hometown girl. Get you a beer?"

"I usually wait until lunch to start tuggin' on the jug. Just got three things. Reckon you've heard us talk about the storm?"

"Auntie Dodd told me it would destroy everything," Anika acknowledged.

"For all her faults, she was dead right about that."

"How long?"

"Storm's on its way. Be here in days, not weeks."

"Can you be more specific?" Anika asked.

Cyclops looked at Sam. "No, but I betcha that little girl can."

"Mayor," Curtis said, "we don't need more intel for this one. If we're confident it's the big one, then we can predict within a day or two how long it takes to travel."

"What's your prediction?" Anika asked.

"She's already five days old," Cyclops said.

"Right," Curtis said. "We got another five days."

"Five days!" Anika said, though it sounded more like a question.

"Maybe six if we're lucky," Cyclops added.

"Luck ain't got nothin' to do with it," Curtis said.

"So everything we do from this point forward," Anika said, "is based on T minus five days."

"Y'all need a plan," Cyclops said.

"Curtis," Anika said, "did Dodd have an evacuation plan?"

"Mostly in her head. Hinged on gettin' town leaders like Ricky and LeSean on board. Start convincin' their people to get out. I doubt she figured that effort would end up with protesters sleepin' in the park."

"I'm not done talking with Ricky and LeSean," Anika said. "Can't we just start with a mandatory evacuation order and see where that gets us?"

"Won't getcha far," Cyclops said. "Those who leave'll be branded cowards. People don't leave Miranda for no storm."

"They might change their minds when they learn a Cat 5's about to take them out."

"The town don't like people leavin'," Cyclops said.

"What do you mean by *the town*? You expect me to believe the town's alive? You're asking me to make decisions based on fairy tales?"

"Call 'em like I see 'em, ma'am."

"Don't matter whether you call it a fairy tale," Curtis said. "People have things baked into their DNA."

"To be honest, Cyclops," Anika said, "I think it's your old timers who keep people from leaving."

"They do what I tell 'em to do," Cyclops said.

"You tell them to follow me?"

"Yes, ma'am."

"And to prevent me from leaving town?"

"Yes, ma'am."

"Because the mayor told you to?"

"Yes, ma'am."

"You gonna keep following me?"

Cyclops looked at Curtis, who gave no direction. "No, ma'am. Reckon not."

"So I'm free to leave town?"

"Wouldn't suggest you try that, Mayor," Curtis interjected. "That's enough talk of treason. You just swore an oath to protect these townsfolk, and we got a lotta work ahead. And I'm fine sayin' the supernatural ain't got no place here, but Sam will play a role. Her gift may be the difference."

Hearing her name, Sam looked up, oscillated her eyebrows, and smiled a devious grin.

"Long way to go and a short time to get there," Cyclops added.

"Cy, anything else for the mayor?" Curtis prodded.

"Want y'all to know that us old timers don't plan to evacuate."

"So much for leading by example," Anika said. "You're starting off this relationship by disobeying orders?"

"Rather not. I'm requesting—in advance, of course—a medical exemption for everyone over eighty."

Anika regarded the gravity of the old timers' request. They were prepared for death. If she agreed to it, Cyclops and many others would likely be dead in five days.

"Most of us will die anyways . . . making a trip like that," Cyclops continued. "We can barely make it to the bathroom, much less Temple or Waco."

"Done," she said. "Curtis, make sure my order includes the exemption."

Curtis nodded. "Reckon you want me to dig you a grave, old man," he said, raising his voice in irritation. "You never was easy."

"Bury me under the porch before you rebuild it," Cyclops goaded.

"And if I can't find you? I figure you'll be washed out in the Gulf of Mexico. Just an old man and the sea."

"In that case, bury my cowboy hat. And pass along my tall tales to the young 'uns . . . just them stories that make me look good."

"That's a short book," Curtis responded matter-of-factly, "but you have my word."

Cyclops nodded at Curtis, put on his hat, and stood up. "I thank you, Mayor."

"I may need a beer after this," she said, eyeing the portfolio. "Hey, you said you had *three* things."

"Reckon so," Cyclops said, sitting back down, sliding the portfolio across the desk. "Must've escaped my mind. Photos from the surveillance you requested."

Anika stared at him before pulling out the photos. "Will I be surprised, Cyclops?"

"Fixin' to find out."

31

The photography was stellar, the photos salacious. "Did they notice him?" Anika asked. "The one taking the pictures?"

Cyclops shook his head. "No, ma'am. Peanut's a true pro. Had he been in Dallas in '63 instead of that Zapruder feller, we'd know who really killed Kennedy."

"Curtis, have you seen these?" she asked.

"Cy showed me this morning."

Sarah Danforth is pure trash, Anika thought. *More than just a home-wrecker—a* family *wrecker. What has she done? What has* he *done?*

After a long pause, Cyclops said, "Ma'am?"

Anika couldn't tear her eyes from the photos. Exhaling, she responded, "I'm not surprised by the affair . . . or the people involved. I am surprised by the carnality of it all. I expected to see them kissing. But not—"

"No, them two ran straight past second base, rounded third, and slid into home."

"These photos are breathtaking—in a bad way," she said, still eyeing the photos and ignoring Cyclops's comment. "Maybe *heartbreaking* is the better word."

"What else you need from me, Mayor?" Cyclops asked.

"Anyone have a recommendation? Curtis?"

"Leave it alone," he said. "Last thing we need right now is to chase varmints down rabbit trails."

"Afraid I can't do that," she said.

"They'll be evacuated or dead anyway in five days," he said.

"But I couldn't live with myself . . . assuming I make it out alive."

"Break the news after we've weathered the storm," Curtis urged.

"Doubt I could live with myself for even five days. Sorry."

"At least let the old timers crank up the rumor mill," Curtis offered, "and leak a photo somewhere."

"I'm fine with your men handling this, Cyclops, but I'm not interested in rumors and gossip. I want something more direct . . . in her face."

"We can leave the photos in the front seat of her husband's truck," Cyclops said.

Anika smiled. "I like that."

"That'll bring things to a boil," Cyclops surmised. "Force him to confront his wife and that other feller, his brother. That should take care of everything."

"Not everything," Anika said. "I want Ethan's girlfriend to see the photos."

"That buck's got doe chasin' him all over the ranch," Cyclops said. "Not sure which one he belongs to."

"Her name's Amber. She's the tall one with green eyes. The one who watches him like a mom watches a baby at the beach."

"Didn't watch him close enough," Cyclops retorted.

"Ethan can't be caged," Anika said.

"Reckon he stays in rut all year long?"

"He doesn't know any better, and no one's gonna change him . . . certainly not a beach bunny hooked on heroin."

"You know what she drives?" Cyclops asked.

"VW bug," Anika said. "You'll find it parked in Ethan's driveway. Has a license plate that reads 'Hard Candy' without the vowels." *HRDCNDY.* "Barf."

"We'll take care of it," Cyclops said.

"And I'll take care of the leadership problem at the MIC," Anika added.

"How so?" Curtis asked, his voice revealing concern.

"Need to visit Ricky and LeSean again. Now that I'm acting mayor, they might listen."

"I'll go with you," Curtis said.

"You can't go with me. You—" She stopped before mentioning that Curtis had killed Ricky's dog and was *persona non grata* at the MIC. She didn't know how much Cyclops knew of Curtis's dark side. For that matter, for all his skeletons she knew about, she wasn't sure she'd seen the darkest parts. "They don't trust you, and I need to rebuild their trust in this office."

"You ain't goin' to the scene of the crime," he declared. "Those men are prime suspects in Dodd's murder. Not much happens at the MIC without their knowin' or doin'."

"Them two fellers is plum dangerous," Cyclops added.

"Appreciate your courage, Mayor," Curtis continued, "but you can't make reckless decisions in your position. You need to protect the office and follow the process."

A true dyed-in-the-wool bureaucrat, Anika thought. *Doesn't he know that process ain't got nothin' to do with it?* "Thanks for the 'safety moment,' guys. But if by 'process' you mean they should meet me here, in my office, then we're tossing process out the window. Those optics are terrible. Looks like a pure power play. Do I have any leverage other than brute force?"

"Not much pre-storm," Cyclops said. "Too late to issue munis."

Anika's face, revealing incomprehension, turned to Curtis, who responded, "Municipal bonds. We considered sustainin' their cash flow as an incentive to close early and evacuate. Dodd vetoed the idea. She didn't want to reward bad behavior. Thought Ricky and LeSean were puttin' profits over safety. She couldn't get past their failure to act voluntarily, to consider the best interest of the town."

"Great," Anika said facetiously. "Looks like our only hope rests on my negotiating skills. And as Cyclops likes to point out, I didn't even attend law school. Curtis, tell them that I'd like to meet for lunch in the park."

"Park's full of protesters," Curtis said, flapping his arms. "If somethin' goes down, we'll be outnumbered."

"We don't have time to play chess," she said. "This needs to happen today."

"I don't like it," Curtis grumbled.

"She's gonna be more vulnerable than Kennedy at Dealey Plaza," Cyclops added.

"You're worried about an assassin lurking in the trees?" Anika asked with a grin.

"No, ma'am," Cyclops said, his eyes open wide. "I'm worried about paid conspirators hiding behind grassy knolls."

"I'll be fine," Anika said, standing up to see them out. "And, Curtis, keep the cavalry at bay, would you? I don't need a strong police presence in the park."

"We'll see," he grunted, clearly unaccustomed to being overruled on matters of security.

32

Before digesting their breakfast and shaking off their morning buzz, the protesters' ostensible fury returned. Anika agreed with Curtis's hunch that Ricky and LeSean had bankrolled the band of professional fusspots. The leaders of the Miranda Industrial Complex, it was clear, originally paid them to influence Auntie Dodd. Of course, anyone who'd spent more than five minutes with the former mayor knew such antics would backfire. Dissent only had hardened her resolve. *Let them eat cake!*

Ricky and LeSean now turned their hired guns on Anika. Satiating the demonstrators' ambition with tacos and *cervezas* only prolonged the inevitable call on performance. They scribbled new slogans on old signs. They set up makeshift drum kits, warmed their vocal chords, and turned up the volume. All this for another day of fussing and false outrage. It wasn't a coincidence that protester energy had increased soon after Curtis had brokered today's meeting in Revolutionary Park. For two guys who loathed small-town politics, the MIC leaders had mastered the tradecraft.

As she crossed the street, adrenaline rushed through Anika's veins. She felt alive for the first time in years. She marched into the heart of the crowd like she was cruising down an incline on roller skates. Intermittent, violent gusts of wind blew her hair, but they failed to disrupt her resolve or cadence. The protesters—taken aback by her courage—stopped their chanting and parted like the Red Sea. Anika eyed her enemies one by one, head to toe, not letting anyone escape her scrutinizing glare. Walking through their disregarded trash, Anika smelled a mixture of salsa, pot, and musky body odor as she trekked to the park's nucleus.

Before leaving the crowd, however, she stopped short of a middle-aged protester with glasses and bushy hair. The woman wore a *Johnny Lives!* T-shirt. Anika felt the heat intensify on her face and under her skin. Her hands clenched into fists, her heartbeat quickened, and her instincts begged her to pounce. Instead, a calm rushed over her. Her hands relaxed, and her breathing slowed. She regarded her situation. Hadn't she committed to be a better person? To be more merciful? Her new position, without a doubt, required it. And wasn't she guilty of a similar offense, wearing a T-shirt with Charles Manson's face on the front? What would his victims' families think of her callousness? She walked on.

Walking deeper into the park, she heard the whining trill (as Bob Dylan described it) of cicadas, and her feelings for Johnny bubbled to the fore. This location exacerbated her emotional pain. The couple had logged many hours among these trees. She remembered their strolls around the park's perimeter, holding hands. She recalled the picnics underneath the largest oak tree near the park's center. She remembered the pull on her heartstrings when Johnny said the "*L* word" for the first time; when he handed her his graduation ring; when they broke out in laughter, realizing the ring was too heavy for her necklace. Her eyes betrayed her, but she wasn't about to cry. Not with everyone watching. No way.

Anika's trip down Memory Lane ended when she spied three sheriff's deputies on horseback. Curtis had positioned them on the outskirts of the park in a triangular formation. As such, he had complied with the details, if not the spirit, of Anika's order. Two of the officers surveilled the park, looking for trouble; meanwhile, Deputy Carl watched Anika's every move. Though she suspected Sheriff Peter Karnes was lurking nearby, she hadn't spotted him.

Karnes concerned her. He liked working behind the scenes. They had never met proper (as Curtis would say), but she knew he'd played a heavy hand in framing her five years ago. Whether her promotion caused him discomfort was of no moment. She now oversaw the police force. Karnes reported to her. She didn't need to kiss his ring (or anything else for that matter). He was accountable to her, yet he hadn't surfaced since before her mayoral installation. She couldn't decide whether to attribute his absence to laziness, ego, protest, or something more sinister. A part of her wished he'd remain hidden in the shadows. He didn't play the role of Miranda's Wizard of Oz, but he had enough power to facilitate or frustrate her plans.

As for Curtis, he was a nervous wreck and unhappy that Anika had refused protective detail. She was traveling into hostile territory on her own. That never happened on his watch, but she had overruled every one of his objections. To be effective in her new role, she needed to exude bravery and strength. An armed escort sent the opposite message. To show her appreciation for his willingness to compromise, she turned around and blew him a kiss as he paced the Alamo's front porch. Unamused by her silliness, his boots didn't break stride, wearing a hole in the plywood.

She meandered east of the park, toward Blouses and Boots Boutique, and loitered outside the store. She softly wolf-whistled to herself, coveting the Lucchese boots through the window—boots that Sarah implied Anika could never afford, boots still beckoning their would-be Cinderella. Beyond the window display, in the middle of the store, Sarah spoke on the phone, waving her hands around. She didn't see Anika, and Anika wondered if she was speaking to Logan . . . or Ethan. Was Sarah already undermining Anika's mayoral authority? Sarah wasn't about to pay homage or have Anika shift the power dynamic. No way the SEC cheerleader would take a backseat to Barrio Barbie and her small-town homecoming crown. But Sarah would soon learn a hard lesson. In the chess game of life, the queen wields the most power.

Anika, even from the park, could see the gaudy painting of Cheerleader Sarah on the store's back wall. Towering over the store, it drew attention away from the high-end products for sale. That, of course, was the point. Sarah didn't operate a boutique primarily to sell blouses, boots, and Western whatnots. She didn't need the money; she didn't care about serving customers. She was selling her brand, crafting her image. Any customers who walked into that store served *her*. In Sarah's world, everything and everyone revolved around Daddy's little girl. She was a woman, it seemed, who got whatever she wanted, whenever she wanted it.

But that was about to change. If the old timers followed Anika's orders, Sarah the Homewrecker's world was hours away from being dropped, kicked, and launched in the opposite direction. Her Highness had no clue what was coming.

Familiar voices pulled Anika from her trance. Ricky and LeSean had arrived, and she re-entered the park for her meeting. There would be no cheeky kisses or other genuine pleasantries this time. The two men sat opposite Anika at the wooden picnic table, hands in their laps.

"Missed you at the installation," Anika began.

"Our beef's not with you, Anika," LeSean said. "We just wanna be left alone."

"Send your protesters home."

LeSean looked at Ricky, who stared at Anika with his arms crossed.

"I'm not an idiot," Anika continued. "And I wouldn't mind you exercising your right to free speech if your protesters didn't throw projectiles at my office and crew."

"Will you continue Dodd's pressure campaign to evacuate the town?" LeSean asked.

"Yes, and I'm upping the ante. Unlike my predecessor, I genuinely care about human lives. We'll be issuing a mandatory evacuation order this afternoon."

Ricky spoke his first words. "Meet the new boss, same as the old boss."

"Guys, we have *five days* to evacuate. Less than *one week*, and this town's toast."

"Who fed you that hogwash?" LeSean asked. "Have you seen the latest weather reports? There's no imminent threat whatsoever."

"Long-term projections have the storm curving north over Cuba and driving up the East Coast," Ricky added.

"I have my own experts who say it's coming right for us," Anika said. "Head-on."

"What experts?" LeSean asked. "Who's telling you this? Senile old men drawing pictures on napkins?"

"Wise counselors," she replied half-heartedly.

"Those of us who oversee the MIC are business leaders, Anika," LeSean explained. "We're responsible for people's livelihoods. We allow families to put bread on the table; we provide wages for room and board. We rely on scientists, not fortune tellers."

"If you'd attended my installation, you'd know that I'm now responsible for people's safety."

"Sorry we missed your flashbulb moment," Ricky carped.

"Let's not get crossways over this," she said. "Our friendship runs too deep, and I'm considering the best inputs available."

"The best inputs are the most reliable inputs," LeSean said. "Not the loudest voices or squeakiest wheels. Certainly not a bunch of hot air bloviated by fanatics. You can't run a town and protect people's safety relying on Ouija boards and tarot cards."

"I can't believe we're having this conversation," Ricky piled on. "I feel like I'm in the *Twilight Zone*."

Anika huffed. LeSean's arguments made perfect sense and should've carried the day. Reliable inputs, no doubt, were the best inputs, and leaders shouldn't be swayed by carneys, swindlers, and town fools. But she was convinced otherwise. She believed LeSean, Ricky, and all the meteorologists in South Texas were dead wrong. "Ricky, I'm just telling you what—"

"No, I've heard enough," Ricky said, standing up. "The Anika I knew was better than this."

"Wait a second, Ricky," LeSean implored, holding out his arm across Ricky's legs. "Anika is family."

"Anika *was* family! Now she's the enemy!"

Anika refused to cower, and her restraint had reached its end. "What a pathetic joke you've become, Ricky! A false caricature of a gangster from the wharf. You're no longer the smart, caring friend I grew up with. What happened to *that* Ricky? All *this* Ricky does is fuss and whine and bully people weaker than himself—all problems, no solutions!"

"Oh, I have solutions!" he said, storming off. "I'm the king of solving problems! Unlike you, I eliminate them before they fester!"

Anika's filter fell off her mouth. "Is that why you eliminated Auntie Dodd?"

Ricky turned around with psychotic eyes. "What did you say?"

"Mister problem solver. Her body was found in your backyard. Care to explain?"

"You're accusing me of killing Dodd?"

"Brother and sister, please!" LeSean said.

Anika stood up to match Ricky face-to-face. "Her body was swinging in your train car. Motive, opportunity, location. Slam dunk."

"You'll never find evidence that I put her life in danger," Ricky said.

"We'll see about that."

"Anika, you're out of line," LeSean added as he stood up to join Ricky.

"How dare you accuse me of murder?" Ricky said. "You're dead to me. Stay off my property . . . or else."

"Sounds like another actionable threat."

"I'm nowhere close to your greatest threat, *Mother*," Ricky seethed, looking past Anika, into the distance, at the man pacing on the Alamo porch. "But I know who is."

33

As the South Texas sun called it a day, Anika, still reeling from her conversation with Ricky and LeSean, reviewed the draft executive order on mandatory evacuations. Her office smelled of flea market popcorn and salted caramel from Timmy's buttery craftwork at the Buffalo Bar. Sam's wrists, meanwhile, worked the Rubik's Cube puzzle on the office couch. Curtis waited patiently in the chair in front of Anika's desk as protesters outside threw rocks that pelted the side of the building.

"This looks good, Curtis," Anika said, handing him the order. "I made two changes. You're sure the age exemption is a good idea?"

"They ain't leavin' anyways, Mayor, so I'd rather not force 'em into insubordination. What about the MIC?"

"I made things worse. They're stubborn, angry, and . . ." She rolled her eyes. "I don't know."

"And dangerous," he said as rocks continued to smash against the Alamo.

"I did challenge them on Dodd's death. Accused Ricky and his Miranda Underground of murder, in fact."

"And?"

"Palms in the air. No hint of suspicion."

"Not a surprise," Curtis said, without any pause or self-reflection whatsoever. "Natural-born killers have zero emotions."

Anika tried not to betray her thoughts. She knew Curtis had killed Sam's dad. As helpful as he'd become to her, she couldn't rule out that he'd also killed Dodd. Anika had no idea as to his motive. He had referred to Dodd as a "runner" and "traitor," but that didn't warrant capital punishment. That he also called Dodd's actions "treason" wasn't something she wanted to consider. Other priorities stared right at her, and time was of the essence. Sam needed immediate medical attention. The hurricane would arrive in four days, and most of the residents remained in town. "I'll let the investigation run its course. I'm more concerned about Ricky and LeSean not evacuating their employees. Do you have any good ideas?"

"Investigation's ongoing," Curtis said, "but I'll make sure it's wrapped up soon. May solve our problems."

A rock the size of an apple crashed through the window!

Anika screamed. Sam dropped the Rubik's Cube and grabbed Faux Pooh. The imbecilic guffaws and groanings of protesters became louder with the window shattered.

Curtis rose to his feet. "I know I sound like a broken record, but it's time, Mayor. The Alamo jail won't hold 'em all."

"Just make them stop," she said, frazzled, her head buried in her hands.

"Fixin' to stop 'em for the night, but unless we do somethin' else, they'll be back at it in the mornin'."

He stared at her, but she refused to make eye contact, not wanting to approve the next step.

"We can build it in two days," he continued, "and I don't see another option at this point."

"Fine . . . but call it something other than a jail or internment camp."

"We can call it the Four Seasons at Four Points for all I care," he grumbled and waddled away like an aged bull rider. He exited the office toward the front porch to tamp down the protests. On his way out, he barked at Timmy, "Fix the mayor's window, you hear?"

As Anika considered her latest order and what lay ahead, she fidgeted with her upper lip and gazed at her sister. "You okay, Samantha?"

Sam nodded but still looked spooked.

Anika wanted to scream again, this time out of frustration. She knew Sam wasn't okay. Sam's life hung in the balance, and Anika couldn't do a thing to help her. *Paralyzed.* The town held them hostage, and no local doctor had the quals to care for Sam. Anika heard Curtis threatening the protesters' lives, including the lives of their offspring. Some protesters showed more courage but less wisdom than others. Eventually, however, they all came to their senses, put down the rocks, and quieted down. Even those with half a brain knew not to trifle with Curtis. Anika knew this firsthand as she contemplated her escape from town—beyond Texas, beyond Arkansas, into Tennessee, into Memphis, into the care of the medical professionals at St. Jude's Children's Hospital. Curtis would be accommodating, it seemed, so long as she did what he wanted—what *Miranda* wanted. But that all would change if she went against him—went against *them*. She couldn't purge the thought from her head: *Is that what happened to Auntie Dodd? The runner? Did the old timers catch her trying to escape town?*

After the crowd hit pause and relaxed, Anika heard the squeaky swinging doors, along with voices. She almost fell from her chair when Curtis reentered her office, this time escorting Logan Danforth. Logan's knees were wobbly, his face puffy, and his eyes bloodshot from bawling. The news was out.

"Mayor, Mr. Danforth's here to see you. I found him in the fetal position on the porch, dodging rocks. He doesn't have an appointment, but—"

"He doesn't need one," she said, walking around her desk.

Curtis nodded, businesslike, and left the room.

"Anika," Logan said, "I was—"

"Come here, darlin'," Anika said, embracing Logan and whispering in his ear. "I heard what happened. Wanna talk about it?"

"No," he said, squeezing her in half, liquor on his breath, tears streaming down his face, his voice broken, "but I need a place to crash."

Of course you do, Anika thought. *When will you learn? She cheats on you, and you're the one kicked to the curb?* "We have rooms upstairs, three unoccupied. Take your pick."

"My own flesh and blood!" he screamed in a childlike outburst, clinging to Anika and startling Sam. "My selfish little brother! It was bad enough that he moved in on *you*. But my wife? Unacceptable!"

Anika couldn't help herself. She couldn't stand by idly while Logan excused Her Highness from this affair. "Sarah's to blame for this, Logan. Ethan's a fool and should be held accountable, but Sarah's the real problem. She's a *femme fatale*. Ethan's a simpleton—no match for her aggressive and manipulative plays."

Anika couldn't detect if Logan was sober enough to process her words as he pivoted the conversation. "I wanna help you, Anika. I wanna help convince Mirandites that we need to evacuate. Let me work with you here until the hurricane passes."

"Of course," she said, disengaging from the hug and opening the office door. A perfect arrangement was taking root. Logan needed a temporary life diversion, and she only needed him temporarily. And part of her felt responsible for his pain. "Need all the help I can get. Hey, Curtis," she summoned, "will you help Logan get settled upstairs? He'll be working with us this week."

Curtis asked no questions. Anika watched him escort Logan away. Logan, haggard and worn, struggled to ascend the stairs with his tiny *Danforth Distributing* tote bag plopped over his shoulder. The bag wasn't big enough to hold a twelve-pack, just some toiletries and a few pairs of underwear. She wondered how much lifeblood Sarah had sucked from his soul. Anika would find out soon enough. Working alongside Logan, she would discern what remained of the man she'd once known. And she'd also learn more about his fallout with Her Highness: the cheerleader, boutique proprietor, and homewrecker. The one Logan married instead of Anika.

She knew her harsh feelings concerning the Danforth dilemma were inappropriate. She was trying to exhibit more mercy, be a better person. But it would have to wait until tomorrow. For now, her righteous indignation demanded a small taste of vengeance.

That brought a smile to her face. A devilish grin. Before she caught herself, she noticed Timmy smiling back at her, as if he could read her sinful thoughts. He winked.

She winked back.

34

The caliche rocks crackled like bones under the tires of the Black Ghost. The car rumbled to a stop at the Church Grounds lodge. Anika killed the engine and exited the vehicle, her eyes locked on Ethan's hippie mobile and Amber's bug in the parking lot. "Sam, stay here."

Luther and Calvin scrambled to their oversized feet. They approached Anika with happy breaths and intrusive noses. Joshua lay aside his guitar and said, "You looked official today at your installation, Anika. Pastors don't like to throw around the word 'pride' very often, but I was proud of you."

"Surprised to see you there. But I'm more surprised to see these Volkswagens in your parking lot. What's going on?"

"Logan's family stumbled into some turmoil today," Joshua said, "and I've agreed to help Ethan and his *friend-girl*, Amber."

Anika rolled her eyes at the euphemistic phrase "stumbled into some turmoil." *Is anyone going to confront the facts and be honest?* "Logan told me Sarah cheated on him," she said. "He's staying at the Alamo tonight. I'm struggling to understand your role in this *affair*?" She liked using that word—it carried a bite but not a punch.

"I've agreed to counsel them. Ethan promised his brother that he'd seek help through the grieving process."

Grieving process? "Okay, well . . . you know there's a humongous hurricane coming toward us. I just issued an order for mandatory evacuation. You have three days to pack up and hit the road."

"I heard about your order. I'll be working to convince members of my congregation to leave over the next several days."

"Are Ethan and Amber staying here together in the lodge?"

"In separate rooms," he emphasized.

"You know she's a user?"

"Saw the track marks on her arms . . . told her I wouldn't tolerate drug use. That's the one big rule."

"That, and the big rule of not visiting your bedroom, right?"

"Glad you remembered," he said, eyeing her suspiciously.

"Sounds like you have quite the task ahead of you, particularly when she starts withdrawals."

"Already started. She's curled up in her bed, sweating and shaking."

"Is the other beach bunny here? Chelsea?"

"No, they mentioned her, but I guess she's allergic to—"

"She's allergic to things that aren't fun," Anika interrupted. "And no offense, but hanging out with a pastor while your normally convenient friends get relationship counseling . . ."

"I get it," he chuckled. "I doubt that's anyone's idea of Disney World."

"I always thought of Chelsea as the ditsy, aloof one, always blowing in the wind and headed for trouble. But she's got a knack for avoiding drama and heartache. Starting to believe she's smarter than all of us."

"Is she also a user?" he asked.

"I'm told she smokes pot like a fiend. I'm not sure if she, like Amber, uses heroin."

"Wish me luck."

"Something tells me you don't believe in luck, Joshua."

"You're a wise mayor. You can pray for me. I will do the same for you. In our current roles, we'll both need providential guidance and protection."

"Ooh . . . 'mayor' sounds way too weird coming from you."

Joshua laughed.

"And I'm still working on this prayer thingy. So," she said, crawling back into the car and turning the key, "wish me luck."

Driving to the guest cottage, she thought about what Joshua had called the *grieving process*. She didn't like any of this. It was all too fishy. She didn't like that term, and she didn't like Joshua's counseling role. Invoking a pastor and using counseling terms made the affair appear more benign—

more like a disease than poor decision-making, more like an alcoholic's struggle with booze than two selfish adults getting caught under the sheets. Rationalization 101.

Joshua was being soft—even for a pastor . . . *especially* for a pastor. Anika understood her Bible well enough to know that consequences flowing from selfish decisions dated back to Eden. And Anika knew this much about redemptive history: the Book of Genesis made no mention of a *grieving process* when God booted Adam and Eve from the Garden for their original sin. God was merciful. God was gracious. God was loving. God was forgiving, according to his explicit terms. But He didn't offer counseling and put the scofflaws through a *grieving process*—unless the grieving process was our first ancestors' arduous trek through a life filled with pain, suffering, and death.

Worse yet, the accusing spotlight continued to shine on Ethan, not Sarah. That meant Sarah was manipulating the fallout. The guilty newly-wed—cornered like a filthy animal by her own treachery—was trying her hand at advanced puppet mastery. Why else would she, and not Logan, be allowed to stay inside their house? And why wasn't Joshua counseling Sarah and Logan? The married couple. Amber and Ethan, as Joshua himself acknowledged, weren't even boyfriend and girlfriend in the traditional sense. The answer was clear. Sarah was employing her brilliant talents at sleight of hand.

Logan was an easy mark for Her Highness's deception. Sarah would need to up her game, though, to avoid her deserved comeuppance. Anika's world had come crashing down after one kiss long ago. No amount of misdirection would allow Sarah, whose sin was exponentially greater, to pull a blameless rabbit out of the hat. And if she tried, Anika would be waiting, front row, with a crossbow and poison-tipped arrows.

Anika put Sam to sleep and spent the next two hours reflecting on her first day in office. As the clock struck midnight, she thought she might hear the roar of the Midnight Rider's engine. Perhaps, if he even existed, he was running drugs tonight without the lights on at death-defying speeds. She wondered how he'd escaped Miranda's borders. She thought, too, that she might hear the customary, haunting music of wolves, coyotes, and owls. But even the wild animals remained silent tonight. Tonight, only one sound skipped over the land and penetrated the skies. The blood-curdling screams of agony and addiction from the lodge. Amber's howling through withdrawals unsettled Anika at first. But after a few minutes, the harrowing cries comforted the new mayor, and the warm feeling of schadenfreude put her right to sleep.

35

"Top of the mornin', Mayor!" Cyrus Kleberg announced as Anika and Sam approached the Alamo, his cowboy hat in his lap allowing the morning breeze to blow the few strands of his white hair. "And a fine day to the beautiful gal with the yella hair."

"Morning, Cyclops," Anika said as Sam grabbed for her big sister's hand, cradled Faux Pooh, and stuck out her tongue. Walking up the porch steps, Anika observed that all but one protester, the one with the crazy eyes, was asleep. Crazy Eyes sat crisscross applesauce and watched Anika's every step without help from his painted glass eye. "What's the storm report?"

"Weather service has it missin' us and surgin' up the East Coast, on target to wipe out the Outer Banks in North Carolina."

"And what say you?" Anika asked.

"She's comin' right for us."

"Why do you say that? Just a hunch? I can't make life-changing decisions on a hunch."

"Some things you just know, Mayor."

"Are you relying on your cubes?"

"More on my gut."

"I just issued a controversial mandatory evacuation order based on your gut?"

"It's served me well for many a decade. But you don't need to rely on my intuition," he said, now staring at Sam, who was still clutching Anika's hand. "There's more reliable intelligence . . . at your fingertips."

"No doubt," Peanut said from the domino table. "All the clues you need are on Goldilocks's feet."

Anika glanced down at Sam's red boots. "The worst day of your life, Peanut, is my Wednesday."

"You holdin' a job fair today, Mayor?" Cyclops said, changing the subject.

"Talking about Logan Danforth?"

"Nah, the pretty one. Gal who looks like a mermaid from the movies, without all them gills and fins."

Anika shrugged. She and Sam walked inside the Alamo to the sound and smell of Timmy's sizzling bacon. "Good morning, Timmy," Anika said, noticing Logan in her old office, standing in front of the whiteboard and writing with an erasable marker. "Where's Curtis?"

"Garage," Timmy said, refusing to break eye contact with the work in front of him.

At that moment, Curtis emerged from the back and greeted Anika and Sam.

"What's Logan doing?" Anika asked.

"Rose before the sun," Curtis replied with a twinkle in his eye. The Alamo caretaker liked starting early. "Workin' on town messagin'."

"He's putting together a public relations strategy?"

"Your words are fancier than mine. By the way, you've gotta visitor in your office. Was fixin' to turn her away, but Logan vouched for her."

"Sarah Danforth?"

"Different one. You want me in there? Figure she's harmless. Says she wants a job."

"No, work with Sam. We need more clarity on the storm. Trained meteorologists are at odds with Cyclops's gut."

"I'll get her started on the graph paper, and then I'll brief you on the status of our investigation."

"Can't wait," Anika said, kissing Sam on the forehead before walking into the office. "Be good, kiddo. Curtis will help you draw today . . . maybe watch you make new patterns with the Rubik's Cube."

Anika had cobbled together enough clues to guess the identity of her guest—*the mermaid without gills or fins*—who sat on the couch with her arms crossed over her chest. "Didn't know if I'd ever see you again."

"Didn't know where else to go," Chelsea said.

"Go for what?"

"Purpose. I need a job."

"Do you have any skills?" Anika asked.

"I'm a quick learner."

"You didn't answer my question. We're in the throes of hurricane preparation and evacuation. I don't have time for charity, and I can't be distracted because your endless summer wasn't as advertised."

"Well," Chelsea explained. "I *was* the top salesperson at Endless Summer Surf Shop for two straight years."

"Of course you were," Anika responded. She hadn't meant it that way—she wasn't even thinking about Ethan's store—but sometimes the right words just worked on multiple levels. "What happened? If you were so successful, then why don't you still work for Ethan?"

"I quit so I could work at the Blouses and Boots Boutique. It's right down the road."

"I'm somewhat familiar with it."

"It was a considerable raise," Chelsea said.

"You work for Sarah Danforth?"

"I did. Technically, I was scheduled to start today. She fired me last night. After my interview, I never set foot in the store."

"What did you do?"

"Nothing, but she thinks I took incriminating pictures of her and Ethan."

"Why does she think that?" Anika asked.

"I was the only one at Ethan's bungalow when someone snuck the photos into Amber's stupid car."

Anika studied Chelsea. The old timers had found their patsy. Cyclops's apparatchiks, ruthless but effective, had orchestrated a photo dump that pulled any hounds off their trail. Not bad for local government work. To be sure, she did empathize with Chelsea. Authorities had framed her too—

five years ago. But she was in charge now and couldn't let tangential issues of fairness distract her. And given her current responsibilities, she couldn't let pity affect her decision-making or drive results.

"Wasn't me, though," Chelsea said. "Sarah's relationship with Ethan is none of my beeswax. Don't care; don't wanna know."

"I believe you." Anika yearned to ask more questions about Ethan and Sarah. *What do you mean by* relationship? *Did you know about the affair? How long has it gone on? Weren't you also seeing Ethan? How does that work? How many others were there? Did he ever tell you we kissed? What did you think about me wearing your clothes?* But she didn't. Maybe later. For now, she focused on the issue at hand. "Any other relevant experience?"

"Beach lifeguard, which shows that I'm dependable, responsible, and diligent."

And physically fit and strong, Anika thought, wondering what skills would be needed if a monster hurricane hit. "I'm assuming you didn't let anyone sink to the bottom," Anika said tongue-in-cheek, "or get sucked out to sea by the rip current." Chelsea's feud with Sarah made Anika like her even more.

"No, but I made a few saves."

"Anything else?"

"I cut hair. Really good with scissors."

Anika leaned over her desk. "Let me see your arms."

Chelsea revealed her tanned, slender arms. She had a tattoo of the Outlaw Josey Wales on her inner forearm. No signs of needle use.

"You can start right now on two conditions."

"Great! What conditions?" Chelsea asked.

"No more weed. And that's not me being judgy. I don't tolerate drugs. Our mission's too important, and I don't employ zombies. And second, I demand full loyalty. That may sound despotic, but I can't be looking over my shoulder at you, wondering whose side you're on. For all I know, Sarah sent you here to spy on me."

"I would never do that."

"Words don't matter in Miranda," Anika explained, "and your timing's suspicious."

"I don't want to seem suspicious. If there's nothing I can say," Chelsea said, "then how can I prove my loyalty?"

Anika regarded her question. "Do you remember seeing those fancy boots in the storeroom window when you interviewed with Sarah?"

"The Luccheses? Exquisite. But I'd have to work several months without food to afford those."

"Right," Anika said. "I want you to steal them and bring them to me."

"I'm sorry. What?"

"I need to know you're all in. Wanna prove your loyalty to me? *Steal* the boots. Bring them here. You have till this evening to figure out a plan. You have till tomorrow to execute it. By sundown tomorrow, we'll know where you stand."

"Wait, I don't wanna steal anything."

"You're not off to a good start, Chels. Listen, that sorry excuse for a human being, Sarah the Terror, fired you for no good reason. She cheated on her husband. She destroyed multiple relationships."

"Yeah, but—"

"But nothing!" Anika said, slamming down her fist. "Did you know that, because of Sarah, your friend Amber was screaming in agony last night at the Church Grounds? Sarah's a terrible person, Chels—a *home-wrecker*. This is what happens when we let outsiders into our town without the proper vetting. She has it coming."

"But I don't want to get arrested," she said, leaning forward on the couch and now whispering in an anxious tone. "I don't wanna go to jail."

"I thought you were an outlaw, *Chelsea Wales*. You think *Outlaw Josey Wales* worried about legal trouble? Besides, who do you think controls the police in this town?" Anika laughed, pointing to hers truly. "Come to think of it, once you pull this off, I might appoint you sheriff."

Chelsea looked at Anika as if the new mayor had become untethered from reality and lost her mind.

"Sheriff What's-His-Face had his deputies arrest me *twice* for no reason," Anika said, continuing her rant, flashing to Chelsea her jailhouse tattoo on her wrist, making clear who was the legitimate outlaw and who was the poseur in the room. "Bad call on his part."

"I don't know. This sounds sketcho."

"Call it what you want. If you want to work here, then you must be *all in*. I'm placing you on a probationary period until those boots are on my feet. If that doesn't happen by sundown tomorrow, then you're fired. If you pull off this daredevil caper," Anika said, pausing for effect, "then I'll quadruple what Sarah promised to pay you. And everyone at the Alamo will welcome you with open arms. Deal?"

Chelsea plopped her head on the couch pillows and looked to the ceiling, eyes wide, mulling over the radical offer. She clearly hadn't expected the job interview to unfold like this.

"Even if you don't trust me about the police," Anika added, "it's only petty theft if you get caught. Slap on the wrist. Maybe burglary if you hatch a plan at night that includes breaking and entering. Even in that case, though . . . two slaps on the wrist."

"I guess I'm all in," Chelsea said with reservation and a crooked smile.

"You wanna be the Outlaw Chelsea Wales, 'you gotta get mean. I mean plumb, mad-dog mean.'"

Anika grabbed a cup of coffee, walked back to her office, and sat down. She knew her conduct with Chelsea wasn't admirable and made her look no better than her predecessor. But she *was* better than Auntie Dodd and, given her outrageous predicament, was allowed some license to misbehave. Before she could take a sip, Curtis returned.

"I hear construction outside. Is that the detention facility?" Anika asked.

"Logan suggested we call it the Hospitality Center. Unless it rains, it'll be done by tomorrow."

"*Hospitality Center*? Curtis, that's very Goebbels-esque. Who made Logan Miranda's propaganda minister?"

"It's hospitality in the sense that we're givin' 'em grace."

"Grace?" She chuckled and rolled her eyes.

"We're givin' 'em grace because they ain't goin' to jail. They have time to think about it. Get that rebellion outta their system." Curtis paused for any questions. Hearing none, he continued. "Speaking of jail—"

"Yeah, what did your investigation find?" she asked.

"What did you *want* my investigation to find?"

Anika now understood how authorities had framed her so easily five years ago. Politics in Miranda was a contact sport like no other. "I'm listening."

"They found probable cause that Ricky killed Dodd."

"Okay," Anika said skeptically, "I'll need the details behind that finding."

"Doesn't mean he did it, but there's enough for an arrest."

"What about LeSean?"

"No evidence that he knew anything about the murder. In searchin' for clues, though, they found probable cause that LeSean's runnin' a meth lab. Again," Curtis said, measuring the reaction on Anika's face, "facts ain't airtight but enough to make an arrest."

However diabolical his methods, Curtis had solved her problem. He wasn't one to choose a sewing needle over an iron hammer, that's for sure. He didn't create; he destroyed. Anika saw right through this hit piece, though, and wasn't inclined to pursue it any further. Even during a crisis, Curtis's solution was a road too far. She was better than this.

"Chelsea tell you she's working for us?" Anika asked. "She speaks another dialect, but the word she'd use for your investigation is 'sketcho.'"

"With all due respect, Mayor, I'm afraid you underestimate the cunnin' of those men."

"Even when they lose their minds, Curtis, they're still my friends. You'll find that I'm a loyal person."

"But loyalty works both ways. You ever finish readin' that stack of papers on your desk? Ones you pulled from the safe?"

Anika didn't respond. She glanced at the pile of documents. She had only read the pages related to Johnny.

"In that pile, you'll find the interview notes of Ricky and LeSean. I suggest you read 'em before tossin' aside my investigative findings."

"Thought you said we didn't have time to chase rabbits."

"Okay, I'll tell you."

"Tell me what?" she asked.

"Them boys told the police you played a role in Johnny's death."

"What? That's preposterous!"

"Check the pile."

"Do you believe them?" Anika asked.

"No, I don't."

"Why not?"

"Because I know what happened to Johnny."

Anika rubbed her neck. "I spent five years in prison trying to figure out how I got framed for his death. They told me if my case went to trial, I could get life without parole. My shoddy public defender convinced me to cop a deal. Were you part of the investigation?"

"No, that was Sheriff Karnes's deputies working with the FBI. Dodd kept me out of it."

"I need to know. Why was there black tar heroin on the scene? Why did Johnny have explosives in his car? Did he commit suicide?"

"No," Curtis said, "it didn't go down like that."

"How did it go down?"

Curtis paused and locked eyes with Anika. "I killed him."

36

"Why did you just confess?" Anika asked, crushed. Her head pounded like she was sitting front row at a Rage Against the Machine concert.

"It's complicated," Curtis said, distracted by escalating voices outside, voices that drowned out the ongoing construction in the park.

"You murdered Johnny," Anika said, her lips trembling. "My love, my everything. And I was framed for it! You stole him from me, along with five years of my life!" Until now, she'd hoped in vain the *Bones Don't Burn* and *Johnny Lives!* T-shirts were true. She had hoped she was wrong about Curtis, who, despite his dark shadows, had treated her with respect. "I'm not sure it's that complicated."

"Let me explain before you draw conclusions," he said, distracted and looking with increased interest beyond the window.

"Explain?" Anika considered telling him she knew he killed Sam's dad. She even thought about accusing him of murdering Dodd, if only to confirm her growing suspicions. On second thought, however, she knew that cornering him wasn't wise, so she kept her emotions raw and to the point. "I hate you."

Curtis buried his face in his calloused hands, and when he looked at Anika again, she thought she saw tears. "You can hate me after you hear the entire story. Right now—"

A thundering crash! Screams erupting outside!

Curtis dashed out the door, past Timmy, and onto the porch. Anika followed with Logan, Chelsea, and Sam in tow. Anika watched the action unfold from the swinging doors.

189

Curtis grabbed the rope coiled around the wall hook. Stepping over Cyclops's cowboy hat and shattered glass, he walked crookedly but with purpose down the porch stairs into the grass, swinging the lasso over his head like a calf roper at the Miranda Rodeo. Machete in hand, Cyclops was a few yards from the protesters when Curtis let the lariat fly.

Curtis had no trouble landing it on target. The rope snaked around his friend's shoulders without a hitch. Curtis heaved on the rope and stopped his quarry in his tracks. Cyclops's thinning gray hair flung wildly in the wind as he writhed in anger, trying to cut the rope with his long blade. But the rope had straight-jacketed him, and he was now at Curtis's mercy. The liver spots on Cyclops's scalp shone in the morning sun as his heavy breaths increased with his labors to free himself.

"I've killed for less!" Cyclops ranted, scanning the crowd with psychopathic eyes.

"You best get back on that porch, you ol' dinosaur," Curtis directed, managing with massive effort to hold the lariat taut as two deputies on horseback arrived. "Y'all go on! I got this under control. Just a minor domestic dispute."

"It's a whole lot more than that, C-Dub! You best get Sheriff Karnes out here!" Cyclops screamed without breaking his stare at the protesters. "We got attempted murder of a senior citizen . . . and veteran!"

"It's 'bout time you simmered down, Cy," Curtis said. Unlike Cyclops, the deputies obeyed him and steered their horses back inside the park.

Cyclops didn't hide his disappointment. "Dinosaur yourself. It's about time you and the mayor brought order to this town. These no-account hoodlums tried to take off my head with that bottle. Yet, *I'm* the one you hog-tied?" Defeated, Cyclops walked to the porch. "Get this rope off me, you sorry excuse for a friend."

"Drop the machete first," Curtis demanded.

"Don't humiliate me. That's like makin' a golfer drop his drawers when he can't clear the women's tees. You're better than that."

"No more violence today, Cy."

After some hesitation, Cyclops said, "You got my word." Curtis released the rope. "But you ain't gettin' my sword."

"Bygones. You know who threw that bottle?"

"Not sure," Cyclops said as he thrust his machete into the large leather sheath attached to his back. "But if I had to guess right or die, I'd figure it's the one with crazy eyes. He's the son of that crooked harbormaster, bred too close to the water on the Lower East Side, a no-good wharf rat with a lowland dialect."

Curtis scanned the mob of protesters.

"What about that detention facility over yonder?" Cyclops asked, signaling that he had bigger plans for the protesters than taking one scalp. "Y'all finishin' that up today?"

"You got my word," Curtis promised. "Not much of a moon last night, but they worked 'round the clock under light towers. Made good progress."

Cyclops eyed the construction, nodded, and returned to the porch.

Staring at Crazy Eyes, Curtis coiled the rope and addressed the protesters. "Final warning. You can protest here in peace until the gale-force winds blow you away; but until then, there ain't gonna be no more violence. Another bottle takes flight and y'all are finished. Am I clear?"

Crazy Eyes stared back at Curtis with a pompous smirk.

"And clean up your trash," Curtis added. "If y'all keep makin' a mess of the park, then I'll declare you a public nuisance and haul you off. Bunch of warmongers and gangbangers."

As Curtis marched back to the Alamo, some protesters mumbled under their breaths, while a few expressed their displeasure with their arms and fingers.

Anika vacated the porch before Curtis returned. The distraction in the yard would go a long way in sealing the fate of the protesters, but it did little to quell her concerns over Curtis's admission. Beyond the confirmation of Johnny's death, which itself wasn't a surprise, something else bothered her. She had not guarded herself well against Curtis, leaving herself vulnerable. Despite his care and shepherding—something she hadn't experienced since her father's death—he was a cold-blooded monster. At best, he was a well-meaning town apparatchik who had little to no control over his thoughts and actions. To be sure, he wasn't pretending to be anything else. Curtis Worden was who he was. He wasn't posing as anything different. He was dangerous, particularly when he didn't get his way—when *Miranda* didn't get her way. Moving forward, Anika would need to do a better job of protecting herself and Sam. She certainly didn't plan to mention leaving town anytime soon.

"We need to talk," he said as he re-entered Anika's office and sat down.

"Protesters are on my last nerve," she said, feeling the *koya* in her office, its effects more like a tailwind than a headwind.

"We need to discuss—"

"I meant what I said about Johnny, and I feel like you've betrayed me eight ways to Sunday. But I don't have the time, energy, or heart to talk about this right now. I may not like you or the measures you take to solve problems, but you're my best option for saving thousands of lives in the next few days."

"But I think—"

"You can spill your beans after the storm. Right now, we have work to do."

He leaned forward, rubbed his chin, and stared at her with curious eyes. She saw her eyes—orange, black, and steely like a tiger ready to pounce—in the reflection of his.

"Where should I start?" he asked.

"Start with the protesters. They're growing more violent and need to go home."

"Someone throws another bottle, and they'll all have a new home . . . in the park."

"Would one person throwing a bottle be enough to detain all of them?" she asked.

"Enough to hold 'em for a couple of days."

"The Hospitality Center looks ready now. What else needs to be done?"

"Bars and roof are up. Need to ensure the doors are workin' properly, and the concrete could use the night to set. She'll be ready come mornin'."

"You putting furniture in there—beds and chairs and such?" she asked.

"We'll have cots. And I'll have two medics on call, in case someone gets hurt or sick."

"What about bathrooms?"

"Reckon two Porta-Johns will do."

"Porta-Johns?"

"Skid-O-Can, Call-A-Head, Royal Flush . . . Porta-John. What do you wanna call it?"

"Ask Logan," Anika chorted. "He runs the new reeducation program. Unbelievable that we've reached this point. Hopefully, they'll heed your warning and behave themselves."

"They won't," Curtis replied without hesitation. His statement was made as if he was describing a future event that had already occurred. Anika wondered whether Timmy or Sam had drawn cubes about the fate of the protesters. Or perhaps Curtis was planning a false flag operation to ensure they ended up behind bars. Or maybe he just knew enough about human nature to make such a bold prediction.

"Unless there's something else on the protesters," Curtis said, ready to move on to more serious accusations, "they found Ricky's prints all over the garage where Dodd was killed."

"Isn't that his garage?"

"Bear with me. We have a ton of circumstantial evidence but no smoking gun. He admitted to being on-site during her death."

"Does he say he's innocent?"

"Of course. Every criminal says that at first."

"Does he have an alibi?"

"It's weak as water. MIC leaders threw a party not far from the garage that night celebratin' the protests. People saw Ricky there most of the night, but no one could attest he was there all night. And no one could say for sure that he was at the party on or about the time when we believe Dodd was killed. Beyond that, his motive was clear—she'd been threatenin' his business and livelihood. And when you read those files," he pointed, "you'll understand the former mayor's blackmail has a long tail."

"Have they ruled out suicide?" Anika asked. She felt silly using the word "they" when she suspected "they" was sitting right in front of her.

"No, but that don't make much sense."

"Why not? People hang themselves, right?"

Curtis shrugged.

"Evidence sounds shaky. Then again," she mused, "I was the victim of false accusations—twice. One of those, I suspect, was your fault."

"That, too, would be a false allegation," Curtis huffed, "but you won't let me explain. As for Ricky, he'll get a probable cause hearing with legal counsel after the storm passes. For now, we've got enough to hold him. Given what we're up against and the thousands of lives at stake, I suggest you lean in on this one."

"Nothing from Timmy or Sam on Dodd's death?"

"Unfortunately, no."

If, as Anika suspected, Curtis played a role in Dodd's death, he would have destroyed any cubes describing the event. And to the extent she could interpret her own drawings, Sam still wasn't talking. "What about LeSean?"

"Like I said, they suspect LeSean's running a meth lab at the MIC. If that's true, then it's little wonder why he don't want to evacuate town."

Anika was skeptical. "It is true?"

"Investigators found hydrocarbon derivatives stored in odd places around the refinery. And LeSean's folks had all the ingredients you'd need to crank out the crystal—anhydrous ammonia, ethyl ether, benzene, hydriodic acid, and so on and so forth."

"But aren't those things you'd expect to see at a refinery?"

"They also found blackened-out windows at one storage facility with burn bits, stained soil, and dead vegetation outside. Hallmarks of an illegal drug lab."

Anika, marveling at Curtis's expertise in chemistry, shook her head in disbelief. She had never witnessed LeSean high on anything but raw adrenaline. And even that was rare, usually around game time. She couldn't fathom LeSean manufacturing drugs. Why would he? His family, treated like royalty in Miranda, was loaded. His compensation at the refinery, whatever the amount, would be sugar on top of his inheritance. But why was LeSean pushing back so hard on commonsense safety precautions?

"Again, Mayor," Curtis said, likely invoking her title to encourage action, "we have enough probable cause for an arrest. Once the hurricane passes, we can revisit the charges."

Curtis had reiterated the main point: detaining Ricky and LeSean had less to do with criminality and more to do with evacuating thousands who otherwise would die. She recognized that, although the charges sounded bogus, Curtis had done his job.

Fixers fix things. That's what they do.

It was now time to do hers, and she didn't hesitate. "Arrest them."

"Will do," he nodded. "Before I go, we have one more problem we need to discuss."

"I told you . . . I don't want to discuss Johnny right now."

"Mayor, with all due respect, Johnny ain't got nothin' to do with it."

"What then . . . or who?"

"Preacher-man."

37

"That full-grown little baby has no clue what he's done," Anika mumbled to herself as Ethan waved like a toddler at a Magic Kingdom parade. He gamboled in the field near the entrance of the Church Grounds, dressed in a Hawaiian shirt, khaki shorts, and flip-flops, and played fetch with Calvin and Luther. The two Danes, intoxicated by the flight of the tennis ball, refused to divert attention elsewhere. Amber, eyes swollen, sat hypnotically at the picnic table on the covered porch of the lodge. She refused to acknowledge the Dodge Challenger driving to the guest cottage as she doodled on what appeared to be a ream of graph paper.

Anika needed to speak to Ethan at some point, but first, she had to find Joshua. The information Curtis had shared about the "preacher-man" caused her serious concern. She parked her car, left the keys inside, and stared at the sunset, which resembled a cured egg yolk hovering overhead. "Don't forget Pooh," she told Sam. Walking to the front door, she peeked at the document in her hand and then stopped in her tracks.

The cottage door was cracked open.

Anika scanned the Church Grounds. Ethan and Amber remained engaged in their activities, not paying any mind to Anika or Sam. "Sam, go back to the car and wait for me."

Anika paused. Alarmed, she didn't know what she'd find inside, so she considered her options and measured the risk. Were Cyclops's old timers still monitoring her? Did Amber find a spare key and wander over to the house earlier? Had Ricky, LeSean, or one of their protesters located the whereabouts of her cottage? Had someone bugged her house? Had they left behind an unwelcome surprise for her? Was someone waiting for her inside . . . ready to cause her harm?

Presently, she found herself without a weapon. (She had left the Bowie knife at the Alamo.) Though her mom had encouraged her to carry mace, Anika hadn't followed her advice. Pepper spray, to be sure, wouldn't help her mom. Barbara Mathis was always too drunk to use it. Overcoming her fear, Anika approached the door . . . and walked in. "Hello?"

No response. No sounds whatsoever. Nothing but the thrumming inside her head.

The *koya*. And it produced a fierce headwind. She felt like she was walking through Jell-O as she entered the narrow hallway. She brushed her hand along the wall to keep her balance. And then, as she emerged from the hallway and entered the living area, out of nowhere . . . a voice.

"Anika!"

She jumped. Paralyzed by fright, the word that was jammed in her throat never escaped, thankfully. It was a word unsuitable for the ears of a preacher-man.

"Anika, I'm so sorry. I didn't mean—"

"Jump scare!" she blurted before taking a breath.

"I jumped too. I was—"

"What are you doing here, Joshua?"

"Replacing your air filters," he said innocently, holding up two rectangular cardboard filters caked in muck. "Filthy."

Anika peered across the living area to the bedroom. The door was closed. Joshua had propped a new air filter nearby.

"I'd be happy to replace that one too," he added. "Not sure how you feel about people entering your bedroom."

Anika smirked. "We know how *you* feel about it. You never explained why you're so sensitive."

"Rather not discuss it. Just know that it's important to me."

"Just a quirk?" she probed.

"More than a quirk. But that's part of it, sure."

"Well, thanks for your discretion, but I'm okay with you entering *my* bedroom. It's your room anyway. Let me make sure it's tidy. You never know when Faux Pooh will leave underwear on the floor," Anika said, handing Joshua a document before walking to the bedroom. "Put your eyes on that."

"Your executive order? I read it."

Anika, now in the bedroom, found nothing tossed on the floor. She closed a drawer and straightened the bed before returning. "Rumor's floating around that you don't plan to follow it, that you sent an email to your church to that effect. Yet, you told me the other day that you'd encourage folks to evacuate. So what gives?"

"I don't crank the wheels of the rumor mill, but I'm happy to share with you the email I sent to my congregation. After considerable prayer and conversations with my elders, I decided to leave the decision up to each member's conscience."

"Conscience? How does defying my order and putting lives at risk sit with *your* conscience? I didn't take you for a David Koresh."

"Comparing Reformed Baptist Miranda to the Branch Davidians isn't fair. For it to be constitutional, your order must provide for a religious exemption. And until we learn more about the final trajectory of the storm, I don't plan on canceling next week's worship service."

"Religious exemption? Doesn't the Bible require us to follow civilian laws?"

"Yes, unless they conflict with God's law."

"How does my executive order do that?"

"It potentially impedes our ability to worship. There's more to it, but—"

"Tell me again how many people are in your congregation, Joshua."

"Five hundred, if you include the children."

"Five hundred?" Anika said with genuine surprise. "You told me you only fill about half that number in the sanctuary."

"I shook some things up when I arrived, and let's just say that some are still soul-searching."

"Meaning what?" she asked.

"Got rid of multiple services, and I started preaching the full counsel of God. The pastor before me preached 'name it, claim it' and the prosperity gospel. I call that a false gospel. I'm teaching the truth about who God is and who we are in relation to him."

"People don't like you calling them sinners, is that it?"

"That, and they don't like to hear they're totally depraved or that God is sovereign over all things, including salvation. I preached on Romans 9, dealing with election, and several hundred protested. They're still on the church rolls, so there's hope, but they've stopped attending worship. Hence, the discrepancy between the number of members and the number that show up."

"The fact remains that you gave license to several hundred Mirandites to defy a town order. In my view, you've encouraged them to commit suicide."

"With all due respect, Mayor, I think you're being hyperbolic; but I'm happy to discuss it tomorrow if you'd like. I promised to take Ethan and Amber out for dinner this evening, so I need to change that last filter and get going."

"Samantha has the hurricane coming right for us," she said as he walked away. "Where's your comfort in this? With local meteorologists? Is it with Amber?"

"Amber?" he said, turning back to her.

"She's quite the artist, it would seem. Nice tattoo of a Rubik's Cube. Do you have her drawing cubes? Is she a soothsayer like Sam? By the looks of her, she looks more like a necromancer—communicating with the dead."

"Be nice. She's suffering through a mighty trial. And, yes, she's dabbling with cubes and certainly has the gift. I told you that multiple soothsayers would come out of the woodwork, and some would possess more talent than others. Her drawings are becoming more precise as the drugs gradually filter out of her body. I haven't seen her work on the Rubik's Cube, but she has potential."

As Joshua finished his maintenance, Anika speculated as to the real reason he'd welcomed Amber. She provided value. But to what end? Why did he want or need a soothsayer in his employ? Was predicting the future merely an interesting hobby? Was knowing what's around the corner a power too potent not to pursue?

Anika feared a more sinister motive. Curtis had described to her Sam's recent drawings, images of a religious militia engaged in battle. There were crosses. Weapons. Guns. What's more, Anika had learned that the number of church members was twice what she'd guessed. That could pose a problem with enforcing her executive order. Some were turned off by Joshua's preaching, but they'd be turned back on by outsiders meddling with their religious rights. That was the third rail with churchgoers and nominal Christians. Anika knew, in the end, they'd all coalesce around a common cause, and there'd be enough strength in numbers to overwhelm Miranda authorities.

Joshua apologized again as he walked toward the door with three dirty filters. She followed him into the eventide and spotted Ethan talking to Sam near the car. Giddy from the attention, Sam's Betty Boop eyes returned, along with a perma-smile.

"I won't let you break her heart too," Anika said half-joking as she hugged Ethan.

"Congrats on your new position," he said, refusing to acknowledge her playful jab. "You've come a long way since coming home. Unfortunately, I've gone in the opposite direction."

"Maybe I'm bad luck," she said as Joshua left them.

"I make my own messes," Ethan acknowledged.

"You're definitely a moron," Anika said, no longer half-joking. "But at least you're a gorgeous moron."

"Helps pay the bills. Also gets me in trouble."

"Don't beat yourself up too much," Anika said, surprised to see Ethan's remorse. Perhaps he was human after all. "This isn't all your fault."

"I hurt a lot of people close to me."

"Maybe, but you have an overbearing girlfriend and a sinister sister-in-law. Set aside Amber for a minute—I'll give her a pass for now—but Sarah shouldn't escape blame for this debacle. I watched her seduce you. Saw that train wreck coming a mile away."

"I understand what you're saying, but—"

"But nothing!" Anika couldn't hold back any longer. "That devil woman is a homewrecker. I have no doubt she put this in motion. And now she's standing back, arms crossed, foot tapping, and waiting for her victims to gouge you with pitchforks. This is unbelievable!"

The color returned to Ethan's face. "Thanks for the pep talk, Anika. You're the best," he said as he departed.

As Sam went inside, Anika sat in the creaky rocking chair on the cottage porch and decompressed under the emerging stars. She watched the trio load up in Joshua's Jeep and leave the Church Grounds for dinner. The dogs barked until the taillights disappeared. Joshua hadn't invited her and Sam to dinner, but that wasn't unusual. Ethan and Amber had issues, and dinner was likely part of the counseling. Besides, to the extent Amber was overcoming drug addiction, being around Anika might be the autobahn to relapse. As much as Anika disliked Amber, the reverse was more intense; or at least, it had been before Amber learned who was the real threat.

Speaking of threats, Anika regarded Joshua. Curtis, relying on Sam's drawings, believed him to be dangerous. But did the cube drawings even work? Or was that a bunch of superstitious nonsense? Anika had no proof that soothsaying was real. Commonsense said it wasn't. From her perspective, nothing predicted had yet to transpire. Those in authority could use soothsaying as an excuse to do whatever they wanted. They could abuse it to destroy their enemies and hold onto power. Until now, flirting with the supernatural hadn't come with any consequences. Putting a target on Joshua, however, upped the ante. She would need more intel—real, indisputable intelligence. And she knew where to find it.

She stared at the lodge. It was dark inside except for one table lamp shining upstairs. Joshua's forbidden bedroom beckoned.

38

Anika turned the knob, leaned into the door, and entered the lodge. Even though she had license to walk downstairs, the *koya* returned before her first footfall inside. Its presence was low in intensity but recognizable, as if a medium-gauge wire had become ungrounded in her head. The place smelled like a cabin after a weekend weenie roast, but no one used fireplaces in this part of South Texas. In fact, air conditioners in Miranda—central air, wall units, you name it—labored non-stop year-round to mitigate the sweltering heat.

She had no idea whether Joshua had installed Ring or other surveillance cameras. But she had to take the risk. She needed hard proof whether Joshua posed a threat—a threat to her leadership, a threat to hundreds of Baptist congregants (including children), a threat to the well-being of Miranda's citizenry. The stakes were too high not to know the truth. Flashlight in hand, she pressed forward, shuffling her feet around some reclining chairs toward the large, butcher-block dining table in the middle of the cavernous room.

Joshua and his troubled pupils had turned the dining table into a study desk. Three Bibles lay opened, spaced out, and stationed in front of three chairs—two on one side, one on the other. Shining the light on pages of Scripture, Anika observed that each Bible was a different translation—NIV, ESV, NKJV—and each was opened to the Book of Revelation. Stacks of books surrounded the Bibles, works written by men named Packer, Spurgeon, Owen, Ryle, and Stott. Anika saw a book on communion by Davidson, one on church discipline by Leeman, and another on polity by Dever. There was even a book written by an author named Pink and two vintage copies of Bunyan's *The Pilgrim's Progress*, the only title Anika recognized other than the Bible. The cover of those two books contained the words, "From this world to that which is to come."

Anika shone the flashlight in the darkness. The beam remained at eye level as she circled in place to survey the area. For whatever reason, she feared the beam would find true darkness—something unwelcomed. A stranger, a cadaver . . . the menacing Grady Twins from *The Shining*.

Come and play with us, Anika.

Reality gave way to paranoia. By working the flashlight around the room, she noticed that death surrounded her. Shoulder-mounted deer peered at her with glassy eyes. Stuffed and tusked feral hogs glared down at her. Mourning doves and bobwhite quail, flying to nowhere forever, emerged from the walls.

The next level. The level where the stairs ended. Three rooms. One on the left, one on the right, and one in the center. She focused her attention on the center room. Even shining the light on this room increased the *koya*, so much so that Anika's breathing increased. The door was shut. *Under no circumstances—none whatsoever—are you allowed in my bedroom,* he had said. She knew this was forbidden fruit.

But she needed to see it.

Approaching the stairs, she looked at the photographs dangling along the stairway walls. Photos of families from yesteryear. In Miranda, however, yesteryear didn't exist in pictures before 1960. That's when the last monster hurricane destroyed Miranda, stripping her to the bones. Photographs pre-dating that event had presumably vanished. Washed away. Etched only in the brains of those who had survived and who were still of sound mind. The quality of the photographs varied depending on the decade. Families from multiple generations and all races eyed Anika between wooden frames. But something was off. These photos weren't passive. Their subjects stared back at Anika with impatient eyes, following her up the steps. Urging her to stop. Beseeching her to go back.

Yet she climbed. One stair at a time. The *koya* increased with each step, crushing her insides like gravitational forces in a fighter jet. Anika summoned enormous effort to conquer each stair. *Left foot—down. Right foot—down.* She persisted . . . one stair at a time. Grabbing the handrail, she pulled, one stair at a time. *One . . . stair . . . at . . . a . . . time.*

She reached the door to the forbidden room. The door with the light escaping through the cracks. Her hands shook. Her eyes watered from the pull. She panted, her chest visibly moving in and out. Her teeth clenched. She switched off the flashlight, turned the knob, and pushed.

From this world to that which is to come.

The *koya* tangled her insides. She experienced disorientation. Her ears and the space in between thrummed. But she continued on until . . .

She was in.

The room was tidy. The lamp on the bedside table illuminated the ceiling and walls. Joshua had made the bed with the skill of a West Point cadet and tucked his house slippers underneath. No clothes on the floor. No unwelcome odors. No trash strewn about. Joshua clearly expected alignment between his sparse furniture and fixtures, but not in a way that evidenced obsessive-compulsive disorder or sophisticated *Feng Shui*. The room's cleanliness, Anika mused, wasn't unusual for a thirty-something bachelor shepherding a sizable church.

But none of that made this a normal room. Someone, presumably Joshua, had painted—maybe with charcoal briquettes, she couldn't be sure—towering letters on the wall above the bed.

YESHUA

Bookcases flanked the bed, filled with works by St. Augustine, Thomas Aquinas, Martin Luther, John Calvin, and others whose names she didn't recognize. Unlike the books downstairs, these editions looked old, and Joshua had stored them behind protective glass. Beyond the religious library, Renaissance-era weapons hung from the walls. Steel pikes, swords, and knives. Wooden axes. Crossbows, arrows, and matchlock muskets. Anika remembered learning in high school about the Thirty Years' War in the mid-seventeenth century. Protestantism wrought by the Reformation challenged the authority of the Holy Roman Empire and thrust Europe into deadly conflict. Given Joshua's fascination with the Reformation (after all, he named his dogs after its two titans), she assumed these weapons reflected that era and war.

Most of his eccentricity, Anika thought, was bachelors-being-bachelors and pastors-being-pastors kind of stuff. Joshua poured himself into his church, so it made sense he'd have books written by ancient theologians. *YESHUA* presumably was a variation of *Joshua*. It looked creepy scrawled on the wall, but that didn't make Joshua a creep. Odd, maybe, but she already had him pegged as weird. What's more, he was a man's man, and she'd known men—boys, really—in high school who would hang their guns, compound bows, and fishing poles on their walls. It was Texas, after all, where many stereotypes proved accurate, and where one could still find deputies on horseback and gun racks in pickup trucks. The photographs near the weapons, though, told another story.

The *koya* stopped as the door shut behind her!

It didn't slam shut by itself like you see in horror movies. It was more unsettling. It closed softly, more methodically, and without a fuss. Anika wasn't dissuaded or deterred, however, nor did she spend much thought discerning what caused the door to close. The room would either accept her or swallow her. Too late now to run. Seeing no other lifeforms, she refocused her attention on the walls. She had come this far; she would find what she was after or accept her fate.

She found it. The reason Joshua didn't want her in this room.

The photos hadn't caught her attention at first glance. Perhaps it was the distraction of other abnormal relics in the room, objects more at home in a store window along Diagon Alley than a second-story bedroom in South Texas. On the surface, these photos and frames were not unlike those along the stairwell. But with a second glance, they captured her breath.

These were celebration photos. Photos of people dancing in the Miranda streets, dancing in the park. Photos of people, drenched in rain, hugging and kissing and holding hands and howling at the emerging sun.

The photos captured the Town of Miranda in other times, different generations. Color photos of survivors from the 1960s—from Hurricane Carla. Black-and-white photos from the turn of the twentieth century— from the Storm of 1900. And daguerreotypes from the mid-1800s—from the Storm of 1840. *Someone took these not long after the Battle of the Alamo,*

Anika thought. *Was this technology even available then? And how did these photos survive subsequent storms?* The Storm of 1840—referred to as Santa Anna's Storm by the old timers—was a thing of legend. In fact, many in the community chalked up that storm to a tall tale.

The devastation depicted in the photos captivated Anika. She couldn't pull her eyes from the desolate flatlands and flanks of wood scattered and piled in makeshift pyres. She saw . . .

"Where are you, Anika?" the deep voice asked.

Anika's heart leaped, but she didn't move. Joshua was behind her at the door. "Where I'm not supposed to be."

"Looks like I'm not the only one defying orders."

"I was just—"

"You need to leave. You should've never seen these pictures."

"Let me explain."

"Certain things can't be unseen. It's no longer safe for you here."

"What's *that* supposed to mean?" Anika asked as she turned to face him. "You would hurt me?"

"Of course not, but I can no longer protect you. You've breached our agreement. I said you could go anywhere on the property but one place—this room."

"You sound like a lawyer . . . and a madman."

"I can sound more like a preacher if you'd like. You've broken our covenant. There are consequences beyond my control."

"You doubled back to check on me? Or did you forget your slippers?"

Joshua forced a smile. "I knew you'd be here."

"Amber must be a fast learner."

"I don't need amateur soothsaying to understand human behavior. It's been the same since the Garden . . . as predictable as the sun rising and setting."

She considered walking away without saying another word, but it didn't stick. "Curtis told me you'd be against us, that you'd even take up arms."

"Do you believe him?"

"I didn't. Why would you do such a thing? I'm only trying to save lives."

"And what do you believe now?" Joshua asked.

"I know you'll tell me the truth."

"What would you like to know?"

"How is it that you have these photographs on your wall?"

"I won't answer that. It's not for you to know."

"Are you in these photos somewhere?"

"That's a little silly, don't you think?"

"Is it?" she asked. "You've asked me to believe in a great many silly things."

Joshua didn't respond.

"Will you be against me in the coming days?" she continued. "Was Curtis right? In addition to these unexplainable pictures, your room resembles a medieval armory."

"I can't predict the future," he replied, "but any aggression from my people will be in kind."

"Do you view my evacuation order as an act of aggression?"

Joshua paused, trying to find the right words. "Let's just say we await the extent of its enforcement."

39

The Black Ghost, with Anika behind the wheel, rumbled to the gate of the Church Grounds on its way to the main road. The clouds had congealed in the sky like cottage cheese, and the air smelled of chocolate daisies. Joshua had allowed them to stay until morning, and dawn had arrived. They hadn't needed much time to pack; they didn't have many clothes and hadn't established deep roots. Sam's face, however, betrayed a deep sadness. Her eyes were moist and heavy, much like the morning air. The sisters exited slowly, as if to accentuate the regret. They both had an arm resting on the door with the windows down as the sun began its ascent over the Gulf of Mexico.

Amber refused to lift her head. She scribbled feverishly on the porch table at the lodge. Even from afar, Anika could tell the color was returning to her face. Ethan stood next to her and waved goodbye like a schoolboy without a clue. He still had little recognition or understanding of true consequence. The extent of punishment to this point in his life, Anika guessed, had involved his mother yelling his first and middle name for emphasis—*Ethan Kelly, you get your hand out of that cookie jar!* A slight disturbance in the force, and he was off to the next adventure in a galaxy far, far away from any controversy. Even after his sordid affair with Sarah, he'd landed in a soft place surrounded by someone to care for him. If, by chance, the hurricane threat passed, it wouldn't be long before an artist chiseled his abs on a new billboard advertisement. Soon thereafter, Anika predicted, he'd return to his normal gig as owner of the Endless Summer Surf Shop, selling cult T-shirts and Mr. Zog's Sex Wax.

But life had dealt a different deck of cards to Anika and Sam. For them, the consequences of expulsion carried a next-level gravity. Joshua's kicking them off the Church Grounds hurt more than a slap on the wrist. Their written relationship with the preacher-man was that of landlord and tenant, and Anika had breached the lease agreement. But this felt worse than a contractual infraction or simple eviction. Although they'd never joined the church—never even attended a worship service—it felt as if Joshua and Reformed Baptist Miranda had excommunicated them. To make matters worse, Anika, who in her role as mayor oversaw the town's law enforcement, felt like a bona fide outlaw.

Joshua stood at the edge of the porch, hands in his pockets, and stared at them. He didn't look disappointed or surprised. He looked resigned—ho-hum, really—as if he knew this day would come. His piercing eyes seemed to say *this too shall pass*. He had told Anika that Samantha could stay. Sam could take Ethan's room in the lodge, and Ethan could transition into the now-empty guest cottage. Anika, impetuous in the heat of the moment, had scoffed at that invitation, thinking the worst of Joshua's motivations. *Does he just want Sam for her drawings?* But as she now considered bunking arrangements at the Alamo Opera House, she questioned whether she'd made the right choice for her little sister.

Calvin and Luther, their cropped ears standing high, sat upright like majestic statues at the front entrance east of the property. The Danes, normally frantic and friendly, were in business mode, like stoic bouncers—or perhaps cherubs—escorting the evictees off the property and guarding the entrance. As the car approached the gate, Anika noticed for the first time the flaming swords on their dog tags. Breaking security protocol, Calvin couldn't help but wag his tail and bark when Anika made eye contact as if to say, *Don't look at me, rules is rules*. Luther had less control over his emotions on Sam's side. She grabbed Luther's neck through the open car window and, with tears flowing, planted a kiss on his head.

Bidding adieu to the large dogs, Anika stopped the car at the main road. Downtown Miranda and the Alamo Opera House were to the left. The back roads exiting town, over the town's only other bridge, were to the right. If she were to make a run for it, this would be the time.

The *koya* returned once she lifted the lever for a right turn signal.

No cars in sight, Anika had no reason to put on a blinker unless she was signaling another kind of turn. She eyed Joshua in her rearview mirror. Seeing the blinker flash in the wrong direction, he had removed his hands from his pockets and was now cracking his knuckles and pacing with rapt attention on the Black Ghost. Sam, too, turned her attention to Anika with wide eyes.

"Speak now if you can find your voice," Anika said. The comment wasn't meant to be callous or cold. "This may be our only shot to survive this town."

Sam shook her head, held up her index finger, and lunged into the back of the car.

"You know I can't interpret your cubes, Sam," Anika continued with deep breaths, her fingernails digging into the steering wheel as Sam dug around the packed boxes in the backseat.

Retrieving her drawings, Sam opened the folder and pointed. The drawings were not of cubes; they were of a bridge. The truss bridge on the outskirts of town. She had drawn triangles formed together and depicting a single unit of wood and iron. Like the tiny stream underneath it, the bridge depicted in Sam's drawings had no name, and it wasn't built for automobiles. It was part of the town's railroad system and hosted two parallel railroad tracks. Anika knew it had enough room for an automobile to pass. In fact, given Johnny D.'s daredevil nature, Anika guessed it wouldn't be the first time the Black Ghost would cross that bridge.

But there was more to the drawings. "Are you sure?" Anika asked, seeing the drawings of stickmen surrounding the bridge. Stickmen carrying guns. Not just guns—automatic weapons. What the town's gun-control advocates called "weapons of war."

Sam nodded.

"You think they're at the bridge right now?"

Sam nodded.

"This is crazy. Did you draw something—cubes, pictures, *anything*—for Curtis or Cyclops that would've referenced this?"

Sam shook her head.

"How would they know?"

Sam shrugged.

Anika slammed her fist on the steering wheel. She pulled out her phone, clicked on the Waze app, and typed in her preferred destination. Thirteen hours to the front door of St. Jude's Children's Research Hospital in Memphis. Once they'd escaped the clutches of Miranda, medical experts could examine Sam's brain tumor as early as tomorrow. But Anika knew that wasn't in the cards. She was stuck. "What's wrong with this place!?" she screamed.

Sam continued to stare at her with concern—concern likely over Anika's state-of-mind, her next decision. Even an eight-year-old knew this choice between left versus right had massive implications. Hands back on the steering wheel, Anika stared forward, gazing beyond the farm-to-market road, beyond the brambles, thickets, and mesquite trees. She blew the hair from her eyes and, after much wrestling and angst, pulled down the lever for a left turn signal.

The *koya* stopped. Sam clicked her seatbelt, and Joshua walked back to the porch. "See you later, mutts," Anika said as the engine roared, and the Ghost sprang forward . . . into a left turn.

Back to the Alamo . . . for now.

40

Anika swung open the Alamo doors before Sam could find Faux Pooh and exit the vehicle. "Where's Curtis?" Anika asked Timmy as he wrapped breakfast tacos in foil behind the Buffalo Bar. Timmy head-pointed to Logan's office without breaking concentration. When she walked in, Curtis stood up to meet her, and Logan, marker in hand, was articulating his public relations strategy on the whiteboard.

"What's going on?" Curtis asked. "Did you see the Hospitality Center? It's ready for op—"

"Whoa!" Anika said, hand-signaling for Curtis to retake his seat. "You've been a busy beaver, Logan!" Logan had covered the office walls with signage, with propaganda. Even without the flashy lights and bustling crowds, the sensory overload in the room reminded Anika of Times Square in New York City.

Some of the messages were expected and appropriate. *Evacuate Now— It's the Law*. And *Do the Right Thing—Save Yourself, Save Your Family*. Some messages were a bit much, but she could temper them with slight edits. *Violating Miranda's Evacuation Order = Jail Time*. And *Riding Out the Storm = Suicide*. And some of the messages were beyond salvage and frightened her with their overreach. *For Safety and Protection, Guns Must Be Temporarily Confiscated*. And *Mandatory Gun Registration at the MIC Today and Tomorrow*.

"What do you think?" Logan asked like an insecure little kid unveiling his Saturday finger-painting project.

"Impressive . . . though I'm not sure why we'd confiscate or register guns. Your job, as I understand it, is to win over hearts and minds, not to incite an insurrection."

Logan looked to Curtis for help, and Curtis stepped in. "Mayor, we're mostly concerned about the religious types. No tellin' what they'll do if forced to evacuate. Those folks have a stockpile of weapons. If they become hostile or form a militia, they'll overcome law enforcement."

"Those people aren't murderers, Curtis. There's a biblical commandment that forbids it."

"Religious types in Texas are stubborn. They've done away with the ceremonial laws; they've cast aside civilian laws. What makes you think they'll follow the moral law? Believe you me, they care more about the Second Amendment than the Sixth Commandment."

Curtis sounded less like her fixer and more like a biblical and constitutional scholar. "That's crazy talk, guys."

"Is it?" Curtis asked rhetorically. "Did you talk to Preacher-man about the evacuation order? Did he agree to follow your law?"

"I raised it with him, but he didn't agree to abide by the EO."

"Like I said, these religious fanatics struggle with authority when times get rough, when the public interest conflicts with their hearts' desires. We saw that with COVID-19 shots, with wearing masks."

"Come on, Curtis. That's—"

"Preacher-man himself held worship services without masks for six months during the latest outbreak. He's supposed to be spreadin' the gospel; instead, he's spreadin' the virus."

Anika struggled to find words.

"You've got a little time," Curtis continued. "Perhaps a couple more days to convince him. Reckon you can make another run at him tonight?"

Anika shook her head and huffed, knowing that, with her next words, she'd fall victim to Curtis's narrative. Before she spoke, Sam arrived and wrapped her arms around Anika's waist. "Sam and I aren't welcome on Church Grounds anymore."

Curtis's eyebrows jumped. "What happened?"

"Long story worthy of a longer discussion," she said, affectionately tugging on Sam's ponytail. "For now, just know that Sam and I will need a room upstairs until the storm passes."

"That's not a problem," he said, "but we need direction on how to handle armed zealots."

"Curtis, you're inviting war if you start confiscating guns."

"Might have one if we don't. If war's inevitable, I'd like to be in it to win it."

"You have intel that suggests a legitimate threat?" she asked.

"Yes, ma'am."

"Did Samantha provide the intel?"

"Yes, ma'am."

Anika rubbed her face and sighed. Sam had been drawing a lot about guns. The burden of governing Bizarro World through a crisis was taking its toll, and Anika didn't try to fake it. "Is there another way to mitigate the threat?"

Logan spoke up. "We can put together a risk-based list and only target those—"

"To be clear," Anika instructed, "we aren't using the word *target* when referring to guns."

"Put together a list to *focus* on those with questionable backgrounds," he corrected.

"How do you define *questionable*?" she pressed.

Logan again looked to Curtis for help, and the fixer obliged. "Criminal history. Hostile social media postings."

"Religious affiliation," Anika poked.

"To be fair, Mayor," Curtis said, "we're trying to solve problems here, not create new ones. We're in emergency mode, and we need to protect our deputies and citizens."

"Bring me a plan that doesn't resemble one used by the SS or Gestapo." She turned to Logan. "Build me a PR campaign that doesn't resemble something fashioned by the Goebbels brigade. Perception matters here, people."

"Anything else you need from us?" Curtis asked.

"Did you say the Hospitality Center was operational?"

"Yes, ma'am, and ready to be populated."

"Just waiting for a rock or a brick . . . or a middle finger?" she asked.

Curtis chuckled. "Reckon it won't be long. Them fools can't help themselves."

"Get Sam to work on her cubes and then come find me. We need to discuss the Joshua situation, and I need an update on our criminal investigation involving our friends at the MIC. Where's Chelsea?"

"Hadn't seen her this morning."

"Guess she decided to move on," Anika said, walking to her office, somewhat disappointed. She thought Chelsea had potential and would add value to her team.

The bad news piling on the morning was taking its toll. Anika's head hung as she opened her office door. But a glimmer soon came to her eyes, and she smiled for the first time in a long time. An unwrapped gift sat on her desk. Though her instincts begged her to rush to it, to embrace it, she demonstrated patience. It was one of the best gifts she'd ever received. She took her time admiring it, soaking in the moment. She marveled at the pair of familiar, ornate cowboy boots that gleamed like the most precious metal ever found on Earth. On the left boot hung a tag. Scrawled on the tag was a message, a message that caused Anika to raise her fist and scream at the top of her lungs: "Let's go!"

To: Cinderella
From: Outlaw Chelsea Wales
Re: All in—Let's go!

41

Anika heard Timmy scream at eight o'clock in the morning as the projectile slammed against the bar. The unidentified scofflaw had heaved the brick over the swinging doors and into the Alamo Commons. No one was hurt, but Curtis wasted no time scrambling to action. Sheriff's deputies mounted on horseback in Revolutionary Park were already in position. As the sun continued to rise, officers on foot surrounded the park. *How convenient*, Anika thought as she peeked through her curtains. Surprised and sleepy protesters emerged from sleeping bags and tents. Given the commotion, Anika rushed from her office to observe the action from the porch.

The old timers made sure to control the narrative, to force the mayor's hand. They left no level of hyperbole unexplored. The gossip on the porch already had eclipsed the doctorate level. *Lucky that brick didn't take somebody's head off. Surprised someone wasn't killed. And*, worst of all, *what kind of person attacks a special needs fella?* Anika knew the playbook; she knew how this would end. She didn't need to wait for the old timers, Curtis, or the sheriff to frame one or more protesters. She didn't need to wait for Logan to post "Remember the Alamo" signs around town, or for Ethan to produce *Save Timmy!* T-shirts and baseball caps to round out the fall collection at the Endless Summer Surf Shop.

She knew the investigation would be quick. Authorities would serve justice like a microwaved Hot Pocket. Push a button and unwrap. Blow on it and choke it down. Due process in this town simply meant *do what must be done*. Crises only sped up things and exacerbated the consequences. During crisis management, few had time to consider the absurdity underpinning the authorities' rationalization of their actions; fewer still had the wherewithal or power to stop them.

Several eyewitnesses recounted the incident. A protester had hurled the brick from behind the orange tent. The only orange tent in the park, Anika observed, happened to be the tent farthest from the Alamo. Not even Tom Brady could throw a brick that far. But facts were pesky things that couldn't swim against the rip current of urgency and expediency. To make things more *sketcho*, as Chelsea would say, witnesses all regurgitated the same vague talking points. White male, late twenties, dark cropped hair, wild eyes—on second thought, make that "wild, wild eyes; one maybe painted." Those orchestrating this farce obviously had Crazy Eyes in their crosshairs. And that made sense. For Curtis and the old timers, he'd become Public Enemy Number One. Anika once again scanned the group of protesters. They were all standing up now, trying to figure out what had happened. They had no clue what the old timers had up their sleeves.

Crazy Eyes, Anika observed, was nowhere to be found.

Curtis, of course, played his best Captain Renault. *Round up the usual suspects!* And the deputies did his bidding without pause or objection, commencing the round-up of protesters in short order. They arrested every protester and escorted them to the internment facility, which Logan, this morning, had unofficially christened the Hospitality Center. Whether that euphemism was less clever than farcical was of no moment. It was time for Miranda to evacuate. And while Anika didn't condone her henchman's methods, she no longer had a choice. All else had failed. Circumstances demanded force.

Not everyone acquiesced without a fuss or fight. Some fought back with harsh words and violent shrugs. Police frog-marched those protesters across the park to the Hospitality Center, giving the term "hospitality" a new meaning. Four others—three men and a raving lunatic who called herself Gypsy Dust—lost their minds and fought back with fists and feet. (Cyclops accused Gypsy Dust of wielding a box cutter, but authorities found no evidence of weapons.) Deputies cuffed those protesters and, to her surprise, dragged them before Anika. She looked down at them from the porch. The hatred and madness in their eyes unsettled her. Gyspy

Dust, in particular, appeared rabid, spit foaming at her mouth and cheeks flushed with hatred. These four protesters weren't paid hands. They represented the true believers.

Anika lost her patience when they screamed obscenities at her, and they disgusted her with their brazen insults and racist remarks. No longer copacetic, she extended her arm with her thumb tilted sideways. And then, with the authority of Caesar, she turned her thumb down—*pollice verso*, a term she remembered from high school Latin—sealing their fate in the Alamo jail cell. Unlike their wiser cohorts, they'd be detained inside, cuffed and stuffed like criminals rather than temporary guests of the town.

As morning progressed and police continued rounding up protesters, a few bystanders joined the fray. This included the occasional do-gooder triggered by what she believed was an abuse of power. It also included the crackpot journalists from local Channel 5, also known as *Miranda's Five on Your Side*. They arrived before lunchtime in two white kidnapper vans with satellite dishes on top. Pretty people dressed to the nines poured out of the vehicles. Anika recognized some of them from high school, maybe from Ms. Stubblefield's theater class. They slid open doors, pulled out expensive-looking equipment, and with the resourcefulness of South Texas fire ants set up their lights and cameras amid the abandoned tents, sleeping bags, and debris across the street.

Diverting her attention from the production, Anika noticed Sarah down the road. Sarah paced outside her store, phone pinned to her ear. She likely was trying to get the attention of the police. A burglar had stolen her prized boots, and she needed help. The phone call would be ugly, Anika surmised. *Pronto, pigs!* would be Sarah's tone (if not her actual words). *Do you know who I am? Do you know how much I pay in taxes?* It was a bad day, though, to need police assistance. More important matters occupied their attention.

Anika glanced beyond the swinging doors. Logan putzed around his office, crafting slogans and signs. Anika figured it was only a matter of time before he crawled back to Sarah. Whatever intimate feelings Anika once held for him had faded. Perhaps his bad judgment turned her off, his naïve belief that Sarah was marriage material. Perhaps Anika conceded that Sarah's spell over him proved too powerful to combat—more addictive than Amber's heroin. Truth be told, despite all of Logan's amazing qualities, Anika had never fallen in love with him. Not in that way. She enjoyed having him on Team Anika, though, and would ensure he remained *all in* until the hurricane passed.

She retired to the porch table where Curtis was caressing his lasso. They sat together for several minutes without saying a word, seldom making eye contact. Anika wondered what to make of their relationship. Like everything else in her life, it was complicated. The old man was the closest thing she had to a caretaker, and yet he was a cold-blooded killer. Not only that, he'd admitted to killing the love of her life. For whatever reason, however, she was drawn to him like a daughter drawn to her father, and it was driving her mad. She figured there wasn't a chapter in the illusive *Mayor's Handbook* that covered daddy issues. "No turning back now, huh?"

"Reckon not, but we gave 'em fair warning. At some point, enough's enough."

"We still live in a free country, Curtis. Hurricane or not, history won't be kind to us for the actions we're taking today."

"If we don't take action today, Mayor, there won't be much history to talk about tomorrow."

"Reporters will make the history," Anika said as *Miranda's Five on Your Side* switched on the lights in broad daylight. A tall woman with red hair stepped into the road with a microphone in hand. "They've got hungry eyes."

"You mind if I tie 'em all up and—"

"Mind your manners," Anika chuckled. That she could smile or laugh at a time like this didn't bode well for her mental state. She felt herself going mad but knew she needed to power through. She noticed several old timers near the porch, drinking Lone Star beer from plastic cups and heating up the smoker for lunch. *Rounding up protesters without due process must be a spectator sport*, she thought. *Not unlike the Miranda Rodeo.* "Where's Cyclops today?"

"With a scout team . . . trackin' down ol' Crazy Eyes."

"Gone all morning?"

"He'll follow that fella around the world if need be. At least to Corpus Christi and back."

"Curtis, we both know Crazy Eyes didn't throw that brick."

"With respect, ma'am, I never blamed Crazy Eyes."

"You implied that Cyclops—"

"Cyclops is chasing after him because Crazy Eyes is a threat. He needs to be arrested."

"On what charges? He wasn't even here this morning. There's no telling—"

"On trumped-up charges, if need be!"

"You're talking like a madman!" she said, before wishing she could take her words back. If Curtis wasn't, in fact, a madman, he likely had killed more people than most madmen.

"I'm tryin' to protect this town . . . to protect you."

"Sam's drawings again?" she asked.

"Yes, ma'am."

"Don't take this the wrong way, Curtis, but I'm worried there's considerable bias—unconscious or otherwise—in your cube interpretations. Or maybe Sam's feeding off your energy when she draws."

"How so?"

"More often than not, Sam seems to target your enemies. And since you're the only one with the ability to interpret the cubes, there aren't controls or safeguards in place to protect against error. Or am I wrong?"

Talk of Sam's motives aggravated Curtis. He fidgeted in his seat. Wagging his finger at Anika, he said, "You question me all you want, Mayor, but that little girl ain't got nothin' to do with it. We don't talk business, and she ain't got no ill motives—unconscious or otherwise. Besides, she didn't draw anything about Ricky or LeSean. That was all my doin', and I stand by it."

"Fair enough," Anika said. She looked away, into the park, keeping her thoughts to herself. She loved how Curtis protected Sam—not unlike he protected Timmy—but Anika had to keep her cool. The yin and yang of love and hate toward Curtis made her want to pull out her hair. "When will they arrest Ricky and LeSean?"

"After they're done with this mess. I told 'em to wait until we figured out . . ." Curtis's voice faded as events in this distance caught his attention.

"What's wrong?" Anika asked, following his eyes beyond the patio.

"Right on cue. Guess they couldn't stay away from all the action."

The brown quarter horse painted with white socks nickered and snorted as it approached the front porch. The deputy riding the horse and wearing a motorcycle helmet said nothing. He was there for backup. His colleague on foot, Deputy Carl, walking in front of the horse with his sidearm drawn for some reason, escorted the two men in handcuffs to Anika and Curtis.

LeSean refused to make eye contact. Ricky, on the other hand, refused to *break* eye contact with Anika, his eyes burning like coals. His labored breathing taxed his lungs and nearly thrust him into hyperventilation. An eerie silence hovered over the Alamo as authorities and arrestees converged. Ricky broke the silence, however, when he made an ill-advised comment in the heat of the moment—a comment that sealed his fate, perhaps forever.

"If you dare stick out that empress thumb again, *Mother*, I'll bite it off."

42

His hands cuffed in front of him, Ricky hurled accusations at Anika as he writhed in animus. "The power's gone to your head, Anika!" he screamed, air-punching his bound wrists toward her. "This town has its grips on you. Snap out of the trance! You once were our beloved homecoming queen, one of the most caring persons at our school. I witnessed time and again how you sacrificed yourself for others. But something's happened. Don't you see what you've become?"

As Curtis left to divert the news crew's attention elsewhere, Anika listened to every syllable without betraying emotion. Ricky's words, however, unlike those absurd insults from strangers, hit their mark. *Sacrificed myself for others?* She wanted to scream, *"And look where that got me! Everyone betrays me! Even my own mother abandons me!"* Despite her strong convictions, her bold actions shredded her heart to pieces. She wasn't the beast they saw through their eyes. Her recent behavior often disturbed her, but she held the lives of thousands in her hands. She wanted to holler—to Ricky, to LeSean, to the other protesters in the park—that desperate times called for desperate measures. Now that she was in power, she believed that to be true; but she knew governing by proverb wouldn't change hearts and minds. It would come across as malarky, as weakness. She needed help with the evacuation, but she couldn't expect naysayers to do her bidding without objection.

Worse than Ricky's piercing words was LeSean's gut-wrenching silence. Ricky's coarse demeanor and harsh reaction made him an unlikeable victim. LeSean, on the other hand, still refused to make eye contact. He had the look of generational victimhood, the look of someone trained as a child to anticipate the abuse of power that comes with racism. Anika remembered the days—not long ago—when everyone lionized LeSean. As the region's best football player, he was the undisputed town hero. If football players in Texas were royalty, then LeSean Brown was the high school king. He never paid for a meal; he never bought his own beer. When he walked into the room, the music grew louder, and the laughs lasted longer. Women wanted to speak to him; men wanted to be like him; and little boys of all colors wanted to *be* him.

Anika also remembered, however, stories LeSean had shared in private. Stories applicable to the Black community. His mom had instructed him to never wear his hoodie in public after dark. Likewise, his dad had told him, if pulled over by police, he was to place his hands on the steering wheel until the officers arrived at his car door. No exceptions. And he was to never question the officers' actions at the scene, however wrong or unfair. Instead, every answer must include the word "sir" or "ma'am," and he darn sure better never interchange those two words.

But none of that instruction mattered because now he was in handcuffs. Anika couldn't bear the thought that she was now The Man that LeSean's parents had feared. She was the manifestation of evil they'd trained him to avoid. In her official role, she was now the subject of those harsh anti-police songs by N.W.A. and Pearl Jam's *W.M.A.* that LeSean and Johnny had listened to during pickup basketball games.

Curtis, however, wouldn't allow his mayor to budge. His prisoners didn't have license to sing in the symphony of injustice. Following Chelsea to the porch, he approached Anika as the news crew packed up to leave. Frustrated by the MIC leaders' behavior, it didn't take him long to pass along his concerns and set things straight. He leaned his head into Anika's ear, gently grabbed her arm, and whispered, "This is all hogwash. Remember how they betrayed you?"

Staring at her prison tat, Anika remembered the dialogue she'd read in the files. Curtis spoke the truth; they had betrayed her for a song. Ricky had fabricated a story about her having a relationship with the Xalisco Boys and black tar heroin. She had never associated with any of that. Those were his connections, not hers. And LeSean had somehow tied her to the explosives, the most unbelievable canard of all. She had aced high school chemistry but otherwise couldn't tell the difference between black powder and a bottle rocket. Mayor Dodd—the grand puppet master—had bent Ricky and LeSean over a barrel, blackmailed them, and fed them false narratives to frame Anika. As some answers concerning her bogus criminal history bubbled to the surface, questions of "why" remained submerged. Why had Dodd, presumably with Sheriff Karnes's aid, targeted Anika and framed her for Johnny's homicide? Was it to protect Curtis, Johnny's real killer? Something more?

Anika's face became flushed. Her resolve hardened. She would govern on facts not feelings. She felt the positive energy from the *koya* flowing through her veins like the dye radiologists flush through a patient's body during CT scans. "Where are they going?" she asked Curtis.

"Jail around back, unless you tell me otherwise."

Anika stared at Ricky like a voodooist.

His rant grew more hysterical. "You'll pay for this, Anika! You're now the enemy!" He howled like a coyote pup lost in the Miranda plains, the last gasp of desperation as the deputy shoved him around the corner of the Alamo. "You were family!"

Anika looked at Chelsea, her eyes as big as sand dollars. "Chels, follow them around back. Make sure the deputies get them in the building. Then bring me that red gasoline can near the garage." Anika noticed Chelsea's eyes checking with Curtis, but he just shrugged.

"Wantin' to mow the lawn?" he said.

"That can filled with gas?" she asked.

"Figure there's a gallon and a half." He quickly discerned what had captured Anika's attention in the park. It was open and obvious. "You'll need this," he said, handing Anika a silver Zippo lighter. Curtis didn't smoke, but fixers often needed fire for other reasons.

Fixers fix things. That's what they do.

"I hate these people," she said as she snatched the lighter and watched the multitudes complain inside the Hospitality Center.

"Don't be too hard on 'em. They can't help themselves. Besides, if governin' was easy, any nincompoop could do it."

Anika seethed. The object left behind by the protesters flapped in the morning wind like a gigantic red cape at a bullfight in Matamoras.

"Want *me* to do it?" Curtis asked. "With all due respect, what you have in mind ain't very mayor-like."

"Maybe I'm a different kind of mayor," she said.

Curtis chuckled. "Ain't no doubt about that." He moved to retrieve the gas can from Chelsea, who was walking up the porch stairs.

But Anika ran out of patience. She stepped in front of him and grabbed the can herself, passing Chelsea on the steps. "Thank you, Chels."

"What's she doing?" Chelsea asked Curtis.

Curtis shook his head and continued to chuckle. "She's about to heat things up." He yelled at Anika from the porch. "Be careful out there, you hear? You'll blow yourself to kingdom come."

Anika unscrewed the cap as she approached the large banner tied with twine between two mesquite trees. As she crossed the road, the screaming, jeering, and cursing coming from the Hospitality Center grew louder. The cacophonic crescendo sounded like a roar as Anika lifted the red can and doused the white banner with gasoline, making sure she saturated each letter—from the *J* to the *S*. She tossed the can aside and admired her work. The black paint that formed the letters now bled to the banner's bottom, but the words remained visible: JOHNNY LIVES.

Stepping back, Anika smiled at her prisoners and clicked open the Zippo. Its flame hopped to life. Wasting no time, she underhand-tossed the lighter through the air. It hit the middle of its target, and the banner exploded into flames. Anika failed to stand her ground as the explosive reverberations blew her backward and singed her eyebrows. She stayed on her feet but could smell the faint traces of burning hair.

Regaining her composure, she noticed her prisoners had taken note. They responded to her antics with complete silence and jaw-dropping awe. Some focused on the flames, but most gaped at the mayor. She had sent a clear message. Not unlike the flames that encompassed the Johnny Lives banner, the mayor was dangerous and unpredictable.

Meanwhile, the circus horn of Cyclops's pre-World War II flatbed truck broke the silence. That was followed by an errant column shift that killed the engine and stalled the jalopy on the road between Anika and the Alamo. Dust caked the windshield, which opened from the bottom with a crank-out knob. A large, presumably inanimate object wrapped in a blue tarp lay in the truck bed. Cyclops crawled out of the vehicle, followed by Moon, Peanut, and Vernis, and lumbered toward Anika with his overalls, straw cowboy hat, and devious smile. "How 'bout-cha? Looks like I missed the cook-off!"

"Y'all find Crazy Eyes?"

"No, ma'am, but we ain't done trackin' that wharf rat," Cyclops said, spitting out his wad of snuff and cleaning his false teeth with his tongue. "But I did bring you a small present from the big city. A tiny token of our appreciation."

"Did you bring me a Civil War cannon? Not sure I'm that violent."

Tilting his head, Cyclops regarded the fire raging behind her, the fury in her eyes, the black marks on her face, and the prisoners screaming and clamoring for release in the distance. "Whatever you say, Mayor." After an uncomfortable pause, he continued, "No, I saw the photo of Selena in your office a few days ago, so I brought you a keepsake—a little sumpin' sumpin'—that'll remind you of her. Forever."

Intrigued, Anika cast her attention on the truck bed.

"Vernis, pull the tarp!" Cyclops yelled.

Selena Quintanilla, born in a nearby town, was the most famous Tejano star in history. Sadly, her budding career ended soon after it began. In 1995, the former manager of her fan club shot her to death with a .38 Special at a Days Inn in Corpus Christi. The famous "Queen of Tejano" had been Anika's age when she uttered her last words, words that identified her killer before her eyes rolled back into her head: "Yolanda Saldivar in Room 158."

Selena meant the world to Corpus Christians. The city had commissioned an iconic, life-sized bronze statue that it unveiled in 1997 at the Bayfront Seawall. On that seawall, the Selena statue had weathered all storms for decades. It depicted Selena leaning against a wall with her right leg bent and her head turned away in reflection. Holding a microphone, she wore the same leather outfit exhibited in the Smithsonian's National

Museum of American History. Thousands of adoring fans, including Anika and Sam, visited her memorial each year, took pictures with the statue, and paid their respects.

Even before Vernis pulled away the tarp, Anika realized the unthinkable.

Selena's iconic statue lay in the back of Cyclops's truck.

43

FIVE YEARS AGO

INTERVIEW OF ANIKA RAVEN

FBI Special Agent Brian Maxwell: Please state your full name and age.

Witness: Anika Raven.

Agent: And your age?

Witness: Eighteen. Sorry.

Agent: Is everything okay? You're shaking.

Witness: I just lost my boyfriend, and I don't know why I'm here . . . answering questions.

Agent: Ms. Raven, I'm sorry about your loss, and I understand it may be difficult answering questions so soon after Johnny Delgado's . . . well, what would you call it?

Witness: Accident? I don't know.

Agent: Accident. Okay.

Witness: Logan Danforth told me this was a murder investigation. Do you believe Johnny was murdered?

Agent: Hmm. Mr. Danforth wasn't supposed to say anything about—

Witness: And he said that he'd hired a lawyer. Do I need a lawyer?

Agent: Ms. Raven, I can't imagine why you'd need a lawyer. This is the kind of routine inquiry that we conduct after any *accident* like this. Of course . . . if there's something that you've done that's causing you concern—something you feel you need to hide—then I can't deny you counsel. We can wait.

Witness: I haven't done anything wrong. I have nothing to hide.

Agent: May I continue without a lawyer present?

Witness: Yes, of course. I don't even know any lawyers.

Agent: Since you mentioned Logan Danforth, can you describe your relationship with him?

Witness: Relationship? We don't have a relationship. What does that have to do with anything?

Agent: Please answer the question.

Witness: He's a friend. We've known each other since diapers.

Agent: Just a friend?

Witness: I don't understand this line of . . . yes! He's just a friend.

Agent: No need to get upset, Ms. Raven.

Witness: I'm not getting upset.

Agent: And to be clear, you *do* believe your boyfriend has passed, correct? You believe that Johnny is dead?

Witness: [Nonresponsive. Sobbing.]

Agent: Do we need to take five?

Witness: No.

Agent: No, we don't need to take five minutes or—

Witness: Johnny's dead, and I don't need a break. Ugh! Why do I have to do this?

Agent: Please let me know if we can make you more comfortable. Would you like a Coke or some coffee?

Witness: No, I'm fine. I just want this to be over.

Agent: We don't have much longer. Is it true that on the night Johnny died you and Logan were together?

Witness: What do you mean by "together?"

Agent: It's not a trick question.

Witness: We went to the homecoming dance *together*, if that's what you mean.

Agent: As friends?

Witness: Yes, just friends.

Agent: Is it true that, after the dance, Johnny witnessed you and Logan kissing?

Witness: What? Yes, but—

Agent: Making out?

Witness: That line of questioning is inappropriate.

Agent: Do you always make out with your friends?

Witness: I'm not answering that! What kind of question is that?

Agent: Calm down. This isn't a trial, Ms. Raven, but it goes to Johnny's state of mind and, quite frankly, your veracity.

Witness: I feel under attack.

Agent: Would you like to take a break?

Witness: No, I want this to be over. Now.

Agent: Ms. Raven, are you high right now?

Witness: What?

Agent: Are you on drugs?

Witness: Of course not! What are you insinuating?

Agent: There were drugs in Johnny's car. Did Johnny do drugs?

Witness: No! Johnny was a straight-*A* student, a model of . . . what are we doing here?

Agent: Some have indicated that you may have connections with the Xalisco Boys from Mexico. Is that true?

Witness: I must ask *you*: Are *you* high!? Who said that? I'm the valedictorian of Miranda High School! I'm going to Rice University! I don't use drugs! I don't engage in nonsense! You are—

Agent: I'm not sure why you're being so evasive, so combative.

Witness: You told me I didn't need a lawyer. You told me this was a routine inquiry.

Agent: Ms. Raven, given the nature of your answers, I need to ask my colleagues to join us.

Special Agents Victor Reyes and Theodore Holder: [Enter.]

Witness: Not sure what that means.

Special Agent Maxwell: One last line of questioning, Ms. Raven. I need to talk to you about explosives.

Witness: This is crazy. *Stranger Things*-like crazy.

Special Agent Maxwell: Are you aware that Johnny's car contained C-4 explosives?

Witness: That's nuts! I'm done talking. I want a lawyer.

Special Agent Maxwell: Ms. Raven, you have the right to remain silent. Anything you say . . .

[Issues *Miranda* warning. Subject Anika Raven is arrested and taken into custody.]

End.

44

PRESENT DAY

The weather report squawked from the radio in Cyclops's lap, snapping him out of his siesta. Things had changed. And not for the good. Even without this news, the morning breeze had a new feel to it, signaling the beginning of a different kind of storm.

Corpus Christi is now in the hurricane's cone, the computerized report declared with programmatic matter-of-factness.

"Hurricane's changed course!" Cyclops yelled. "She's comin' right for us!"

Anika and her staff, including Timmy, congregated on the front porch with the old timers. This was news that carried great enormity. The hurricane had shifted course and, instead of snaking northward—over Haiti, through Jacksonville, toward the Outer Banks—now barreled westward through the Gulf of Mexico. Straight for South Texas. For some, the news came as a shock; for others, it confirmed the accuracy of their intelligence; for Cyclops, it vindicated his "gut feeling."

For Anika, it was a test. A test of her leadership, of her mettle. She had managed consequential issues in recent days, hours, and even minutes, but this crisis was different. It was existential. And now everyone was looking at her, including Curtis. She knew he couldn't help her with this moment, the moment she voiced her first words in response to this news. He could try to fix it if she messed up, but it's hard to stuff panic back in the tube—

even harder to characterize chokers as champions. And Miranda needed its mayor to be a champion if the town were to survive Hurricane Lorenzo.

"This shouldn't be a surprise," she said loudly but calmly, turning to address the old timers. "Some of you have prepared for this moment for years. Thanks to some great intel," she winked at Cyclops, "we're out in front of this and ahead of schedule. Evacuations have begun, and they will continue. The hurricane has changed its course, but let me be clear: *we will not change ours*."

"Hear, hear!" Peanut shouted.

She continued with the crowd focused on her every word. "Don't make panicked decisions, trust the process, and stay focused. Let me or Curtis know if you need any guidance or assistance. More to come, but that's enough from me," she said, slapping her hands together. "Let's get back to work! We have lives to save!" she exhorted, looking again at Cyclops, who was nodding with a proud tear running down his cheek. "Lives to honor!"

Chelsea, Logan, and Timmy returned to work as Cyclops listened to the weather report in his rocking chair. Curtis joined Anika at the porch railing overlooking the park. He was struggling for the right words, but his eyes said everything. "I'm . . . uh . . ."

I'm proud of you, Anika. Or was it, *I'm sorry, Anika.* Maybe both. She would never know for sure because words escaped him. It didn't matter. Either way, her response was the same. "I know," she said.

The park bustled. Deputies continued to detain unruly citizens in the Hospitality Center, and construction workers framed its roof to make way for the skylight's plastic panels. Nearby, joggers, picnickers, and other law-abiding bystanders watched Moon, Peanut, and Vernis struggle to raise the Selena statue in the middle of the park. Meanwhile, whatever remained of the JOHNNY LIVES banner fueled the final flames of Anika's amateur pyrotechnics show.

It also fueled questions Curtis had yet to answer.

She stared at his profile as he gazed at the statue. Her eyes took measure of every facial feature, every nuance of his expression. Was now the time to ask him? He said he welcomed the conversation, and she no longer feared he would hurt her. Not physically. At least not unless she tried to escape. But she feared something else. She feared hearing truths she couldn't unhear; truths she couldn't accept; truths that, once heard, would haunt and paralyze her. *Why did you kill Johnny? Why was I framed for it?*

It took all her discipline and might, but she demurred. "What else? I don't want Lorenzo catching me unprepared."

"Plenty to do, but I reckon we've got the hurricane prep covered."

"What about levees and floodwalls?"

"We don't have levees. Our footprint is different than what they got up there in New Orleans. We do have a seawall, though."

"Is it sound? Can we do anything to buttress it to prevent a breach . . . build it up to prevent overtopping?"

"There won't be any breach or overtoppin', per se."

"What do you mean by *per se*?"

"A Category 5 hurricane will obliterate our seawall . . . lickety-split. Nothin' short of heaven's good graces can prevent that."

"What about pump stations?" she asked. "Have we done all the necessary maintenance and operation on critical infrastructure?"

"Pump stations ain't got nothin' to do with it, but you're startin' to sound like a pro."

"I do my homework. Google- and YouTube-trained mayor."

"No drainage pumps in these parts."

"Sure we're not missing anything?" she probed.

"Responsibility for maintenance and operation of critical infrastructure are diffused throughout federal, state, and local authorities. Managin' that is a mess, and it won't matter anyway. We'll see a mighty storm surge and wind speeds over one hundred and fifty, causing flying debris. Worse yet, the seawall will fail before the eye of the hurricane reaches us. And once the seawall fails, billions of gallons of the Gulf of Mexico will flood South Texas."

"Sounds terrible."

"Toppled trees, power outages, displaced rattlesnakes washed away by flash flooding. I'd rather drown than have a rattlesnake bite me."

She rubbed the side of her face. "Nothing else on infrastructure?"

"We'll focus on the roads and insist on contraflow. I'll call TxDOT tomorrow and—"

"TxDOT? Contraflow?"

"Texas Department of Transportation will order contraflow, or lane reversal, once Lorenzo gets closer, but sometimes they're late. We need I-37 goin' north in all directions by tomorrow afternoon. Railroads will be operative until the floodin' starts but of little use because—"

"Lack of volume with limited tracks and cars."

"Right."

"What else?" she persisted like a field general.

"Utilities will be down soon. Internet'll be down. Cell towers compromised."

"Do we have generators?"

"We have generators at key facilities throughout town, including the hospital and at the Alamo. Hurricane's gonna knock out power right after landfall. Based on current projections, I reckon that'll be around noon on Friday."

"Less than seventy-two hours. At least it'll be daylight." Small in the grand scheme of things, questions concerning Scotty Mathis's body—still frozen in the morgue—surfaced. "What about Sam's dad?"

Curtis's pregnant pause illustrated an ounce of sympathy, even if his answer didn't. "Reckon his body won't thaw out before the sharks get him."

"Eek. I feel like there's something else."

"There is something else," he said, his eyes turning toward her for the first time during the conversation.

Anika wondered whether this was the moment. The moment when he'd raise the issue of her leaving with Sam. Was now the time, with the hurricane just days away and most of the preparation finished? She hoped that he'd come to his senses, realize she was of little importance, and release them. Release them from the hurricane's path. Release them from Miranda's clutches. Release them from floating rattlesnakes and hungry sharks. Release them from certain death by drowning or cancer. *Release them to medical care at St. Jude's.* "What is it?"

"There's the problem with the preacher-man."

Of course. The preacher-man. Curtis was like the main character in the movie *Heat*, she thought. The one who has freedom in his sights but throws it away just to settle scores. "You said no chasing varmints down rabbit holes. What threat is he at this point?"

"Varmints ain't got nothin' to do with it," Curtis fussed. "He's the primary threat."

"There's a hurricane barreling down on us that says otherwise."

"Before that, Mayor, there's a war comin'. Tomorrow or the next day, before the storm hits. It's a war that he'll start, but it's one we'll need to finish if we're gonna survive. That's why we've gotta confiscate those guns from his church members."

"Chelsea's working with the deputies on a plan to seize the guns. I just approved the list."

"I also have a team outfittin' a couple of vehicles. Just in case things get bad."

"Outfitting vehicles? Let me ask you a question, Curtis," she said, bending down and picking up a leaf on the porch floor. "What do you see here? Go ahead and take it."

"It's an oak leaf," Curtis said, holding it up to his eyes.

"When you look at that leaf," she pointed, "do you see a midrib that runs down the middle?"

"Yeah, but how did you know that doodad is called a midrib? Never heard that word."

"I was valedictorian, remember? I made an *A* in biology."

"Yes, I remember," he said as the loud hammering stopped in the distance.

"And breaking off from that midrib are several veins that extend out left and right. You see that?"

"Right."

"Now, when you look at that pattern, does it tell you anything?"

"Like what?" he asked, keeping one eye on the leaf and another on the construction workers in the distance. They were yammering in excitement as they raised the first large plastic sheeting for the Hospitality Center skylight.

"As if something will happen, or not, based on whether the veins are—"

"It ain't like that, Mayor," he interrupted, shaking his head, spitting in disgust between his feet, and tossing the leaf over the porch railing. "Readin' cubes ain't like readin' the lines on some dang leaf."

"Well, before we start disarming citizens and prepping for *war*, we need to make sure—"

"Anika Raven!" yelled a woman walking toward the patio with her beau in tow and cowboy hat in hand. "Police say they can't help me without your permission!"

"Sarah Danforth!" Anika said with genuine surprise and a fake smile. "So good to see—"

"What is this nonsense?" Sarah complained. "I requested police assistance long ago! They won't even check the town surveillance cameras near my store! What kind of operation are y'all running here?"

"I'm so sorry, Sarah. Are you in danger?"

Sarah stopped short of the Alamo porch, hands on her hips, staring up at Anika in outrage. Soliciting help, she grabbed her new shiny boy toy who'd followed her. It was clear, however, that he was out of his element and wouldn't engage. His body language suggested that if his new princess had hoped for Obi-Wan Kenobi, she'd chosen the wrong jedi. Shaking her head in disgust, Sarah pointed her cowboy hat at Anika. "I don't need to come *beg* from you!"

Anika wasn't long for this spectacle. She couldn't allow Sarah to undermine her authority publicly. "But yet here you are, literally hat in hand, asking about the operation *I'm* running. My question stands: *Are you in danger?*"

"Of course I'm in danger! Someone broke into my store and stole a new pair of Lucchese boots. Those boots are worth more than—"

"More than what?" the voice came from the swinging doors. Anika turned around. She hadn't noticed Logan before now. He had returned to the porch, summoned by the Pavlovian enticements of the shrieking, familial voice. Chelsea stood beside him as he continued addressing his wife. "I see you have something else new . . . beyond footwear."

"I'll handle this, Logan," Anika said, her face heating up upon noticing Sarah wasn't wearing her wedding ring. Anika didn't want to emasculate Logan, but he was no match for his estranged wife. "I've had enough of this harlot. She tramples on everyone around her."

Sarah, shell-shocked by Anika's vicious response, calculated her next move. It didn't take combat training to know when one was outnumbered and outflanked. Her new lover refused to protect her honor, and she was staring up at a porch full of enemies unwilling to budge. "I want justice."

"I'll have the sheriff's deputies meet you first thing in the morning," Anika declared.

"You promise?"

"I promise. Please leave now."

As Sarah hiked back to her upscale boutique, Anika grabbed Curtis and followed Logan and Chelsea inside the Alamo. The four of them congregated in Logan's office. Anika closed the door and addressed Logan. "Are you all in, Logan?"

"I'm not sure what—"

"Look at me!" she said, her finger pointed at him. "*Are . . . you . . . all . . . in?*"

"Yes. Whatever it takes."

"Chelsea," Anika said, "I need another special project from you. Actually, I need *two* things from you this evening."

I want justice, Sarah had said. Tomorrow, Anika would give it to her.

45

The rooster crowed, Timmy blasted "Reveille" over the porch speakers, and Anika threw open the swinging doors. No one else moved or made a peep. The early-rising old timers on the porch held their dominoes (and their breaths) as Anika emerged onto the porch. The pipe fell out of Peanut's mouth and crashed to the floor. Anika's eyes were alive and sinister, her smile prodigious. And her head was now much lighter. . . hosting a new buzz cut.

Cyclops broke the silence. "My heavens, girl! Where'd your hair go? Saints be silenced . . . you're as pretty as the mornin'," he said. "Didn't think you could look more beautiful than you did yesterday. I was *wrong*."

"First time he's admitted to bein' wrong," Moon said. "Find shelter 'fore the lightning strikes!"

"That man's never been more right 'bout bein' wrong," Peanut said, picking up his pipe without taking his eyes off Anika.

"Good morning, boys," she said, walking down the steps in her Johnny Was blouse, tattered blue jeans, lightning bolt earrings . . . and brand new Lucchese cowboy boots. They fit perfectly.

"Penny for your thoughts!" Cyclops shouted.

Without looking back, Anika raised her fist and yelled, "Justice!"

In the distance, near the middle of the park, workers had finished construction on the Hospitality Center. They loaded up their tools and materials from the jobsite: excess plywood, nails, Plexiglas, and whatnot. They left behind a few ladders, along with a generator, lighting, and rolls of plastic sheeting. The roof, with its rectangular patches of skylight, was

239

up. Most occupants remained in their cots. The around-the-clock hammering had likely kept them awake much of the night.

It would take time, Anika thought, for them to understand that she wasn't some tinpot despot. In keeping with the detention center's euphemistic name, Timmy would soon provide the hospitality. He would serve the guests coffee and his award-winning breakfast tacos, along with veggie and vegan options. (Always perfecting his craft, Timmy was excited—if not a tad nervous—to unveil new variations of tofu and gluten-free tacos.)

But first thing's first; justice needed serving.

Anika sat on one end of the park bench across the street, facing the Alamo. Timmy appeared through the swinging doors with his apron on, wiping bacon grease from his hands as he scampered down the steps. He crossed the street, sat next to Anika, and put his arm around her neck. Timmy had found his happy place. Not only had he joined Team Anika, but also she'd invited him to this morning's inaugural staff meeting.

Chelsea and Logan arrived with painted skeleton faces, an antic Anika had pre-approved. In addition to white makeup and black lipstick, they had painted black circles around their eyes, black splotches on their noses, and black stitching around their mouths. Anika didn't fully understand the gesture. That Chelsea would paint her face didn't faze Anika; Outlaw Chelsea Wales was half-crazy on a normal day, and this was not a normal day. Logan's participation, however, surprised her. It wasn't his style. But then again, he'd stayed up late at the bar, soaking his sorrows in Lone Star suds and listening to lovesick tunes. Anika guessed that a heartbroken-inspired hangover had impaired his morning judgment.

She had excused Sam and Curtis from the staff meeting, which was a good thing because the bench only seated four. Sam, meanwhile, drew cubes in Anika's office, and Curtis and a few others—mechanics and body-shop types—outfitted a large vehicle in the Alamo garage. Curtis called it "war preparations." Anika didn't know what to think about that, but she couldn't think about it right now. She waited patiently as deputies on horseback took position in strategic areas of the park. Anika also spotted a deputy on the witch's hat roof of the orange-and-white-striped Whataburger building. His bolt-action rifle rested on a bipod stand near the rooftop air-conditioner. Curtis hadn't taken any chances on security. Though he worked behind the scenes, his cautious hand and obsessive planning operated in plain view.

The music ended and Four Points fell silent. Queuing his next song, Timmy issued Anika a devious grin and flashed the remote control for his jukebox. She patted his leg as he waggled his eyebrows. She glanced at Logan at the end of the bench. No telling how Logan would respond to the main event. He stared forward into nowhere, looking more eccentric than spooky, seemingly haunted by failure, betrayal, and consequences wrought by crushed expectations.

"You okay, Logan?" she asked.

He continued his catatonic stare but signaled a thumbs-up.

Anika noticed Peanut staring at her from the porch table, his pipe reloaded. He had recently shared an interesting story. In 1995, he had retired from the Southeast Texas field office of the Bureau of Alcohol Tobacco and Firearms, or ATF (now ATFE to include Explosives). Two years earlier, he'd been in Waco, Texas (about five hours north) for the ATF and FBI standoff with David Koresh's religious cult, the Branch Davidians. To torment Koresh and encourage his followers to surrender, federal law enforcement played Nancy Sinatra's "These Boots Are Made for Walkin'." Koresh never surrendered, and his maniacal stubbornness led to the tragic deaths of seventy-six followers, including many innocent children. But Peanut's story had inspired Anika.

The song began when Sarah came into view and Timmy hit play. The iconic and memorable bass line with quarter-tone descent set the stage. Optics being everything, Chelsea had deployed policewomen to effect the arrest. And she allowed no handcuffs. The two female deputies—replete with brown uniforms, seven-point badges, and eight-point caps—flanked Sarah and held her arms as they marched her from her boutique toward the Alamo. To get from Sarah's store to the Hospitality Center, crows wouldn't fly over the park bench. Anika considered it important, though, that this prisoner march follow the Miranda parade route. People would witness her administration serving justice. They would understand that those living lifestyles of the rich and famous couldn't escape punishment.

They would see—with their own eyes—that no one could mess with her or her staff. Or else.

"Wait, wait, listen," Sarah pleaded to the deputies as they escorted her down the middle of the road. "Where are you taking me?"

"Come along, ma'am," one of them said.

"But you don't understand!" Sarah bellowed. "I didn't know she was undocumented." This was another *Captain Renault, call your office* moment. Employing undocumented workers in Miranda was the equivalent of *There's gambling in this establishment?*

"That's the least of your problems," the other deputy said.

"Wait a second! I don't know anything about explosives. Somebody planted those. Listen, why would I have explosives?"

"You can tell the judge all about the C-4 in your supply closet," one deputy said.

"And we'll see what else the bomb squad finds," said the other.

Chelsea's more ruthless than I am, Anika thought. *She must've worked with Curtis on the explosives setup. Brutal . . . no, brutally effective.*

Sarah was within field goal range of Anika's park bench when she realized her immediate challenge. That's when reality set in; and that's when she lost it. That's when her desperate pleading metamorphosed into insanity. The sheriff's deputies clutched her arms tightly as she peddled her feet in the air and screamed, "Stop! Stop! You can't take me to jail! I didn't do anything wrong!"

The deputies marched toward the Alamo with purpose and without emotion. There would be no more talking. No negotiation. Anika noticed that, despite Sarah's writhing, the cadence and synchronization of the deputies' footfalls rivaled any Fightin' Texas Aggie Band halftime show.

Twenty yards away, Sarah fell in line. She hadn't accepted her fate—that would come later, during the storm—but she was losing steam. But then she spotted Anika on the bench and reverted to lunacy. Sarah fussed and fought and kicked and screamed. No one on the bench, not even Timmy, escaped her wrath.

"You! With that stupid tomboy haircut! You pariah! You thief!" Sarah screamed as she struggled to break loose. "She's wearing my boots! She stole them! *She's* the one you should arrest! Not me! She's a thief and a scoundrel! She set me up!"

Anika smiled, crossed her legs, and dangled her boots. Rubbing Sarah's nose in the boot heist proved more painful to Her Highness than a literal boot to the face. And Sarah didn't respond well to Anika's silence.

"Turn off that ridiculous song, you nitwit!" she yelled at Timmy. Timmy, unaccustomed to criticism, took the ableist insult in stride. He had to grab Anika, though, who didn't take the slight well—*at all*. She was poised to stand up, charge, and tackle Sarah after that discriminatory remark. Timmy, however, wouldn't let Sarah's calloused heart and foul mouth ruin his good time. He lifted his remote control, taunted Sarah as he slowly moved his finger to it, and then—his eyebrows waggling once again—mashed "Replay."

As "These Boots Are Made for Walkin'" restarted, Anika high-fived Timmy as Sarah howled. Sarah's words, already scathing in tone, grew more offensive in substance. She shouted curse words young children had never heard and the old timers had long forgotten. Her normally clear eyes—now cloudy and bloodshot—bulged from their sockets. She frothed at the mouth, and high-frequency wheezing noises accompanied her speech.

Madness!

"And *you* . . . *Missssy*," she hissed, directing her ire to Chelsea. "You played a leading role in this set-up! You're a traitor and a tramp! And to think I considered hiring you in the first place! *Trash!*"

Chelsea's skeleton smile reflected her genuine mood. She wanted to stand up, dance a jig, and chant, "Sticks and stones can break my bones . . ." But she had something more provocative in mind, something more sinister. Chelsea pursed her lips and blew Sarah a kiss; then she placed her hand on Logan's leg and rubbed it. Slowly. Passionately. Her eyes never left Sarah's, and her smile never left her painted face.

Sarah—unnerved but undeterred—saved the crescendo of contempt for her husband. "You're a weak fool, Logan! Go look in the mirror at your face! I'm embarrassed to call you my husband! You've always been something less than a man! We're finished! You hear me? *Finished!* I don't ever—"

"Shut up, witch," he said calmly. He spat toward her, careful not to threaten the deputies. Chelsea's hand climbed from his leg to his neck, a gesture meant to prevent him from overreacting.

Anika and her staff watched (what forever would be called) the *Sarah Spectacle* until the policewomen marched her into the Hospitality Center. Anika's choreography of the event likely surprised her former high school classmates. She wasn't known for vengeance or marked by a short temper. Instead, they'd crowned her queen in large part because of her grace and mercy. But times had changed, and extraordinary behaviors demanded commensurate measures. Anika kept promising herself she would be better, maybe return to her old self. Perhaps, one day, Anika would apologize to her enemies, starting with Sarah. Meanwhile, she needed to protect herself, her team, and others in town, even if that meant resorting to harsh measures for jerks and ne'er-do-wells.

The Sarah Spectacle conveyed that sentiment. It had the added benefit of great theater, something the Alamo Opera House had lacked for decades. But Sarah was the least of Anika's problems. A storm approached, and a more consequential battle brewed. Standing from the park bench, Anika knew the coming hours would be crucial to her and Sam's survival.

46

Anika refused to fixate on Logan's altered state of consciousness. His painted skeleton face made that difficult. A man on top of the world a few days ago, now a picture of crushing defeat. He looked psychotic. Larger trouble loomed, though, and she had no time for handholding or therapy. Whether it was the hangover, the heartbreak, or watching the po-po perp-walk his wife Salem-style, Logan needed to snap out of his hallucinogenic state. Fast. And he needed to overcome adversity if Anika's team hoped to succeed. Category 5 hurricanes didn't care about lovesick fools feeling sorry for themselves.

"Logan," Anika said, returning to the Alamo, "I need you engaged. One hundred percent. I need to know—"

"All in!" he screamed like he'd acquired Tourette's.

Keeping stride with Chelsea, Anika placed an arm around her. "Wash the paint off your face before confiscating guns. Otherwise, some cowboy will shoot you on sight. At least twice."

"Yes, ma'am," Chelsea giggled. "Of course."

"And Logan can't go with you," Anika said in a hushed voice. "He's not right. Too unpredictable, too vulnerable."

"Understood. I'll help him wash off the paint and encourage him to post his signs around Four Points."

"Good luck, Chels. And make sure someone picks up Sarah's Range Rover and drives it around back . . . to the garage." *To Curtis's makeshift armory*, she failed to add as she climbed the porch stairs toward the swinging doors.

"That was somethin' fierce, Mayor!" Cyclops said, rocking in his chair, his face radiant, his pipe billowing plumes of smoke. "My goodness me."

"Like them yanks say up north: *wicked good*," Vernis added. "The stuff of legend, really."

If Peanut wanted to say something, his mouth forbade it. It remained agape and dysfunctional as he stared in awe at Anika.

"Moon, y'all do me a favor and help Logan post signs, okay?" Anika said, pushing open the swinging doors, not waiting for a response.

Anika walked to her office. Sam lay in the fetal position on the couch, paper covered in cubes strewn on the floor. Her blonde hair fell like a mop over her face, and the morning sun glistened off the peach fuzz on her legs. Sam needed help. She needed a doctor. Anika suspected the tumor in her head was growing. Again, however, Anika had limited choices. She could curl in a ball herself and hope the world's problems would pass. She could fret, moan, cry, and complain. Or she could follow her dad's instruction, quoting Winston Churchill: *Never, never, never, give up!*

She pressed on. She needed to have an honest discussion with Sam. They needed to go somewhere safe. Somewhere where the rooms weren't bugged, where inquiring minds didn't linger. "Samantha," she said, grabbing the Rubik's Cube from her desk and brushing away the hair from her sister's face. She heard the old timers filing into the Alamo Commons, their boots shuffling on the dusty hardwood floors. They were loading up on breakfast tacos, she guessed, before helping Logan post his propaganda around town. "Get up, girl. I know you're exhausted, but we need to walk." She leaned down and whispered, "We don't have much time."

A drawing on the floor caught Anika's attention. Like Sam's bridge drawing, it was more architectural than cubical. Anika folded and pocketed it. "Let's go," she said, and Sam opened her eyes and grabbed Anika's hand. The two scurried through the Commons toward the porch, past the old timers. "Timmy," Anika announced, "Sam and I are going for a stroll." Though she addressed Timmy by name, her message was meant for older ears. *When Curtis asks, tell him we're fine.*

"Understood," Timmy said dutifully without lifting his head.

Anika's next request, made before she reached the swinging doors, was genuine and without pretext. "Also, please tell Curtis to check on Mom at the convalescent center."

Not long into their walk, they reached Whataburger. The owner had bolt locked and chained the front doors, but the lights were on inside. Sam still in tow, Anika walked to the glass doors and knocked. Janice O'Brien (real name Maria López from San Luis Potosi, Mexico) was sweeping the floors (Anika had read Auntie Dodd's file on her). *A hurricane's coming,* Anika thought, *but she's sweeping her floors. Of course she is. That's what proprietors—those who don't take their opportunities for granted—do.* Janice, startled by the rapping on the doors, collected her wits and motioned Anika to come around the building.

Janice was waiting when they reached the service door. "I'll be gone in the next two hours, Mayor. I promise," the anxious Whataburger owner said. "I was just—"

"You're fine, Janice," Anika said as they walked inside. *We aren't Immigration and Customs Enforcement.* "Thank you for heeding the evacuation order."

"Just cleaning up before the storm," Janice said, grabbing her broom as if to make her point. "We're not serving food."

"We're not police, Janice, and we're not hungry. My sister and I just want some peace and quiet for half an hour. You mind if we have a seat in the corner?"

Janice was bewildered but accommodating. "Not at all," she said, leaning on her broom and casting a glance at the corner table. "Be my guest."

As they slid into the bench seats across from one another, Anika grabbed the small, square ketchup packet on the table. The smell of bacon grease, French fries, and milkshakes—caked into the walls, tables, and ceilings—brought back fond memories from Anika's childhood.

She tossed the Rubik's Cube on the table, and it landed with a thud. "I need to tell you a secret, Sam. I feel terrible about keeping it from you, but I did it for your own good."

Sam stared at her.

"The reason you can't talk right now, the reason you're so tired . . . is because you have a brain tumor."

Sam sat still, eyes locked on Anika, with no change of facial expression.

Surprised by her sister's stoicism, Anika asked, "Did you already know this?"

Sam nodded.

"Did Auntie Dodd tell you?"

Sam shook her head.

"Curtis?"

Another shake of the head.

"How did you find out? The cubes? You can feel it?"

Sam shook her head, pulled a pencil from her pocket, and grabbed a Whataburger napkin. As Anika watched, Sam scribbled a word on the napkin, folded it, and slid it across the table.

Anika snatched the napkin but stared at Sam before opening it. Then she unfolded it and looked down.

Pastor Joshua.

"Joshua shouldn't have told you," Anika said, taking a deep breath, allowing her anger to melt into acceptance. "That's my responsibility. Did he tell you anything else?"

Sam continued her stare, twitched her nose a bit, and nodded.

"When we get back to the Alamo, you'll need to write down everything he said. For now, though, I want to say . . . I'm sorry. I'm sorry I didn't tell you first. Will you forgive me?"

This time her response wasn't delayed. Sam nodded immediately. "What was so secret in Pastor Joshua's room?" Sam wrote on the napkin.

"A bunch of scary weapons and weird pictures from long ago," Anika replied.

Sam turned over the napkin and continued writing. "Why were the pictures weird?"

"They were taken long ago and weren't supposed to have survived other big hurricanes."

"That makes them weird?" Sam scribbled.

Anika was done lying to Sam, but she chose her words carefully. "They were also weird because I thought I saw Pastor Joshua in some of the really old ones. Freaked me out, and it made him angry that I saw them. Who knows? Maybe it was his ancestors who looked like him. Exactly like him."

Sounds from the distance interrupted their exchange. Something outside. They heard the rise in commotion from guests in the Hospitality Center. Fussing, chanting, and clanking objects against the bars. Soon after, Anika heard the militaristic footfalls of police coming their way, followed by sounds of static communication over police radios. Chelsea, too busy to see Anika and Sam in the window, led her police unit, assembled to confiscate the guns. Marching eerily similar to a German goosestep, she had the blacklist in her hand. Her bulletproof vest bulged through her shirt. She had removed the skeleton paint, but she'd styled her hair in Princess Leia buns. Anika hoped Chelsea would heed her advice and steer clear of the real police work—the actual gun confiscation. Witnessing her in action, however, didn't inspire confidence that she'd avoid danger. Chelsea was an adrenaline junky. All bets were off.

Anika turned her attention back to Sam. "Has Curtis taught you how to interpret the cubes?"

Sam shook her head.

Of course not, Anika thought. *Curtis would never relinquish the source of his power.* "What about Joshua?"

Sam tilted her head and nodded.

"Do you understand what you draw?"

Sam shrugged.

"Are you able to interpret all of it?"

She shook her head.

"But you understand most of it?"

Sam squinched her face.

"Some of it?"

She nodded.

Anika smiled. This was a key development, and she was proud of her little sister. Her smile, however, didn't last. "I have another secret. Something I can't tell anyone else, especially not the others on our team. Can you keep a secret? Sisters in the bond?"

Sam nodded.

Anika placed her forehead in her palms. "I'm really scared, Sam." Sam squeezed Anika's hand. "I'm not equipped for this. I don't know what I'm doing." Sam squeezed her hand harder, this time as a show of comfort and support.

A show of *confidence.*

Once again, sounds from outside distracted them. Logan and several old timers shuffled past the window carrying signs. Signs of encouragement, signs loaded with propaganda. Like Chelsea, Logan didn't glance inside the Whataburger fishbowl. Unlike Chelsea, his face advertised despair and defeat rather than adventure and purpose. Like Chelsea, he'd washed off the paint. Unlike her, he'd replaced it with a sad clown face.

"Back to Pastor Joshua," Anika continued. "Do you know if you've been drawing cubes about him? About him coming after us before the storm?"

She nodded.

"Curtis talks of some battle before the storm hits . . . a battle with Joshua and his church. Does that ring a bell?"

She nodded.

"Does that scare you?"

She nodded.

"Can you tell who wins?"

Sam paused and looked out the window, toward the park. Returning her gaze on Anika, she shook her head.

Anika slid the Rubik's Cube toward her. "Can you try using this? Land on a pattern you can interpret?"

Sam stared at the Rubik's Cube, grabbed it, and nodded.

"We're on a wing and a prayer, Sam. Maybe we can pray silently together?"

They held hands again and bowed their heads. After a period of quiet that felt like minutes, Sam, ·for the first time since Anika's homecoming, spoke.

47

"Our Father in heaven," Sam prayed, "hallowed be your name; your kingdom come, your will be done, on earth as it is in heaven . . ."

After Sam finished the Lord's Prayer, Anika's eyes were as large as Whataburger flapjacks, and her bottom lip felt like it was resting on the table.

Without any explanation, Sam winked at her sister, picked up the Rubik's Cube, and got back to work.

"Sam!" Anika screamed before lowering her voice to a loud whisper. "Don't act so casual! You're talking? When did this happen?"

Sam cracked a smile. "Just now."

"Does it feel . . . strange? You know, to be talking again?"

"It's a little weird, to be honest, to hear my voice. Almost forgot what I sounded like."

"Amazing," Anika said, throwing up her hands and shaking her head in disbelief. And then a thought emerged, and she placed her hands atop Sam's (which were still cradling the Rubik's Cube) and leaned over the table. "You can't let anyone know about this. Not yet."

"Why not?"

"Because we're on a war footing, and we can't trust anyone, other than ourselves."

"What about Curtis?"

"That old bird's tricky. We can't trust him, but we need his help."

"I like him," Sam said. "And I draw a lot for him."

He killed your old man in cold blood, Anika thought, *and that was just for starters. He'll kill us, too, if he catches us trying to escape town.* "Keep doing what you're doing, but remain silent. I doubt you'll be drawing much more for him. Hurricane Lorenzo's almost on top of us."

Sam nodded and looked distracted.

"What's wrong?" Anika asked.

"I'm worried about you."

"How so?"

Sam hesitated. "Never mind."

"If something's on your mind, spit it out. Sisters in the bond, remember?"

"You're always nice to me. I just . . ."

"Yeah."

"I don't want you mad all the time. Since you came home, you've been a little—"

"Mean-spirited?" Anika asked.

"But that's not who you are. You're the nicest person I know."

"Fair point," Anika admitted. "It was mean to frog-march Sarah Danforth down Main Street."

Sam laughed.

"But she deserved it, right? So bad."

"I know everything's scary for you right now," Sam said.

"Promise I'll be nicer when this is over. There's still good in my heart, and hopefully, people will understand my decisions after the hurricane."

"I have faith in you."

"What else is bothering you?" Anika asked.

"I miss Mom."

Anika needed to remember she was more calloused than Sam. Her sister gave their mom the benefit of the doubt, whereas Anika had run out of patience for the never-ending hassle and heartbreak. Barbara Mathis had abandoned her children and deserved no additional grace, but Sam saw things differently. Anika felt obligated to ask the obvious follow-up question. "What about your dad?"

"I miss him too . . . but it's different."

It's different because he's dead but not in the ground yet, Anika thought. *That's too much for an adult to process, much more for an eight-year-old.*

Anika pulled out the drawing she'd snagged from Sam's floor pile and placed it on the table. Unlike her cube work, it contained words, numbers, and two-dimensional shapes. The shapes on the front included a trapezoid (in the upper righthand corner) and several triangles (in the middle). On the back, an orb sat atop a rectangle (in the center of the page), along with the word "Latitude" written at an angle (on the bottom lefthand side of the page) and the word "Longitude" written at an angle and upside down (near the middle at the top of the page). To make the drawing more confusing, Sam had added another triangle (in the far righthand corner of the back of the page). Taken together, the multi-folded drawing was an indistinguishable mess.

"Do you think this is an important drawing? I can't make heads or tails of it."

Sam nodded (either out of habit or convenience).

"What are these triangles? Looks like the Giza pyramid complex in Egypt."

Sam, now re-engaged with Anika's interest in her drawing, giggled, "I don't know what Giza is, sis. Those are Mayan temples. I learned about them by watching the History Channel."

Anika smiled. Through all the recent crises and Sam's silence, she'd forgotten that her little sister remained a child. Still innocent, still playful. But life—that is, *Miranda*—had forced her to grow up early. It wasn't fair, but the saying *life isn't fair* was a worn-out cliché for a reason, particularly when staring death in the face. "What about this shape in the top right corner? Looks like a rhombus . . . no, I guess that's a trapezoid. My geometry's rusty."

"I don't know what you call it, but that's the important part of the front page."

"You know what it means?"

"I have a picture in my mind. I think I know how it works."

"How what works?" Anika asked without waiting for an answer. She was ready for the back page. "That doesn't make sense to me. What's on the back? Looks like a golf ball on a tee in the middle?"

"I don't know why I drew that."

"And there's a triangle at the bottom-right?"

"That's important."

"And the words 'Latitude' and 'Longitude?' Those are big words for an eight-year-old."

"I know what they mean. We learned about them in my accelerated learning class at school. But I don't know why I wrote them."

"Do you know why you wrote them at an angle and upside down?"

Sam nodded, and her eyes opened wide.

"Tell me."

"Better yet," Sam said, grabbing her drawing from Anika. "I'll *show* you."

Taking a deep breath, Sam rotated the paper clockwise to a horizontal position. She folded the top-left corner until it was flush with the bottom. The effect of her fold was the trapezoid on the front page, marrying up with the triangle on the back, yielding a larger right triangle.

Their eyes met. "Not sure what to make of it," Anika said. "Maybe a blockade of sorts? Perhaps another impediment town officials will build to block the roads . . . to keep us from leaving town?"

Sam tilted her head, as if to question her sister's hypothesis, and folded the paper again. This time, the page itself made a right triangle, and the words fell into their proper places. The word *Latitude* was couched next to the smallest angle; the word *Longitude* ran alongside the opposite leg of the triangle. "Or a ramp . . ."

A ramp. Amazed, Anika grabbed the folded triangle from her sister, stared at it, and unfolded it. Staring at the image that looked like a golf ball on a tee, she said, "I know what this is. Let's get out of here."

CHAD BOUDREAUX

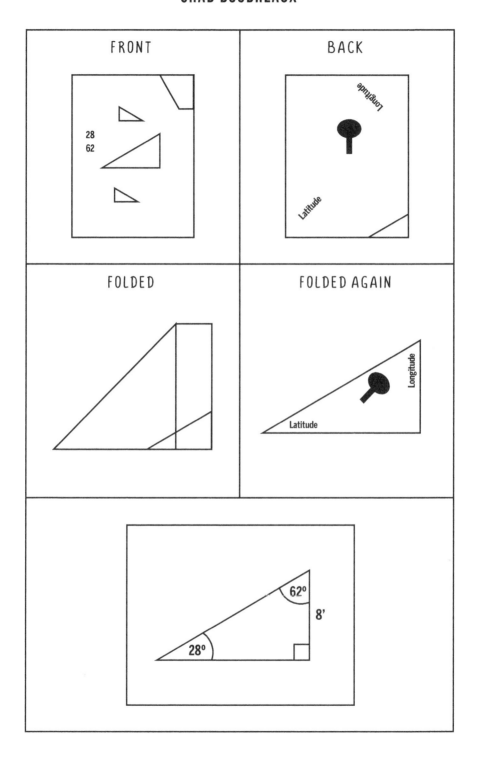

The Miranda water tower was on the edge of the Flats. Never before had it brought to Anika's mind a golf ball on a tee, but when considered in light of Sam's drawing, the resemblance was unmistakable. And where else would one put such a ramp but right here, on the banks of the Miranda River?

Intermittent wind gusts forced Anika to hold the railing near the top of the tower. The air was salty, the seagulls fussy. The birds had their own hurricane escape plan. They would soon be flying in treacherous, spiraling winds toward the calm eye of the storm for protection. Looking down, Anika regarded the Flats as a spot of hopelessness. The spot where Johnny D. died. Rumors aside regarding *whether* Johnny died—all the *Johnny Lives!* malarky was nauseating, especially after Curtis's confession—credible speculation existed as to *when* he died. Before the explosion or after (before he landed . . . or after). Zero speculation, however, existed as to *where* he died. She knew where Curtis had murdered him. Right down there, on the edge of the Flats, in the river shallows.

She hated this place.

But with Sam's drawing, this place of hopelessness offered her the greatest opportunity for hope. *For escape.* Johnny had owned the right vehicle, but he hadn't had a ramp. He had jumped over a hardened dirt pile unsuitable for mountain bikers, much less a four-thousand-pound muscle car. And beyond that, he never had a chance. The Ghost had plenty of muscle, but it didn't have the same odds as the black Trans-Am in *Smokey and the Bandit* or the orange Dodge Charger in *The Dukes of Hazzard*. Someone—likely Curtis or one of his henchmen—had loaded Johnny's trunk with explosives. For whatever reason, Curtis wouldn't let him escape. *Miranda* wouldn't let him escape. *The town don't like people leavin',* Cyclops had said. A push of the button and . . . *boom!*

Anika need to be wilier, less impulsive than Johnny if she and Sam were to escape—to survive. She believed she could outwit Curtis; she was less sure about outwitting whatever controlled him.

As she had directed, the contractors arrived at the Flats with the excess materials (sheets of plywood, two-by-fours, nails, screws, and such) from the Hospitality Center. They smoked cigarettes, wore hard hats, and drove in the nondescript, white contractor trucks (with the bloated, ten-lug chrome hubcaps) commonly found near orange detour signs or construction sites.

If Curtis viewed the construction with suspicion, he hid it well. The purpose of what he called "that contraption" was key. Would it be used to facilitate vehicle travel or, rather, to impede it? Was it a ramp or a blockade? Anika called it the latter, and as the cherry on top, she made Sam write the word "Roadblock" on her drawing. With all the surrounding busyness of battle preparations, Curtis didn't waste much time mulling the project. Sam had drawn it, so it must be important.

Cyclops was the one who had spooked her. Not with his suspicion but with his perception; his puzzle-solving prowess. While others contemplated the contraption's purpose, he wrestled with the words "Latitude" and "Longitude." Why was "Latitude" written in the lower left angle of the triangle? Why was "Longitude" written along the triangle's opposite leg? The improbability of his hypothesis was only outdone by its brilliance. And that's what spooked Anika. Anika had always questioned those interpreting Sam's drawings. She had questioned both their effectiveness and motivation. Before now, reasons had existed beyond the supernatural to explain Sam's drawings and their interpretations. If Cyclops was right, however, it became harder to dismiss supernatural causes. Put differently, the odds of dumb luck made that a harder proposition. No one questioned Sam's IQ, but she didn't know squat about designing ramps.

His hypothesis was as follows: What if the geospatial coordinates of the water tower also served as the dimensions of the blockade (or ramp)? That is, the *latitude* was the angle's size, and the *longitude* was the blockade's height. A quick internet search had revealed that the latitude of the Flats was roughly 28.5N, and its longitude, roughly -96W. That meant the relevant ramp angle would be twenty-eight degrees and the ramp's height—after converting from inches—would be eight feet. Even for the engineering disinclined, that made sense.

Chelsea's math wizardry had come in handy and provided the rest. A quick formula she had jotted on a napkin yielded the remaining dimensions needed to build the contraption. If everything proceeded as planned, Chelsea would need to devise one more formula. Anika couldn't ask her for that now, though. Miranda's will (whatever that meant) likely held power over both Curtis and Chelsea. Anika had to assume, when loyalties conflicted, Chelsea would choose her town over her boss. But eventually—before her planned escape—Anika would need Chelsea to calculate vehicle velocity. That is, how fast the Ghost must travel before reaching the ramp and clearing the Miranda River. She couldn't go too fast, but she couldn't go too slow.

A shiny object beyond the river, off in the distance, caught her eye. An idling vehicle. A dark blue metallic-colored muscle car with a hot rod engine protruding from the hood. The driver appeared to be a male, although she struggled to discern his features. He stared at her. She squinted her eyes until . . .

Anika jumped. Her phone buzzed in her back pocket. Careful to keep one hand on the railing, she answered it.

"There's an FBI agent here to see you," Curtis said, his voice serene. "Says he knows you."

Anika didn't feign surprise. She didn't expect this visit before the storm, but she knew they would eventually come for her. She hadn't kept in touch with her parole officer. "Okay."

"If you want, I can take care of it."

She knew how Curtis took care of such things and opted for a less *permanent* option. The last thing they needed (before or after the storm) was a cavalry invading the town in search of a missing federal agent. "No, I'll speak to him."

"Can't let him arrest you. Reckon that's his plan."

"Understood," she said, making her way to the tower's ladder. "On my way."

Before descending the tower, she gazed again into the distance. The man in the vehicle had vanished.

48

Curtis escorted Special Agent Brian Maxwell from the holding cell down the hallway and deposited him in Anika's office. Before closing the door on his way out, he gave her a serious eye, the message unmistakable.

He leaves you alone, or he doesn't leave at all.

No one had touched Maxwell—he was, after all, a federal agent armed with a revolver and a radio—but Anika could tell he was miffed. No doubt Miranda's current atmosphere surprised him. Auntie Dodd, who'd duped Maxwell five years ago with fake evidence concerning Anika, no longer called the shots. (She was swimming with the fishes, of course, but Maxwell didn't know that.) Ricky and LeSean—who had also duped Maxwell long ago as part of Dodd's conspiracy to frame Anika—occupied the holding cell he'd just left. No telling what they'd said. They had likely woven a narrative of political corruption and false imprisonment.

Beyond that, Maxwell had surely spied the statue of Selena glistening in Revolutionary Park. It was hard to miss. Authorities in Corpus Christi had reported it stolen, and the scandal had garnered national attention. He probably also saw the large detention facility in the park holding scores of outspoken prisoners. That's not the kind of thing that goes unnoticed. What's more, Anika was expecting, at any moment, Chelsea and her squadron to return with wheelbarrows of guns—pistols, AR-15s, shotguns, you name it. And to top it off, Maxwell's quarry now governed the town from behind a replica of the Resolute Desk. A living picture of small-town politics run amok. *Eat your heart out, LBJ.* Anika's veins traced through her lithe, muscular arms, her hair was trimmed like Joan of Arc, and her blazing orange eyes burned a hole through the back of his head.

"Here to arrest me again?" she asked, spotting Timmy through the window. He exited the front door and walked down the porch steps. Curtis didn't want Timmy in harm's way.

"I was."

"*Was?* What changed your mind?"

"Intuition, I suppose," he said with his head on a swivel.

"Intuition serves you well, Special Agent Maxwell."

"It's kept me alive this long."

"You're still young. Plenty of time to make a mistake, to commit an unforced error."

"Maybe it's not just intuition. Maybe it's the concern that I'm outnumbered by men who won't enjoy seeing their new mayor marched out in handcuffs."

"Some in these parts are fond of me," she said. "And not just men."

"So you lied," he huffed, cutting through the small talk. "You're not surrendering."

"I told the truth the first time we met, and you sent me to jail. I lied this time to protect myself, to prevent that from happening again. And believe it or not, maybe even to protect you."

Maxwell struggled to process Anika's words.

"You look uncomfortable," she continued. "Can I offer you some water?"

"Not thirsty, thanks."

"Perhaps a breakfast burrito? I'm told they're the second best in Texas."

"Not hungry," he said, wriggling in his chair. "There's something heavy about this place. Feels like . . . I don't know."

"Spit it out."

"Dark magic."

"Come on, Special Agent Maxwell," Anika chuckled with a boldness indicative of someone who'd turned the tables of power. "You believe in fairy tales? There's no such thing as magic."

"But there's such thing as evil."

"True, but you must define evil for it to make sense. I know a pastor, for instance—his name is Joshua—who says we live in a fallen world, immersed in sin, and that what we see all around us is the result of humankind's total depravity. You may not agree with him, but at least he's attempted to define evil. He has a point of view. Do you believe I'm totally depraved, Special Agent Maxwell? Do you believe I'm *evil*?"

"I'm not here to discuss theology or religion. You've violated your parole. Period. End of story. The rest is neither here nor there. Besides, what I'm talking about is more tangible than all that mumbo jumbo. It's like an increased gravitational pull that comes in spurts. I can't put my finger—"

"The pull you feel is called the *koya*."

"The *koya*?"

"If you're religious, you'd call it spiritual forces. If you're agnostic or atheistic, you'd attribute it to a mixture of weather and physiology. Or perhaps some complex psychological phenomenon driven by your fight-or-flight functions. Now, if you're into voodoo or hoodoo . . ."

"What do you think causes it?"

"I don't know. Theories vary," she said, although Joshua's supernatural worldview had started taking root. So far, his theory of spiritual forces provided the only sensical explanation. "I know I'm cursed, though. Your presence here today proves that theory."

"I don't understand what happened to you, Anika. You had your whole life ahead of you. Destined for success."

"*You* happened to me," she said, clenching her jaws. "You and Auntie Dodd took *everything* from me. Dodd and her two accomplices in that holding cell lied to frame me for a murder I didn't commit. I've read her files. I know what happened. I know the truth."

Maxwell fidgeted, his eyes locked on Anika's. She had learned in jail that psychologists train FBI agents to study eye movement. To look for signs, for tells. Eyes had a mouth of their own even when suspects refused to talk or talked too much. Maxwell was exercising his tradecraft. "Interesting that you'd bring up Mayor Dodd and her two accomplices. You threw her accomplices in jail. I'm curious. Where did you throw her?"

Maxwell was fishing without bait. "We're done here."

"We are *not* done here. You can't just run a town, Anika, like you're the mayor. This is ridiculous. You're barely old enough to vote. And you can't vote anyway because you're a convicted felon."

"Thanks to you."

"The real mayor won't return my calls," he continued, breaking eye contact. "She's AWOL. I'll assume—at least for now—you had nothing to do with her disappearance. But you've moved into her office. And you stole an iconic statue. You've put your political enemies in jail. You have a huge holding pen in the park for . . . who are those people?"

"Lawbreakers." She borrowed a term from his vernacular but almost said *evildoers*. Maxwell had some facts wrong, but she didn't feel the need to quibble or help him round out things.

"Someone told me they were protesters."

"Of course LeSean and Ricky would tell you that," she said. She didn't need Maxwell to reveal his sources. "They hired those hooligans to intimidate me with a show of force."

"I didn't say—"

"Listen, I don't have the luxury of parsing language. Nor do I have time to play games. Call those criminals whatever you want. Call them 'mostly peaceful protesters.' Call them 'insurrectionists,' I don't care. We warned them countless times to forego violence, and they refused. *Period. End of story. The rest is neither—*"

"I get it," he said, rolling his eyes. "What are your plans for them when the hurricane comes?"

Anika shrugged. She knew the answer but wasn't telling.

"Come on, Anika! This is nuts!"

"I didn't ask for any of this. I don't know why they asked me to help them . . . to lead them. But they did. And I have one or two days left."

"You've decided to become a fugitive? You have no desire to be rehabilitated? No desire to do the right thing?"

"*The right thing?* What a joke. You sound like a walking Hallmark card. I told you the truth the first time we met, and you made a choice. You chose not to believe me. Right now, you have another choice, this one more consequential than the first. So what's it gonna be, Special Agent Maxwell, intuition or ambition?"

"What would you have me do? Walk away?"

"I want you to do the right thing!" she said.

"This place is a powder keg about to explode. I can't turn a blind eye to you thumbing your nose at the law. I can't unsee all this crime, corruption, and . . . whatever you call that colossal outdoor prison you've constructed."

"You—meaning the federal government—have bigger problems than little ol' me. If we don't evacuate thousands in the next several hours," she explained, pointing outside, "they'll die. Crushed by debris. Blown away by storm winds. Electrocuted by lightning. Washed into the Gulf by flooding."

"I get all that, but—"

"Here's my deal for *you*, Special Agent Maxwell. Let me do my job. Let me stay in town for the hurricane, and I promise to surrender if I survive."

"Your promises are worthless."

"Whether I keep my promise doesn't matter," Anika said. "If I survive this hurricane and run away, then you can reenact that Tommy Lee Jones role in *The Fugitive* and 'check every warehouse, farmhouse, henhouse, outhouse, and . . .' I can't remember the last one."

"Doghouse," he chuckled, showing a slight crack in his veneer.

"Check every *doghouse* in the area," she nodded, realizing she'd lived in the proverbial doghouse since coming home. What she said next crushed her spirit because she knew it was true. "If I were stupid enough to run, I couldn't outrun your horses and hounds."

Maxwell rubbed his face and sighed. Anika's hold on power was real but temporary. If she survived the next forty-eight hours, then their roles would be reversed. The FBI or the Marshals would quash Anika's rebellion without breaking a sweat. Any cavalry coming for Anika, any siege of the town, would make Waco look like child's play. "Remind me: What was the young man's name?"

She stared at him, wondering why he'd asked, and replied, "His name was Johnny Delgado."

"You told me you didn't play a role in his death. Now that you've served your time, is that still your story?"

"Yes."

"Do you know who did?"

"Auntie Dodd," she said immediately. Her answer was incomplete. She could've included Curtis. Auntie Dodd had been the diabolical puppet master, but Dodd's aide-de-camp (now Anika's right-hand man) had copped to doing the dirty work. Accusing Curtis, however, wasn't in her best interest. He was listening to this conversation and, if required, would make quick work of the special agent and mayor. Of course, she could've accused Miranda, but that would've confused Maxwell. Besides, some evil you just didn't tempt if you wanted to survive.

"You read her files," he said. He paused and looked outside, as if to collect his thoughts, as if his next question would be the most consequential of his career, maybe his life. "Do you have proof of your innocence?"

She bit her bottom lip, and tears swam in her eyes and streamed down her face. She dared not fight them. She couldn't have stopped them if she'd tried. She couldn't speak, so she just nodded. For the first time in years, hope returned. Maybe she was naïve; maybe it was false hope. But it was hope, nonetheless. As tears pattered her desk, she placed her hands on her cheeks and just kept nodding.

"Give it to me," he said.

Anika hadn't expected this moment, but she was prepared. She rushed from her chair to the corner of her office. She grabbed the banker's box with all her red tabs screaming *Read Me First!* She walked the box to the couch and dropped it next to Maxwell. His eyes, aimed at the photo of Johnny on the credenza, never moved.

"Did you make copies?" he asked.

She nodded.

He knew she was innocent. And she knew that he knew. *Pyschologists train FBI agents to study eye movement*, and he'd gleaned something from her eyes. Something that wasn't there—something he'd missed—five years ago during her interview. Truth. Or maybe now, this time, he knew she had no reason to lie about Johnny Delgado. She had served her time.

Authorities couldn't try her again for the same offense. Double jeopardy 101.

Soon after Anika retook her seat behind the desk, Curtis walked in and asked, "Everything okay?"

"Special Agent Maxwell was just leaving," she said, wiping her eyes, hoping she was right. *He leaves you alone, or he doesn't leave at all.* "And he's taking Ricky and LeSean with him."

"Why would I do that?" Maxwell asked as he stood up and grabbed the box.

"Because you'll want them close by after you read the evidence in that box," Anika said. "And if you choose not to read it, then you'll assume you left behind two victims of false imprisonment to die a heinous death. Either way, leaving them here will make it harder for you to live with yourself."

Whether she'd convinced Maxwell that taking her prisoners was *the right thing to do*, or whether he'd surmised it was the *safest* thing to do, Anika would never know. But it didn't matter. Curtis would make sure Ricky and LeSean left town in the backseat of Maxwell's cruiser. Of course, their departure only solved her most immediate problem. Clear and present danger lay ahead. As Maxwell walked to the holding cell to gather his new prisoners, Curtis returned and asked, "All good with Eliot Ness?"

"I would've said Johnny Utah, but yes. I believe Special Agent Maxwell will leave us alone until the storm passes. After that, all bets are off."

"I have bad news. Chelsea's back. Showed up empty-handed, and her report ain't good. Ain't good at all."

49

MORNING—DAY BEFORE IMPACT

Chelsea's gun confiscation efforts had failed. Her team had exhausted the list—thirty homes in total—and had collected only three pistols, twice as many rifles, and a couple of shotguns. Most gun owners on the list had abandoned their homes for the Church Grounds. But not all had abandoned their neighborhoods peacefully. Stories told by some neighbors painted a picture of rage and disbelief. And *revenge*. Someone had warned them in advance. A mole within Anika's administration or someone else who could predict the future. Perhaps someone who was learning to master the cubes.

Someone with a Rubik's Cube tattoo.

The preponderance of the evidence pointed to Amber. Why else would non-Christians be meeting at the Church Grounds? Did Joshua have his own list of gung-ho gun owners in town? More likely, Joshua had interpreted Amber's cubes, taken action to scare those on the list, and used it to build his anti-government coalition. *The government's coming after you,* he would say. Coming to take their guns forever, coming to deprive them of their Second Amendment rights. Coming to put their names on watchlists and reduce their identities to barcodes. Now the most troublesome gun owners—those who modified semi-automatic AR-15s to shoot like automatic M-16s—weren't just miffed. They were angry. And they were girding for battle. Preparing for a showdown at the Alamo.

Chelsea's gun confiscation efforts had backfired.

"Sorry, Anika. I didn't mean to—"

"Not your fault, Chelsea," Anika said from behind her desk, eating a breakfast taco filled with brisket as the pouring rain pelted the Spanish tile roof. "I should've been smarter. You were following orders."

Chelsea and Curtis sat in the chairs facing her as the weather bayed. Neither said a word about the mayor falling off the vegetarian wagon, even as the myoglobin from the rare meat dripped down her chin like blood. Logan, too, had a hint of red face paint around his lips. He rocked gently on the couch as he clutched Faux Pooh. Sam, working the Rubik's Cube, sat next to him with headphones on (music helped with the headaches), listening to Harry Styles on a cassette tape played by a vintage Sony Walkman she'd found in a desk drawer. The old timers had hazed the driver of the gray-blue Amazon van when he parked in front of the Alamo. Peanut gave him a wedgie on the porch after he'd dropped off Sam's new cassette tapes.

"We've stirred up a hornet's nest," Chelsea lamented.

"Hornets or not, playbook's the same," Curtis said. "Don't fire unless fired upon."

"Nobody's firing anything," Anika said. "There's no reason for violence. Hurricane Lorenzo's about to kill us, so why the discussion of war? I'll talk to Joshua."

Curtis cringed. "You don't know him as well as—"

A psychotic scream!

An indecipherable, acrimonious screech from the road. Its piercing howl interrupted their conversation and reverberated in the office. All but Sam snapped to their feet and coalesced around the window covered in a waterfall of descending raindrops.

"Speak of the devil!" Chelsea said.

"That's not Joshua," Anika replied.

"Ain't the devil, neither," Curtis said as if he'd once palavered with the prince of darkness (or perhaps they shared a more intimate history). Seeing enough, he moved from the window, toward the exit.

But before he could reach the door, another scream came from the road, this time a female voice. "Anika! Help me! Anika, please!"

A crash inside the office!

The Rubik's Cube exploded into miniature cubes as it slammed against the wall. Everyone froze. The moment would pass in an instant, but Anika would never forget it. Nor would she ever understand it. Not fully. The *koya* was intense. A fierce thrumming. Blood-curdling, heart-wrenching, it was decibels louder and more palpable than anything Anika had experienced. She witnessed the others—all but her little sister—bending over and holding their ears. Anika would never forget the look of psychotic rage in her sister's innocent eyes. What's more, she'd never forget the look on the others' faces. Their eyes in that moment would forever be etched in her memory. Eyes painted in shock. Eyes of uncertainty. They didn't know what to fear more: the evil marching toward them from the road outside . . . or the little girl inside the room with them.

Sam jumped from the couch, tore off her headphones, and in a penetrating voice that could summon the angels above and demons below, screamed, "Mommy!"

Crazy Eyes jerked Barbara Mathis by the hair. Keeping one eye on the Hospitality Center and his fake eye on the Alamo, he marched his hostage straight ahead. The earlier downpour had eased to a hard sprinkle, but powerful wind gusts bent the park trees' smaller branches.

"Curtis, how did this happen?" Anika asked as she joined him on the porch. The old timers rubbernecked with interest but without words. For her safety, Sam remained in Anika's office, watching from the window, palms mashed against the glass. "Didn't you just check on her?"

"Must've happened this mornin'. Ain't heard a word from the rehab center."

"You think he busted her out?"

"Reckon he just *checked her out*. She's allowed visitors, and they can check her out for a meal."

Anika looked perplexed.

"You said you didn't want *strict confinement*," he continued, defending himself. "Them was your exact words."

"Listen, Curtis, I didn't want Mom in a straitjacket. That did *not* mean I wanted strangers taking her to lunch. Do I really need to explain the nuance when—"

"I'm sorry, Mayor," he interrupted. "Never thought this would happen. Not sure how that wacko found her. Not even Samantha predicted it."

The dark sky allowed a sliver of light to glisten off the switchblade in Crazy Eyes's hand. His knife, while small, was big enough to demand attention. And it garnered the attention of the mayor, who walked down the stairs of the porch.

Mascara oozed down her mother's face, which was pasty and blistered. She wore the sad, destitute countenance of an alcoholic and drug addict coming off a months-long bender. Her eyes, however, told a different story, one of a substance abuser who'd hopped back on the all-day train to Neverland. Children of addicts can spot an active user a mile away. Anika was only thirty yards from her mom. The mayor's mother was snot-slinging drunk or, as Cyclops would say, more sauced than Kansas City barbeque. It didn't take creative catnip formulas to lure Barbara Mathis into danger. Crazy Eyes had somehow figured that out. A bottle or more of cheap wine—maybe some Mad Dog 20/20—would do the trick. But Crazy Eyes hadn't figured out everything. He didn't know, for instance, that when Mom had an appointment with Dr. Drunk, she arrived early and stayed late. And once there, she proved hard to handle. Crazy Eyes was experiencing that now, dragging her by her bloody knees as she pitched from side to side and caterwauled in the rain.

Meanwhile, some of the Hospitality Center guests had lost their minds. Though most had huddled on the dry side of the facility—the side where the windblown rain couldn't reach (for now)—a few puttered in the sprinkling rain (closer to the action), held onto the bars, and egged on the maniacal and now infamous Crazy Eyes. Encouraged by their cheerleader, Sarah Danforth, they banged and rattled the prison bars and chanted, "Let us go!"

Cyclops retired inside the Alamo and, before long, returned with the wheelbarrow of confiscated weapons. Curtis, along with Peanut, Moon, and Vernis, swept up four long rifles. The gray riflemen all lined up, their scraggly eyebrows and squinty eyes hovering over the scopes, with rifles resting on the balustrade's railing. They looked like seasoned mall rats playing Big Buck Hunter in the arcade. If the weapons had contained laser scopes, then red dots would've covered Crazy Eyes's forehead.

The situation called for a firm resolve, but Anika needed to exercise caution. The closer she edged toward Crazy Eyes, the closer the edge of his knife blade waved near her mother's throat. "Hands off her!" Anika shouted. Her words, while not profound, were authoritative.

Crazy Eyes lacked the calm that accompanied evil genius. That allowed for more options from the negotiations playbook, but it didn't bode well for a quick surrender. "Let the hostages go!" he yelled.

Hostages? She didn't like the sound of that. This guy was crazier than she'd imagined, and she'd never watched the Masterclass on hostage negotiations. She glanced at Curtis on the porch, his gun leveled on the lunatic. She saw Sam standing in the window. She could hear Sarah's shrill chants overshadow those of her fellow inmates. Anika inched closer to the road as she responded. "We don't consider them hostages. And we don't want to charge them criminally."

"Why are you caging them like animals?" he asked as he dragged Barbara along the road.

"Just letting things cool off," Anika said as the chants continued. "Please be careful with my mom. She's not well . . . and she's bleeding!"

"You can't rule by royal edict, Mayor! You can't violate our First Amendment rights to speech and assembly! You can't hold them without due process!"

You can't put a knife to my mother's throat, you freak! "Listen," she said, putting up the palms of her hands, "we need—"

"Get back!" he screamed. His head shook wildly as his eyes tried to keep up. He jerked Barbara's head back by her hair and placed the blade to her trachea. "Tell them to stop aiming . . . those . . . guns . . . at . . . *me*!"

"Wait!" Anika yelled as Sam began to beat on the windowpanes.

"Do it now, or I'll slice her throat!"

Anika heard Cyclops on the porch say, "Careful not to spook him, boys. A man who ain't got nothin' ain't got nothin' to lose."

"Put the guns down!" Anika shouted, signaling with her hand, keeping a hawk's eye on her mother. Curtis and the old timers relaxed, removing their rifles from the railing. Curtis probably figured Mommy Dearest was expendable, and Crazy Eyes wasn't hurting anyone else with intemperate language and a switchblade. In fact, if he hadn't been responsible for cleaning up the mess, Curtis would've already squeezed the trigger and allowed a bullet from a .30-'06 cartridge to straighten those eyes once and for all.

"Anika," her mother said with garbled desperation, barely loud enough to be heard over the music, "let the people go. Why is everyone—"

"Be quiet, Mom!" Anika barked. She had voiced those exact words (and much worse) as a teenager and had felt ashamed. Now, however, there was no shame. She didn't voice them to sting, deliver a blow, or show disrespect. This was business. She could see that Barbara's talking agitated Crazy Eyes. Her slurring voice grated on his conscience.

"Enough yelling!" he said. "You clowns are driving me nuts!"

"Please relax," Anika said. Crazy Eyes was coming unraveled, losing control. She grew more worried. His blade had drawn blood from her mother's throat, blood that was dripping down her neck.

But he didn't relax. "If I kill her now," he shouted, "then I'll be a hero. You'll have to let everyone go." He had reached a bad spot. Maybe a place of no return.

Bedlam!

Anika closed her eyes, coming to a stark realization. Crazy Eyes wasn't looking for a prisoner swap, nor was he looking for a solution. He sought martyrdom. Anika had run out of cards to play, other than to order the guns back on him. The best bet was always on the house, and Curtis manned the house. He could take out Crazy Eyes with one shot before the knife dug any deeper and inflicted permanent damage.

But out of the blue, something happened. Something that changed everything. Fear overtook Crazy Eyes. Not just fear. *Absolute terror.* He stared at the porch, losing his footing as he stumbled around, entranced like he'd witnessed the angel of death. His breathing grew heavy, and his lips throbbed. He swallowed like his Adam's apple was trying to escape his throat. His about-face caused the Hospitality Center inmates to stop chanting. At that moment, Anika assumed Curtis had re-aimed the rifle at Crazy Eyes's head. But no. When she turned around, she saw nothing of the sort. Instead, she saw something else. Something else entirely.

Samantha, in her red rain boots, was walking down the steps.

50

The *koya's* thrumming ceased when Sam's rain boots landed on the creaky wooden steps. Decades later, a surviving bystander at the scene would tell her grandkids they could've heard a pin drop as Sam strolled down the stairs. But that wouldn't be true. Even during calms before storms, Mother Nature barks and meows. And besides, the sounds of deputies on horseback arriving on scene cut through the silence. The horses' whinnies, grunts, and snickers reminded onlookers that Miranda law enforcement would eventually clean up the mess. That included the prospect of cleaning up dead bodies, a reminder that life in Miranda was cheap. Sounds of authority, coupled with the sight of armed militia on the Alamo porch, meant only one thing. Absent a successful hostage negotiation, fate had numbered Crazy Eyes's minutes on earth. The only question was how much pain, and how many casualties, he'd cause in the meantime.

Horses weren't the only source of noise. Cyclops, growing anxious, couldn't stay quiet. "Curtis," he said with an uncharacteristic tremor in his voice, "you reckon Goldilocks oughta get back inside?"

Curtis blew him off. He had no choice. His primary interest was the maniac with the mangled eyes, but a close second were the police officers seeking guidance. They didn't ask questions; their inquisitive stares provided clear communication. Slowly and horizontally, Curtis sliced his hand through the air, sending a clear signal: *Let it ride . . . for now.*

For reasons she'd never understand, that was Anika's instinct too. *Let it ride.* Let Sam continue walking toward an unhinged lunatic bent on murder and mayhem. No one in her right mind would allow that. The mere thought was crazy. *Insanity!* But Anika did just that, allowing her young

273

sister to march into imminent harm and possible death. And her refusal to grab or speak to Sam wasn't caused by fear or cowardice. Her body was mobile, words of warning on her lips. Rather, she believed it was the best option, even though she had no clue of Sam's intentions. *Let it ride.*

Once she reached Anika, Sam said, "Stay here." Those two words destroyed whatever strategic advantage the sisters had enjoyed with the old timers when Sam had stayed quiet. In fact, several on the porch gasped when they heard Sam's voice for the first time.

Fidgeting and frightened, Crazy Eyes held up his knife with one hand while his other hand kept a tight hold on his hostage's hair. "I don't want any trouble with you!" he screamed as Sam approached.

Barbara, still on her knees, was at eye level with her youngest daughter—a daughter she hadn't laid eyes on in weeks—but said nothing. It was as if mother knew baby daughter was—somehow, someway—the right person for this job, perhaps born for this role. Born for this moment in the rain, wearing the perfect footwear for once. Even if she didn't arrive from central casting, Sam played the part. She didn't waste time before commencing negotiations, or maybe she was making demands (Anika struggled to hear). Anika could only see the back of her sister's blonde head and, above that, the maniac's terrified stare. One eye darted left, the other right, but his nose pointed at Samantha. He looked down at her, locked on her every word. After a few minutes, he lowered the switchblade and tossed it aside.

Anika wanted to draw closer. She needed to understand what was transpiring. She knew, however, that any movement would be ill-advised. Sam—somehow, someway—was making progress. Sam was taming the madman!

Sam's magic touch soon bore fruit. Crazy Eyes stopped yelling, stopped talking, and started nodding his head. The negotiating was over, it seemed, and Sam was advising the sheriff's deputies on next steps. Crazy Eyes placed his arms behind his back as the deputy snapped on the cuffs. The deputy then escorted him to the Alamo holding cell as Barbara lay on the street curled in a ball. Not until another deputy helped her to her feet did she come to her senses. She begged, pleaded, and cursed all the way through the park, past the Selena statue, and into the Hospitality Center as onlookers ogled in shock. *How could those girls put their mother in jail?* they no doubt thought.

Even Anika's conflicted heart ached as she watched the deputy haul off her mom like she was FBI's Most Wanted. But Barbara would sleep it off, wake up clearer-headed, and get over it—eventually. For now, Anika thought she had Sam's plan figured out, a plan in their mother's best interest. Anika didn't know how Sam had cut the Gordian Knot, but she believed she understood what her little sister was thinking.

Sisters in the bond.

For all the urban legends that would follow, the primary thrust of the stories recounting the Crazy Eyes hostage situation would remain true. Facing one of the greatest crises in Miranda's storied history, an eight-year-old girl wearing red rain boots had single-handedly averted mass carnage and saved countless lives.

For a moment.

MIDDAY—DAY BEFORE IMPACT

Exhausted, Sam was passed out on the office couch when Anika arrived. Bystanders and porch dwellers had sung, "She's a Jolly Good Fellow" (sounding more like "feller") and passed around Goldilocks like a beach ball at a Miranda Marlins baseball game. Unlike its host, the cancerous tumor in Sam's head wasn't asleep. Instead, it grew restless, and Sam was running out of time. Anika obviously wasn't a doctor, but some things you just knew. Sam's tete-a-tete with Crazy Eyes, while impressive, shouldn't have zapped all her energy. Anika had a million questions for sissy. How did she do that? Was it magic? Was it the *koya*? Was it divine providence? How did she calm and disarm that madman so easily? In terms of importance, though, one question floated to the top: *Why was he so terrified of her?*

But those questions would need to wait. The storm would slam Miranda in hours, and much work lay ahead. The rain had restarted in earnest, and radar forecasted no more breaks until the eye of the hurricane reached the Alamo. Time to kiss the South Texas sun goodbye. Hurricane Lorenzo had arrived, and he would only get worse with each passing hour as night progressed into day.

Anika strode with purpose across the Alamo Commons to Logan's office where the others had gathered. Before entering, she lingered at the doorway and gazed at Timmy as he worked behind the bar. Twenty minutes ago, he'd starred in the Alamo spotlight, dancing and singing with his eyes closed, arms spread, and palms open to the heavens. The porch junkies had spun him in circles and chanted, "Go, Timmy! Go, Timmy!" like tourists on a booze cruise off the Packery Channel. If he survived the storm, Timmy would no doubt lead a long, healthy life. But he would require a caretaker. Someone to save him from becoming a hopeless wanderer.

"Who will care for Timmy?" she asked as the others sat at the conference table.

"He'll be fine with me," Curtis said without hesitation.

"The hurricane will destroy this place. Then what?" she pressed. "He'll have little purpose."

"They rebuilt her before. Reckon we'll rebuild her again."

"That'll take two years, Curtis. Timmy needs a soft landing. He can't take an insult to his—"

"What would you have me do, Mayor!?" Curtis growled. "Go beg the genie in the bottle?" She had hit a nerve. Timmy was Curtis's Achilles' heel.

"I want you to consider what's in Timmy's best interest," she said, "not your own."

Curtis slammed his fist on the table, causing everyone but Anika alarm. He huffed and puffed and . . . sulked. Finally, with Anika staring down at him without blinking, he admitted, "You're right, doggonit." He buried his haggard face in his large, calloused hands. "We could send him with Preacher-man."

"Joshua?" Anika asked, surprised to hear Curtis voice that option. "You said Preacher-man was coming for us. You said we're going to war against him."

"If he brings war, then we're goin' to war. But his followers won't lay a finger on Timmy."

"How do you know Joshua will survive this so-called war? For that matter, how do you know he'll survive the hurricane?"

Curtis pointed to the whiteboard.

Anika read the words and stared at Chelsea and Logan. They returned her stare. Everyone but Curtis was perplexed.

"I asked Sam the same question," Curtis continued. "What's gonna happen to Preacher-man? Instead of drawing cubes, she jotted down some Bible verses."

"From the Book of Daniel," Logan said. He had obviously done some research. "Chapter Seven."

Anika returned her attention to the whiteboard, and Chelsea said, "Looks like Samantha's been doing more than negotiating with domestic terrorists."

> In my vision at night I looked, and there before me was one like a son of man, coming with the clouds of heaven. He approached the Ancient of Days and was led into his presence. He was given authority, glory, and sovereign power; all nations and peoples of every language worshiped him. His dominion is an everlasting dominion that will not pass away, and his kingdom is one that will never be destroyed.

"And you think that means we —"

"I may not like what it says, but it's easier to interpret than the cubes," Curtis interrupted.

"He wins; we lose? Is that what you're saying? If that's the case, then I'll drive to the Church Grounds right now and surrender."

"Quit talkin' nonsense," he replied. "No one's surrenderin'. It just means Preacher-man escapes. Lives to fight another day. Doesn't mean he wins. Sam's cubes predicted a battle, but the results are unclear. At least to me."

The burden of Anika's selfishness dropped on her shoulders like a pallet of bricks. She had insisted that Curtis consider Timmy's best interests, but was she doing the same for Sam? If so, why hadn't she turned over custody of Sam to Joshua? Her escape plans relied on the successful construction of a wooden ramp and the harebrained idea of jumping a four-thousand-pound muscle car over a river. Wouldn't Joshua take Sam to St. Jude's for medical care? How was the current plan in Sam's best interest when she could drive away safely in Joshua's Jeep?

Because that's the plan Sam had scribbled on a Whataburger napkin, she reminded herself. But Sam was eight. Eight years old! And her powers were suspect, even after today. Magic didn't exist. *But there is such a thing as evil,* Special Agent Maxwell had said. Sam—or Anika, for that matter—wasn't moved by spiritual forces, was she? Joshua had exaggerated the idea of divine providence, right? The *koya* was harder to explain, but there had to be natural (that is, non-supernatural) explanations for its existence. Whatever drove the decision-making, Anika believed she and Sam must stick together to survive.

Sisters in the bond.

But something else gnawed at her. A potential red herring her mind refused to abandon. Something in Auntie Dodd's files. She had skimmed over the folder at the time, but now it beckoned. She made a mental note to revisit her copies, particularly after what she'd witnessed at the water tower.

"Curtis, I have another question for you."

"Shoot, kiddo."

"What do you know about the Midnight Rider?"

Chelsea and Logan exchanged glances. They had all heard the wild stories.

"Folklore," Curtis replied as he stood up to stretch his legs and massage his neck.

"Folklore, huh?" she said. "If that's true, how is it that I saw him from the water tower?"

"Mistaken identity," he said as his knees cracked.

"Dark blue muscle car . . . hot rod engine growing out of the hood?"

Curtis fell back into his chair with shock in his eyes.

Make that *two* Achilles' heels.

51

NIGHTFALL—DAY BEFORE IMPACT

The team met in the Alamo Opera House's Theater Hall. Unlike Anika's and Logan's office rooms, this cavernous space blunted the violent sounds of rain and thunder bent on disrupting discussion. Many almost-famous musicians and actors had performed here in the '60s and '70s—mostly Tejano up-and-comers and country music has-beens. According to the old timers, the feel of the place had been more Branson, Missouri, than the *Louisiana Hayride*. Someone had long ago kicked out the stage's footlights, but the thick, ornate, dark-red curtain with gold fringe still hung majestically from the rafters. As the mayor's team gathered in the theater for the first and last time, she imagined the ghosts of audiences past awaiting one last show.

Timmy sat in the middle of the auditorium (Row T, Seat 7), eating a bag of buttery popcorn among a sea of empty seats. The four others sat at a scuffed, wobbly table placed in the middle of the old stage. Curtis had pulled back the curtain to make room for the charts that Chelsea and Logan had placed on easels in a half-moon around the workspace. The stage lighting provided ample visibility. Curtis had turned on several colored lights (green and red, mostly) to achieve the appropriate brightness. As such, the ambiance resembled more Christmastime at Macy's than an office setting, but no one mistook Curtis for Santa Claus, and the temporary meeting space would do the trick.

The men had bussed the dinner plates, racking them on shelving offstage. No one would be cleaning those dishes tonight (or ever again). Timmy had cooked cheese enchiladas with red corn tortillas and chili gravy. He had used a recipe purloined from the Old Mexico Restaurant on the opposite corner of Four Points. The recipe called for more garlic than normal (and a healthy dousing of Gephardt's Chili Powder), but Anika had savored every bite. This would be their last supper together, and the last time anyone would use the Alamo stove. The garlic wouldn't fend off domestic terrorists or tame the *koya*, but vampires beware. At this point, Anika mused, fending off vampires would be a walk in the park.

Logan, still without an appetite since Sarah's betrayal, had abandoned his Mexican food in search of a wardrobe from mothballed boxes. He had returned from behind stage with a costume that—with its green tights, brown Renaissance vest, and medieval hat resembling a paper boat—was a convergence between Robin Hood and Peter Pan. He sat at the far end of the table with his arms crossed. His mind elsewhere, he acted aloof but remained engaged enough to function. Sarah had snuffed out his spirit. Crushed him. Transformed him into a pathetic shell of his former self. Anika knew, unless Chelsea could make inroads into his psyche, Logan would need professional counseling to overcome his grief. Unfortunately for Logan, if all went as planned, Anika wouldn't be around to help. She had more pressing caretaking responsibilities and a date with St. Jude's.

Logan's outfit clearly distracted Curtis, but the Alamo fixer had bigger things competing for his attention. He and Anika had reached an impasse on key issues. He refused to discuss the Midnight Rider, and she wouldn't entertain talk about why or how he had killed Johnny. Those elephants in the room, left unaddressed, impeded productive dialogue and problem-solving. Meanwhile, his hands rested on a weathered book in front of him. Anika didn't know why. She assumed he'd open it eventually, perhaps after they wrestled with essential business. But she stared at it until Chelsea, who sat nearby, sneezed. Chelsea still donned the Princess Leia hair buns. Despite her flare, she'd become a formidable teammate—everything she'd promised in her interview and more. Not only was she dependable, loyal, and physically capable, but she also carried with her a heart of gold and a mind sharper than Crazy Eyes's switchblade. Anika would encourage her to take an IQ test if Chelsea survived the storm. To be sure, she had aced every test since joining Team Anika.

"Let's get started," Anika said. She and Curtis had already resolved that Joshua—somehow, someway—would take custody of Timmy, so the status of the evacuation became the first item of business. All agreed that, despite piquing the church folks and the usual fusspots, Anika's executive order had proven successful. Those who'd heeded the government's warnings would survive. Most had left town before the deluge arrived, before TxDOT had ordered the contraflow that opened all lanes in one direction. Those who wouldn't (or couldn't) leave town numbered about ten thousand. If any riding out the storm survived, FEMA would arrive with water, ice, food, and medical supplies. The Town of Miranda would eat, and her portions would border on gluttonous, but Team Anika had robbed her of an all-you-can-eat buffet.

The next issue concerned electricity and fuel. They were needed to run engines, vehicles, weapons, and communications. Anika had zero experience with city administration and planning, but she knew that without electricity and fuel, all would be lost. Any battle against Joshua. Lost. The battle against Hurricane Lorenzo. Lost. Even without LeSean Brown, the Miranda Refinery had continued to provide enough energy to survive through the storm and beyond. Under Curtis's direction, the old timers had stored thousands of barrels of refined oil and identified a handful of oil and gas experts inside the Hospitality Center. What's more, they'd stationed commercial-grade generators in all key locations, including the Alamo. The question now was whether they had done enough.

As if on cue, something popped, and the lights went out! Darkness. Only Timmy had brought his smartphone, but for whatever reason, he couldn't get the light to work. No one had brought a flashlight or smartwatch. Chelsea started to panic until Curtis said, "Hold tight a second for the generator." But seconds came and went, and darkness remained. Anika kept calm. She didn't feel the *koya* moving at all, and Curtis remained at her side. In fact, she was close enough to Curtis to sense his growing nervousness. Any thought she had of Curtis killing her at that moment (rather than protecting her) drifted away.

The team, however, was helpless. And the darkness was starker, more disorienting than normal, as if they were wrapped in Vantablack or enveloped in a black hole. With the lights out, the smell of Timmy's popcorn became more acute, and the sounds of their creaking wooden chairs on center stage muffled the sounds of cracking thunder and howling wind. Anika assumed everyone shared the same thought: *Is this a natural or man-made problem?* With each passing second, their thoughts drifted to the latter. Curtis, miffed by the generator failure, scooted his chair back. Time to investigate. He could navigate the Alamo corridors—indeed, every nook and cranny—in his sleep. Before he stood, however, something popped again, then a motor started, and then . . . the lights flickered and came back on. Everyone exhaled. Sounds of relief ricocheted off the walls and echoed throughout Theater Hall, testing its acoustical limits for the first time in decades.

Lights back on, Curtis turned to the main issue: preparing for battle. Anika struggled to pay attention. Fancified battlefield charts didn't impress her. She viewed fighting before a hurricane to be a fool's errand. She certainly wasn't fighting Joshua. Instead, she planned to purchase a one-way ticket out of town with Sam in the passenger seat. Her disengagement on this topic, however, stemmed from a far greater truth: she didn't believe a battle was forthcoming. Things didn't add up. This felt like Hatfield-McCoy balderdash conceived by someone—namely, Curtis—raised on John Wayne movies. Joshua was in the business of saving souls, not destroying them. He wasn't violent, and fighting during a hurricane made zero sense.

Of all the areas where Anika feared Curtis was manipulating Sam's cubes, this was at the top of the list. She remained highly skeptical of his wartime interpretations. Curtis wanted war, or someone (or some*thing*) with war in mind had a hold on him. Perhaps legend itself was influencing him; maybe something spellbinding in that beat-up leather book. Did that book catalog the stories of Miranda wars occurring ahead of the sixty-year hurricanes? Battles that begat unspeakable bloodshed that storms washed away? Deadly conflicts that never made it into accredited publications, never captured by reputable journalists? Anika would revisit Curtis's "cubistry" with Sam, but she wouldn't sanction more fighting. Fighting fellow townspeople during a deadly hurricane was the height of absurdity. She wouldn't let it happen. And even if she failed, she'd be long gone with all fools and trouble in her rearview mirror.

"Anika?" Curtis asked. "Anika, you still with us?"

"Earth to Anika!" Timmy joked. He was now sitting farther from the stage in the cheap seats (Row WW, Seat 2). He figured out how to use his phone light and was shining it around the auditorium.

"Sorry," Anika said. "Lost my focus."

"Wanna talk about post-storm items?" Curtis asked.

No words came to mind. Anika didn't know how to respond. Curtis had put her on the spot as if he'd read her thoughts. And he'd asked with some skepticism, as if to say, *You gonna be here after the storm blows over?* Her eyes bounced around the table. Everyone waited for her response like she was the star witness in the crucial part of a high-stakes trial. She eventually found Curtis's eyes, and the two stared at one another stoically. Not one of them blinked. Not one of them spoke. But they somehow communicated. Or at least Curtis communicated. He said, *I can't save you if you run.*

"Let's discuss the Hospitality Center guests," she said, breaking eye contact with Curtis. Her demurrer was as clear to Curtis as his communication was to her. *Message received.*

Curtis cracked open the leather book and put on his dollar-store reading glasses. The Alamo's fixer putting on glasses of any kind was like the Lone Ranger riding a tricycle—it just didn't fit his persona. Anika, however, showed more interest in the book's content than Curtis's appearance. Besides, with Anika's hair chopped off and Peter Pan and Princess Leia huddled around the table, Curtis was winning the "least awkward" contest.

Reading from the book, Curtis had no time to recount all the stories of old. Stories shared around Miranda dinner tables and passed down from generation to generation, from grandpa to granddaughter, like priceless heirlooms never captured in a will or trust. He hit the high points, however, sharing snippets of tales (some truthful, others no doubt legend) that may save (or end) their lives in the coming hours. He spoke generally of wars that preceded the deadliest hurricanes. He discussed how the town always rebuilt anew like scorched land produces more fruitful crops with richer soil. He described the battle between good and evil (although he never aligned himself with one or the other). Time being of the essence, he arrived quickly at the most important part: Revolutionary Park. He spoke as a figure of authority but also one beholden to the script. Depending on the facts, Anika thought, that made him either a reliable teacher or a useless idiot. Anika guessed he was a little of both.

Anika was resolved to govern without regard to superstition, wives' tales, or urban legend. She believed in good and evil (and had experienced her share of both), but she also believed rational explanations could deny the existence of magic. Her belief system was challenged, though, when it came to Revolutionary Park and the lives of those in the Hospitality Center. Despite all the crazy actions she had taken (and planned to take tomorrow), believing the stories about the park held the highest stakes. The fate of multitudes, including her mother and some around the table, likely rested on her decision to hold or release them.

"We built the Hospitality Center where hurricanes don't go," Curtis said. "That area and about fifty feet around it will be safe. People in that space will weather the storm . . . they will live."

"How can you be sure?" Anika asked.

"I vote with my feet. I plan to sit on the bench right outside the bars. No cover but tree-top canopies."

"You understand how I might be struggling with the decision to leave them detained, right?"

"Yes, ma'am, but they'll surely die if they ain't in that protected cell. Storm's gonna take everything else to the roots."

"Everyone okay if I leave that decision up to each inmate tomorrow morning?" Anika asked. "They either trust and believe or they don't?"

"No!" Logan shouted. The question sprung him to life. "You need to make that decision for them."

"I disagree," Chelsea said. "Each person needs to make his or her own decision. To believe or not to believe. We can't put that burden on the mayor."

"Let's put it to a vote," Anika decided. "All in favor of allowing the inmates, or guests, to make the decision themselves, raise your hand."

Anika and Chelsea raised their hands. Logan and Curtis didn't. "It's a tie!" Logan declared. "And ties go to the status quo, meaning everyone in the Center stays put, including your mom." But everyone knew that Barbara Mathis wasn't the person on Logan's mind.

"Sorry, Logan, we're all one team," Anika said as she pointed to the upper rafters. Up there, in the darkness, a bright light emitted from a phone. And it revealed something that broke Logan's heart and stirred him to leave. As he walked away from the table in anguish, Anika said, "Maybe Sarah will make the right choice."

Timmy was raising his hand.

52

THE DAY OF THE STORM

The bugle call Degüello, which means "provide no quarter," derives from the Spanish verb to slit one's throat. On March 6, 1836, Mexican General Santa Anna, accompanied by two thousand Mexican soldiers besieging the Alamo in San Antonio, played Degüello before attacking the Alamo near dawn. At that moment, the nearly two hundred Texians holed up inside the unremarkable Spanish mission would've known their fate. Their chapter in the Texas Revolution against Mexico was nearing its end. Two weeks earlier, their commander, William B. Travis, had penned a letter soliciting aid to support his brave but fledgling garrison. His letter closed with the words "Victory or Death," which he underlined three times.

Aid never arrived, and the Texians got victory *and* death. Santa Anna's men killed everyone in the Alamo, but the battle cry, "Remember the Alamo!" reverberated throughout the land. The Texians had killed enough Mexican soldiers at the Alamo that Sam Houston would later crush Santa Anna's army at San Jacinto. Texas history and folklore lionized those who died at the Alamo, heroic men like Davy Crockett ("King of the Wild Frontier"), Jim Bowie (namesake of Anika's knife), and Travis (namesake of Travis County, home of Austin, Texas). The Alamo chapel, relatively small in size, holds a special place in Texans' hearts and imaginations. Indeed, every Texan learns about the Battle of the Alamo in seventh-grade Texas History.

And that included every guest holed up in the Hospitality Center and every would-be vigilante from the Reformed Baptist Church of Miranda marching toward Four Points.

Timmy played Degüello through the Alamo Opera House speakers before the first hint of dawn. He played it at full volume so any ne'er-do-wells would hear the deafening bugle horns over the howling wind, crackling thunder, and violent rain, through the plexiglass surrounding the Hospitality Center, throughout Revolutionary Park, and beyond. And he played it on repeat so everyone would be on notice—on notice that the mayor's office wouldn't tolerate physical violence or challenges to authority, that it would quash any attempted *coup d'état*.

Awoken by bugle calls, Anika started her day by checking on Sam, who'd slept on the office couch. Sam remained cuddled up with Faux Pooh but without covers. Anika knelt beside her, pushed away her sister's golden bangs, and reached for the right words. She presumed Curtis had bugged the room, but she needed to talk. D-Day had arrived, and important questions remained unanswered. Hurricane Lorenzo loomed large, Joshua assembled his evangelists, and Miranda, with all her jealousy, waited in the wings. Anika whispered in faint tones. "Your head hurt?"

Sam nodded.

"Can you walk?" Anika asked, her hand shaping her sister's tousled hair.

Another nod.

"Can you talk?" Anika asked.

A beautiful smile. "Yes."

And then . . . a muffled question, soft like a baby's snore. "You think it's built . . . and in place?"

Sam grabbed Anika's hand and squeezed it. The answer was yes, but she winked and said loudly, "I don't know what you're talking about."

Anika didn't know whether Sam's confidence stemmed from real intel (from Chelsea, perhaps) or a gut feeling, but it didn't matter. The liklihood of them making it alive to the ramp was slim, lower than the odds of the ramp being ready. Beyond that, the odds of a successful jump and surviving the landing were anyone's guess. Single digits at best. "I'll come get you when it's time. Until then, no more heroics or . . . whatever you did to Crazy Eyes."

"No more saving your bacon?" she quipped.

Anika couldn't wait any longer. "What did you say to Crazy Eyes?"

"I asked him if he had any loved ones in the cage. His girlfriend's in there."

"You knew that because of your cubes?"

"That's what he told me."

"Makes sense."

"I told him I wanted my mom in that cage with his girlfriend. It's the only place she can survive the storm."

"Why was he afraid of you?"

"He thinks I can predict the future. He also thinks I'm evil."

"Because he knows about your gift?"

"No," she chuckled, "because I threatened him."

"How so?"

"Told him that if he didn't surrender, I'd tell Curtis to blow his brains out."

"Yikes."

"And then I told him you'd torture his girlfriend."

Anika stared in disbelief.

"Had to talk tough," Sam continued. "Unlike you, I *did* watch the Masterclass on hostage negotiation, and Mom was in trouble."

"Right. No more saving lives for you. It's time for us to save yours." Anika kissed her forehead and tried not to worry about the growing cancer that lay behind it. "You need to rest if we're to survive."

Sam wouldn't let her big sister pull away. She stared into Anika's eyes, handed her Faux Pooh, and said, "Be careful, sis. Something evil's coming for us."

"Is it the bogeyman?" Anika asked, back to a light whisper.

"I think so."

"*Who* is the bogeyman? Do you know?"

Sam shrugged, pulled Anika's ear to her lips, and whispered, "It's my turn to share a secret."

"Oh?"

"Sometimes the bogeyman doesn't even know that he's the bogeyman."

Anika greeted Timmy and exited through the swinging doors. The rain blew sideways. Four Points was saturated, but roughly a third of the Alamo porch remained bone dry. The musky, earthy scent of a South Texas downpour accompanied the smell of breakfast tacos and pecan-roasted coffee beans. Tree limbs in Four Points lunged toward the ground. Anika couldn't determine wind speeds, but she knew before the end of the day, Hurricane Lorenzo's winds would surpass triple digits. They would uproot trees, smash windows, fling pedestrians to their deaths, overturn and displace cars, and destroy houses and stores—all but a small remnant of life and development wiped from the map.

Anika cared mostly about the trees near the Hospitality Center in Revolutionary Park. As predicted, the wind had less of an impact on them. They weren't immune from the storm, but they weren't as affected. At least not yet. And the Hospitality Center itself was holding up well. Those who failed to pay attention got wet, but the roof and plexiglass kept most areas dry. She suspected her mother, even if sober by now, was failing to pay attention. Before Anika could check on her, however, Cyclops climbed the porch steps.

"Figure Timmy woke Davy Crockett from the dead with that bugle," he said, holding a broken umbrella adorned with the Texas flag. It would be the last umbrella he'd ever need. His elderly wife, whom he introduced as "the Missus," walked beside him. More old timers arrived behind them—including Moon and his fourth wife, whom he introduced as "the Mistress"—all dressed to the nines. Each wore exquisite, borderline obnoxious apparel from another era. The men wore Nudie suits, dress shirts with sequins, and their best cowboy boots and straw hats. The women sported ornate dresses. For aid and comfort, the geriatric group carried reusable grocery bags (H-E-B) filled with dusty bottles of aged whiskey and vintage moonshine. Their ride from sobriety to eternity, Anika observed, would be fast and furious. Given the smell of alcohol, they'd hopped on that train hours earlier with the Alamo front porch likely their final destination.

Before the old timers found their seats, a new problem emerged. Scores of people emerged from the shadows. People Anika didn't recognized. Wharf rats, longshoremen, shrimpers, and migrants, all spilling into Four Points. They stumbled around in the rain and wind like zombies, seemingly with no purpose or destination.

"In my grandpa's bedtime stories," Curtis said, joining Anika on the porch, a pistol at his side and radio in hand, "he called them the Lost Colony."

"What are they doing here?"

"Homeless and roustabouts who didn't evacuate. They got no place to go. Bars are closed. Half-houses, mental institutions, all the government-run outfits—they're all boarded up."

The radio in Curtis's hand crackled and squawked. *All officers are in position, and all assets are in the area: cars, trucks, ATVs, horses, and—"*

"Nobody fires a shot unless fired upon, ya hear?" he directed.

"Roger that."

Curtis turned to Anika as Chelsea walked onto the porch. "Y'all ready?"

"Ready for what?" Anika asked.

"Preacher-man's comin' around the bend. Gotta posse with him."

"What?" Anika said, craning her neck. They had planned for this all night and into the morning, but the speed of Joshua's arrival surprised her. She wasn't expecting a champagne breakfast, but she hadn't finished her first cup of coffee. "Already? Logan's not here!"

Luther and Calvin led the procession. Cropped ears perched high, they pranced majestically in the storm's elements. About fifty marchers followed. Joshua, his head shaved to the skull, walked in the middle. He no longer looked like a Young Life acoustic guitarist; he looked more like the captain in Star Trek with the aerodynamic head. He wore Birkenstocks and a full-length white rain slicker that resembled a shiny catholic robe. Ethan and Amber flanked Joshua as they marched side by side but not in lockstep. The chants sounded more like a hymn as the crowd approached and sang in unison.

Come, ye sinners, poor and needy
Weak and wounded, sick and sore
Jesus ready, stands to save you
Full of pity, love and power

"Y'all best be ready for a full-on, all-out brawl with that bunch," Cyclops goaded.

"You boys pullin' on the jug need to sit this one out!" Curtis admonished as the crowd grew closer, the singing louder. "You'll get us all killed! Told you we needed you sober! You ain't no good to us this mornin'!"

I will arise and go to Jesus
He will embrace me in His arms
In the arms of my dear Savior
Oh, there are ten thousand charms

A rusted white bus drove alongside them with the words Jesus Saves spray painted in red on the sides. Someone had emblazoned a cross on the front, and, at least from Anika's vantage point, the inside resembled Elvis's Jungle Room at Graceland. But Anika remembered her time with Johnny at Delgado Auto Pros. She knew that, when it came to vehicles, looks could be deceiving. She heard the engine purr, so she assumed the bus's innards were top of the line—like its all-terrain tires.

"Curtis, they don't have weapons," Anika observed, her worry turning to hope. "They're just here to evangelize!"

"We don't know that for sure," Curtis said, his hand on his sidearm. "That highfalutin' dog-and-pony show is more than needed to blather on about God."

"They wouldn't be out here in this mess if they was up to any good," Moon added.

Come, ye thirsty, come and welcome
God's free bounty glorify
True belief and true repentance

Every grace that brings you nigh

The evangelistic parade found no neutral observers. A few lunatics, freaks, and other wanderers repented and believed the gospel, fell into the procession, and started mumbling words in tune. Others not so much. They responded with raging fury, wailing, and gnashing of teeth. Out for bloodshed, they didn't wield weapons but simmered in hate. This included Sarah, who—enraged by the thought of anyone proselytizing in a storm—led Hospitality Center guests in a diabolical fit of wrath. Meantime, Anika observed that her mom remained disengaged and clinging to her wet cot. Anika's heart, calluses and all, begged her to extract her mother from the cage; her mind told her to trust the plan, to trust Sam.

> *Come, ye weary, heavy-laden*
> *Lost and ruined by the fall*
> *If you tarry 'til you're better*
> *You will never come at all*

Once the procession reached Revolutionary Park, one of the wayfarers emerged from behind a tree. Without warning, he charged one of the marchers and threw a right hook to his jaw. Bystanders screamed from all angles. Most, including Anika and Joshua, begged for calm. The aggressor wouldn't abide, however, and the victim of the blow fought back. He punched his way out of a hold and delivered his own round of jabs, body blows, and one devastating uppercut.

> *I will arise and go to Jesus*
> *He will embrace me in His arms*
> *In the arms of my dear Savior*
> *Oh, there are ten thousand charms*

Anika heard the sharp crack of a gunshot from the porch!
She saw the bullet strike the marcher in the back of the head. As the singing stopped, she saw him collapse to his knees, then to his side. Every-

one looked at Moon. The smoke floated around his gun. Even in his ine-briated state, Moon had remembered where to find the wheelbarrow of confiscated weapons. He was too drunk to hit the backside of a barn, but when his blurry eyes saw three men instead of one, his ol' Pappi Moon-shine had taught him what to do.

Shoot the one in the middle.

53

Curtis aimed his Colt revolver at Moon. By the snarky, unrepentant look on Moon's wrinkled face, he was begging for a bullet. Pulling the trigger, Anika knew, would put Moon out of his misery—save him from the hurricane—but Curtis wasn't in a gracious mood. Not after Moon's reckless stunt that likely killed a man and put other lives in jeopardy. She feared Miranda's appetite for death and hold over Curtis, so she placed her hand on Curtis's shooting arm . . . just in case.

As the storm advanced, the thunderclaps, sustained wind, and relentless rain persisted. Those outside the Alamo, however, tuned out the harrowing sounds of historic weather. Silence blanketed Four Points. The bugles of Degüello had stopped. The singing had stopped. The chanting had stopped. The screaming of curse words and demands for justice had stopped.

Those able to peel their eyes off Curtis's Old West revolver placed them on Joshua. He walked like a white knight with stately purpose to the man lying face down on the road. With one athletic motion, he bent down and swooped the limp body over his shoulder. Standing erect and with zero sign of struggle, Joshua eyed those on the Alamo porch with disappointment before walking to the JESUS SAVES bus. To Anika, his silent message spoke volumes. He pitied those involved in the violence and, without a word, exhorted them to wake up. *Snap out of your slumber, fools; life's cheap in Miranda.*

Three participants in the gospel parade—presumably those with medical acumen—walked toward Joshua. They grabbed the injured man, whisked him into the bus, and began life-saving measures. As Joshua returned to the action, the sheriff's deputies revved the engines from ATVs, patrol cars, and other vehicles, including Miranda's two school buses. Unlike the church's bus, though, these longer buses—now painted yellow and black, like a southern yellowjacket—had more curb appeal than performance capability. Of course, Sarah's supercharged Range Rover, now plated with armor and a performance exhaust system, was new to the fleet. Anika, however, only cared about one car—the Black Ghost. And it remained parked in the Alamo garage with a full tank of gas.

But before the crowd could catch its breath, sounds of fury emerged from the side of the Alamo. The angry cries of a madman!

Logan sprang like a cheetah released from a cage. He sprinted so fast toward the crowd that Anika, at first, only saw a green blur. It didn't take long, though, for her to see the shiny metallic object tucked in the small of his back—her Bowie knife. She wanted to yell "Stop!" but no sounds came forth. The sight was too surreal to allow for words. Even Chelsea, now standing next to her, remained paralyzed.

Logan still wore his hybrid Peter Pan and Robin Hood outfit, but it was torn as if he'd spent the night thrashing it up in anger. Or in preparation. Perhaps, Anika thought, he'd stood in front of the mirror mumbling threats as he played diabolical seamster with the Bowie knife. Whatever the case, he now had a green and black bandana carved from his ensemble and wrapped around his head. His face was still pasty white from prior paintings never washed off. And he was running headlong into the crowd with reckless abandon.

Running for his brother!

Logan attacked his prey. Ethan, stronger than his elder brother, stood his ground but did nothing to avoid the blows. Logan launched into him like a blitzing linebacker tackles a defenseless quarterback. Ethan soared through the air and crashed into the puddled ground. Ethan took the form of a lifeless punching bag. When Logan's fists curled and his knuckles tightened, Ethan refused to protect his Hollywood face. He understood the reckoning and accepted his punishment. Logan had lost his mind. He wailed in sorrow and anger as he landed one fierce punch after another, shedding the blood of his younger brother, a brother he'd spent his entire life adoring and protecting.

Anika glanced at the Hospitality Center and saw Sarah the Home-wrecker enjoying this! She was holding the bars, relishing the fight. This was too much for Anika to stomach. She could countenance—up to a point—two rough and tumble brothers resolving their differences through fisticuffs. Under no circumstances, though, would she allow Sarah to revel in the carnage. Sarah's evil pride fueled her bad behavior. She enjoyed watching grown men fight over her. It stroked her ego. It put her back in the spotlight.

Chelsea, too, had seen enough. She beseeched Anika to stop the fight. Caring little about the vain honor of men, Anika didn't need much convincing. She walked briskly down the steps into the rain, and Joshua (apparently of a similar mind) walked in the same direction. Fight time was over. Ethan had taken enough of a beating, and anything more could cause permanent damage.

In an instant, though, Anika's walk turned into a sprint. Logan pulled the knife from the small of his back. He gripped it with two hands over his head, ready to thrust it downward, ready to slay his little brother! Ethan was willing to die or unable to defend himself after absorbing so many punches.

Anika and Joshua both threw up their hands and screamed the same panicked words at the same time, *"Logan, no!"*

But their screams fell on deaf ears. The only thing anyone heard was the click of the hammer on Curtis's revolver. It would do all the talking. "That'll be enough reckonin' for one day, Logan," Curtis said as he walked behind him, thrust the muzzle of the barrel against his head, and grabbed the fifteen-inch knife from his hands.

The sight of Ethan's blood unsettled Anika. She could smell or even taste its bitter saltiness. Amber knelt and consoled Ethan. Curtis used his free hand to grab Logan's hair and pull him to his feet. Before he holstered his gun and left the scene, however, Curtis dropped his stare on Joshua. "The first two was on us, Preacher-man. The next one is on you. Y'all need to get in the Hospitality Center or vamoose," he spat, "before everyone dies."

Joshua knelt next to Amber and tended to Ethan. He paid no mind to Anika, and he refused to respond to Curtis or abide by his commands.

"Sorry, Curtis," Logan said. "Don't shut me down just yet. I'm still useful."

"Ain't gonna be no more fightin' today," Curtis said. "Yer gonna look after Anika's momma."

Curtis escorted Logan to the Hospitality Center. Those marching in the gospel parade spread out among the Lost Colony and began proselytizing. Before long, a line of fifteen, maybe twenty, wandering miscreants loaded into the church bus. Others didn't want anything to do with God, Jesus, or people in general. They snarled, cursed, spat, spoke with their fingers, and chose to wallow in the mire amid the howling wind and torrential downpour. The more Joshua's group evangelized, the louder the sounds of rage and discouragement escalated throughout Four Points. Before the opera of discontentment reached its climax, though, it was cut short again by another surprise from the Alamo front porch.

A Lost Colony malefactor had used the distraction to sneak past everyone. He grabbed the wheelbarrow containing the cache of confiscated weapons, ran as fast as he could holding onto its handles, and crashed it through the side railing. Pistols, rifles, and shotguns scattered along the ground, and the culprit tumbled right behind the loot, nearly breaking his neck before falling onto his stomach. But the weapons wouldn't stay scattered long. The culprit's ragtag militia of Lost Colonists snatched up the guns and found positions behind nearby trees.

Anika, along with Joshua, Amber, and Ethan, found herself in the open, vulnerable and without cover. Everyone but a bludgeoned and disoriented Ethan questioned whether the firearms were loaded. Dissidents firing shots behind the trees quickly answered those questions. Bullets and pellets peppered the church bus. New converts scrambled to climb aboard and duck into their seats. Rifle shots clinked off the Selena statue, a reminder that a bullet would never harm her again, but also that everyone else faced potential death. One Lost Colonist fired repeated shotgun shells. His blasts caught the attention of even the most inebriated old timers on the porch.

But even in the heavy wind and rain, the smoke from gunfire betrayed the Lost Colonists' location. Miranda's finest sprang into action. ATVs roared toward the grove of mesquite and oak trees. The armored yellow jacket buses drove into tactical position. Once there, Deputy Carl, straddling an ATV out of range from all but rifle fire, pulled out a bullhorn and instructed the assailants to drop their weapons. That request was met by a hopeful pause . . . and a rebellious shot. And that one shot was all the deputies needed.

Officers dropped the windows in the armored school buses. Rifled barrels emerged. There would be no standoff. These were officers trained from handbooks with a chapter dedicated to Waco's lessons learned. Authorities would massacre any of the lunatic fringe who threatened innocent lives. To that end, scores of guns sent a fusillade of bullets into the grove of trees. The buses shook with the unrelenting recoil. Though muffled by the rain, the crackling sounds of gunfire deafened even the hard of hearing. Trees splintered, the earth trembled, and bodies fell. The entire showdown ended in less time than the gunfight at the O.K. Corral.

But Amber's scream and the Great Danes' howls signaled that it hadn't come without cost. Everyone in Four Points could see that one of the Lost Colonists had painted the preacher-man's white raincoat a shade of red.

Joshua had been shot.

54

The persistent rain lightened to a sprinkle, but the wind increased its fury and ripped three Revolutionary War flags from their moorings. Sam walked on the porch with her stuffed animal in one hand and, for additional support, Timmy's hand in the other. Faux Pooh shone like a bright orange sapphire in a sea of gray. The mayhem outside had caused Sam and Timmy concern. Luckily, the shot to Joshua's shoulder had missed his vital organs. It required immediate medical attention, but it didn't prevent the preacher-man from finding his footing. Amber tended to Ethan, so Anika went to Joshua. Even in the heat of battle, the thought of two men she cared for suffering serious injuries crushed her spirit.

"You have a medical team on your bus," Anika said, grabbing Joshua's hand. "You need to go."

"The bullet zipped clean through me," he said with a smile, craning his neck around his shoulder. "Feels like a bee sting." Joshua stared at Anika with his penetrating, authoritative eyes. They looked bigger with him bald. "You know, there's room on the bus for you and Sam. You just need to turn away from this chaos and climb aboard. The choice is life or death."

"We have our own way out," Anika said, pulling away from his hand.

"Please, Anika! Let me at least take Sam! She's sick. I can get her help."

"What makes you so sure you'll escape?"

"I always do."

"Let me guess: divine intervention?"

"Something like that," he said with a slight grimace. The pain in his shoulder seemed to have taken root. "Depends on your worldview, I guess.

Are you even aware that your detention facility—your outside jail—has the same dimensions as Noah's Ark?"

Anika stared at the Hospitality Center, startled by this revelation.

"Genesis 6," he continued. "God used the Ark to protect His people—His remnant—from flooding. And even now, His people are baptized when we come out of water. If you don't believe in providence, then you must think I have a pocket full of rainbows. What are you relying on?"

"Intuition, I guess." She couldn't muster the courage to tell the whole truth: *superstition, mostly.* "I'm sorry I let you down, Joshua," she said as Curtis approached. He had left Logan with Chelsea near the Selena statue. "I'm trying to be a better person."

"Anika, God justifying you has nothing to do with you doing better. Your salvation is based on faith alone, in Christ alone. When you turn from your sins and trust in Him, you get Christ's record, and he gets yours. Stop trying to clean yourself up and just believe."

"Where are y'all going?" Anika asked, changing the subject.

"Florida, most likely. There's usually a sixty-year storm in that area."

"Well, maybe I'll see you on the other side."

"That's my great hope. Godspeed, Anika Raven."

She nodded slowly.

"One more thing, Anika, before you leave," he said, making sure Curtis was still beyond earshot. "Not sure what your escape plans entail, but this town will never let you go without a fight. Miranda rarely lets anyone leave once, much less twice. When the moment of truth comes, you'll need to believe."

"Believe? That's it? Those are your final words of wisdom?"

"Believe, Anika!" he yelled, holding up his fist. "In your moment of greatest challenge and doubt, you'll need to *believe* with all your heart, soul, and mind!"

"You gonna live, Preacher-man?" Curtis asked as he arrived.

"Figure I have one or two more lives left. Like you said, this one's on me."

"Reckon so," Curtis said, staring intently at Joshua . . . and then at the porch.

A strange synergy overtook the two men. They began communicating, it seemed, without voicing words. The silence lingered until Joshua said, "I'll take good care of him, Curtis."

Curtis ran his fingers through his hair and kicked the dirt like a spoiled pubescent overcome with emotion. Anika had never seen him this way. He was shaking his head wildly and refused to make eye contact. "He's all I got left," he said sadly. "Miranda's done robbed me of everything I ever loved."

Joshua remained steadfast. "Even if he survives the hurricane, he won't survive the aftermath. There won't be anything for him until after the rebuild."

After regarding the circumstances, Curtis screamed, "Timmy!"

Timmy broke hands with Sam and dutifully walked down the steps. When he reached Curtis, he looked up with a questioning stare.

"You need to go with the preacher-man, Timmy. He's gonna—"

"But I wanna stay with—"

"Ain't gonna be no interruptin' now, ya hear? And I don't negotiate. You do as you're told."

"Yessir," Timmy responded as he looked at the others soaked with rain in the huddle. "Should I get on the bus?"

Curtis nodded.

"I'll miss you, good friend," Anika said. "You made a difference."

Timmy hugged Anika. He handed her the remote control to the jukebox and pulled a napkin from his pocket. The words on the napkin, crafted in his handwriting, spelled out "Timmy's Doozy of a Playlist" and contained a list of twelve songs (one with an asterisk).

Before Timmy left for the bus, Curtis grabbed him. The old fixer squeezed him like there would be no tomorrow. For many, there wouldn't be. The embrace was animalistic, clumsy, and almost violent in its affection. But it was sincere, and it was meaningful.

If Timmy ever doubted that someone loved him—if anyone ever doubted that bad men are capable of love—all doubt ended at that moment.

Sam waved as the church bus drove away. Anika and Curtis reunited with Logan and Chelsea below the swaying oak trees that provided a canopy over Selena and the Hospitality Center. No one said a word. Watching Timmy drive off unsettled the group, and it brought home a stark reality—a finality—to everyone in the area, including those detained. The end was near. The hurricane was on top of them, and it was about to rip this town to its core. Was the legend of Revolutionary Park correct, or was it just a deadly wives' tale? Would this hastily constructed facility of two-by-fours, plywood, and plexiglass hold when brick and mortar and steel and concrete located elsewhere would fail? Was this what Joshua meant, Anika thought, when he said she had to *believe*?

A line of thirty-two willing Lost Colonists waited to join about sixty detainees. Anika's mom remained one of the lot, and her situation stirred up tension in Anika's heart and mind. Barbara Mathis sat in the far corner by herself. Anika could see her clearly beside the gray Porta-John, amidst the strewn cots and stacked pallets of plastic water bottles and MREs. Her wayward eyes signaled sobriety, but her body swayed like she'd lost her marbles. Anika walked nearby and tapped on the plexiglass. As before, when Anika spoke to her or tried to capture her attention, Barbara said nothing. She wished she could rush her mother to safety, but she trusted this was the safest place. Besides, nearly one hundred other lives depended on her judgment. Keeping her mom interned signaled she would join them soon. Anika had to trust not only that the hurricane would spare her mother's life, but also that Logan, Chelsea, and Curtis would survive and care for Barbara after her daughters had departed.

Sarah, with tireless energy, continued to wail, kick, and scream like a lunatic. She wanted out. Logan stood on the other side of the plexiglass, begging for calm, begging her to stay in the facility. In response, she punched the plexiglass and spat at his face. Her reckless and disruptive behavior found Curtis's last nerve. Logan, not without persistence, tried to change Curtis's mind. Logan argued that Timmy had left, so his decisive vote in Theater Hall no longer counted. *Ties go to the status quo.* His attempts at persuasion, however, failed, and he'd exhausted his rights of appeal.

"Ladies and gentlemen," Curtis declared with an unusual, stately presence, "the choice is simple. If you wanna live, you'll hole up in this here Hospitality Center. If you wanna die, you'll go elsewhere."

A rumbling of concern and discontent coursed through the facility. Inside, people chatted, fussed, shook their heads, and shrugged. Outside, Chelsea grabbed Logan's hand and, yearning for his attention, stared at him without a blink.

"The choice is yours," Curtis continued, jingling keys and opening the door. His gun remained holstered but ready to draw. "Ain't gonna be no negotiatin' or hijinks, and we ain't got time for no questions. It is what it is. That's all I've got to say."

To no one's surprise, the blonde firecracker walked out first, followed by six others. To Anika's delight, Barbara wasn't among the defectors. Those leaving dispersed like delinquents escaping after-school detention. Logan, standing with Chelsea, pleaded with his wayward wife to stay. "Sarah, please reconsider!"

Ignoring him, Sarah started with Anika. "Keep the boots, *mayor*. I'll make sure they bury you in them. You're trash, no matter what's on your feet." She turned to Logan and rolled her eyes. "You're such a loser, Logan. Always have been. The only thing I'll reconsider is our marriage vows . . . because we're finished."

Chelsea squeezed Logan's hand until she cut off the circulation. He would need to withstand two storms today—Hurricanes Sarah and Lorenzo—and she planned to help him weather both.

"When I saw you fighting Ethan," Sarah continued, "I finally thought you'd be a winner. But you couldn't even finish that. And now look at you. You're dressed like a clown and holding hands with another loser."

As Sarah strode off, Chelsea grabbed Logan's face with both hands, puckered her lips, and kissed him passionately. He resisted at first, but then he succumbed. Anika noticed that, after that sensual kiss, he never looked back at Sarah. He never saw her jogging back to her boutique, back to where she'd be surrounded by her life-size portraits and burnt orange and white pompoms. Back to where she'd be the center of attention once again . . . and perform one last cheer.

"Time to load up," Curtis said, using his arm to direct Logan and Chelsea inside. "Mayor, I reckon you oughta grab Sam."

Anika, now drenched, took a deep breath. The fateful moment had arrived. What happened next would forever shape Anika's life (and Sam's). In fact, what occurred in the next few seconds would determine how much longer Anika had to live. Walking toward the porch, she felt the *koya* overtake her, turning from accelerant to resistance. Sam stared at her with her golden hair blowing wildly. Sam knew it was time to go, and with nothing but Faux Pooh in her hands, she had already kissed her mom through the plexiglass and was packed and ready.

Only one line of questions remained. Did Curtis know? Did he have any suspicion whatsoever? Did he really believe she would join the others in the Center? She could hear his footfalls now. He was walking behind her. Was he coming to say his goodbyes to the old timers? And where was Cyclops? Why was he not dancing and drinking with others in his normal spot?

Sam's eyes grew larger. Something was wrong. The tension growing, Anika looked behind her and saw his stone face. "You following me, Curtis?" she asked nervously.

He didn't respond. The haunting rhythm of his footsteps increased. She could hear him drawing closer. She could feel his presence, could feel him closing in, could almost feel his breath on her neck.

And then, just as she reached the porch, he stopped and said, "Figure it's time we had that conversation."

Anika stopped cold, her foot resting on the bottom step of the stairs. "Got plenty of time for that later."

After a long, uncomfortable pause, he replied, "I know what you're up to, Anika. I know of your plans to leave."

Anika winced. This was the moment she'd feared. She found herself without a weapon—without a way to fend off an attack. But she continued up the stairs. She forced herself to keep climbing. She needed to fight through the *koya* and get out of the wind and rain. She needed to grab Sam, run to the Black Ghost, and leave town. Forever.

But when she finally reached the top step, she almost lost her footing and tumbled down. She nearly collapsed after her legs went limp, after Curtis's next words sucked the oxygen from her lungs.

"Them T-shirts people are wearin' . . . well, Anika, they're right. *Johnny Lives.*"

55

"You told me you killed him," Anika said, her jaw tightening. Curtis now stood in front of her near the swinging doors, out of the rain. "Or did I just make that up?"

His hands—normally balled in a fist, even on a calm day—hung loosely, but he fidgeted as he spoke. "I made him disappear."

"With explosives, you mean? That's an interesting variation of the disappearing body magic trick."

"Yes, and no."

"I saw your stash of C-4 in the garage."

"I loaded down the trunk with explosives and detonated 'em—true. But Johnny wasn't in that car when she blew. You see, I needed everyone other than Dodd to figure he was dead."

"How'd you make him disappear?"

"That's a long story."

"Johnny wasn't the only person you made disappear. You landed me in jail."

"Dodd said we needed a patsy or stooge to protect our secret. I never meant for the police to finger *you*. Never thought for a moment Dodd would have you arrested. She didn't even know you. But you were her most convenient Oswald, I reckon. Certainly wasn't part of my plan . . . been trying to make up for it ever since you came back."

"By making more people disappear?"

"Them's bad people, Anika. Out to do you harm, to hurt that little girl. I got no regrets about what I've done. I ain't a good person—never said I was—but I'm trying to get better. Reckon some of us just get dealt a rotten deck of cards."

Reckon so, Anika thought. *Now you're speaking my language . . . or I'm speaking yours.*

"I fix things," he continued. "That's what—"

"That's what fixers do," she interrupted. She needed to strike with questions now, before he snapped out of his woe-is-me mode. "Why did Dodd care so much about Johnny?"

"She doted on that boy," he said, his eyes turning glassy. "Loved him like the ones she'd lost."

"You didn't answer my question."

He looked around as if nature was eavesdropping, ready to punish him for treason. "More this town than Dodd, you see. Johnny interfered with the mayoral succession plan, and Miranda didn't like that much. Dodd had talked to him about takin' over one day. He was her heir apparent. But he didn't want to live here anymore, especially after seein' you kiss Logan."

The picture was finding its frame. "Johnny tried to escape, but Miranda—this heaven-forsaken place—wouldn't allow it. Is that it?"

"It's treason when—"

"Whatever. I'm sick of hearing that nonsense. How did Johnny know Dodd so well? He never mentioned her when we dated. Wait, you're the fixer in this town. Why did you, of all people, help him escape? You're no Good Samaritan. You turned against the town . . . you were insubordinate. That's not like you, Curtis. That wasn't in your interest unless . . ."

Tears trickled down his sandpaper cheeks. They started off muddied, like droplets trapped in a broken faucet for years. Once the spigot creaked open, however, they flowed free and clear, indistinguishable from the raindrops.

"Wait. *You* are the one who knew Johnny best," she said, with her hand pressed against her forehead. "Oh, my—I'm a moron! It was right in front of me this whole time, and I missed it. Johnny knew Dodd because you worked for her. You knew him better than she did; you knew him better than *I* did. He was family, wasn't he?"

Curtis stared at her with bleary eyes, his bottom lip jumpity (as Cyclops would say), but he said nothing.

"He was . . ." she continued. "He *is*—"

"Johnny's my only grandbaby."

Anika turned around to look at Sam, who was listening to every word. Sam's expression signaled a similar shock. She hadn't known. For whatever reason (shame, maybe), Johnny had never mentioned his complicated grandpa. Anika stepped forward with little hesitation, grabbed the broken fixer, and pulled him to her with both arms. "Oh, Curtis," she said as he balled on her shoulder, "let it all out."

"Sheriff Karnes was gonna arrest my baby boy," he bellowed as Anika patted his back. To her credit, she didn't experience the usual surprise that overtakes young people when their elders lose their bearings and fall to pieces. Perhaps that's because she still hadn't digested the news—*Johnny Lives!* "Likely hurt him real bad," he rambled defensively. "The sheriff's the real enforcer. Ruthless. He doesn't believe those with skills and talent should ever leave town. Takes it personal. Once he found out Johnny was bent on leavin', I had to make Johnny disappear before the sheriff found him."

"I still don't understand why—"

"Anika, I can't stop 'em from chasin' after you. Y'all don't have much time."

"But I need—"

"You need to go!" he said. "I'll tell 'em you said goodbye." But there was another concern that made it hard for Anika to leave. Eventually, Curtis put his finger on it. "We'll take good care of your mom. Look over yonder at Logan and Chelsea," he pointed. "They're already sittin' with her. If you leave now, there's a chance you'll make it."

"Right," she said, snapping out of her trance and turning around. "Sam, time to roll."

Sam darted inside the Alamo and, before the swinging doors came to a rest, returned with the Sony Walkman. "I put in new double-A batteries," she said, handing the device to Curtis and hugging his waist. "You can listen to it in the park until the hurricane's gone."

"Not sure how I'll get along without you, girl," he said, choking up again as he kissed the top of her head.

"We'll meet again one day," Sam said, skipping away with Pooh and blowing her mother a farewell kiss from afar. And for any doubters who could read lips on the porch, she turned around, stared into Curtis's eyes, and mouthed words of hope beyond her years.

Cancer won't beat me.

The message stunned Curtis. Before Anika and Sam scuttled off, however, he gathered his wits and stopped them. "Anika, wait! Johnny's car. It wasn't fast enough to make the jump. I replaced it with a better engine, but you'll have to use it. Even with that ramp contraption y'all built . . . if you hesitate or fail to put the hammer down, you'll crash."

"You coached me well at the Flats. I'm ready."

"One more thing. I plated the back of the Ghost with armor. That will help with weight distribution and, heaven forbid, any gunfire. But you still may be too heavy in the front. If y'all survive the jump, those seatbelt straps will be your angels, ya hear?"

It was amazing. He had worked secretly and meticulously behind the scenes for years, planning for this day, to get her to this moment. "We'll miss you, Curtis. Thank you for everything."

"You can thank me by staying alive."

"Before I leave, I need to know: Is Johnny the Midnight Rider?"

Curtis smiled, but, before he could answer, Anika heard the voice of an unwelcomed figure walking toward the porch. "Yes, Curtis, let the answers fall," Sheriff Pete Karnes said. "This is quite the palaver."

"This don't concern you none, Pete," Curtis said with a novel tremor in his voice.

"Oh, I beg to disagree," the sheriff declared. "Looks to me like I got a mayor on the lam, and her trusted fixer is a criminal accomplice."

"What's your issue with me, Sheriff?" Anika pressed, trying to leverage any remaining authority she had over the police force.

It soon became clear that she had none. "Missy, unless you march directly into the Hospitality Center, I'm placing you under arrest for the murder of Scotty Mathis. Do not pass go, do not collect two hundred dollars. Might also charge you with treason."

"You know that ain't no credible charge," Curtis said.

"Treason against the town of Miranda!" Sheriff Karnes yelled, pulling his gun from the holster. "Treason against the great State of Texas herself! Well, it just don't get more treacherous than that, does it? Like the good mayor here, I've certainly killed for less."

"She didn't kill nobody," Curtis insisted. "That was my doin'."

"I'll deal with you in a minute, old friend," the sheriff said. "You've been up here bearin' your soul like a fool, boo-hooin' like a coyote caught in a foothold trap. Never pegged you for a big baby."

"What do you want from me?" Anika asked. "Sam and I aren't your concern."

"Goldilocks is going in the park with momma," he said, pointing with his gun and waving it around as he spoke. "You can go with her, or I'll toss you in the clink with ol' Crazy Eyes. If he doesn't kill you, the hurricane'll finish the job. Your choice."

"Arrest *me*, and let them girls go," Curtis said. "I'm the only criminal here."

"You're next on the list. If the wannabe mayor takes one more step toward that garage, it'll be the last bad decision she ever makes."

Curtis was done negotiating. His hand inched closer to his revolver. But before he could make his move . . .

"That goes for you too, Curtis!" the sheriff said, crouching in firing position and leveling his gun. "You're not due any more bad decisions. Your hand moves any closer to that six-piece, and I'll shoot it off! You hear good? You keep that iron cold!"

"Curtis was wrong, Sheriff!" came the drunken screed from the other end of the porch. Moon was stumbling and swaying with catatonic eyes and a rifle in his hands. "He ain't the only criminal here. I used this here rifle to shoot a man 'bout an hour ago."

"Put that down, Moon," the sheriff said, refusing to take his eyes off Curtis. "You're as drunk as Cooter Brown."

"Ol' Cooter was a patriot, by gosh. Anybody says otherwise is peddlin' fake news."

"Sit this one out, Moonshine, and I'll let you sleep it off."

"Long arm of the law ain't that long, Pete," Moon continued. "Ain't nobody goin' to be arrested today. I see eight of you, and I'm aiming at the two on the right."

"You couldn't hit the side of a barn with that fieldpiece, floatin' in all that shine."

"Reckon the feller I shot would argue otherwise."

Moon made a valid point, and Sheriff Karnes looked to be rethinking his situation and contemplating another risk assessment. "I got no beef with you, Moon. Go back to your drink."

"If you gotta beef with Curtis," Moon slurred, "then you gotta beef with me. Double beef," he chuckled, putting up three fingers with his free hand, "with queso."

Karnes returned his attention to the barrel of his pistol. "You and my pops went to school together, Curtis, served together. We can work through this. You tell him to drop that gun."

"Appreciate you, Pete."

"But I can't let her go," the sheriff said, making it clear Miranda maintained control over his discretionary function. "You know that."

Curtis stared at Anika and Sam before returning his attention to the sheriff. "But you *can* give me your gun, Pete. Give them girls a fightin' chance. Give 'em a head start. That's worth sparing your own miserable life, ain't it?"

Karnes looked at Moon, shook his head in disappointment, and walked up the porch steps. Moon's threats had convinced Karnes to hand his pistol to Curtis.

"Anika, you were a great mayor," Curtis said. "You'll be missed but not forgotten. Remember what I said, though, if you want to live. Pedal down and give her wings."

Anika smiled and put her arm around Sam.

"If y'all think that makeshift ramp is facing the right way," the sheriff scoffed, "then y'all are stupider than you look. We had that contraption pegged from the get-go."

Curtis took the pistol, grabbed Karnes's arm so hard he could feel his pulse, and returned his gaze to Anika and Sam as the yellow-jacket-colored buses drove toward the porch. Their windows dropped open with a loud clank in unison to make way for the guns.

"Remember the Alamo, Mayor!" Moon shouted.

"Girls, you need to run," Curtis said. "You need to run as fast as you can!"

56

The sheriff's deputies had killed the generator so the garage door wouldn't open. The garage itself risked collapsing in the high winds. It was nothing more than a large metal kit, built with the same quality products as a mobile home. Its rafters swayed; its sides shuttered. Anika feared Mother Nature was about to go haywire, not only destroying the garage but also everything in it. And that was the least of their problems. Sheriff Karnes had dashed any hopes that the ramp would be ready. Drawing on her dad's timeless lessons for overcoming adversity, Anika tried to focus on one impediment at a time.

She needed to get the Black Ghost out of the garage. The *koya* pounded her head, however, and made it hard to function. On the one hand, she didn't know whether the car had the muscle to penetrate the garage with brute force. Curtis usually anticipated every challenge, but Anika couldn't be sure that he'd retrofitted the door for an easier breakaway. On the other hand, she couldn't open the door manually. Even if she had the wherewithal and strength, she couldn't risk authorities arresting or shooting her while she tried. Deviating from normal practice, she didn't spend much time weighing her options. There was no time. Instead, with Sam in the passenger seat, she started the car, threw it in reverse, and jammed on the gas.

"Latch your belt and hold on tight, Sam. This may be a short ride, but it's gonna be bumpy."

The Ghost roared. Its tires spun. Smoke spewed everywhere. And within a second, the Dodge Challenger accelerated backward like a lightning bolt and crashed through the garage door. Out in the open. Out into the pouring rain, gale-force winds, and airborne debris. The large door, which had detached from the railing and flung open in one piece upon impact, now swung back down. It barely missed the car's hood as it careened back into its natural position with a monstrous crash.

Before Anika could gain control of her vehicle, she screamed as it rammed into the paramilitary bus waiting for them behind the garage. The sound of crushing metal and plastic was unnerving; the smell of oil, coolant, and other fluids palpable. The collision had catapulted the armed deputies who'd positioned themselves in opened windows. Most lay on the bus floor, disoriented. The damage to the Ghost seemed minimal—she had traded a bumper for some yellow paint—whereas the bus was out of commission. Anika had crashed into its engine compartment, and the Ghost's fortified backside had disabled the bus's front axle. The driver tried mightily to maneuver the bus forward, but (to borrow another Cyclops term) that cowboy was riding a hobbled horse.

Anika didn't wait around to exchange insurance cards. The assailants had regained their wits and would soon regain their positions. Anika had neutralized the bus, but the deputies' legs and guns still functioned. She mashed the pedal and rocketed from the scene. Turning onto Bowie Street, however, she again lost control of the Ghost. It hydroplaned atop large puddles at the intersection and spun out in the wrong direction. The car's engine coughed, spat, and grunted but continued to flex its muscle. Meanwhile, the windshield wipers whisked away the raindrops barely enough to reveal the frightening object coming right at them.

"Say hello to the other bus," Sam said.

"Never a dull moment," Anika added, equally collected. She threw the Ghost in reverse and mashed the pedal once again. The speedometer needle buried itself past zero in the wrong direction as the vehicle accelerated backward at a rapid clip—some ten, twenty, thirty miles an hour. The bus, however, gained. "Don't be scared, Sam," Anika said, craning her neck behind her. "I'm about to try a maneuver that Moon taught me from his family's bootlegging days."

"Why would that scare me?" Sam said sarcastically. "Might as well go out in style."

Anika, with the car flying in reverse, jerked the wheel clockwise, popped the clutch, and stabbed the brakes. The Ghost's momentum transferred as it spun around one hundred degrees into a J-turn (or as Moon called it, a Rockford turn). The car's nose bearing straight, Anika popped the clutch again and threw the Ghost into forward gear. It didn't take long for the high-performance machine to reach meteoric acceleration. Within seconds, houses and commercial buildings became a blur, and the police bus faded into the distance.

Located north of Bowie Street, the Flats were a few miles away. Even with flooded streets and obstacles blowing every which way, the travel time at this speed was less than five minutes. Anika checked her mirrors and exhaled.

"We're in the clear . . . for now," Anika said.

"But not out of the woods," Sam added.

"Right. Maybe Sheriff Karnes lied about the ramp to scare us."

But once they arrived at the Flats, they learned he'd told the truth. The fat end of the ramp faced them and served as a barricade. Not only that, the scene was so surreal as to be absurd. Hordes of protesters, dressed in bright colors and filled with rage, surrounded the barren plain. They could barely keep their footing against the ferocity of the wind. Those with the sturdiest of placards held them up with statements such as "TRAITOR!" and "TURNCOAT!" and "HOW DARE YOU LEAVE US HERE TO DIE?" One that caused Anika alarm said, "DIE, YOU FILTHY PIG!"

But nothing—not the barricade, not the maniacs—threatened them like the sight ahead. Anika idled the Ghost forward onto the Flats. She would approach the threat with caution but head-on. Curtis, for all his preparation, hadn't thought to armor the front of the car or bulletproof the windshield. Or perhaps he'd refused to disrupt the car's weight distribution. Either way, the Ghost couldn't defend against the weaponry aimed from Sarah's Range Rover. Sheriff Karnes, accompanied by his most elite unit, had beaten them to the site and was positioned between the Ghost and the launch point at the river.

Anika couldn't see the officers' faces through the windshield. She only saw their weapons pointed at her from outside the Range Rover's windows.

Soon, she heard Sheriff Karnes's demands, bellowing and crackling from a bullhorn. His cloudy words muddied his clear desire—he wanted them arrested or dead. Given the circumstances, arrested meant dead, so the result would be the same. Things looked dire. Anika could scarcely move an inch without eliciting deadly gunfire. The sheriff's nasty and insulting screed persisted, rivaling the evil chorus of shrieks and howls of maniacal protesters.

Their luck had run out.

Or had it? The Range Rover catapulted off the ground before Anika could duck her head, before she heard and felt the explosion's deafening blow. The blast obliterated the vehicle in an instant; flames engulfed whatever remained. Sarah's overhauled Range Rover was no more, no doubt destroyed by a hidden box of C-4.

Fixers fix things. That's what they do.

As the sky dumped buckets, scores of zombie-eyed protesters dropped their placards and ambushed the Ghost. They would overtake the vehicle in seconds. At the same time, a green forklift—with its Come and Take It flag flapping in the wind—came out of nowhere!

"Look, Anika! Look behind the fire . . . at that machine! Look at the man in the cowboy hat!"

"Cyclops! He's driving to the ramp!"

The *koya* pulled Anika with G-like forces. She and Sam locked their doors as the zombies bent on destruction attacked the car. They beat on the Ghost mindlessly and barked crazy statements about humanity, evil, and loyalty to their town. A teenage girl with green hair and frothing at the mouth snapped off the car's windshield wiper blades and bloodied her knuckles trying to break the glass. It felt as though the rabid crowd would turn the car over.

Cocooned amid a raging battle, Anika and Sam tried not to panic. They kept their focus on Cyclops, who had forklifted the ramp and was maneuvering it into launch position. They checked their harnesses that served as seatbelts. Faux Pooh looked on from the backseat as maniacs pounded the car with palms and fists. Anika revved the engine, and the car rocked right and left as it roared. Anika noticed the clops of mud caking the windshield.

"Can you drive without wipers?" Sam asked.

"If we go fast enough, the rain should wash that away. We'll find out soon enough."

"You think Mom will be okay?" Sam asked.

"Her chances are better than ours," Anika replied before pivoting to a lighter subject. "What do you think Curtis is doing right now?"

"Sitting on the bench outside the Hospitality Center, trying to figure out the Walkman."

"What cassette did you leave for him?"

"Harry Styles," Sam giggled.

"What should we listen to?" Anika said, pulling out the napkin with Timmy's playlist.

"Violent Femmes?" Sam offered.

Anika tracked down the napkin with her finger. Timmy had chosen the song for them. His choice was marked by an asterisk. "Nope. Timmy's still the DJ. 'Run To the Hills' by Iron Maiden."

"Same as Johnny," Sam said.

"Yep, but this time, we make the jump."

Cyclops almost had the ramp in position. In fact, he was waving his hat, signaling to Anika that he was close enough for her to come his way.

Sam loaded the eight-track cassette, and Anika gunned the accelerator. The car spun around three hundred and sixty degrees, slinging mud and flinging a handful of meth heads onto their stomachs and backs. Anika heard machine gun fire as bullets clinked off the Ghost's backside. The police bus they'd outrun had arrived and turned into attack position as police unleashed a staccato of fire from one hundred yards away. The gunfire only stopped after it claimed the lives of two protesters.

Anika aimed the car at the ramp and looked at Sam. "This is it. No turning back. What's the Rubik's Cube say?"

Sam held up the puzzle, which had no discernible pattern. "I don't care. I'm ready."

"I love you to the moon, Sam."

"Love you, too, Anika. To the moon . . . and back. Thanks for coming home to save me."

"Sisters in the bond!"

"Now it's time to rock n' roll!" Sam said as she pressed play.

"Pooh, you ready?" Anika asked.

"Pooh was born ready!" Sam laughed. "Sewn together ready!"

Music blared, tires spun, and bodies tumbled over the hood and flew aside as Anika mashed the accelerator again. Her head crashed against the seat as the Black Ghost launched forward, climbing toward its top speed like a fighter jet flying off an aircraft carrier. The pelting rain washed some of the mud from the windshield, but she was largely driving blind. She tried to maintain control—to keep the vehicle on a straight path—as the sisters screamed in unison, "Let's go!"

As the river beckoned, the Ghost traveled so fast that some of her parts started to shake and rattle. Anika's knuckles turned white around the steering wheel. If she mashed the accelerator any harder, it would go through the floor. Since she couldn't see ahead, she had to rely on faith that Cyclops would drop the ramp in time. Their lives depended on it.

And the idea of faith triggered another thought. Anika had remembered Curtis's direction—seatbelts on and pedal to the metal—but now her attention turned to Joshua's counsel. He had exhorted her to believe. To believe she would make the jump, to be sure. But he wanted her to believe in something more. *In your moment of greatest challenge and doubt,* he had said, *you'll need* to believe *with all your heart, soul, and mind!* In this moment, she tried to muster all the belief inside her.

But would it be enough?

Anika Raven, the former homecoming queen of Miranda High and its current mayor, closed her eyes, clenched her teeth, and believed with all her heart, soul, and mind as the front tires crashed onto the lip of the ramp.

And the Black Ghost sprouted wings . . . and took flight.

EPILOGUE

ONE YEAR LATER

Curtis rocked in his chair and fussed at the carpenters for taking down the Bob Wills poster and hanging the swinging doors crooked. He was mad at the world. Logan, he thought, worried too much about being a newlywed and not enough about rebuilding the Alamo Opera House. *Where is he, anyway?* Curtis wondered. *I never took off an afternoon.* What's more, the construction of buildings in Four Points was taking too long. And without a hurricane threat this year, it made no sense. From the Alamo porch, the landscape was littered with vertical two-by-fours but very little plywood. This newer generation made all sorts of excuses, he thought. Coronavirus, supply chain, work-life balance—*blah, blah, blah.* They relied too much on those fancy-schmancy electronic tablets. Everyone knew that experts used paper blueprints to build complicated things. Though effective, Mayor Chelsea Danforth wasn't nearly as tough as her predecessor.

"Anika would've whipped them workers a lot harder," Curtis huffed.

"Good leadership's hard to find," Barbara Mathis replied.

"Chelsea just needs more reps. Problem is the labor force. They'd rather play them video games than work."

Barbara took a sip of moonshine and declared, "Some things never change."

"Reckon you're right," he said, gazing at her bottle. He walked down the stairs, crossed the street, and wandered into the park.

He spent the lion's share of his time these days in the park. Soon after the hurricane had passed, he returned the Selena statue to the Corpus Christi bayfront in the dead of night. Last week, however, on the one-year anniversary of the storm, Logan presented him—presented the entire town of Miranda—with a similar statue. This one, though, was not in honor of the Queen of Tejano but of another Texas hero. Curtis had fallen in love with it soon after Chelsea ripped off its tarp. He couldn't stop staring at the inscription.

ANIKA RAVEN, MAYOR OF MIRANDA, TEXAS (HURRICANE LORENZO).

FORT LAUDERDALE, FLORIDA

The sun's rays glistened off the crashing waves as the seagulls squawked *ha-ha-ha* overhead. The birds stalked the girl hurling crackers into the Atlantic.

"Do you think my second toe is bigger than my big toe?" Anika asked as she looked over her pregnant belly in her lounge chair. Her tan was out-of-sight good. Even her head, now fully shaved, was dark. But her feet were swollen, and she was feeling insecure.

"Your feet are perfect," the young man said, "just like most things about you."

She rolled up her *Southern Living* magazine, leaned over, and smacked him on the chest. "Most things?"

"Would you let me read my novel, please?" he said, shaking his head with a chuckle. "Need to learn how Blake Hudson gets out of this pickle."

"Where do I fall short of perfect?" she asked, staring at the diamond on her left ring finger. She aimed it in the sun where it cast a glare on her husband's face.

"You ask too many questions, for one."

"You don't answer my questions," she said, "that's why."

"Like what?" he asked.

321

"You know what."

"This topic again?"

"How did you become the Midnight Rider? What was it like? Where did you live?"

"We've gone over this a thousand times, Anika."

"What did you smuggle? How was Dodd blackmailing you?"

"You're right. I'm not answering your questions. Not those, at least. Ask me later . . . much later."

She patted her stomach. "Do you think Joshua will be as beautiful as you?"

"Well, as his father, I must say that if he's half as beautiful as his mother, he'll be the prettiest baby in Florida."

"What about Texas?"

"Texas too."

The girl with the crackers approached. Like Anika, she had a shaved head, but hers had a huge scar across it. Anika had only shaved her head in solidarity and support. *Sisters in the bond.* "Anika, can we get ice cream?"

"You just had ice cream," Anika said.

"Please!"

"Let's wait until dinner, okay? That's a long walk on hot sand."

"Johnny, will you walk with me?" Samantha pleaded.

Johnny put down his novel and bounced from his chair before he could say yes.

"Sucker," Anika said with a smile. "Hurry back, you two."

As they walked off, Anika felt the knot in her stomach. It wasn't the baby knocking. It was something else. Pangs wrought by surprise, maybe . . . or fear. When she had told Sam to wait on the ice cream, an old feeling had returned. A feeling she hadn't felt in over a year, not since the Flats. She had felt the *koya.*

As she watched a healthy, cancer-free Sam walk away, she chalked up the feeling to her rabid imagination running wild. Life was good. No reason to buy trouble when it wasn't for sale. She uncurled her magazine and returned to her article on how to paint a nursery. Her biggest questions were blue or orange paint, carpet or hardwood floors. But something forced her to look up again, to look at her little sister.

Sam, who was holding Johnny's hand, looked back at Anika.

And winked.

Anika felt the *koya* again, and the thought hit her like a punch to the face.

Sometimes the bogeyman doesn't even know that he's the bogeyman.

She dropped her magazine in the sand and covered her mouth with both hands. She remembered all the focus on Sam from the very beginning. The way Sam had summoned her to Miranda. The way she always influenced events around her. The way she could draw and work the Rubik's Cube in ways that arguably predicted the future. Her ability to manipulate events. Her ability to negotiate with domestic terrorists, like Crazy Eyes. The fear—absolute terror!—she instilled in friend and foe alike when her emotions ran high. The power she wielded in her area of influence.

Does Sam feel the koya? she thought. And she remembered the intense pull and thrumming in her office when Sam learned Crazy Eyes had taken Mom hostage. *Was Sam the cause of the* koya?

Sometimes the bogeyman doesn't even know . . . that she's *the bogeyman.*

"Nah," Anika said aloud, exhaling, picking up her magazine, and turning the page. "Bogeywoman ain't got nothin' to do with it."

THE END

TIMMY'S DOOZIE OF A PLAYLIST

- YOUR CHEATIN' HEART, HANK WILLIAMS
- WHAT I LIKE ABOUT TEXAS, GARY P. NUNN
- CLAY PIGEONS, BLAZE FOLEY (BEST EVER!)
- THE FRONT PORCH SONG, ROBERT EARL KEEN
- TIME OF THE PREACHER, WILLIE NELSON
- BOOGIE WOOGIE BUGLE BOY, THE ANDREWS SISTERS
- A BOY NAMED SUE, JOHNNY CASH
- BIG BALLS IN COWTOWN, BOB WILLS
- BIDI BIDI BOM BOM, SELENA
- THESE BOOTS ARE MADE FOR WALKIN', N. SINATRA
- DEGÜELLO, DIMITRI TIOMKIN
- ✱ RUN TO THE HILLS, IRON MAIDEN

✱ ~~BUY MORE BUTTER~~
✱ ~~WASH APRON~~

TEAM ANIKA!

ACKNOWLEDGMENTS

To my wife and first reader of all my books, Kristi Boudreaux. Thank you for your love and grace.

To Cortney Donelson, my editor, thank you for your guidance, encouragement, and skill.

To Chris Treccani, the master of design, who gave life to my words through images.

To my lifelong friends from Corpus Christi and wildly successful beta readers, Kristin Riddick and Tania Missad. You escaped "Miranda" for Los Angeles and made it. I will forever be grateful for your time and candid feedback.

I am also thankful for Reuben Rosalez, who kept me honest with this project and with *Scavenger Hunt*.

Finally, I would like to thank my publisher, Morgan James Publishing, and my publicist, PR by the Book.

325

ABOUT THE AUTHOR

Chad **Boudreaux**, a native of Corpus Christi, Texas, is a Washington insider hired by the US Department of Justice the night before the September 11, 2001 attacks—launching him immediately into counterterrorism work that earned him high accolades at an early age. His success in the Justice Department carried him to the US Department of Homeland Security, where his role as deputy chief of staff allowed him to work directly with Secretary Michael Chertoff, advising him on significant policy and operational and legal issues facing the Department. He is currently the chief legal officer of a publicly traded, Fortune 300 company and America's largest military shipbuilder. Boudreaux leverages his unique, high-level experience in global security matters and his extensive legal expertise to craft breathtaking, insider stories of mystery and intrigue that are ripped from today's headlines and sure to shock his readers. His first novel is titled *Scavenger Hunt*.

A free ebook edition is available with the purchase of this book.

To claim your free ebook edition:

1. Visit MorganJamesBOGO.com
2. Sign your name CLEARLY in the space
3. Complete the form and submit a photo of the entire copyright page
4. You or your friend can download the ebook to your preferred device

Morgan James BOGO™

A **FREE** ebook edition is available for you or a friend with the purchase of this print book.

CLEARLY SIGN YOUR NAME ABOVE

Instructions to claim your free ebook edition:
1. Visit MorganJamesBOGO.com
2. Sign your name CLEARLY in the space above
3. Complete the form and submit a photo of this entire page
4. You or your friend can download the ebook to your preferred device

Print & Digital Together Forever.

Snap a photo

Free ebook

Read anywhere

Printed in the USA
CPSIA information can be obtained
at www.ICGtesting.com
JSHW020043070724
65927JS00002B/2